Sailors always know when a storm is coming.

The MONARCHS

ANACOSTIA MILLER

HOT TREE PUBLISHING

FARLIGH
VIOLETTA SILVER'S HAVEN
THE WILDS
THE FAE OCCUPIED GULLIES
FISHERMAN GULLY
BLISS THATCHER'S COLONY

THE IVORY KEYS
BOR
FARLIGHT KEEP
PIKE ESTATE
THE ISLES OF FARLIGHT
WEST ALGAR SEA
SHIPWRECK BAY
LUCKY BARTRAM'S OUTPOST
ANCHORAGE COVE

THE MONARCHS

THE GUARDIANS OF FARLIGHT ISLES
BOOK TWO

ANACOSTIA MILLER

HOT TREE PUBLISHING

For information, contact the publisher, Hot Tree Publishing.

WWW.HOTTREEPUBLISHING.COM

EDITING: HOT TREE EDITING

COVER DESIGNER: BOOKSMITH DESIGN

E-BOOK ISBN: 978-1-923252-08-0

PAPERBACK ISBN: 978-1-923252-09-7

To all the men who have been told vulnerability is weakness.
You've never been stronger.

PROLOGUE

Thick curtains shrouded any natural sunlight beaming into Varric's study. Empty. Not a guard in sight. His study was meticulously pieced together. Not a speck of dust anywhere.

Immaculate.

Vastly different than it looked when Maeve betrayed him.

It took two weeks to piece himself back together, but he refused to let anyone see what lingered under the surface. The insides of his cheeks were raw where the taste of blood lingered.

Every time he thought of his daughter, his jaw clenched, and fury blurred his vision briefly. He should've known that appealing to her better nature was pointless. Maeve's invulnerability was the final piece he needed.

He thought that after everything he'd done for her—all the *sacrifices* he made for the little brat—she'd willingly offer her hand. *Varric* was the one who gave her a home. He gave her power and status. Anything she could've wanted.

Yet Maeve rewarded him with *betrayal.*

He could've easily found the source of her powers after enough study. Taken her apart and put her back together over and over until he had what he needed. But he didn't.

Well, if the ungrateful brat wouldn't give him her power willingly, then he'd just have to take it with force. All he had to do was get her away from the pirates, and then he'd have both the leviathan and Maeve.

Draconite *and* immortality.

Whatever became of Maeve's husk wasn't his concern. He'd discard her and likely never think of her again.

A white-gold crown was embedded among his graying curls. He fiddled with a sparkling black amulet with flecks of blue that flickered when it caught the dull lantern light.

The crack was still there....

Maeve had the power to shatter draconite. Another layer to the strange fae girl he stumbled upon twenty-odd years ago.

Varric's stormy eyes gave nothing away. No thread of remorse. No guilt. Just stoic disinterest. Under the surface, his head swam.

Whatever she was, the dragon *couldn't* have her.

Varric *owned* her. The pirates stole her.

A swirling portal opened up in the center of the throne room, spitting violet and white as the seam between the countries became paper thin. Varric didn't look surprised.

He had been expecting a visitor.

The light undulated violently, a blinding brightness obscuring the figures that fell through it. A draconite crystal rolled across the floor, cracking and spasming as the magic leached from it to keep the portal open.

Draconite shattered as the portal slammed shut like a door. Blue light flitted through the air, swirling as it sought escape before evaporating through the heavy curtains.

Varric's expression of disinterest changed as two figures grappled on the ground. One, Varric recognized.

Thallan. The Face-Stealer.

A man Varric didn't recognize slammed on top of Thallan's body, both hands latched around Thallan's throat as he brutally strangled the Face-Stealer. The man's fine white hair was in disarray, matted at the side where blue blood coated his scalp.

Thallan flailed, slamming their hands against the floor, trying desperately to get away. They changed colors as their life faded away. Their face morphed. Their muscles twitched and writhed as they tried to keep their chosen form, but it flittered to and from.

Thallan's face fell slack, eyes devoid of color. Peachy skin dissolved into gray. The masculine form they had taken melted into long, sinewy limbs. Thallan's true face.

Varric didn't intervene, just watched.

He had no need to keep Thallan alive.

The unknown man was dressed only in satin pajama pants, his lilac skin shimmering with filth and sweat. His pierced ears were pulled into exaggerated tips, and tattoos were inked over all visible skin. A fresh slash dripped blue blood onto the palace floor.

A Skadian elf. Though not just any Skadian elf.

Blue-blooded royalty.

The elf roared with seething rage and slammed Thallan's head down against the concrete floor, violently shattering the back of his skull until Thallan's violet lifeblood stained the tiles.

Thallan was already dead, but the elf didn't stop.

Varric watched, interest twinkling in his eyes. He noticed wet tracks streaking down the elf's face, his jaw locked in a snarl.

This wasn't senseless violence.

This was vengeance. Magnificent carnage.

An opportunity.

The Skadian elf trembled with unconcealable rage as he rose to his feet, hands and feet splattered with blood. Yellow eyes darted around the throne room before slowly landing on Varric. He bared sharp canines in a vicious snarl. His blue tongue clicked against his teeth as if he was barely holding himself back from continuing the violent rampage.

Varric could *use* that violence.

The elf was distraught. He wasn't particularly old—probably midtwenties to his early thirties—but the pain in his eyes held unfathomable anguish beyond his years. Varric judged him as young enough to be an heir to the royal family and old enough to be *the* heir to the throne.

With feigned fear, Varric put up his hands. "Where did you come from?"

The elf seethed but didn't answer.

"I know them," Varric said, gesturing to Thallan's contorted corpse. "Thallan… a Face-Stealer. They work for the Royal Leviathan."

Not a complete lie. Thallan used to serve the royal family before they joined Varric during the coup. Even after receiving status and political power, Thallan kept coming back to Varric for *more*.

More. More. More.

Riches, servants, or even new faces. Thallan was never satisfied, but that greed served Varric well, until now.

Varric chuckled in an attempt to defuse the tension. "Or I suppose *worked* for him."

The Skadian elf thrummed with grief. Varric could practically taste it. Suddenly, he disappeared from sight, blinking out of existence before reappearing right in front of Varric. A billowing fog surrounded him, icy energy flowing around him like smoke and winter.

A magic unique to the royal Skadian family. Inherited just like their blue blood.

"Where am I?" he growled, his voice thick with a Skadian accent.

"Farlight Isles. I'm King Varric Cross. I seized the kingdom from the leviathan tyrants."

The Skadian elf homed in on his words. Varric knew

royal dark elves could sense lies. Hear heartbeats. They were so overcharged with magic that the Skadian empire never needed any allies. The royals fought on the front lines during war and carried battles on their shoulders to minimize casualties.

A waste of perfectly good magic.

But that also meant that the other kingdoms feared Skadi.

Varric's heart rate never changed. He was completely in control of the situation.

"They killed my wife," the Skadian elf whispered. "Where can I find them? How can I get back to Skadi?"

Varric hummed. "Skadi is a long way from here… especially after the Grand Sorceress pushed the islands into the ocean."

The elf lowered his shoulders, no longer visibly threatening. He was listening.

"But I have an idea that could get you back home. I think we might be able to help each other," Varric revealed. "The Royal Leviathan, the one who sent the Face-Stealer, also took something precious from me. You get your revenge, and I help you get home."

"What did they take from you?"

Varric pressed a hand over his chest. "They took my beloved daughter. Bring her back to me. Deliver the leviathan. Then I will send you home."

1

MAEVE CROSS

Who am *I*?

Or, I suppose, more importantly, *what* am I?

The events of Farlight lived in my mind, never too far away. I busied myself with menial assignments most of the time, enough to be distracting. But once I finished the task at hand, the thoughts came back.

I didn't know how to cope. The only other person who knew I wasn't Varric's daughter—or human—was Ronin.

In the midday sun, Ronin sparred with Wesley. He was pushing himself too hard, as usual. He had barely started to heal, and he was at it again, pretending he didn't hurt. His usually tawny complexion was visibly pale, and I noticed tremors when he moved too fast as well as a clammy sheen across his forehead.

I noted the way his mouth would slightly screw to the side in discomfort before he moved forward to strike Wesley. Nothing more than a show to save face.

Each of Wesley's hits was hesitant. Sweat from the summer sun dampened his brow. He wore his brightly colored bandana to protect his skin from the heat, but even so, the ocher of his skin deepened in the telltale sign that summer was here.

The only time Ronin would let his exhaustion peek through his facade was when we were alone together. Which wasn't as often as I'd prefer. But between meetings and all the work we had to do on the ship, there was hardly time for it.

When I'd been lucky enough for him to hold me as we slept, he'd wake up with a start in the middle of the night. I'd listen to him retch his guts out, and whenever I'd ask him if he was all right, he'd pretend.

He'd distract me.

He'd lie.

Such a pretty liar.

I knew he was in pain. I knew he was sick, still purging the vitrophine from his system, but I just…. *I wanted to take it all away.* My heart ached for him.

For his touch.

For the chance to soothe his pain.

I loved him, but that was proving to be just as painful as when he'd left me with nothing more than a letter and cold imprint of where he slept beside me.

Even during intimacy, he held me an arm's length away. A chasm had cracked the ground beneath our feet, trapping us on opposite sides.

The one person I could truly confide in… stuck in his own head. Meanwhile, my mind was racing, clouded with everything that had happened to us, truths wrestling with what I used to believe.

My childhood was a lie, and I struggled with it *alone.*

I understood why Ronin was distant. Showing any sign of weakness was dangerous. Most of the crew stood behind him, but the few who didn't could spell disaster. It only took one shipworm to sink a ship.

We didn't need to deal with a mutiny while he recovered and I hunted for the truth.

Where did I come from? Did I have parents? Who were they?

Why was Varric in Fisherman's Gully?

What the Hells is a sentry?

Those questions kept me awake at night, swimming through my head, while I listened to Wesley, Luella, and Andra sleep in the officer bunks around me. It didn't matter that there were more important things to worry about.

We had an impending war to prevent. Monarchs to unite against Varric. People to save before his fanaticism burned the Isles to ash.

But I couldn't help it.

Varric wasn't my father. I wasn't a princess. That piece of me had been hacked away.

Lost forever.

I mourned the person I used to be. It was like she… died.

Well, technically, I *did* die.

I shook off the memory, but the ghost of a scalpel still kissed my throat. I vividly remembered growing cold as blood colored my hands and plummeting into a never-ending darkness. The fleeting wonder of what would be waiting for me when I hit the bottom.

The sight of utter devastation on Ronin's face branded the inside of my eyelids. I could still picture the twinkle of awe in his eyes when I came to his rescue, just to be snatched away in front of him.

Sometimes it seemed as if he didn't believe I survived and was nursing the pieces of his heart while suffering through every day of his recovery. Meanwhile, I *starved*, aching for him. For reassurance.

I wanted to feel alive, while Ronin treated me like I died back in Farlight Prison.

Neither of us knew how to cope with it, so we resorted to sex. The distraction granted a moment of bliss.

A *moment* of feeling alive.

Then I was a ghost again. Ronin could rarely tolerate holding me afterward, leaving me feeling *used* when I went back to my own bunk and dreamed of nothing. The emptiness in my belly got worse every day. We were frayed like a split seam, but every time I tried to stitch it back together, Ronin pulled it apart. I didn't think it was intentional, but that didn't make it any easier.

I don't know what to do....

The wind blew at the back of my head, rustling my hair as I dangled my legs from the top deck. Various shiphands climbed the rigging, adjusting sails to catch more wind.

Then my eyes found Ronin as he pushed himself to the limit.

Wesley's dark eyes gleamed with pain. His mouth drew down at the corners as he pulled another punch. Fighting to pass the time wasn't a new practice on the ship. They did it all the time. But I knew the difference between the brawls Ronin used to take part in for entertainment and his training regimen now.

Nothing he did was for enjoyment.

It was like he *wanted* to suffer.

I missed how he would stroke my hand in passing or press a tender kiss against my throat. Now those small gestures came few and far between. Unless we were having sex, he rarely touched me.

I missed *him*.

A broad-brimmed hat came into my periphery as Luella —or in private, *Lulu*—climbed the ladder up to where I was sitting. "You look awfully lonely up here," she commented, sitting on the lip that hung over the lower deck.

"Just thinking," I said wistfully, eyes on the man I had foolishly fallen in love with.

Luella nodded, not saying anything. But her company was more than enough.

"Can I ask you something, Lulu?"

She grinned, finding humor in the cutesy nickname that didn't suit her at all. "You just did, love. Ask me another."

"Do you ever feel alone even when someone is right next to you?" I wondered.

She leaned back, looking up at the sky as the sunlight enveloped her. Moments like this, I realized how Andra fell head over heels in love with her. Crimson hair billowed around her freckled face, her intense green eyes pondering.

When we met, I thought she was terrifying, but as I got to know her, I learned that she had quite a twisted sense of humor. She enjoyed the fact that she put people off. She loved making them jump in fear.

At the same time, when she said something, she meant it.

"I think we all do sometimes." She tilted her head to the side. "What happened in that room after Varric trapped you and Levi in it?"

She was nothing if not intuitive. I gazed down at the sailors, my heart a hard rock in my chest. "A lot happened. But even after all that, I can't help but feel… unwanted."

A gruff grunt left her lips. "Don't be foolish, Mae. If you weren't wanted, we would've left you at that prison."

I scoffed, the noise sounding ruder than I intended. "Forget I asked."

"You dwell too much on what other people think."

I gazed at the brawling ring, aching for connection. I *wanted* Ronin so badly that I couldn't seem to focus on anything else. There must've been a frown on my face because she poked me hard in the side, causing me to squeak and jump. My eyes darted over to her. "What?"

"Stop that. You look like a lovesick puppy."

I huffed, my chest squeezing and fluttering like butterflies swarmed my throat and then plummeted down to my stomach to make me sick. "I can't help it. I *miss* him. He's right there, but he's so far away."

"Give him time, love." Luella patted me on the shoulder, the closest gesture I'd ever get to comfort. "There's more, though, isn't there?"

I paused, debating whether or not I should tell Luella everything.

"Listen here. You don't owe anyone your thoughts. Not a single fucking person. But I'm all ears for you, lass."

I'd kept to myself since we returned from the prison, but everything felt so godsdamn heavy that my shoulders were beginning to sway. After another pause, I said, "Varric isn't my father, Lulu."

"Aye." Luella gestured to my ears, taking me back to the moment in the greenhouse when she backed me into a corner to examine the scars on them. "I had my suspicions."

"Both you and Ronin knew?"

She shrugged. "We didn't know *why* Varric took you as a ward and masqueraded you as his daughter."

Should I tell her about my unnatural healing?

Fuck it.

Luella didn't interrupt as I told her about what happened in that room. How Varric stole me from Fisherman's Gully. My death. All the unknowns. She nodded along, mouth fixed in a firm line. Her intense eyes held mine in a concentrated lock, never once looking away.

"Explains the blood. And how you survived your drowning." She leaned back on her arms, breaking eye contact to look up at the clear blue sky. "I knew Varric was cruel, but that's an innovative type of cruel."

"And I don't know *what* I am either."

She made a throaty noise and said, "I can't recall any fae with immortality. And that doesn't explain why Varric went to Fisherman's Gully at all. To my knowledge, the merrow shoal was impartial during the war."

Fae....

"What makes someone fae?" I asked. Most of the civilians

in Farlight were human. I'd seen elves occasionally at royal parties. I didn't get much exposure to fae at all.

"The concentration of magic in the blood. Humans are typically *ungifted*. They have to learn magic. Elves are in between, while fae have a very high concentration of wild magic. Some say elves are descendants of fae and humans, but others speculate that elves split off into human and fae, but who knows."

"So… Ronin and Conway would be fae?" I asked.

"Yes. And Lucky Bartram. He's the son of a dryad." She paused, tapping her chin. "You know, Conway would be a good place to start poking around about your origins. Swing by Butcher's and see if he knows anything. Quietly, of course. Immortality is something people would kill for, so keep your head down."

She made a good point.

"Would Lucky help me?" I wondered. "He's a monarch, so he has influence. I'm sure he's seen a lot in his day."

Luella didn't seem completely opposed to the idea, even if she was cautious. "Lucky is fairly self-serving, and he has some long history with Seabird. That might be more complicated than you think."

"All right." I nodded, piecing together a plan in my head. "What else can you tell me about the monarchs?"

"You know, you do your best work on a whim, but I do love it when you plot." She cast me a sideways grin. "Let's see. Hmm. You've met Lucky, but he has a reputation of breaking hearts. Including Bliss Thatcher's. Bliss, on the other hand, is known for their cutthroat mentality. They live at one of the Gullies, fairly isolated. It will be difficult to convince them to be in the same room with Lucky."

Ex-lovers rarely came back together amicably. *Speaking of….* I wondered if Ronin's ex-lover would even consider working with us. "What about Violetta Silver?"

Luella chuckled under her breath. "The third monarch is a blood-cursed trickster."

"Blood-cursed?" I inquired. I'd never heard that term before.

With a hum, she explained, "When an elf fucks around with the wrong deity, they become blood-cursed. Cursed to sustain themselves with blood, devouring flesh if they succumb to the curse, becoming mainly monster. She's learned to live with it and uses it to her benefit. Levi could tell you more. All I know about her is that she's an elf who loves stealing shiny things and fucks around with her mate, Pinky. She could charm you out of your breeches. Just ask Levi."

I nearly choked, making Luella laugh again when my cheeks turned red. I doubted most people responded well to someone joking about their lover's past fling. "You're awful."

"Hey, just because he's recovering doesn't mean I'll stop talking shit." She waved her hand dismissively. "But let me remind you that no matter where this journey will take us, I've got your back, even if I like to poke fun."

"It should go without saying that I've got your back too."

She shot me a toothy grin. "I know, love. The only reason I haven't killed you yet."

"What about my sparkling personality?" I teased, feeling much better than earlier.

"Don't push it. I'm complimented out." She flashed me a wink before gripping the ladder to slink away without saying goodbye.

I shook my head at her, a small smile pulling on the corner of my mouth. Across the deck, Andra was directing shiphands in the rigging and pointing at those who missed a spot swabbing the deck. Luella passed her, pressing a casual kiss on her cheek before disappearing under the deck for her quartermaster duties.

Luella had several lists to make. One for restocking *The*

Ollipheist for the next expedition and another for our journey through the Isles from monarch to monarch. I knew she planned on restocking at every port, but in case of storms or sirens, we had to be prepared for the worst.

"Mae!" Andra called, stealing my attention away from my thoughts. "Break time is over! I need an extra pair of hands."

I perked up. "Aye, ma'am!" I shouted, grasping the ladder to slide down to the main deck.

I could feel Ronin's gaze, and it made the butterflies inside me start flapping again, those nerves returning. I missed feeling comfort with him, but now anxiety had replaced it, teetering on the line of fear.

Anxious that I'd say the wrong thing.

Anxious that I might hurt him.

Afraid to lose him.

I shook my head, giving Andra my attention as I waited for her orders.

2

MAEVE CROSS

On *The Ollipheist*, new sailors worked as a cabin boy, no matter their station or experience. We had a large influx of them from the Farlight Prison. Everyone started on the lowest level of the hierarchy. They floated from various crews to help where needed until their first year was up.

The promotion was standard. As was the increase in pay.

Then they would move to another ship, leave the life altogether, or choose which crew to join, whether it be ship crew, gunnery crew, or even night crew. The only exception was when the crew head decided they wanted a cabin boy to join their charge early.

That was the case for Luther. It was hard to believe that the same scrawny boy who'd knocked me off the ship had found his calling in the galley with Butcher. Not as red-faced or soft-spoken anymore, he barked orders to the other cabin boys like a natural.

The hour before dinnertime was always hectic.

Cabin boys were moving in and out of the cramped galley, which wasn't much more than two narrow countertops, a large sink, a charcoal oven that billowed smoke out the windows, and a handful of burners. I assisted in the preparation by dicing onions, slicing off mushy parts of potato for composting, and chopping carrots for the three massive stewpots.

Nothing stamped the midway point in a voyage like Butcher's infamous garbage pail soup. It was tastier than it sounded. This stew would simmer for days, feeding sailors with all the scraps that wouldn't last the next two weeks.

"Your knifework is getting better, Mae!" Luther commented enthusiastically as he moved around me to gather more vegetables from the cold box cooled by water rushing through the pipes before siphoning into the filter system.

I beamed, flashing him a grin full of teeth. "Thanks!"

He nudged me playfully before pointing over at one of the new faces that was blocking up the small space. "You! The dishes are pilin'. Get to it or get out!"

Butcher glanced over at him, his single eye gleaming with pride. He stood next to me, leaning on his braced leg while his knife glided expertly over the cutting board. He rolled his sleeves up his forearms, revealing several silver scars.

I imagined he'd been quite similar to Luther once upon a time. Red-faced and young. His formerly pale, rosy skin was now tanned from decades in the sun, and he was far from scrawny with a stocky frame and massive arms that he used to get around when the aid for his missing leg wasn't cutting it.

Glancing down at his hands, I noticed scars and chunks of flesh missing but long healed. I replicated his motions, trying to make sure I used my knife correctly. It was muscle memory to Butcher now, but I was still getting the hang of it.

"Luther," Butcher called out. "Get 'em sea biscuits. The first pot is ready for bellies."

With a salute, the young man shouted back, "Aye!"

He turned his attention to the cabin boys, instructing them to bring the pot and bowls and utensils to the mess for hungry sailors. They got right to work, leaving Butcher and me alone in the galley.

"You've been spendin' more rounds here, lassie. Is there a reason why?" Butcher asked.

There was. More than one. I was following Luella's advice to get to Conway through Butcher. It felt insincere, but I also didn't know how else I was going to get to the bottom of the massacre at Fisherman's Gully.

Or my identity.

Perhaps the most nefarious mystery, why Varric was there if he was on good terms with the merrow.

"Do I need a reason to be here?" I countered. "Maybe I just enjoy your company, Butcher."

Not the whole truth, but also not a lie. I genuinely enjoyed the old sea dog's company. He was delightful to chat with and even more delightful to learn from.

He chuckled. "Don't give me that cheeky rubbish."

"Fine. Fine," I relented, thinking about which reason I wanted to start with. I couldn't dive right into asking him about his husband.

There was another reason I sought out his company. Perhaps it was more selfish than the first, and it definitely sounded more pathetic the longer I thought about it.

Just spit it out, Mae.

"One reason I'm here is because I'm learning a lot. What spices to use. How to use a knife…," I trailed off, heat finding my cheeks.

Butcher waited patiently, even though the noise from the mess steadily got louder as more sailors sat down for dinner.

"Last time we were at Anchorage Cove, Ronin cooked for me. I want to return the favor," I said, my face boiling as I admitted it aloud. I *did* want to cook for Ronin so the foolish man would sit there and relax once in a while, but that wasn't the *entire* reason I wanted to cook for him.

Many of my daytime fantasies included watching Ronin

knead bread dough and wanting it to be *me* under his hands rather than flour and water. I imagined making a mess of the flour, getting the powder in my hair as he took me to the highs I *always* thought about.

The things I would do to that man....

"Aw. That's sweet, lassie." He nudged me with his shoulder, tearing me from my indecent thoughts.

I missed the intimacy with Ronin afterward, but *during*, I couldn't find it in me to care about anything else. Just that he took the painful, longing *ache* away.

I'd fall into a million pieces if he barely brushed me in passing.

Pathetic.

Push it down, Mae. Give him time.

"You know, I don't think I'll ever get used to Cap's real name," Butcher murmured. He seemed to fall into a deep thought, rubbing his stubbly chin before getting back to his task.

"What do you think about it, then?" I asked.

"I think it'll be a tough road. But Cap was good to me. Took me in even after I served in Varric's navy."

I stopped what I was doing. "*You* used to serve in the Royal Navy?"

He nodded, mouth twisting into a frown. "It's how I lost my eye. I know firsthand what that man is capable of. I can tell you right now that the amulet around his neck isn't the source of his power."

"What do you mean?"

"Sure, that trinket bypasses natural limits for human magic, but that man could manipulate someone into killing their own children even without it. I've seen it." Butcher shook his head fiercely. "I know it can be hard to hear these things about your flesh and blood, but you need to know *who* this man is."

He's not my father.

I kept my mouth shut, offering my ear. "Okay."

"I wasn't much older than you when I joined the service. Not to fight. I wanted to cook. They made me fight." He squeezed his eye shut. "The situation was a powder keg. Power turns people into monsters, especially when the helpless are involved. My rankmates were ordered to burn down a village unless the people surrendered. When they did surrender… my CO still killed them."

"That's awful." I didn't know what else to say. I heard a little of this story from varying perspectives, including from Enya talking about how Varric had wronged every sailor one way or another, but it was different hearing it from someone on the side of the aggressor.

"I deserted. When they found me, they took my eye and lined me up for hanging."

I remembered this part. "That's when Conway saved you."

At the mention of his husband, a fond smile pulled at the corner of his mouth. The tension left his shoulders. "I didn't deserve to be saved, and I definitely don't deserve him."

"You don't mean that. Conway loves you."

"Doesn't mean I deserve it." He sighed and laid his knife down. "It's nothing compared to what happened to Conway. To think that I knew some of the soldiers who had orders to kill the merrow…. It makes me sick. But after everything, Conway and I still have each other. The one good thing that came out of this whole blasted war."

I cast him a sidelong look, getting some peace of my own to know that he managed to find a little good among all the bad. "I'm happy you found each other." After another few beats, I asked, "What happened at Fisherman's Gully?"

"Not my story to tell, lass."

I chewed my lower lip, bringing my eyebrows together. "Would Conway tell me about it? Why were they attacked?"

Butcher considered before nodding. "If it matters to you, we can talk about it over dinner back at Shipwreck Bay." He paused, his one eye focusing on me. "Why do you care so much about Fisherman's Gully?"

I rubbed my arms, pondering my response. "It doesn't make sense for Varric to attack potential allies, so I think it would help Ronin to know *why*. If we know even a little snippet of his motivation, it could really help us in the long run."

"If it'll help Cap… then say no more."

Warmth spread through my chest as I smiled, feeling lighter inside. "Thank you, Butcher."

He nudged me playfully. "Anything for my favorite lassie and my captain."

3

MAEVE CROSS

With two bowls of dinner warming my hands, I climbed the steps toward Ronin's cabin. The sun lowered onto the horizon, casting everything in an orange glow. The ocean was breathtaking. The scent of brine in my nose, the warm breeze on my skin, and the sight of the sunset—it felt like paradise.

It never ceased to amaze me.

I gave Plankwalker a friendly nod as he set the course for the night helmsman—Mooney—to make their job a little easier after everyone went to sleep.

"Evenin', Mae," Plankwalker greeted, gesturing to Ronin's door. "Cap just turned in for the night."

I nodded in thanks, using my foot to kick the door in an attempt at knocking. It only took Ronin a few moments to answer, his jaw strained, hands gripping the door for support. As usual, he put up a front to hide it.

But I clocked his discomfort instantly. The subtle shake in his legs as if he'd been on them too long. The tight strain of the tendon in his neck. I wanted to kiss it. Stroke away all the discomfort.

He looked clammy, his throat bobbing as if he was swallowing down pain.

Let me take it away. Let me take care of you.

But he wouldn't… and I couldn't push him. He'd shut me out, and this time he might not open the door again.

As soon as he gazed down at me, his eyes softened. He looked as if he had a million things to say to me but had no idea how to. Instead, he only said, "Hey, sweetheart."

The low timbre of his voice made my knees wobble. My belly fluttered. Nervousness and longing flushed through my entire being, from the tingles at the top of my scalp to the tips of my toes.

I want you.

I ached for him from a distance, but it was even worse up close.

My cheeks warmed. "Hey."

"Did you bring me dinner?" he asked, noticing the bowls in my hands. He swallowed again, hiding how utterly nauseous he was. He'd never admit it to me, anyway.

"No, I was going to eat both bowls myself." It came out teasing, but if he couldn't stomach anything, I didn't want to force him to eat.

The corner of his mouth pulled up, a dimple puncturing his cheek, making those butterflies swarm as I drank in his smile. I was so damn lovesick that everything he did made my knees shake and my skin tingle.

"My mistake." He crossed his arms, leaning heavily on the doorframe, appearing nonchalant to anyone who didn't know better. "Well, at least come in so I can watch you eat two fucking bowls of stew."

I giggled softly, passing him to place the bowls on the table next to the window.

The door closed with a quiet click as he groaned, then pressed his back against the door to get his balance. I sat down at the table, watching him take deliberate steps toward me. He didn't want my help, but that didn't make it any easier to watch him struggle.

Gods, just let me help, you blasted stubborn man.

"Are you all right?" I asked when he sat down across from me, visibly falling slack with relief once he was off his feet. That glorious throat of his bobbed, and I wanted to press my lips to it so it would stop trembling. "And don't lie to me."

He sighed. "I'm fine, Mae."

He wasn't.

But I didn't push it. If he didn't want to talk about it, then no force in the entire realm would change his mind. It reminded me of that time he told me how a rival pirate captain tied him down to pluck his fingernails out one by one until he revealed the location of Anchorage Cove's wealth of coin.

The rival captain didn't survive the encounter. It took several months for his nails to grow back, but Ronin thought it was a small price to pay.

But I wasn't a rival.

I wasn't an enemy.

I was someone who loved him more than anything, and with every lie, he drifted further and further away.

He ate a few bites of the stew, and I couldn't help but rub my hands together and watch him. He took a deep breath to steel himself with every nibble.

I ached to smooth the wrinkles on his shirt. Kiss his throat. Comb his hair. I wanted to pull him back so he would stop drifting away from me. He needed a reminder that he wasn't alone, but maybe that frightened him more than loneliness.

Suddenly, I didn't feel hungry anymore. I was more interested in the dip between Ronin's collarbones. His sleeves rolled up over his forearms. The way his throat bobbed when he drank something. The needle holes in his arms were still red and irritated. Some had faded, but the more recent ones were raw, as if he kept scratching at them.

His shoulders were narrower than they used to be, and the muscles of his arms were slightly atrophied, but he seemed to be getting his strength back faster in his arms than in his legs. He wore his hair down to hide the matted areas he hadn't been able to comb out yet.

Weariness hung on his face, deepening creases, but it didn't make him any less beautiful.

If only he'd let me touch him.

My heart thundered at the thought of closing the gap between us to taste his lips again. My skin would sing and pebble with goose bumps if he so much as breathed on me.

I wasn't hungry for dinner; I was hungry for *him*.

Starved.

I wondered if he could hear my breathing shallow at the mere thought of touching him. Tingles ran rampant down the nape of my neck, coiling at the base of my spine. My eyes lingered on his throat and the valley of his chest where his shirt hung open half unbuttoned.

My passion for him only seemed amplified by the distance.

"Yes?" Ronin asked, quirking an eyebrow at me. "Why are you staring at me?"

I looked away. Heat flushed my face, and I gulped down all the lustful thoughts of ripping his shirt open to hear the buttons ping off the wooden floor.

"What are you thinking about, sweetheart?" The tone of his voice remained unbothered but was toeing the line of condescending.

I wrung my hands together, my face incredibly hot.

"Look at me when I'm talking to you."

My mouth went dry as his presence overwhelmed me.

The smell of cedar and seawater filled my lungs, but it wasn't enough. "I just…. I want you. I *ache* for you…."

His eyes were soft, something I couldn't identify flickering in the dark depths. "Eat something, Mae."

I swallowed, cheeks getting even hotter as I tried not to let the rejection get to me. A huff of breath left my lips as I ate a few spoonfuls of stew, biting my tongue to keep from arguing. I could feel the intensity of his eyes on my face, and I tried—quite poorly—not to give my disappointment away.

A throaty chuckle broke through my thoughts. "Baby," he started, drawing my gaze back up to him to see a dimple in his cheek, easing the sting of his rejection. "That's not a no."

"Oh?" I perked up, excitement prickling the back of my neck.

"Stop worrying about me. I can see it all over your face. Eat something."

I waved him off with a dismissive hand and teased, "Me worried about the Great Captain Leviathan? Never."

His eyes flashed again with that emotion I couldn't place. It was gone as soon as I noticed it. "That's what I thought. Don't make me repeat myself."

I scoffed. "What was that?"

He laughed under his breath, knowing I was baiting him as usual. The sound of his laugh made my belly feel fuzzy, warmth expanding in my chest. If I could make him smile all the time, I would.

We ate our dinner between banter, teasing here and there. This time he wasn't floating further and further across a chasm, only at arm's length.

I enjoyed myself so much that I had almost forgotten one of the things I wanted to talk about.

"When we get back to Shipwreck Bay, would you come with me to Butcher and Conway's place? He invited me to dinner," I asked as I stacked our bowls to place outside the door for the cabin boys.

"Of course, Mae. You don't have to ask."

"I'll always ask," I returned, closing the door.

He didn't reply, but the gentle curve of his lips told me he appreciated it. He watched me as if mustering one last surge of energy to get up. "Is this about Fisherman's Gully?"

I rubbed the back of my neck. "Varric says that's where he found me. In the care of the merrow shoal." My voice got quiet. "I need to know. And *you* need to know why he was there to begin with."

"You're right about that," Ronin concurred. "Though Fisherman's Gully was a massacre. I doubt Conway will want to talk about it."

"But he might. And I have to hold on to that. Maybe he knows who I am."

He made a throaty noise. "That's true. He might. But are you ready to admit it? You can't close that door once you open it."

That piece of information could be the floodgates in a storm. But I'd made my decision.

I made it a long time ago.

I chewed on my lower lip, gears turning in my head. "I won't be ignorant anymore."

My answer satisfied him. "All right. Then I'm with you." Ronin pushed himself off the chair to take a seat on his bed. He groaned in relief, falling backward onto the furs. "I love this fucking bed."

"I have to agree. Your bed is considerably more comfortable than the officer bunks," I teased, striding over to him to help him take his boots off.

He fell slack as I lifted his leg to pull them off. His calves tensed, the muscles nearly pulsing with overexertion. I tested to see if he would tolerate my touch by running my hand up his calf.

Instead of pushing me away, he sighed, tilting his head back against the pillows.

"Is this okay?" I asked, continuing my ministrations as I moved on to the other leg. I removed his second boot and ran my hand up that one too.

I glanced up to see his eyes closed, his arms folded behind his head. He grumbled, "It feels nice. Keep at it."

"Would it kill you to say please?" I commented, kneeling on his bed to stretch over him, working away the exhaustion from the day.

My shirt dipped to reveal the curves of my breasts. Ronin's breath caught as he touched me tentatively through my blouse. I arched my back, craving everything he'd give me.

More....

My eyelashes fluttered as I unconsciously pushed into his hands.

A euphoric sensation swept up my body, pebbling my nipples and tensing my belly. The ache intensified, throbbing between my legs like I'd been on edge all day.

He pinched my oversensitive nipple, tearing a desperate noise from my lips before I could stop it. He twisted it, and I rewarded him with a breathy gasp.

I melted into a puddle of pure liquid desire for him.

Sex was easy.

Simply two bodies seeking out gratification. No traumas or hard conversations. Just sex.

It had to be enough.

But it isn't enough.

"I'd rather make *you* say please. It always sounds so pretty on your lips."

I unconsciously curved my throat toward him. If I replied, my voice would shake. His mouth hypnotized me, the world around me growing hazy, like a vignette had surrounded him. I reached for his forearms, tasting him with my touch.

His eyes never left mine, their pupils devouring the irises.

My breathing grew heavier as every filthy thought I'd been suppressing came to the surface. I was recalling how many times we'd been together—and how many times I wanted to do it again.

I craved him in the early morning before the sun woke up.

He captured my dreams when I fantasized about having all of him. All the dreadful thoughts. The agony. The scars. The light buried within the darkness. I wanted *everything*.

I don't want to feel alone.

Make me feel alive again.

He groaned softly when I walked my fingers down to his belt. Twisting them in the waistband of his trousers, I felt his skin burn through the fabric, his eyes half lidded as he let me continue. I ached to feel his skin. Feel his body on mine again. I needed the calluses on his hands to leave scratches on me. Marks that wouldn't go away.

"You're awfully needy, sweetheart," he teased, removing his hand from my breast to return it behind his head.

Touch me again.

He lay there, all spread out for me, eyes dancing with excitement. My breathing came out faster and harder. My cheeks flushed down to my collarbone. A boiling heat erupted within me.

Give me everything.

"Is that a complaint?" I rebutted breathlessly. "I can stop."

Empty threats. We both knew that.

I wanted to help him forget about whatever tangled thoughts or trauma had been weighing him down. And he was going to help me forget about all the questions I didn't know the answers to.

Ronin played along with my threat, mischievously saying, "If you stop, I might have to find the energy to hunt down those cuffs for teasing me."

I straddled his waist, earning a low groan. I rolled my

hips against him, shuddering and tossing my head back when a bolt of electric desire shot down my spine. Heat pooled at its base, swelling my clit as I rocked against him again.

He hummed, watching me, his eyes flickering down my body. I traced his chest, unbuttoning his shirt slowly. I grazed every new strip of skin, drinking in every reaction.

"But what if I'm having fun?" I asked, continuing to trail featherlight brushes down his chest. He shivered and arched into my touch. "I like the way you're looking at me right now."

His pupils had now fully devoured his irises. "Stop playing this game, Mae."

"I like this game." I dipped down and kissed his neck. Listening to something that resembled a growl get stuck in his throat, I stroked a sensitive part of his neck with my tongue, nipping and suckling. "I know the rules."

His hips bucked upward, and the noise he made unleashed another wave of prickly desire down my body. My eyelids fluttered as I moaned against his shoulder, inching farther and farther down. I unbuckled his belt and unlaced his trousers. I veered back, greedily eating him up with my eyes.

And he was a banquet.

A sight for *me* and me *alone.*

Shirt splayed open. Chest heaving. Breeches unlaced. Face flushed and lips parted with shallow breaths. His eyes were hooded as he grasped the pillows. I wanted to commit the desperate way he was looking at me to memory.

The word *beautiful* wasn't enough.

Everything seemed to pale in comparison to the man underneath me. Warmth swelled in my chest as I leaned down to kiss him, murmuring, "I love you," before capturing his lips.

He returned the kiss, releasing the pillows to place a hand

on each of my hips, curling them around me. I cupped his jaw, the stubble prickling my fingers.

You're not close enough....

I deepened the kiss, giving him everything I had because I wasn't sure when this intimacy would be taken from me.

With one movement, he rolled us over so he could hover above me. His eyes bored into mine as he pulled back, breath puffing across my lips. "I love you, too, Mae."

I'd become so accustomed to his lies that I wasn't sure if I believed him. But those soulful eyes drew me in, and I let myself fall victim to his honeyed tongue. My heart fluttering in my chest, I was weak in the knees, even lying down. "Kiss me some more."

Our lips molded together as Ronin pulled my shirt off, tugging on my trousers impatiently. The room seemed to get hotter with each layer of clothing shed. He pinned my hands over my head with one of his, making me arch my spine toward him. I parted my legs around his hips instinctively, rocking us together, needing to feel connection.

Needing to feel *alive*.

His cock throbbed against my skin, swollen with need. Wetness pooled between my legs as I tilted my hips up, rocking my needy sex against him. I whimpered, a plea almost leaving my lips.

His eyes blistered with desire, face pinkened with a lustful blush. It wouldn't last forever, so I'd drink up every ounce of affection to keep me warm when I went back to my own bed.

A bead of fire had ignited under my skin, eating me alive. I needed to burn. I needed to let the fire consume me and be reborn once it had finally swallowed me.

"Ronin," I murmured as his cock slid against me, velvety smooth, perfectly slick with our mutual desire. He pulled his hips back, and a whine bubbled up from my throat.

His mouth descended on my throat, nipping the soft skin there. "We both know what I want."

"*Please*," I whimpered.

I could feel his lips pull upward against my neck. "So pretty with your sweet voice."

A guttural noise of pleasure left my lips when the crown of his cock notched exactly where I wanted it, sinking in. I cried out softly, murmuring another plea.

His arms shook around my head, grip loosening on my wrists.

My inner walls fluttered around him, clenching as pleasure tightened the base of my spine. I could already feel rapture unfurling across all my muscles, tingling my skin, flushing my cheeks.

His eyes screwed shut. "Yeah. Choke my cock like that."

A whimper fell from my lips. "That filthy mouth will be the death of me," I gasped, my legs completely falling open.

"There are worse ways to die," he replied somewhat cheekily, taking my earlobe between his teeth and pulling.

"Ronin." His name turned into a plea as I tried to rock my hips back and forth to get him to move.

I needed more.

I needed to forget.

I needed *him*.

He grunted, releasing my hands to grab my hips. He leaned back on his knees, pulling me with him to stay fully sheathed. "Would it kill you to be patient?"

"Yes," I whined, painfully full and completely unsatisfied. "Would it kill you to fuck me like you mean it?"

"You're infuriating," he said, sliding out to slam back inside.

My eyes rolled back. "Oh, *godsdamnit*. Do that again."

"Say please."

That condescending tone again. Any other time I'd argue

and string this along. But I was too far gone to fight even if I wanted to. "Oh, Ronin… *please*. Take me. Please."

He grasped my hand and took two of my fingers into his mouth. His tongue swiped around them, moistening the skin. Heat tightened in my belly as he positioned it between us. "Touch yourself for me, sweetheart."

"Gods…," I murmured as I slid the swollen bud between my slicked fingers. I was saturated even without him putting my fingers in his mouth.

He pulled back and pounded back in. His eyes were on me, groans of desire falling past his lips. The hunger in his eyes made my belly flutter with every thrust.

"You're so fucking beautiful." He tilted his head back, losing himself in how I felt. He grasped my hips, moving me up and down his cock, pounding against a tender spot that had my head reeling. "Get there for me, baby. Let me feel you strangle my cock again."

I couldn't respond, too deep in the moment. My core tightened, warmth flooding my limbs as I rubbed circles on my clit, clenching around him with my impending orgasm. He moaned my name, fucking me harder, driving us toward the edge of euphoria.

He swelled, reaching the pinnacle of pleasure shortly before I did. Filthy noises spilled from his lips when he finished. I whimpered his name, my entire body going slack as the waves of it washed over me, thrashing me so hard I could barely breathe. He captured my mouth again with a kiss that took my breath away completely.

It wasn't passionate the way we'd just taken pleasure from each other.

No.

He kissed me as if I'd disappear at any moment. As if he had so much to tell me.

As if he *needed me more than anything.*

I pulled him closer, burying myself in the comfort of his touch.

I wasn't going anywhere.

His chin rested on top of my head. He didn't say a word. I didn't know what was going on in his head, but the way he held me close told me that he was *trying*. His lips pressed against my forehead as he took in a deep breath.

That night, I didn't go back to my own bed. I fell asleep with Ronin stroking my hair while I nuzzled his chest. His body went slack and he finally—*finally*—accepted comfort.

4

RONIN MURDOCH

Moonlight spilled in from the windows at the stern of the ship. A silver glow kissed Mae's skin as she curled up under the furs, naked aside from one of my shirts. Her loveliness did nothing to get me out of my head.

Her soft wheezes didn't comfort me.

How dare you lie down next to her like you didn't let her die. Pathetic worm.

Nausea welled in my stomach, crawling up my throat. I tried so hard to fight it, but I lost, rushing to my washroom to purge my fucking guts into the chamber pot. My arms shook, a cold sweat saturating my forehead.

I clawed at my chest, trying to get out of my own skin. My panic suffocated me as I sat there, limp from how much all the retching took out of me.

Fucking vitrophine.

I couldn't even sleep it off because of the nightmares. Memories of the haze Pike kept me under. The ghost of unwanted touch everywhere. A million bugs crawling and slithering around me.

I don't even know what those pirate hunters did to me, but I can feel it.

Sometimes I was coherent and sometimes I wasn't. But their touch remained.

Every time I closed my eyes, Varric greeted me by sliding a scalpel across Mae's throat, my legs stuck unmoving in tar beneath me, banging on some invisible wall while I soundlessly screamed her name. In my dreams, an eel like the Cross coat of arms would slither from the tar, clamp around my throat, and drag me into the sludge.

I could never get out. In the black, all I heard was Mae dying. I'd listen to her crying my name, choking on her own blood. *Needing me*, but I couldn't break out of the tar as it filled my lungs and encompassed me with this overwhelming weight.

But she didn't die.

I'd felt her warmth in my arms all night. The scent of her hair lingered in my nose. My skin still tingled from where her breath billowed across my bare chest.

She's real.

She didn't die from Varric's hand.

She was right *fucking* here.

I pressed my hand into my chest, trying to offset the growing pressure. It didn't work.

Mae had traveled across the sea for me.

For how I was. Not for the damaged goods I had become.

She loved me as I was.

I retched again. Nothing came up, but my body lurched uncontrollably. My stomach clenched as agony squeezed my chest. I couldn't stop. I couldn't control it.

Mae can't know.

She can't know how sick I've become. She can't know that every day, I ache to go to my mother's stash of opioids just to go to sleep. Only to take the edge off.

That's what I would tell myself.

But I knew myself well enough to know that I'd start

relying on it. I relied on the fuzzy feeling of vitrophine for that split-second relief. I'd do the same with opioids.

I knew what happened to men who relied on drug-induced escape. I'd been to those dens to retrieve sailors under my charge. There was no excuse for me.

They relied on *me*. I'd suffer for as long as I needed to. Without help.

I didn't need anyone's fucking help.

I ground my teeth together as my legs bunched under me. The muscles strained, hardly able to support my weight as I pushed myself to my feet. I ached from sparring with Wesley, but that didn't stop me.

I had to keep pushing. I *needed* to be strong.

The horrible feeling of pressure forced a throaty noise of discomfort from me as I tried to force my tendons back into their rightful place, straining the healing muscles when they weren't ready.

I feel so godsdamn sick.

I didn't have time for it. I just wanted to feel right again.

Nothing feels right anymore.

I pretended that I didn't feel the pain as I stood up to open the window in the washroom, hoping I'd settle my stomach so I'd stop dry retching.

She can't see me like this.

I threw it open, inhaling the sea air.

The briny scent twisted another sensation of dread from my bones.

Since Pike captured me, I hadn't been able to shift. Every night, I tried. The sea was an old friend, beckoning the sea beast within me to indulge in a swim.

But the tattoo didn't hum under my skin.

Dull and lifeless.

Faded like I was.

When Mae asked me what would happen if I couldn't shift, I never thought I'd be trapped in my skin. Unable to escape. Every night Pike had me, I could feel my leviathan squirm, desperate to unleash itself, but the vitrophine stole my control.

I would lie there, dizzy and incoherent, while Pike and his pirate hunters did whatever they wanted.

As the days went on, it became unbearable. My pulse pounded in my ears, my head reeled, and when it finally felt like my heart was going to split my chest, my leviathan *stopped.*

How in the Nine Hells was I supposed to unite the pirate monarchs? They'd never follow me. Then one by one, they'd bend to kiss Cross's rings.

There wasn't room for failure.

There wasn't room for weakness.

I was a shadow of the man I used to be, and I didn't know if I'd *ever* be the same.

Thickness formed in my throat as I looked out at the vast sea.

I'd been having dreams of my leviathan flying away from me, leaving me to sink into the tar. I'd hear a rumbling voice call me a pathetic worm and tell me I wasn't worthy to be a Royal Leviathan.

The phantom sensations of my leviathan stirred like a lost limb I was only imagining still existed, my spirit cleaved from me as viciously as an arm. Strike after brutal strike until all that remained was fleshy, bloody ribbons of muscle and sinew.

Who am I without my dragon?

What would my father think of me? What would my mother think of me? Would she think that I turned my back on our family?

I pushed the thought away and stepped over to my sink to wash out my mouth with filtered water until the nausea subsided. I brushed my teeth with a bristled toothbrush until I couldn't taste the sickness in my mouth anymore.

My eyes lingered on a second toothbrush in a separate rinse cup near mine that Mae used when we spent the night together.

Mae can't know. No one can know.

With soft, staggering steps, I sat down to look at myself in front of the mirror. The man who looked back was a stranger. He couldn't be me. Not with matted hair, sunken eyes, and gaunt cheeks. My shoulders were narrow, lacking the strength I used to have.

It'd been two weeks since Farlight Prison.

Since my forced bedrest and the start of my vitrophine withdrawal.

Since I'd gotten proper care for my atrophy.

With anxious fingers, I tried to pick apart the mats on my scalp. By now, I'd gotten most of them out, losing so much of my hair in the process. There were still several mats on the side of my scalp, under the crown of hair on my head.

I *hated* the way I looked. The way I felt.

I didn't want to look at the mats anymore. I grabbed a small dagger off the bench and sawed the big chunks away. I was sick of it. I wanted to cut it *all* off.

I need control over this.

"Ronin?" Mae's sleepy voice washed over me.

I closed my eyes for a moment, shoulders stiffening. Tremors shook my hands, and fear paralyzed me.

If I look at her, will she be drenched in her own blood?

Would I see her lifeless eyes? Neck split open like a torn seam?

Would she be breathing?

Get a fucking grip.

I gave her a sideways glance. She leaned against the doorway, looking so fucking beautiful with my shirt sliding off her shoulder. Even in the dull light, I could see the rosy pinkness dusted over her cheeks. Relief slackened my form.

She's alive.

"Go back to bed, sweetheart."

"Did you go for a swim?" she asked, stepping into the wet room and glancing at the open window.

"Yes," I lied. My heart tightened. I turned my attention back to the man in the mirror.

Fucking coward.

She wouldn't love you if she knew.

Do you want her to see the pathetic worm you've become?

I could feel her eyes stroke the side of my head to the balls of hair in my hands and on the floor. "Let me—if you don't mind."

The longing in her voice released a shiver down my spine.

Everything in me softened. I wanted to accept the comfort. I *wanted* her.

Conflicting thoughts ripped me in two.

I love her.

I wish she didn't love me.

I held out the knife, and Mae gave me the warmest smile as she accepted it, then stepped up to my back. My skin buzzed at her proximity. I ached for her touch, but I still couldn't help flinching the moment her fingers brushed the side of my head.

Her reaction was immediate. She withdrew her hand, taking a full step back from me.

No. The last thing I wanted to do was push her away. I caught her hand, relaxing as I initiated the touch. "It's not you, Mae."

"I know," she replied. "I just don't want to overwhelm you. I understand. It's okay."

Because she needs to handle you with gentle hands meant for a sniveling child.

"You're not," I said, more sharply than I meant to.

She didn't believe me. It was apparent all over her face, even though she tried to hide it.

Please don't pull away from me.

Please don't touch me.

Two contradictory emotions warred within me, but I knew what I wanted.

I reached out, cupping her soft, warm face between my palms. Her lips parted instantly, and she leaned into my hands as if starving for my touch.

She was.

I starved us both.

I stood up, ignoring the pain in my legs, and dipped my head down to capture her mouth. Her chest molded into mine, both of her arms curling around the back of my neck. My scalp tingled with delight, allowing me a reprieve from the crushing pressure that threatened to cave my ribs in.

Kissing Mae felt right.

I stroked her cheek, trying to fit everything I couldn't say in how I kissed her. Her soft tongue swiped across my lower lip, and I let her in. I nipped her pouty lip, and she gasped, pulling me closer.

I reared back, breaking the kiss.

She was a sight for sore eyes. Mae blinked up at me almost sleepily, pupils blown with excitement, skin flushed down to her collarbone. Gods, she was beautiful. The corners of her mouth pulled upward in a smile that weakened my knees.

"Okay," she decided. "Sit and let me at this hair."

My own mouth drew up into a smile because hers was so damn infectious that I couldn't help it. It silenced the doubt.

The intrusive thoughts.

Not forever, but for now.

"As you wish," I replied, sitting back down on the bench.

She turned up the oil lamp to brighten the room, bathing her in a soft yellow light. It brought out the dark freckles that decorated her nose and peppered her collarbones and her shoulders. I thought about pressing my mouth to each beauty mark, bathing her in affection to show her everything I didn't know how to say.

I couldn't help staring at her behind me in the mirror, her nose crinkled with focus. She drew her lower lip between her teeth, petal pink. Her round brown eyes narrowed as she gave me her full attention.

The fingers on my scalp didn't feel so foreign anymore. For now, I'd be able to tolerate it. Only because it was Mae.

She made me feel safe.

My guard slowly went down as she cut away chunks of matted hair. Every passing moment freed me. I wasn't attached to my hair, but such a simple thing altered my internal view of myself.

The man in the mirror looked more familiar. More put together. The hair on top of my head remained long with my scattered locs intact, but the sides were now cut down short. I was still able to wear it up or down.

However I liked.

Relief ebbed throughout my body, relaxing the anxiousness in my fingertips, which I'd been twisting the whole time.

"You look good," Maeve murmured, pressing a kiss on the side of my neck.

My skin tingled, nearly crying out for her. I needed her touch, needed everything she was willing to give me.

Warmth flooded my chest. "Yeah?" I asked, letting myself lean into her, tilting my head back against her chest. She was always so soft.

She beamed. "You always look good, but a fresh haircut helps. Do you like it? I've only practiced haircuts on Gunny."

I let myself stare up at her, melting like butter in a sizzling skillet. Inevitable. "That explains his terrible haircut last week."

Mae rolled her eyes, setting the blade on the bench. "Rude."

"You like it."

She giggled under her breath, and the sound might as well have been fucking music. "Perhaps."

Her wide brown eyes fell on me again, and she stroked the side of my face through my beard with her thumb. The way she looked at me….

I don't deserve it.

"Now, give me a serious answer."

"Fine. Fine. If you insist," I relented, glancing at myself in the mirror. It wasn't a perfect haircut and had some uneven bits here and there, but I liked it. And I liked it even more because Mae did it for me. I kissed her cheek, warm under my lips, before murmuring, "I like it. Thank you, sweetheart."

Her face pinkened that lovely hue I liked. "You're welcome."

For now, I felt okay.

The nausea subsided, and I took her into my arms again when we went to bed. I pressed my face into her supple chest, and she stroked comforting circles down my back until I fell asleep.

And this time, the nightmares stayed away.

5

MAEVE CROSS

When I woke up, Ronin's face was pressed into my chest, his bulky arms tight around my waist. His breath puffed out across the collar of the shirt where it fell open. Despite the angle we had tangled ourselves in during the night, I was quite comfortable.

Cozy and satisfied.

I combed through his hair with my fingers, stroking close to his scalp where the hair was shorter. He groaned in his sleep, burying his face closer. I basked in the affection, letting it refill the well that had run dry.

His hair was coarser than mine. The strands were thick enough to thread a needle. I admired him as he slept, enjoying how relaxed he looked in my arms. When he let himself be vulnerable around me, it was a gift.

I don't think he knows how beautiful he is when he lets me in. When he lets me see the parts of him he's too stubborn to reveal to anyone else.

He'd busied himself with taking care of the crew, but he never let anyone return the favor. I ached to take care of him.

With a rumble of his chest, he roused himself from a

seemingly deep sleep. He pressed himself farther into my hands, seeking out as much of me as he could tolerate.

His dark brown eyes met mine, the blue flecks glimmering. "Good morning, sweetheart." His voice was thick with sleep. He stroked the side of my jaw, kissing me deep enough to make my heart flutter.

Morning breath be damned.

I sighed, kissing him back before he pulled away. "Morning. Sleep well?"

"I did. Just not enough." He made this throaty noise before burying his face in my chest again. "I'm not ready to face the crew yet. I'm so fucking exhausted."

His breathing got all uneven when I ran my fingers through the loose strands of hair, my nails gently scratching his scalp. He practically preened as if he were a cat curling up in my lap. I was surprised that he didn't start purring.

That in and of itself filled me with incredible pride.

It'd been so long since he let me touch him freely. Without sex. Just intimacy.

"Then lie with me for a while. What do you have to do today?"

"Too much to do," he murmured, making no move to get up.

"You've been through the wringer, Ronin," I said, running my nails down to the nape of his neck. "You can rest every once in a while."

He sighed. "No. I can't." He drew back, propping himself up on his elbows to hover over me.

My eyes went all half lidded when I looked up at him. Even though he had satisfied me last night, my hunger couldn't be sated.

"Rest would be seen as weakness. And weakness sows a seed of doubt."

"But—" I tried to start, but Ronin pressed a finger to my lips.

"I know you want to help. And I love you for that. For your soft heart and your smart mouth." He paused, running his finger down my throat to the dip between my collarbones as if he debated leaning down to nibble on it.

Please do.

But he sighed and met my eyes again. "But you don't know these people like I do. New sailors challenge authority. Test boundaries to see how much they can get away with. I can't allow it. If I have an insubordinate crew, then the monarchs won't give me the time of day."

I grasped his hand, encouraging him to touch me before he pulled away. I wasn't ready for the bubble to pop. I wanted him to cup my face in his big hands and kiss away all my worries. "They're just people, Ronin."

"It's more complicated than that." He caressed my jaw before pushing himself up completely. His back flexed as he stretched, briefly distracting me from the problem at hand.

I followed him, sitting upright. "Then help me understand."

He hummed as if debating how to divulge that information. With a hesitant glance over his shoulder, he made his decision. "All right, baby."

The word *baby* made my belly tumble and flip over itself. "Go on, then. Get to it."

"Always impatient," he teased, reaching for a strip of fabric to tie his hair up. He paused for a moment, as if remembering his haircut, and his frame relaxed even more. He released his breath and pulled his hair completely up.

I enjoyed seeing him so open. Without his walls and without his lies. At least until he threw them up again, and the fissure between us grew larger and larger, like a crack in the foundation threatening to crumble what we'd built.

Don't think about that now.

"First of all, Lucky is in love with my mother," Ronin stated.

It took me a second to respond. "What?"

"If you ever see him and my mother in the same room, it's obvious. Makes you almost feel bad for him. But my mother has always been one for monogamy, and my stepfather was the jealous type."

Ronin stretched again, and I reached forward to touch his back, wanting to stroke the enticing muscles that were recovering nicely.

He flinched when my fingertips ghosted over his skin. I shouldn't have snuck up on him like that.

"Sorry." I withdrew my hand, recognizing that he'd hit his limit for the morning. I tried not to feel hurt by it, but it only got harder every time it happened.

"Maybe later. Right now, it would be too much," he said, eyes apologetic. Those dark, soulful eyes swam with so much. Guilt. Shame. *Pain.*

I wish he would tell me what he's thinking.

But he wouldn't. I didn't want to make him feel guilty, so I dropped it. None of this was his fault. I had Nathaniel and Varric to thank for how distant he'd become. "It's all right. Go ahead and continue."

"My mother never talked about it, but the twins and I speculated that most of Lucky's disdain for her was because he never got over the fact that she chose our father and not him."

"Would that disdain be enough for him to hold it against you?"

Ronin nodded. "Absolutely. I can't blame him. I'd feel the same way." He got up, steadying himself on wobbly legs to pull on his breeches.

Warmth found my face, and a foolish question flew past my lips before I could stop it. "You're talking about me, right?"

He tied the laces on his trousers and glanced at me from over his shoulder. The corner of his mouth twitched, and he raised a thick dark eyebrow in amusement. "No, I'm talking about my cat, Mae."

My face boiled, and I threw my legs over the edge of the bed. "Right."

Two big hands came into my view as he placed them on my thighs, the possessive gesture drawing my eyes up to his. "If I'm being completely honest, sweetheart, I've never been much for relationships at all," he admitted. "Someone getting too close to me was a liability. So, I'd fuck around a bit, but I never sought more."

I looked away again, unable to stop myself from sticking my foot in my mouth. "What about Violetta?"

"Look at me," he said, pulling my attention back to him again. "Violetta and I were never serious. She's nothing like you. I've *never* been with anyone like you. All right?"

Somehow my face got even hotter, and my heart ran rampant in my chest. "All right."

"I love you, Mae. You and your silly questions." The corner of his mouth quirked up, those dimples taking my breath away as I returned it.

Say it again. Never stop telling me you love me.

I swallowed and nodded, pulling away to dress myself. I took his shirt off and put on one of mine, followed by my trousers. I tied them off at the knee, my eyes darting over to Ronin as he sat on his bed to fiddle with his boots.

Gods, he is so handsome. All the time. I didn't think I'd ever get used to how he made my belly swarm with butterflies.

He tugged on his boots, grunting with discomfort but brushing it off quickly.

If he had been up for it, I would've climbed in his lap and kissed him until he forgot about all those pesky responsibilities bogging him down. Maybe in that postcoital bliss, he'd tell me what was going on in his head.

Why had he woken with a start before slinking out of bed

in the middle of the night? If it was a nightmare, he wouldn't talk about it. If it was his vitrophine withdrawal, he kept it to himself. I wanted to help him, and *he wouldn't let me.*

Though, I'd been thinking about other things. Including the fact that my wedding tonic was *definitely* out of my system now, and he still hadn't elaborated on *why* he couldn't have children with me, which bothered me even though the last thing I wanted to do was bring a child into this war-torn mess around us.

I'd never given children much thought beyond the fact that I did *not* want to be a mother. Not now, maybe not ever, but as strongly as I felt about it now, I knew I couldn't rule that part of my life out completely. I was only twenty-two. I didn't know what I'd want when I finally got a taste of peace.

Every other time we'd been physical, it'd been *just* sex. No pillow talk. I'd go back to my own bed while Ronin gave me nothing but ice.

But he seemed more open now than he'd been the past few weeks.

Ask him.

"There's one more thing I wanted to ask about," I mentioned, cheeks warm as I used the foot in my mouth to my advantage.

"Shoot," he replied, looking over his shoulder at me.

I laced my fingers together, my belly all tight with nerves. *We need to have this conversation, even if I dread it.* "You mentioned once that you couldn't get me pregnant even if you wanted to…."

Both his eyebrows flew into his hairline. "I did."

I was quiet for a moment, waiting for him to say something else.

He didn't, instead reaching to his nightstand for his belt.

Like pulling teeth. I huffed. "Care to elaborate a little?"

"No."

My lips pressed together into a thin line, and my glare loosened his lips on the matter.

He chuckled a little under his breath as he replied rather cheekily, "Why're you so interested? Do you want to carry my babies?"

Heat rushed to my cheeks, no doubt coloring my ears pink. For a split second, my heart pounded even harder as I gazed at him staring up at me with those disarming dimples. He had no right to look at me like that.

Just then I noticed how thick his lashes were, half lidded over his dark eyes. His gaze felt soft, full of adoration. All it took was a look and my knees became pudding.

He doesn't know the power he holds over me.

That scared the absolute daylights out of me. He didn't know how many pieces he held of me, while I barely held any of him.

I gulped the fear down, trying to distance myself from my vulnerability.

I didn't want to get hurt again.

I was having sex with him, but I hadn't forgiven him for how he left things the last time we were in Shipwreck Bay. That would take time.

"No. Of course not," I muttered. "My wedding tonic is out of my system. I'd rather not end up pregnant while pirate hunters and a fanatical king are after us."

"Fair. All right." Ronin stood up and buckled his belt, then got his sash to house his gear. "Then you have nothing to fear, sweetheart. There's no such thing as a hybrid fae. We're not biologically compatible."

A slap across the face would've hurt less. My heart clenched as I crossed my arms, trying to throw up some sort of armor around the fragile muscle. "It feels pretty godsdamn compatible to me."

"That's not what I'm talking about, love." He stepped

toward me, looming over me with that damn air of condescension around him. "Stop frowning."

"I'm not frowning," I retorted, averting my gaze completely.

He crooked a brow. "*Okay*, sure. Whatever you say. To put it as plainly as possible, fae can only have children with humans or their same type of fae, because humans are essentially a blank slate to accept the magic in our blood. Fae blood tends to fight the other for superiority."

"Oh." Some part of me was relieved, but the other part felt… disappointed. The emotions tangled tighter as my eyes flickered over to him.

I couldn't keep his gaze.

"Why are you looking at me like that, Mae?" he asked, no longer the man I spent the night with. He was all business, and his tone reflected it.

Why doesn't he care as much as I do?

The crack between us felt deeper than before. "I don't know. I suppose we never talked about the future. *Our* future." I hated how quiet my voice became. I knew there were other things we needed to worry about, but thinking about the future gave me hope for the present.

He had to care about that, too, right? Did… did he even want a future with me, or was this just an extension of our fling? Was he just going to fuck about a little longer before deciding to leave me another letter?

The knot in my belly tightened, calcifying into a rock.

He turned away from me, firmly shutting that emotional door between us.

Come back to me. Can't you see how much this hurts me?

He shrugged on his jacket and opened the cabin door. A harsh sigh flew from his lips. "One day we will talk about this. But it can't be now. I don't have time to ponder the future."

I nodded in defeat. "All right. I know."

"We have work to do."

I brushed by him, not looking back because I feared that vulnerability would rear its head and everything would hurt even worse.

"Aye, aye, Captain," I uttered bitterly.

"Are you still interested in being trained for rigging?" Andra asked, pulling me aside while the rest of the ship crew got to their duties.

I looked up at the vast maze of netting, lines, and crew members resetting the sails to crack with the wind. Tapping my fingers together, I couldn't help a broad smile sweeping across my face, excitement blooming in my chest. "Yes!"

Andra laughed. "I love the enthusiasm, Mae."

"Where do we start?" I asked eagerly. Perhaps too eagerly, but I'd been wanting to scale the netting since I saw the rigmates climbing through the maze of ropes and canvas my very first morning on the ship.

And this would be a nice distraction from the churning of my stomach.

It wasn't so much the conversation with Ronin itself. It was the utter lack of interest from the man I loved so damn much that every time I thought about it, it threatened to tear that fragile muscle in half. And I *knew* my unnatural healing wouldn't help me with that.

I didn't even *want* children, but I wanted a future. I wanted *something* with Ronin. Something hopeful to make me fight that much harder. It bothered me so much that if *he* wanted children, then everything we fought for wouldn't matter.

Our future.

None of it would matter. *We wouldn't work.*

Pushing those thoughts away, I gave Andra a big grin, putting on a brave face. Thankfully, she wasn't looking at me, or her damn intuitiveness would've seen it. Then I'd spend all day in the rigging with her asking me if I was all right.

And I couldn't lie to save my life.

"Come over here," Andra said, guiding me over to the base of the netting tied carefully to the side of the ship with a bowline knot.

The king of sailing knots—or so Gunny told me—used for just about anything. Easy to untie but could withstand a great deal of pulling.

"Tie your safety first," she instructed. "We have harnesses here."

I retrieved two of them from the stash kept nearby for this purpose as well as for siren attacks. It was nothing more than a tangle of line with loops to stick my legs through like a pair of trousers. Two straps went over my shoulders with a closing hook to lock around ropes.

"You'll use this hook to attach yourself to the mizzenmast so you don't go falling off the canvas into the big salt. I think Ronin may actually knock me off the half wall if anything happens to you."

Or he'd finally be rid of me and my *silly questions*. I'd wash ashore somewhere and be someone else's problem.

"Oh, I'll be fine," I commented, gulping down the sour taste in my mouth. I followed her lead when she showed me how to tie the loose ends around my waist.

Her dark eyes pinned me with absolute seriousness. "When we're up in the rigging, you need to listen to everything I say. We're fortunate to be one of the few ships that use safeties, but even these fail sometimes."

"I hear you," I replied, giving her my complete focus. "I'm ready."

Andra tugged on my safety to make sure it was tight

enough for her liking. "All right. Let's go. The netting can be tricky. Do not let go until your feet are secure."

Throughout the afternoon, Andra and I traversed the rigging as I learned the proper technique to climb it. With every few feet we climbed, we'd hook our arm into the netting and move the safety hook farther up.

It was tedious and time-consuming, but every time I slipped, I was thankful it was there to catch me. I knew that even if the fall killed me, I'd get back up again.

But it would still hurt like the Hells.

My arms ached from constantly pulling myself up or hooking one in so I could help tighten a few of the knots that had loosened throughout the day. Or when Andra would stop to show me what to pull and retie to readjust a canvas to the wind.

While I struggled, the rigmates moved around us, throwing a cheerful "Hello" to me every once in a while. It was second nature to them. One day, I'd be able to move just as effortlessly, but like wielding the cutlass, it took practice.

Exhausting, sweaty, and blister-covered practice.

No wonder the rigmates were unbelievably toned. I'd frequently catch them arm wrestling in the mess. They'd even gamble and have lighthearted competitions over drink.

One time, I foolishly thought I could win, and they threw me across the bench. The mess erupted in laughter, and my opponent helped me to my feet and brushed me off.

"Better luck next time."

Mortifying in the moment, but I could look back and laugh at it.

Those memories were some of my favorites, along with the soft moments Ronin and I used to share when we looked up at the stars and wondered if the Gods were really watching us. I was more optimistic than he was, though it did feel like the Gods had dealt us a shitty hand.

Again, that unsettling feeling rose in my belly and welled in my throat.

"Up here, lass," Andra called out, sitting on a platform in the middle of the mast. The platform lined up perfectly with one of the sails, just a foothold away from the ties holding everything together.

I joined her, but not without attaching my safety hook to a notch on the platform. I was out of breath but thrilled as I gazed down at the little heads rushing around the deck below us. Andra sat quietly next to me, glancing my way as if she wanted to say something but wasn't sure how.

After several moments of breathing heavily, rigmates moving around us, and Luella shouting orders on deck, Andra sighed. "Are you all right, Mae? You seem distant."

"Do you want children?" I blurted before I could stop myself. *What is with me and my mouth today?*

Both of Andra's eyebrows flew up. "What? You... you've only known my brother for a few months. How long have you...? That's not nearly—"

I needed to cut her off. "Because I don't know if I do."

Instantly, relief swam over her face. Followed by confusion. "I... I mean, I'm in a committed relationship with another woman. A biological child isn't something either of us want. Maybe one day, we'll take an orphan into our care...."

I looked away, frowning. That didn't make this awful feeling go away. I didn't know what it was or why it was there, but it only seemed to swell inside. "Oh."

"Why do you ask?"

"I don't know." I shrugged it off. "Let's go down. It's almost mealtime."

Andra's hand shot out and stopped me from getting up. "No, you don't. Tell me what's going on." Her voice was full of worry, and the fact that she was concerned at all made me feel like an unhoused duckling tucked under a wing.

I softened, aching for some type of reassurance that I wasn't a foolish girl asking silly questions. "I never wanted kids. So I don't know why I'm so upset to hear that's not an option."

"I see." She didn't pry about the logistics.

Thank the Gods.

My chest ached as if my heart would drop out and take me with it. "I don't understand why I feel like this. And Ronin… doesn't seem to care."

"Don't dwell on him. He's not talking to anyone right now." She rubbed the back of her neck. "Believe it or not, Luella and I went through this. Luella has experienced a lot of pain in her life, and the prospect of having children dragged up trauma that I didn't want her to go through again."

I nodded, encouraging her to continue.

"When Lu told me, I didn't know how to feel. But after years of processing it, I came to terms with it. I'll save you some time. This feeling? It's grief. You're grieving what you'll never have. Possibilities you *don't* have." Andra put her hand on my shoulder, and that complicated feeling started to unravel like the first tug on a knot.

Andra was only a year younger than Ronin but several years older than me. For the first time, I had an older sister looking after me. Offering me wisdom to make my journey a little easier. I'd never had guidance or powerful women to look up to.

The weight inside lightened. She was right. It didn't matter if it was something I wanted or not. It was one more thing I couldn't have.

"But at least you've already jumped over that hurdle." Andra nudged me with her elbow. "Levi may be older than you, but I promise you, this is uncharted territory for him too. And when you're new at anything, you fumble. What's important is how you recover."

"You're right," I answered, mulling over her words again and again. The pain wasn't completely gone, but it helped. I looked over at her. "Thank you."

"Anytime, Mae," Andra replied. Then she slapped me on the back and got to her feet. "Breaktime is over. Get off your hind end. There's more to do."

And just like that, the moment was over, but my spirits were a little lifted. "Aye, aye, ma'am!"

6

RONIN MURDOCH

I'M SUCH A FUCKING PRICK.

I knew I had self-destructive tendencies, but they'd never manifested so badly before. Mae allowed herself to be vulnerable with me. She asked a simple question that she had every right to know the answer to, and I belittled her.

Why couldn't I stop myself?

My heart ached the more I thought about the future with Mae. How badly I wanted her by my side. But I had a million other things to deal with before I even considered the future.

It was a pipe dream. Nothing more than a fantasy.

I squeezed my eyes shut, regretting instigating anything with her.

She deserved someone who could give her a real answer. Give her everything she wanted. Be strong enough to keep her safe.

I should've been strong enough.

But I wasn't.

She deserved someone who could be an immoveable force to keep bastards like Pike or Cross from ever fucking touching her again. She deserved someone who could've *saved her* instead of watching her choke to death on her own blood.

Mae deserved the whole fucking world and someone who wasn't lying to her.

But I was too damn selfish to let her go.

I remembered her death vividly. Every single fucking flutter of my eyelids played that harrowing scene over and over again. Even now, when she was in the room with me, I blinked and for a split second, I saw her throat split open.

My stomach churned as the nausea flared again, making my mouth water.

I gulped it down, focusing on the thick canvas map rolled out on my desk in front of me. Luella pulled out a small pouch of items to represent each of the monarchs. She placed the items along the map to dictate their last known location.

Lucky—a carved knucklebone from Wesley's set.

Bliss—a golden coin.

Violetta—a single earring from a set of fine jewelry.

"First, we go to Lucky's Outpost. It's on the other side of Shipwreck Bay, not even a two-day voyage along the coast," Luella strategized. "I've prepared correspondence to the monarchs, alerting them of our arrival. I'll send them once we get back."

Leaning on my desk, I looked over Wesley's shoulder. We were dressed only in our shirts and trousers, our officer jackets hanging on the coatrack. The weather was changing, moving from spring into summer. Wesley had even tied his trousers at the knee to adjust to the heat.

Luella sat across from us in one of the plush chairs nailed down to the planks so they weren't knocked over every time we hit a wave. "He's the closest. Makes the most sense."

Her broad-brimmed hat cast a shadow over her eyes before she took it off, hanging it on the coatrack right next to mine. Her red hair was plastered against her neck. She tossed it over her shoulder, but it seemed to be bothering her, so I reached into one of my drawers and passed her one of my ties made from fabric scraps.

She dipped her head, snatched it, and tied her hair up. Wordlessly, she tapped at the side of her head, indicating the place where my hair was short, and gave me an approving grunt. There were times that Luella and I could have full conversations without uttering a single word.

Wesley seized our attention when he tapped at the various marked locations on the map. The pirate colonies moved around, but The Big Three had settled in corners of Farlight far away from Varric's army.

Lucky was located on the other side of Shipwreck Bay in an outpost along a ship graveyard. We marked our route to ensure we had the correct amount of supplies for our small crew. The waters wouldn't be as harsh since we'd be sticking to shore currents and not the open sea.

The plan was to visit each of the monarchs and convince them to come back to Shipwreck Bay to forge a formal council to unite us against Cross's inevitable siege. Shipwreck Bay was neutral ground.

Less likely to end in a gunfight. One of the few rules of the port town.

Not officially put into law, but they were common knowledge. No territory fighting. No spilling blood. No violent robbery. Honor among thieves. Even the common bandits or pirates unaligned with the monarchs knew how to behave themselves there.

Sure, sometimes those rules were broken, but they were enforced by the residents who lived there. Shipwreck Bay could be dangerous, but it was also a safe haven for families, merchants, and anyone escaping the war. They looked after their own.

The monarchs respected that. They had all the power to burn the port town to the ground, but considering Shipwreck Bay had taken them in when they needed it, it became an unwritten code of conduct.

"Also," Wesley said, marking a spot where we knew there was rocky terrain, "I've been meaning to ask about what crew we're taking. The ketch only has room for ten, at most."

Luella shrugged. "I figured it'd be us mates, Levi, Seabird, and Mae. Let the rest of the crew enjoy shore leave."

"Not Mae," I stated. I wanted her safe, not in a position where the monarchs could hurt her if things went awry. I didn't care if she had unnatural healing or restored vitality, I'd be damned if she so much as scraped her knee.

"Yes Mae," Luella retorted. "Lucky Bartram let us go. She bought his sloop. It would help to have someone he recognizes with us without… all that history you lot bring to the table."

I frowned. "Mae and I got into a fight with him at the port town. It's not a good idea."

Luella scoffed loudly. "Do you want to risk her stowing away again?" she countered, the corner of her mouth twitching. "She's not going to listen to you. Might as well invite her. She's coming regardless."

Unfortunately, she had a point. "I hate that you're right."

"You picked a stubborn one, mate. Not my fault."

My lips pulled into a half smile. Mae was as stubborn as they came. One of the many things I loved about her. "Fine. Who should we leave in charge at Anchorage? I was thinking either Gunny, since he has leadership experience, or—"

"If it's all the same to everyone else, I'd like to stay," Wesley interrupted.

Luella and I looked over at him.

He looked up from the map. "I don't know what's going to happen once the council forms. I'd rather spend whatever certainty I have with my family. And no one is a better choice to leave in your stead than me. I'm the liaison between you and the crew. You should take Gunny with you. It could do you well to have an artillery expert."

I respected that. "All right. I'll miss you out there, mate, but you should spend this time with your family."

"I agree. Hug those babies for me," Luella tagged on.

Wesley smiled, always beaming from ear to ear. "It's a deal. Plus, it'll be good for me to be there to bribe the tavern to let us host all the monarchs at once. A gamble, but hopefully it'll be worth it. Not to mention, we need to hire more sailors to replace the ones we lost when Pike took the ship, as well as the ones who are leaving when we dock."

While *The Ollipheist* could operate with a crew of eighty, I preferred to have three shifts for maximum efficiency. And when people died, it was necessary to have extra hands to fill their boots.

Pirating wasn't easy and often came with injury and loss. The least I could do was even out the workload so my sailors could rest.

A soft knock sounded at my door before it opened, and my mother stepped in. "Evenin'."

As always, my brother stepped over to give her an affectionate hug, earning a kiss on the cheek. "Good evening, Mama."

A lump formed in my throat as I glanced at her, not making a move to hug her like I used to. Wesley and Andra had adapted their greetings to accommodate my new aversion to touch. My mother, on the other hand, hadn't. She didn't know how to address me anymore.

So, she'd stand here with her hands by her sides, expecting me to make the first move or spill my guts, but I'd do neither.

"Mama," I acknowledged, turning my attention back to the map. An uncomfortable silence hung in the air. "Is there something you need?"

"Can we speak alone?" she asked.

Fuck no. "Whatever you need to say, you can do so in front of my mates."

I knew it sounded cold. That I'd thrown up a wall of ice between us.

She wanted to understand what Cross did to me at Farlight Prison. What Pike did to me when he had me isolated on the ship. She wanted to *fix me* like I was fucking broken.

"It's all right. I can go—" Wesley started to say, gesturing to the door, as visibly uncomfortable as I was.

"Stay," I ordered sharply. I used my brother as a shield, and he knew it. "What do you need, Mama?"

She looked between me, Wesley, and Luella and sucked her teeth, disapproval written clearly across her face. I didn't care that my response made her angry. I wanted her to leave me the Hells alone.

"It's not important. We'll talk another time." Without another word, she turned and left, closing the door behind her.

After the door clicked, Wesley whirled around. "Stop doing that. I hate it."

"I'm not doing anything," I retorted. I didn't spare him another glance, tracing the route on the map with my fingers. I bristled, ignoring his glower.

He wasn't going to let it go, and frankly, he shouldn't. But that wasn't going to stop me from being a prick to him too.

"You're putting me between you and Mama. Just like when we were kids. Cut it the fuck out." He huffed out a harsh breath between his teeth. "Whatever reason you have for pushing her away, leave me out of it."

Between me and the twins, I was the eldest. Not by much, only a little over a year, but that became my role. Wesley was the baby boy, and I was the one who grew up too fast. When my mother had something to say to me that I knew I wouldn't like, I'd have Wesley there to soften the blow. She would always be softer with him than with me.

Unfair to my brother, but life was fucking unfair.

"Fine," I said, dismissing the topic altogether.

Wesley opened the door and slammed it behind him. I gulped down another bout of sickness. It weighed heavily in my body, and I didn't know how much longer I could keep down the few nibbles I'd had for breakfast.

"They'll never get it, Levi," Luella said, leaning back in the seat. She'd been so quiet that I'd almost forgotten her presence altogether. "I do."

Luella had never led an easy life. Between the plague that ravaged her childhood town and the unhealthy competition between her and her siblings, she'd been chewed up and spat out. She understood me better than anyone. Even Mae.

"I appreciate that."

"Need me for anything else?" she asked, reaching over to grab her hat.

"I'm going to need you to make a supply list for the trip," I ordered.

"Already done, Cap." Luella stood up, perching her hat on her head, and headed toward the door. She paused, looking over her shoulder to cast me a sideways glance. "Look, it's good to talk to someone, but you don't owe anyone an explanation. Not me. Not Seabird. Not fucking anyone."

I met her gaze and offered a small nod. Then she left too.

When I was finally alone, I sank into my seat. I tasted bile in my mouth, my stomach tensing painfully.

"Damn it."

I got up and threw the door open to the wet room to puke my guts out. My head pounded with every awful lurch. I just wanted it to be over, but I didn't have time to let myself fight the withdrawal symptoms.

We were racing a clock.

Who knew when Pike would stage another attack.

Or what Cross had planned next.

My arms shook violently as I fought to hold myself up. Everything fucking hurt, and I thought I might be spending another evening on the floor of my wet room, dreading the next time I retched.

It didn't happen as often. The spells of sickness were fewer, and there was more time for recovery between, but I was so tired of the pain that my body *craved* more vitrophine.

I craved the brief moments of haziness when my limbs felt numb.

The cravings were gradually going away. The withdrawal was petering out, but that didn't mean I was out of the woods yet. It certainly didn't mean it had gotten any easier.

Almost there. Hold on a little longer.

When it was finally over, long after my stomach was empty, I shakily leaned against the wall. The boat swayed, adding more agony to my pounding headache. I shut my eyes tight, willing myself to take back control of my body.

I need to control this.

"Me-row."

A chirping noise drew my attention to the space between the wall and the floor. Lieutenant Commander Lazlo wriggled through the narrow opening and sat across the washroom from me. He blinked owlishly, fluttering bright green eyes. Sitting comfortably in front of me, he groomed his fluffy mane.

Relief swam through my muscles as a soft smile came over my face. I offered my hand out. "Good afternoon, Lieutenant Commander Lazlo."

He meowed, sashaying toward me to bonk his nose against my hand. I accepted the invitation to scratch his ears and under his chin. He released a loud purr, curling on the floor against my leg. His purring vibrated the floor, easing the anxiety and nausea plaguing me.

The massive, fluffy beast of a cat comforted me. He

nuzzled my leg, bumping his nose against me for more attention. Lazlo didn't care about the details. He never asked
questions or judged me for being weary.

I didn't know how long I sat there with my cat, but I
needed it. Eventually, he climbed into my lap, and I scratched
him to his heart's content. I leaned my head against the wall,
slowing my breathing and petting my cat until life felt a little
more tolerable.

7

MAEVE CROSS

ANCHORAGE COVE SAT JUST on the edge of the horizon. The closest thing I had to home aside from *The Ollipheist*. Though, as I stood on that pier and gazed up the hill to Ronin's cabana, the memory of that heartbreaking letter struck me.

When he ended things between us without so much as a goodbye. I felt just as alone now as I had then.

Granted, over the past two months, so much had changed. *I* had changed. Last time I was here, I was certain of who I was, but now I had more questions than answers. And to find those answers, I would have to throw open doors and dig up things better left forgotten.

Worst of all, if I didn't like what I learned, I couldn't force those doors shut again.

I had made my decision. I would not choose the path of ignorance.

Whatever pain lingered in those memories would grant me clarity I desperately needed. At least I'd have some closure. More than I could say about my relationship with Varric.

Varric laughed as the skin around my throat parted, spilling lifeblood down my chest and dripping onto my feet.

Crimson. All crimson.

Eerily similar to those dreams I had about my childhood. Two deaths by Varric's hand. Both times, he'd slit the tender skin of my neck to watch me choke to death on my own blood.

It haunted me. I felt every moment, right down to the part where I plummeted into darkness, the cold breath of the Reaper never far away but never close enough to whisk me to the afterlife.

Varric—the man who was supposed to be my father—laughed when I died. He watched me as if I were nothing more than a rodent performing tricks for his amusement. Ice flooded my veins, welling in my neck where I could feel the cold sharpness of a blade.

I understood Nathaniel's motives. He was an awful man, but he was predictable. He got off on hurting people. He acted almost explicitly through self-pleasure.

Varric, on the other hand, was playing a game I didn't understand. I didn't know the rules. I didn't know the goal. He was several moves ahead of me, but if I could piece together one motive, follow one thin line of the web, tug at one thread—it could unravel everything.

If only I knew his motives.

One step at a time, Mae.

I leaned against the half wall, watching the waves lap at the ship's hull as we closed in. I rolled my loose sleeves up my forearms, a thin sheen of sweat sticking my hair to my forehead and a heavy sigh on my lips as the ship crew gathered supplies and prepped the ship for docking. Plankwalker maneuvered around sharp rocks and the jagged remains of sunken ships.

The blue-tinged water was clear to the bottom, where fish swam among the reefs.

How I wished to sink my hand into the water just to feel the soothing embrace of the ocean and get some sort of reassurance that I was doing the right thing. Going the right way. But all I had was my gut and my wits.

And my friends.

More than I'd ever had before.

"Mae," an authoritative voice uttered from behind me.

Enya. There was a lilt in her voice, sharp and bitter.

I turned, looking over my shoulder to see her standing there, arms crossed, her mouth a thin line.

"Yes?" I asked, tilting my head slightly to the side, wondering why she was looking at me with such a blaze in her eyes.

She'd been avoiding me for the better part of the trip. Not unusual. Between teaching new sailors how to read and tending to small wounds, she frequently kept to herself. However, she used to look at me rather dismissively, but lately, she'd been shooting daggers at me with her eyes.

"Come here," she ordered, whisking me away to a quieter part of the upper deck near the bow where I could get a good view of the ship cutting through the water.

She kept her distance from me, her three-fingered hand clenched tightly around her other forearm as if desperately seeking something to hold on to. She looked angry, and she was directing all that aggression right at me.

Fantastic.

"Are you all right, Enya?" I asked cautiously. Last time I saw her this angry, she was moments away from cracking Varric's head under her boot.

"No." The answer, barely more than a hiss, seemed like it got stuck between her teeth. "My son won't talk to me, so you *will*."

It was an order. Cold prickles danced on the back of my neck. In response, I folded my arms tight against my chest, leaning back against the half wall. "If he doesn't want to tell you, then I won't either."

Ronin's trust was more valuable to me than she was.

She took a step forward, grasping my arm hard as she yanked me toward her. The aggressive action took me off guard, a gasp flying from my lips as I stumbled. I tried to pull away. "Get your hand off me, Enya."

"You *will* tell me what happened to *my* son in that room. What did your father do to my boy?"

Her eyes narrowed into slivers, and I got the glimpse of the woman Luella had warned me about. The protector. The one who didn't take kindly to stowaways. The woman who would do anything to protect her children. Including backing me into a corner to interrogate me. Even kill me if necessary.

Something else flickered across my mind.

"Come with me, Your Majesty. I must get you to safety."

A hand fastened over my gauntlets, all five fingers, gripping hard. "Not without my boys. Please. I must get to my sons."

I blinked it away, not letting it shake me. I didn't shrink from Enya's gaze, steeling myself under her scrutinizing stare. She didn't scare me. "Intimidate me all you want, Enya, but I *will not* break Ronin's trust."

Her grip tightened, eyes becoming accusatory. "Why didn't Varric's spell work on you?"

What?

The spell in Antediluvian....

Then I remembered it. In that awful room, the spell moved *through* me while it propelled everyone else out of the room. My eyebrows came together, trying to make sense of it, but there was still a piece missing.

Who am I?

"I don't know."

Her mouth screwed into a snarl, her teeth almost completely bared as she hissed, "Liar."

This was pointless. Even if I wanted to tell her what happened, I doubted she'd believe me. Especially since I didn't have any answers to the mountains of questions she'd likely ask me. "Believe what you want."

Her grip nearly bruising my forearm, her lips parted, ready to hiss another accusation.

Suddenly, Wesley's voice cut through the tension. "Mother."

Enya released me immediately, nothing more than a red mark where she'd grabbed me. The violence left her eyes as she looked over at her adoptive son and grew soft.

Andra was close behind him. "What's going on here?"

Enya looked at me, her mouth still set in a hard line. "Apparently, nothing of importance." Then she turned, leaving me in the company of Wesley and Andra.

"Are you all right, Mae?" Andra asked me, gently laying a hand on my shoulder. "What happened?"

Wesley frowned. "This is about Levi, isn't it?"

Hesitantly, I nodded. "She wanted to know what happened. Though she was quite aggressive about it." I rubbed the red mark on my arm as it disappeared.

Wesley dipped his head down, sighing deeply. "She means well, Mae. Levi has always kept his cards close to his chest, but our mother isn't taking it well. We can see that Levi is hurting, but there's nothing we can do until he lets us in."

I wanted the conversation to be over. "I get it, but the harder she pushes, the deeper he'll go." *Then he'll shut us all out.*

"You're right, Mae." Andra gave me a nod and her brother a knowing look before getting back to her duties.

"Is he all right?" Wesley asked, lowering his voice. "You don't need to tell me anything else. Just tell me if he's okay."

"No, he's not," I answered honestly, matching his volume. "He tells me he is, but he's lying."

He sighed. "I know. Fuck, I just wish he'd talk to me. He

won't even tell me what happened when Pike had him captive." Wesley crossed his arms, visibly upset. "He used to tell me everything, and now I'm just sitting here wondering if *I* did something wrong."

Ronin wouldn't tell me what happened that month when Nathaniel had him strung out on vitrophine. I teetered on the line between wanting to ask and not wanting to know at all. I knew Nathaniel's brand of cruelty. I was afraid to know what he did to Ronin.

How could I possibly take that pain away from him too?

I reached up to squeeze Wesley's shoulder in a gesture of comradery. "It's not just you. There's a lot of that going around."

A short breath left his nose. "I wish I could say I was comforted by that, but I'm not."

I repeated the advice Luella gave me. "We need to give him time, Howler."

He hung his head. "I just want my friend back. I hate seeing him like this." Wesley's hand came down to pat me on the head. "Even if he doesn't want to talk to me, I'm glad he's got you. You'll take good care of him, yeah?"

My heart squeezed hard, nearly stealing the breath from me. "You know I will."

He stared at me for a long time, those kind brown eyes awfully sad even though he was smiling. "Levi isn't going to be easy to get along with, Mae. Every time he's gotten himself in a bad way, he shoves and says awful things."

Unfortunately, I was learning that very quickly. I looked away, unable to hide the frown pulling my lips down.

"Do me a favor, eh? Don't take it lying down." He paused, the smile falling off his face. "Don't let him be a fucking prick just because he's going through it. You are *not* his pawn."

That vulnerability came back, thickening in my throat. "But what if I end up pushing him away?" It was a raw question, but I didn't know what else to do other than let him push me around.

"Then he will have lost a good thing, and it'd be his own blasted fault," he replied with complete seriousness. "Levi is my mate, but you're my friend, and if you ask me, you took him back too easily after he pissed around last time."

My cheeks burned.

"He cares about you. That much is obvious, but because of that, he'll hurt you. Don't let him." Wesley watched the doubt cloud my eyes, the shy *newness* of my feelings. "But know this, Mae—if he hurts you, Wraith and I will bury him at sea."

I looked away again, rubbing my hands together. "Hopefully it won't come to that."

He was quiet for a moment. "Hopefully not, but I *will* lay him out if he mucks up as badly as he did last time."

Wesley thumped me on the back, signifying the end of the conversation.

"Come now, lass. More prep to do before we drop anchor."

THE SUN STARTED to set once we docked. The sailors who survived rejoiced to be alive, kissing spouses and children. The new sailors grouped together, some joining Gunny and the gunnery crew, others invited to fish with retired sailors. A handful of them went on their merry way.

On the dock, I noticed Conway, slender and tall, his milky eyes fixed on the planks, arms folded. His fair skin almost reflected the color of the water. He was waiting for his husband. Anxiety fluttered in my belly at the sight of him. Having dinner with him and Butcher made me nervous. But I would have Ronin with me.

Why didn't that comfort me the way I hoped it would?

He promised he'd be there for me, but his words were empty.

Butcher's aid clanked on the wood behind me before his beefy hand cupped my shoulder. I looked up, briefly comforted by his warm smile. "Good evening, Butcher."

"Evenin', lassie. We'll meet in a fortnight. Plenty of time for stories then. Rest now."

"Understood," I agreed, gazing past him at Ronin, who was wearing the mask of indifference in the company of his crew. But I knew how exhausted he was. I knew how much he needed to rest.

Gods, I do too.

The last time I was in Anchorage Cove, Ronin had just broken my heart. I hoped he wouldn't do it again.

Butcher patted me on the back and descended the gangway. Conway could sense him, lighting up and following the shadows on the dock until he found his husband's.

Conway embraced him, finding his lips and kissing him. The barrel-chested man cupped Conway's face, brushing his cheeks with his thumbs. Even if Conway couldn't see Butcher in the traditional sense, he inhaled his husband's presence, staring in his direction with all the love in the world.

The same way Luella looked at Andra—and how I wished Ronin looked at me.

I swallowed down a painful lump, trying not to dwell on it.

Conway looped his arm around Butcher's waist, taking the place of one of his aids as they walked up the stairs and off the dock.

"Are you ready to go?" Ronin's voice enveloped me, soothing and warm like a cup of tea on a chilly morning. "Unless…." He paused, causing me to turn around to look up at him. "I wouldn't hold it against you if you wanted to stay elsewhere. I know I haven't been the best company."

That's putting it mildly. But like everything else, I chose to let it go.

My fingers ached to stroke his frown away. "I want to stay with you if you'll have me, but if you want to be alone, I understand."

The blue flecks in his eyes flickered as he looked away from me. His eyebrows came down in an expression that looked an awful lot like shame. "I'd enjoy your company. Though I can't promise much else."

"I don't need anything else," I answered. "Just you."

His throat bobbed as if he was swallowing down what he really wanted to say. His eyes shot back over to me, his entire frame softening. "Do you want to talk about…?" I could only assume he was referring to how we'd left things the other morning.

"We don't need to," I said. "I was upset because there's a big difference between *I don't want children* and *we can't have children.* You know?"

With a nod, he replied, "Trust me, I know. I shouldn't have brushed you off like that. I just have a lot on my mind."

I chewed on my lower lip. "It's fine."

It's not fine.

"My mates are handling the rest of the disembarkment. They're rather insistent that I get some rest. I suppose I need it. Though I don't know how much I'll be able to sleep." He ran a hand through his hair, bracing his weight against the half wall with his other hand. "We'll regroup in the morning to discuss our next expedition."

I crossed my arms, propping out my hip. "And you're not leaving me behind this time, right?"

"I'm not making that mistake again, sweetheart."

On the stroll to his cabana, he walked slower than usual, taking his time to soak in the outdoors. His gaze lingered on the abyssal water next to the drop-off, an indiscernible expression fixed on his mouth.

"What is it?" I asked.

"Nothing," he answered, steeling his gaze as he took slow, deliberate steps up the steep hill. "Why did I build this house on a godsdamn hill?" he grumbled, pausing before taking another few steps up.

"You built it?" I inquired, slightly out of breath. I supposed it made sense. How else did any of this get here if he didn't build it?

"I did. With the help of Wraith and Howler." He reached the crest of the hill, body loosening in relief. "About five years ago during shore leave after an incredibly successful raid."

I followed Ronin inside, and he closed the door behind me. "Where did you live before?"

"Live is a strong word. I bounced from inn to inn. Slept in my cabin. Occasionally stayed with Isa and Howler." He paused. "I needed my own space outside the ship."

"Their kids didn't let you sleep in?" I teased.

Ronin smiled, shrugging off his jacket and then placing his hat on the rack. "It wasn't the kids. It was my mother." He paused. "I love her, and I respect all the sacrifices she made for me. But I couldn't spend every waking moment with her."

I rubbed my arm where she'd grabbed me earlier.

"It doesn't matter. I'll start dinner. I've got flour for bread, and the fishermen have a good catch." He sighed, legs quivering as he prepared himself for another task.

"Sit down, Ronin," I ordered softly.

His eyes shot over to me, and he quirked an eyebrow. "Excuse me?"

"I don't like to repeat myself," I replied, sticking my tongue out to emphasize the words he frequently said to me.

The corner of his mouth pulled upward, puncturing a dimple in the side of his face. "Cheeky."

"And demanding," I added. "For the love of the Gods, put your feet up for a moment."

His eyes lit up as he chuckled. "Aye, aye, Captain."

"Now, while I knead this bread, you might as well tell me the plan. You've been plotting away in your cabin for most of the voyage." I remembered a quick bread recipe that Butcher liked to use. But it would still need to rise. Just enough time to prepare some fresh fish. I could roast vegetables later when I had enough time to pick them up from the community garden.

"I suppose," Ronin sighed and took his shoes off before sagging in relief against the chaise. "First, we go to Lucky's Outpost. It's less than a two-day voyage around the island."

"What's the plan when we get there? Won't we sneak up on them?" I wondered.

"Wraith is sending out correspondence specifically so we don't startle them. We don't need a rain of gunfire when we pull up to their pier. This has been a long time coming. I'm sure Lucky is already expecting us."

I nodded along, glancing up at him every so often as I added a warm water and yeast slurry to the flour, then took my time to knead it into a pliable dough. The more I worked the flour, the less sticky it got. "And then?"

"Then we pay Bliss a visit. They're on the formerly occupied Fisherman's Gully."

Chills swept up my spine as flashes of memories assaulted me. The death that had haunted my nightmares for as long as I could remember. My jaw clenched, and my fingers became stiff. I squeezed my eyes shut, fighting for control of my mind.

When I opened my eyes again, Ronin was in front of me, leaning on the countertop. His eyes were full of kindred understanding. Hesitantly, he rested his hand on top of mine. "You don't have to go."

I gulped down my discomfort.

Discomfort is a privilege.

"I'm going."

"Whatever happens there, you won't be alone." He squeezed my hand softly, sufficiently melting all the ice away.

His touch soothed me, relief spreading through all the rigid muscles. "No. I won't be." I caught his eyes again, bringing his hand up to press a tender kiss against the back of it, all rough and scarred. "Neither will you."

I almost didn't notice the flush bloom on his face as he pulled away to rub the back of his neck. "I should go sit down."

He never blushed like that when he had me or tore all sorts of ungodly noises from me with his mouth and fingers. But small, intimate gestures set his face aflame.

He's never had this, has he?

"Yeah, put your feet up. Let me take care of you tonight," I replied.

At that, his face seemed to darken more, his eyes unbearably soft, as if he didn't understand why I was here with him. "All right," he decided hesitantly. He sat on his chaise, reaching over to his side table for a book that held a strip of fabric marking his place.

Having Ronin's trust was a fragile endeavor.

More precious than anything else.

His trust was glass with a crack already down the middle. He had suffered so many losses that his heart couldn't take another. The fact that he'd let me in so deeply was a gift.

I won't squander it.

That night, after dinner, he helped me tidy up the dishes, and I turned in for the night in the private bedroom under the loft, but I didn't hear him get up to purge his stomach. I didn't hear him at all, so I hoped he was getting the rest he needed.

8

MAEVE CROSS

Butcher and Conway lived in a small townhouse near the tavern, their home a slender building sandwiched between two others and connected through a communal rooftop garden. It looked quaint, and I would never be able to tell it was located in the heart of the port if it wasn't for all the noise.

The port became significantly louder at night than it was during the day when I usually perused the shops and merchant stands. Working women from the brothels accepted coin from sailors coming into the pier, who would hoot and holler in return.

I'd become accustomed to seeing the women in taverns and inns, never far from the guards who ensured their safety. From time to time in my youth, I'd hear about the palace guards buying women for the night, the rumors always hushed, since prostitution was illegal in Farlight Harbor.

The nobles considered sex a *dirty* activity, always met with gossip and prying questions. Meanwhile, I never saw the harm in it as long as all parties were protected and consenting. An opinion that was very, *very* scandalous in the company of the nobles.

Ronin stood in front of me and cupped my waist in his big hand, stroking my flesh through the thin linen blouse with his thumb. My skin tingled with delight as my eyes traced the line of that hand up his arm and shoulder to the handsome face that accompanied it. But his eyes weren't on me. I glanced over my shoulder to see that he was glaring daggers at the sailors across the pier.

Sailors who were, in fact, averting their gazes from me when they noticed my captain.

I raised an eyebrow as he looked back down at me, pinning me instantly with those intense eyes. The corner of my mouth twitched as I drew my lower lip between my teeth. He stood up straighter than he'd been able to during the voyage, holding himself up tall. I couldn't perceive the mild pain from his injuries reflected on his face.

All day long, Ronin had more energy. His legs didn't sway as badly as they had been. He didn't look clammy or overcome with sickness. I watched him devour breakfast as if he hadn't eaten properly in weeks.

Which he hadn't.

He seemed happier, enjoying the interim before we embarked on Lucky's Outpost. When he'd woken up that morning, I also got a nice show of his morning exercises. I'd sipped tea and watched him stretch, emphasizing his returning mobility.

Not as vigorous as his routine before his capture but adapted to fit his needs. I certainly preferred it to sparring. He was less likely to hurt himself, and nothing perked me up faster than watching sweat bead along his neck and down the planes of his chest to disappear into the waistband of his trousers.

Sometimes he didn't want to be touched, and that was fine. I'd devour him with my eyes instead of my fingertips. Especially when he was visibly getting stronger. The rest served him well. He'd catch me every time, sticking the tip of his tongue out before he asked me if I liked what I saw.

I'd always answer, "Of course not."

It entertained me to see him glowering at other sailors, a frown on his face and a hand secured on my waist. I couldn't help but laugh a little under my breath. Ronin always looked so grouchy when we were out, daring anyone to approach us.

Then when he was alone with me, his eyes would dance, and I'd take in his smile lines and that little wrinkle between his eyebrows. He'd tease me, and I'd give it right back to him. All that banter usually ended with us tangled on the floor or against a wall.

We still hadn't talked about any of the things we'd been dreading, but I was afraid to disrupt the normalcy. I just wanted to enjoy my peace before it was snatched away again.

"What?" he asked, a light dusting of rosiness washing over his face, almost hidden by his beard. It had filled out during our journey and was now neatly trimmed, not nearly as unkempt as it was on the ship.

"What're you doing?" I rebutted, a teasing lilt in my voice. I knew exactly what he was doing. I did the exact same thing when I noticed how much attention he got in port.

"Nothing," he replied, removing his hand from me. "It doesn't matter."

"No, it doesn't. But—" My hand shot out, grasping his and returning it to my hip. "—I rather like *nothing*."

A glimpse of a dimple punctured his cheek before he gave my hip a playful squeeze. "Are we going to stand out here all night, or are you going to knock?"

My heart fluttered in my chest. I jittered with nerves. They welled up in my belly and pitter-pattered in my chest like a horde of fluttering insects. Or perhaps something bigger, like a booming flock of birds.

As eager as I was for answers, a part of me wanted to turn

around and remain ignorant. As if nothing good would come from digging up old graves.

But I needed to be brave. Some things needed to be dug up to be laid to rest properly.

My hands were shaking as I secured the handle of the breadbasket over one arm and reached out with the other, rapping quickly on the door with my knuckles.

My throat thickened, but I gulped it down.

"Not too late to run, sweetheart."

I steadied my shoulders and replied, "I don't run."

His thumb stroked my hip again. "I know." The tone of his voice, a quiet rumble that betrayed the fondness he felt for me, weakened my knees. "I'll know things are really about to go to shit if you leg it out of here."

My belly twisted uncomfortably, everything bubbling inside urging me to shut that cracked door and lock it tight. Soft footsteps sounded from the other side of the door. Then the knob twisted, and it came open.

"Captain Leviathan," Conway greeted, milky eyes fixated on our shadows on the ground. He turned to me. "Mae. Nice to meet you again." He stepped to the side, sniffing the air. "Is that bread for us?"

I nodded before realizing Conway couldn't see the gesture. "Yes," I said firmly. "We didn't want to come empty-handed."

He smiled, a jagged row of teeth poking out from between his lips. "Thank you. Butcher is on the terrace. Take that up with you if you don't mind. I'll be up shortly."

"Thank you," Ronin replied, gently guiding me inside so Conway could close the door.

The inside of their home was as boisterous as Butcher's personality. Art pieces hung from the walls. Chipped paint and curling ivy decorated the banisters and climbed up the decorative trim. Fishing nets and gear were propped by the door. Every inch of the townhouse had some sort of liveliness to it, whether it be foliage, herbs, or flowers. Conway clearly had a green thumb, and it trailed him inside his home just as steadfastly as it did outside.

We followed Conway's instructions and climbed the stairs to the terrace. Ronin held on to the worn handrail in case he needed it, but he didn't seem to have much difficulty. I wondered if Butcher struggled with the stairs or if his arms were so bulky because of how frequently and freely he used them to pull himself along.

The top of the staircase on the third floor opened up onto a beautiful rooftop garden full of fresh fruits and vegetables. Well-loved plants bloomed and blossomed. Some of the flowers closed under the moon, while others unfurled right before my eyes. It was ten times the size of the greenhouse on *The Ollipheist*, and it was just as beautiful.

Had Conway also designed the greenhouse on board?

I spotted Butcher sitting at a set table under an ivy arch. Glasses, plates, and drinks awaited us. My nerves increased tenfold when I realized how much work they must've put in to provide a nice dinner.

"Oi, lassie! Cap!" Butcher said cheerfully as he stood up, grasping his aids to greet us. "Fine night, ain't it?"

"It is," I answered. "Oh, this is for you!" I offered the basket, setting it down on a free side table to not take up too much space.

"Well, thank you, lass. Come. Sit. Have a drink!" Butcher encouraged, gesturing to the table and sitting back down.

I obliged, and Ronin followed, sitting next to me as Butcher poured us two fingers each of rum. I sipped my drink nervously, and Ronin gently bumped our knees together under the table in a gesture of affection hidden from Butcher's eye.

"Does Conway know why we're here?" Ronin asked.

Butcher dipped his chin. "Aye, Cap. I didn't want to blind-side him. He has agreed to talk about it, but first, we're going to enjoy our dinner. Then we can get to the real reason you lot joined us tonight."

I heard Conway's feet tapping up the stairs until he appeared, carrying a tray of food before setting it down in front of us, laden with seasoned roasted vegetables and golden-brown chicken. The savory scent wafted up to my nose, making my stomach grumble impatiently. The smirk that curled the side of Ronin's mouth told me that he heard it.

I'd been so concerned about everything today that I hadn't eaten much before worrying about something else. Even Butcher's husband seemed to notice as he chuckled and served us our portions before sitting down.

The merrow clasped his hands together, dipping his head down in some kind of prayer.

"To the Goddess Cliohde, we thank you for our meals to warm our bellies..."

I knew that prayer.

Memories flashed before my eyes.

Grilled fish and sundried seaweed. Laughter and joyous conversation. An older woman with glittering tattoos like orange fish scales across her arms reaching toward me to offer more food. I remembered my belly being warm and full. Gentle humming soothed my fears.

A lean man with milky eyes had given me a toy carved from driftwood. I couldn't remember what it was, but I remembered curling up with it under a blanket when the nights were too quiet, a memory long forgotten. He would sit next to me during meals and recite the prayer for me slowly, carefully sounding out each syllable with an exaggerated shape of his mouth.

Tears filled the corners of my eyes as I thought about how I would laugh at the silly man making funny faces.

I'd relived all the bad memories, but the good ones were finally starting to show through the blur.

My eyes flickered up to Conway, and I said the next verse with him. *"And to keep us safe among the violent current."*

He stilled, his chin shooting up as he stared at me. His eyes focused on the shadow I made on the table, the moon at my back. In an instant, his hands came forward, touching my face as if he were searching for something. "Muirgen," he uttered. His fingers traced my cheekbones, my jaw, and my forehead. His eyebrows came together. "Is that you?"

"I… I don't think…," I answered quietly, my throat feeling thick as I did. The name was familiar, but it wasn't mine.

"I see." His hands dropped from my face. "Excuse me."

"My heart…." Butcher reached out to him.

Conway shook his head repeatedly. "No." He moved quickly to the door, closing it hard behind him.

Heavy silence hung in the air. I twisted my fingers together, guilt churning in my stomach. I didn't think my response would send Conway away. "Did I muck it up? I'm sorry."

Butcher sighed, looking longingly at the door as if debating getting up to chase after his husband. Ronin was silent next to me, but the feeling of his hand squeezing my thigh comforted me.

I looked away, face hot, belly twisting and turning. My eyes settled in my lap, and I couldn't find it in me to be hungry anymore. "I'm sorry," I murmured again.

"Lass," Butcher said. "Muirgen was a little girl from Conway's shoal. An orphan who he looked after, and he was there when Cross himself cut her down, right next to his mother."

"I'm sorry," I repeated. I didn't know what else to say.

"I'll be back," Butcher said, standing up and grasping his aids. "Please, eat. I worked too hard to let it go cold." He shuffled over to the door, clearly going after his husband.

"Well, now I feel awful," I said, shoulders sagging.

"Don't," Ronin replied, hooking his finger under my chin to draw my gaze up to his. Those intense dark eyes bored into mine, just as intoxicating as when I first saw them. "This gave us a way out."

I furrowed my brows. "What do you mean?"

"It means we can still keep your identity a secret for now. If you want, that is." He stroked my jaw with his thumb. "As far as anyone knows, you're Cross's daughter. Let's keep it that way."

I nodded firmly. "All right. But I'm a terrible liar. What if this Muirgen is me?"

Ronin just about rolled his eyes. "Obviously."

"*Obviously?*"

"A little girl cut down next to the former matriarch. An orphan. Yes, *obviously*, you adorable, dense little thing."

I gaped, face flushing hot. "Excuse—"

He rocked my chin back and forth, cutting off my retort before letting me go. "Let me ask the questions, and you can come to your own conclusion."

My cheeks burned, and I bit my tongue to keep from snapping back at his condescending tone. I despised that voice. And I hated it more that it was the exact same tone he took with me when we were in bed together. Every time he used it, I was confused, aroused, and angry all at the same time. "Fine."

"Fine?"

"*Fine.*"

His dimples weakened my resolve. Why did I have to fall in love with *him* of all people? Not someone nice like Gunny. Or funny like Wesley. Or even straightforward like Luella. I had to fall in love with a cheeky bastard.

He reached forward and stroked my cheek with the back of his hand, the gesture all affection.

I practically melted.

That's why. I had no say in it to begin with. I was helpless.

The door to the terrace opened, and Butcher and Conway came back up together. The merrow squeezed Butcher's arm before letting go. "Apologies. I knew what tonight was about, but...."

"There is nothing to apologize for," Ronin answered. "Come. Let's discuss."

Conway steeled himself, puffing his chest out as he came toward the table and to the chair he'd occupied before. Butcher stared at Conway as if he were his whole world, face crinkling with worry. Then his eyes moved over to me, and he offered me a small, reassuring smile before rejoining us at the table.

We ate in silence for a little while. The chicken was still warm, though the vegetables were now cold. But even so, they still tasted lovely, lush with fresh herbs and butter. I couldn't complain even if I wanted to.

"Cross came out of nowhere," Conway offered quietly.

I put my silverware down, giving him my full attention. Ronin continued to eat, listening and absorbing. Butcher reached over to hold Conway's hand, and the two interlocked their fingers as if Butcher were the anchor holding the ship from drifting away.

"Fisherman's Gully was neutral territory. Cross knew this. He said that as long as we didn't stand against him, he would let us live peacefully. We agreed. What else were we going to do? Fifty merrow, mostly children and elderly, against an army of hundreds? Our warriors defended us against siren clans or predators. We were in no way, shape, or form a threat to Varric."

Conway's mouth contorted into a frown, milky eyes darkening as he bared his teeth. His nails seemed to get longer as Butcher held his hand. I watched his shoulders tremble as rage colored his cheeks pink.

"One day, he visited our shoal unannounced. Looking for

something. Determined that we had it. I remember him shouting that he knew we were hiding a sentry weapon or artifact."

I grew cold, skin prickling as it washed over me. *Sentry?*

"We didn't know what the fuck he was on about. But he didn't believe us. I heard the first body fall. The wet squelching of blood. I heard…." His voice grew thick. "I heard Muirgen cry. She was just a *child,* and she was crying when her voice was cut short."

Butcher's eyes filled with compassion as he squeezed his husband's hand again.

"He gave the order to kill everyone. Raze the village. Find the weapon." Conway rolled up his sleeve with his free hand, revealing a jagged deep scar, raised and purple among the tattooed scales on his arms. He traced it with his finger. "I felt the sword cut into my arm. I saw the shadows of the massacre. Smelled it. The blood in the water attracted sharks. Kuru. Predators. Water splashed as they devoured whoever tried to escape by water. I… I…."

"It's all right," Butcher whispered. "There's no shame in surviving."

Tears filled the corners of Conway's eyes. "I *hid.*" Despite what his husband said, shame textured his tone. Thick and full of self-hatred. "I heard my shoal dying, and I hid in the reefs, hoping my blood wouldn't bring sharks to my hiding place. I was a coward."

"Dead men keep their fucking mouths shut," Ronin stated firmly. "That's the point. Who would be able to tell the tale if you'd died? Who would've saved Butcher from the gallows? Shame has no place at this table. Death doesn't discriminate. You're alive."

Conway gulped, burying those feelings, pushing the powerlessness down hard. "It haunts me."

"Violence haunts us all," Ronin concurred. "Thank you for sharing this. I know how difficult it can be."

The merrow nodded, his tears dotting the table and moistening an unused napkin.

"Now I'm going to ask a few questions," Ronin stated after a moment. "All right?"

Conway's milky eyes shot up, following Ronin's shadow to approximately where his face was. "Aye."

"Do you know what the weapon was?"

Me....

My throat thickened as the realization grasped me. Varric's words echoed in my head. *I don't know what you are... but I can't wait to find out.*

I was the unknown factor in Varric's plan.

A confusing myriad of feelings assaulted me, but one shone above all else.

Hope.

"I could deduce that it was some sort of artifact. Whatever it was, Varric tore apart the Gullies looking for it. I don't think he ever found it."

Ronin leaned forward, dead serious. "You mentioned Muirgen before. Who was she?"

"A little fae girl. We found her on the beach one day when she was a baby and assumed she'd washed ashore after a shipwreck. It was a miracle she survived. We took her in." Conway got quiet. "I regret every single day that I wasn't close enough to save her."

"You can't save everyone," Butcher offered softly.

Conway shook his head. "She was too young to die."

Ronin didn't answer, but he placed his hand on my knee, physically drawing my attention to how hard I was bouncing my leg under the table.

"That's all I know, Captain. Now, I'm going to ask you to leave," Conway said harshly, completely overwhelmed by the conversation.

Too much uncovered at once. Too much grief dug up again.

The chair scraped the ground when Ronin stood up, gesturing for me to follow him. "I understand. Thank you for your time, and for dinner. Let's leave, Mae."

I followed Ronin to the door, stopping to dip into a curtsy even though Conway couldn't see me. "Thank you."

Butcher gave me a nod, gesturing with his hand for me to leave.

9

RONIN MURDOCH

ON THE WAY back to my cabana, I could feel my knees buckling.

Godsdamn it.

I'd been having such a good day that I'd forgotten to pace myself. My legs weren't ready for a trek across the island, but I pushed anyway. Mae subtly wrapped an arm around mine, offering some support even though I hadn't asked for it. I flinched, unable to help it, and I fought the initial instinct to pull away.

If I pushed her away, I'd hurt her. I didn't want to hurt her.

It would be better if you did. Burn that bridge. Destroy this relationship. She'd be safer without you.

Without the broken man you've become.

You couldn't save her once. You'll fail again. And this time you don't know if she'll get back up. She'll die, and it'll be your fault.

You deserve to be abandoned.

I ground my teeth together, pushing those awful thoughts away. I bit down so hard, I tasted blood. Her fingers wound through mine like a powerful current, pushing me out of the deep water toward the shallows, but I wanted to fucking sink.

"Ronin?" she asked as if a question had been brewing in her thoughts.

I couldn't say I was surprised, given how quiet she'd been since we left Butcher and Conway's.

I struggled to get out of my own head and be present. *She needs me now.* "What is it?"

"Do you remember when the sirens attacked our ship?"

"*Our* ship?" I echoed, slightly teasing to hide how much I enjoyed that thought.

Mae pulled away from me, scoffing, "Yeah. *Our* ship. It's my home now too."

I missed her touch immediately even though I pretended I didn't.

Home. What a beautiful word. My eyes softened as I looked down at the crown of her head, loose brown curls blowing in the wind. Almost as beautiful as *my* Mae. Warmth filled my chest as I continued, "Yes, I remember the sirens. What of it?"

"One of the sirens called me something when I got between her and Howler," Mae murmured.

"Sirens don't speak Common." Contrary to popular belief, they did speak, but it was an old dialect, masked in trills and caws.

Mae furrowed her brows, stalling her steps. A bout of anger swelled in my belly as my entire body ached to collapse. It pissed me off.

"Baby, if we stop walking, I don't know if we'll ever get back," I said, audibly annoyed at my shaking legs. "Come on." I took another step, and my legs completely gave out from under me, toppling me into the dirt, both of my hands catching me. "Fucking Hells."

"Ronin!" she gasped, running to fuss over me.

When she came into my peripheral view, I snapped. I

couldn't stop the hurtful words falling from my lips. "I don't need your fucking help, Mae. Back off."

"Too damn bad!" she replied, gripping my arm to tug me to my feet with a loud grunt.

I felt my eyes darken as I looked at her down the bridge of my nose, now steadied on my feet. The rage inside me amplified. So godsdamn angry at my weakness, angry at the circumstance, and even more fucking angry that she wanted to help me.

"I don't like to repeat myself, but I will. When I say *back off*, I mean it."

"And when I say *too damn bad*, I mean it too." She put her hand on her hip, taking a downright *bratty* stance with me.

Look at how she pities you. Even she can see how pathetic you've become.

Another hurtful statement seethed inside me.

I *wanted* to hurt her.

I *wanted* her to hate me.

I wanted to destroy this.

Maybe if I pushed her far enough, she'd be safe. If I broke this fragile love between us, she'd live. She'd find someone else. Someone whose lineage wouldn't threaten her every second.

She wouldn't die for me again. I wouldn't let her.

Her eyes bore fire, and the soft roundness of them grew dark. "You *don't* get to talk to me like that."

A lump formed in my throat. My heart pounded under my ribs, and the rage churned in my belly like a rancid brew. "I will talk to you however the fuck I want to."

Hate me.

Just hate me, Mae.

Realization was a thick, unrelenting band squeezing my chest. I didn't want her to hate me. I didn't want her to leave, but if she kept digging, she'd see me for what I was. She'd see the man too weak to save her from her death.

She'd see the man laid out under Pike's boot, covered in his own filth until those pirate hunters bathed me again. I didn't know what was worse. I was powerless to stop any of it.

My leviathan spirit didn't stir. It was gone, and I was unworthy to wield it.

A pathetic worm.

She stared up at me and uttered, "Say that again."

I didn't.

Then she took a step forward and jabbed me in the chest with her pointer finger. "I said, *say that again.*"

A tic formed in my jaw as I drew my lips into a thin line. I wanted her to turn around and leave for her own sake, but I was too selfish for it. I was an unpredictable riptide, pushing and pulling her away from shore into the trenches with me.

"If I wanted to be pushed around, then I would've stayed with Nathaniel."

Her words felt like a strike across my face as I remembered all the horrible things Pike had told me in my cabin. How he used his wives. Treated them like dirt because they deserved to be under his boot.

He described everything in detail. Each horrible thing he'd done to his wives and wanted to do to Mae. He tortured them until they stopped breathing. I remembered him going on and on about how badly he yearned to watch Mae take her last breaths.

It fed my nightmares.

All I could do was lie there and fantasize about death as he humiliated me for his own amusement. Sometimes I imagined Pike's bloody demise. Sometimes my own.

I tried to gulp down the lump, averting my eyes altogether. Shame flushed my face. I was destroying the one good thing that had come out of any of this.

I can't stop myself.

"Fine" seemed to be the only word I could utter around the thickness in my throat.

"*Fine,*" she scoffed. "You know what? Never mind. You're being a prick."

Why do I keep fucking it up?

She drew her lower lip between her teeth and sighed. "I'm going to stay at Isa's. I don't want to fight." Mae put her hands up, turning around so all I could see was the narrow line of her shoulders. "I'll just go."

Conflicted feelings mashed together in my chest. I wanted her to run far, far away from me, but I also couldn't bear the thought of losing her.

Why are you so selfish?

My heart ached in my chest as my hand shot out to stop her. I grasped her wrist before she could move away. "No, please. Don't go."

She turned her head to meet my gaze again. "I'm not going to stand here and let you walk all over me."

"You shouldn't." I let her wrist go. "I'm sorry, Mae. Please stay."

"If you start being a prick again, I'm leaving," she stated.

I nodded even if I couldn't promise it. I replied, "Tell me what the siren called you. I want to listen."

Her shoulders drooped, but she softened. I didn't deserve it. She was too fucking good to me. We walked toward my cabana as Mae continued, "The siren called me *Sentry.*"

I never thought I'd hear that word again. "What?"

"I thought I imagined it among all the noise, but I don't think I did. Especially after I threw Nathaniel's sword into the ocean and heard it again. Is that a type of fae or... or what? I don't know."

This was clearly something she'd been thinking about for a while. Part of me was a little bothered that she hadn't told me sooner, but I hadn't been the best company. And I'd be a fool not to consider that her entire world had turned upside down since Farlight.

Sure, I wasn't much better, but at least I knew who I was and what I'd lost. Nothing challenged my sense of identity.

Her identity had been torn away, reshaped, and shoved back into an ill-fitting socket.

"It's odd," I answered.

"What is?" Mae asked.

"*Sentry* is a title, not a type of fae," I replied.

Her eyebrows furrowed when she looked at me, urging me to continue.

"The royalty in other kingdoms have *knights*, but the Royal Leviathans had *sentries*."

"What happened to them?"

I didn't remember much of them. Leviathans were at their weakest in their human form, so we required warriors to protect us on land. Another reason Varric only harvested from us while we were in our human form.

He'd never be able to tie down a fully shifted leviathan or remove one from the water.

The sentries fought valiantly during the coup, but Varric's forces had the element of surprise. Though my mother talked about one sentry who'd bought her just enough time to save me. "They died during the coup. Picked off one by one until my family was vulnerable."

"Oh...."

"You're the artifact he was looking for, weren't you?" I asked, already coming to my own conclusion.

She rubbed the back of her neck, visibly conflicted. "I... I think so, but that only gives me more questions."

I already knew she was fae, but if Varric had been looking for her all those years ago, I wanted to know why.

I grasped her hand, pulling it up to my mouth to press a kiss on it. "Then we'll find this out. Together. Like everything else."

The declaration felt empty. I wasn't in the right place to be the support she needed, and that only made me hate myself even more.

But she looked at me as if she didn't notice how hollow my words were. Finally, that frown melted away, the soft gleam in her wide doe eyes brightening. "Thank you. For being with me tonight."

"You don't need to thank me, sweetheart."

"I know." She smiled up at me, the visual disarming. It was painful to see how much she adored me.

I don't deserve it.

"Do you want to go swimming with me tonight?"

I wanted to, but that only reminded me of the severed part of myself that I couldn't touch. "I don't know if I have the energy for swimming."

"Fair enough," she said, eyes twinkling. "Shame I won't get a good show."

Gods, I love her. I chuckled. "You get a good show every morning."

"I don't know what you're talking about." She giggled under her breath, curling her arm around mine. "Scoundrel."

"You love it," I retorted, the banter between us reinvigorating me enough to power through the rest of the walk.

By the time we arrived at the cove, I ached to swim. Feel the ocean around me again. The deep water beckoned me... and reminded me that I couldn't shift. The leviathan spirit under my skin didn't stir. I couldn't feel it at all.

The part of me that felt so natural before felt disjointed now.

Broken. Pathetic.

Stop it.

I gritted my teeth together, pulling away from Mae to shut my mind up. I needed a distraction. Desperately. Something to fracture the thoughts whirling in my head, telling me just how useless I'd become.

Here I was, the last of my kind, losing the only ties I had left to my father.

My brothers.

My people.

Fucking disgraceful.

"Get out of your head," Mae said, tossing her jacket onto the coatrack once we got inside. "I can practically feel you disappearing next to me."

"I don't know what you're talking about," I deflected, even as her voice grasped me and dragged me back to the surface before I could succumb to the darkness beneath me. But the sticky tar still had its claws on me, and I couldn't break away completely.

Mae didn't reply. Slowly, she undid her sash, and her shoulders sagged. I knew I was doing everything in my power to slam the door between us.

Cutting her out.

Everything felt so far out of my control that it made me physically sick.

When it came to touch, it was easier when I initiated. The one thing I had power over.

And I needed to feel control now.

"Come here," I ordered, grasping Mae's blouse to pull her over to me.

She gasped, nearly falling into my arms as her face brightened to that pink hue I liked. My beautiful woman still blushed like a virgin whenever I looked at her. Her skin would prickle. Her eyes would get all wide, her inky pupils devouring the warm brown.

She let me take the control I needed.

I'll give it back to her one day, but that day isn't today.

I captured her mouth, tightening one of my hands in her blouse while with the other, I grasped the back of her hair, taking it into my fist and pulling enough to make her lips part and sigh. The taste of her mouth blurred all thought, enrapturing me with lust. She made all these little noises against my lips, reaching into my parted shirt to feel my skin.

Delight tingled the back of my spine, crawling up to the nape of my neck where all my hair stood on end. Everything about kissing Mae ignited the heat in my belly, thickening my cock against her stomach.

She was maddening. Intoxicating. I grew drunk off her taste. Stronger than any bite of liquor on any long night when I had nothing but a bottle of brandy to keep me company. Soft against my hands, pliant against my lips, she eagerly returned every kiss, pulling me harder into her as if she couldn't get enough of me.

Gratifying.

I stroked her tongue with mine, inhaling her scent through my nose, taking note of how she wriggled in my arms, arching her neck. Insatiable.

But I was the same way.

I reached for the laces of her nice breeches, tugging to release her from them. I wanted *everything*. I selfishly wanted every single thing she was willing to offer me. I wanted to drown in the sensation. Everything else could wait until the morning. I could let the dark thoughts take over again.

Sleep could wait.

Lucky could wait.

That whole fucking war could wait.

I only cared about making Mae come as many times as physically possible.

I pulled away, attacking her neck instead of her mouth. Sampling the soft flesh while she arched helplessly against me, I groaned as she tilted her hips, trying to notch me where she wanted me.

"Ronin," she whispered. The breathy sigh was a bolt of pleasure right down to my aching cock. "We're leaving in the morning," she objected, but she didn't push me away.

"I can think of a few things I'd rather do than sleep," I muttered, nipping her throat. "But if you want to stop, just say it."

She released a noise of pleasure, her head falling back as I continued my assault on her neck. I fisted her hair again while slipping my other hand into the front of her trousers. Mae moaned my name as my fingers came into contact with her saturated sex, damn near soaking me as I stroked her needy cunt, playing with the swollen pearl at the apex of her thighs.

I needed to bury myself inside her. Hear her cries of pleasure. Feel her silky cunt clench around me. My fingers. My tongue. My cock. All of the above. I wanted to forget all the fucking bullshit I was going to deal with for the foreseeable future.

I needed everything.

And I needed it *now*.

Her small hands grabbed me closer, her eyelids fluttering. "Wait...."

She didn't have to say anything else. I pulled away, removing my hand instantly. My face blazed, desire like molten honey in my veins. My cock throbbed painfully, but if Mae wanted to stop, then we stopped.

End of fucking story.

My chest rose and fell rapidly, and I knew my pupils were blown to oblivion, as were hers.

Her mouth was pink, swollen from all my nibbling. She was all soft pants and tempting lips. While her mouth demanded more, that wasn't what her eyes were saying. I hated the way she looked at me.

Like I wasn't a selfish bastard.

Like I wasn't a fucking liar.

Like she *loved me*.

I hated the way it made my heart skip a beat. It was so

much easier when we pretended it was just a spot of fun. Easier when I could treat her as one of the faceless women I'd invite into bed only to forget about. A mutual thing. I doubted the women remembered me either.

But who was I kidding?

I'd never treated her like a fling. I didn't take flings to my cabana. I sure as fuck didn't tell them my name. Even before she damned me with her kiss, I'd admired her, but now I couldn't deny that I loved her. I wanted her. I *trusted* her.

And I was still *lying.*

She reached for my hand, and I hesitantly offered it to her. Mae took another step toward me and pressed my palm against her chest, where I could feel her heart pounding quickly.

"Do you feel that?" she whispered.

My palm flattened as she breathed harder, smiling up at me, cutting through all the thoughts welling inside me.

"Do you feel how excited you make me?" She took my other hand and placed it on her waist. She reached forward to my chest, feeling my heart pound in tandem with hers. "Slow down. This is the last time we'll be here for a while. Let's just enjoy this. Just *be with me* right now."

My shoulders slackened, and I melted into her touch, letting her get up on her toes to kiss me. I cupped her face with both hands and kissed her back, letting the gentleness of the moment wash over me. She unbuttoned my shirt slowly, then reached up to push it off my shoulders. I let it fall, following suit as I pulled back to lift Mae's shirt over her head.

The sight of her made me ache. Peachy sun-kissed skin. Soft breasts. Pink nipples begging for attention. "Will you let me put that pretty tit in my mouth, or is that going too fast?" I asked, eyes darting between her eyes, mouth, and tits as if I wasn't sure what I wanted to be looking at.

"Well—"

"I need more of you, sweetheart. I want to remind myself how exquisite you taste when you come."

Her nipples pebbled further, and the hair on her arms stood up on end. "You don't mince words, do you?"

"Never have. Never will." I grasped her waist, hooking my other hand under her chin to watch how dark and sleepy her eyes could get.

It made me feel devious as I pushed her up against the front door, hovering over her. She drew her lower lip between her teeth, watching me with wonder.

Drawing out every touch felt undeniably decadent.

I'd forgotten how much I liked watching her squirm. I stroked her trembling belly with my pointer finger, enjoying the soft whimper that followed.

I wasn't thinking about all those dark thoughts. Only her.

Mae was *everything*.

I sank to my knees in front of her. Her eyes went wide as I stroked her thighs, touching every new strip of skin as I pulled her breeches down.

"Ronin," she murmured again, lifting one foot at a time so I could rid her of all clothing.

I didn't kiss her tempting thighs. Instead, I let my breath puff over them, making her wriggle her hips. She released a whine, head falling back against the door with a resounding *bang*. I ghosted my fingertips over her hips. Her thighs. Barely a touch.

Slowly, I leaned in and kissed her thigh, sucking marks all over her supple skin.

A gasp filled the air, and I could *smell* how wet she was. Her stomach trembled, the muscles clenching and releasing as I continued teasing her. Her thighs shook as she parted them, revealing her godsdamn *soaking* cunt.

"Look at you," I murmured.

"Ronin," she whimpered, parting her thighs further.

"Don't know how to say anything else, sweetheart?" I teased, nipping her hard enough to leave a red mark that faded just as quickly as it appeared. "Touch yourself."

She obeyed, using her slickness to swipe her clit between her fingers, panting and puffing as she struggled to hold herself up against the door. She moaned my name again.

I love how good my name sounds on her lips.

"You're doing so well, baby," I encouraged. The longer I watched, the more my mouth watered. My cock throbbed. It felt like such sweet torture.

Finally, after several minutes of her playing with herself, I leaned in and gave her a firm lick. She gasped, her hands going to either side of the door to support herself. I slid my tongue from her slit to the swollen pearl aching for my attention.

Divine.

The noises spilling from her lips surrounded me. I grasped her thigh, pulling it over my shoulder to get a better angle to suck on her clit. She screamed, one of her hands slamming into the door at the potent sensation.

Incoherent noises fell from her lips, sounding an awful lot like begging. I moved one hand between her thighs, using two fingers to slide in and out of her cunt. Her breaths became shallower, her body growing taut. Tasting even more decadent as her hands dove into my hair, pulling.

When we were intertwined like this, I didn't have to think about anything else.

I groaned into her cunt, getting even harder knowing I was about to push her over the edge. Her head banged against the door as she screamed my name again, clenching tightly around my fingers as she came. Her muscles tensed, eyes rolling back as her hips took over, damn near fucking my face when the pleasure hit her.

Before I could pull away and bask in her beautiful flush, she shoved me backward until I fell onto the floor.

She got on top of me, unlacing my breeches clumsily.

"Not in the mood to slow down anymore?" I teased, biting back my need to come when she pulled my cock out. I knew she wanted to ride me, but that wasn't going to work for me. "Get on your hands and knees."

Mae stared down at me, flushed and shaky, but she obeyed. She climbed off me, then got down on her hands and knees on the floor of my entryway. She curved her back at a mouthwatering angle so I could get a view of her cunt when she spread her legs.

My desire for control was satisfied as she presented herself for me.

"Don't move," I demanded, enjoying how her thighs trembled and her hair fell messily over her shoulders. I admired the curve of her spine and how her breasts hung down. My body tightened. "My pretty girl."

She whimpered, and I cruelly watched as her thighs got damp from excitement. We'd fought earlier, but she still gave herself over to me.

How far would she let this go?

I stopped that train of thought immediately.

"Can you handle me like this, sweetheart?" I asked. *I'll always ask.*

"Yes," she answered breathily, wiggling her hips in a desperate demand for me to get on with it.

She wasn't going to get what she wanted easily. I controlled when and how hard she met her liberation.

It was the one thing I *could* control.

Thanks to her, my cock was already out of my trousers as I knelt behind her, stroking my fingertips down her spine. Goose bumps cascaded across her skin in the wake of my touch.

The involuntary reaction was beyond gratifying.

I grasped my cock, rubbing it back and forth from her shy little clit, along her slit, and back again. Her breathing got heavier, her arms shaking as she fought to hold herself up.

"Tell me how bad you want me," I ordered, rocking back and forth, not entering, only saturating myself in her arousal while her thighs shook.

"*Please*, Ronin. I need you." Every word was tight, coming from a desperate place. I couldn't help but feel as if her statement wasn't about sex. "If I don't have you, I'll cry."

"I don't want you to cry," I murmured, just barely entering her.

Her spine bowed, walls fluttering helplessly while I sank in deeper. She clenched around me, soft as silk. I groaned, letting the delicious sensation wash over me.

Mae cried out, whimpering my name as I started to move against her. She collapsed onto her elbows, completely at my mercy. Her voice was lust drunk, slurring, "Gods, just *take* me."

I gritted my teeth on another shallow thrust. "If it's too much, tell me to stop."

"Never," she moaned with a bitten-off whimper.

"I'm serious, sweetheart." It didn't matter that I was acting like a greedy fucking bastard. I'd never forgive myself if I took this too far.

She nodded, chest rising and falling rapidly. "I will."

"Arch your back," I said softly, kissing her shoulder.

She obeyed, arching deeply while she propped herself up on her elbows. I grasped her hips hard, dragging her flush to my pelvis as her cunt swallowed me completely. My name rumbled from her chest, and she released incoherent pleas as I pounded into her again. Her body shuddered and clenched around me. She backed up against me thrust for thrust as we gave in to each other that much harder.

Finally, my head was fucking quiet.

A sob broke from her chest as I watched where her body

devoured mine, my abdomen slick with her desire, my cock glistening every time I pulled back to push forward again. She wasn't capable of speaking anymore, blindly chasing the sensations I gave her.

Mae always required a little extra effort to reach her peak, but I didn't mind. It was worth it to watch her shatter, knowing how hard I worked to get her there.

She tilted her head back, and that lovely mane of hair was too tempting not to grasp onto. She rewarded me with another mouthwatering scream. I felt her getting closer, wetter, tighter.

"Break for me, pretty girl."

Breathtaking.

"Please," she begged. "Please. *Please.*"

My hand left her hair to wrap around her, reaching for where that swollen bud was aching for attention. "Take it, then. Take what you want."

She clenched around me once, making my eyes roll back.

"You feel fucking perfect, sweetheart. Gods, *yes.*"

She released a wail of pleasure, her entire body stilling. Her walls crushed me, choking my cock as her orgasm moved through her body, leaving goose bumps in its wake. I removed my hand from her clit and grasped her hips. I guided her back and forth, harder, faster. She was practically limp, face on the floor, ass in the air, milking me for everything I was worth.

Heat bunched at the base of my spine as I tumbled over the edge shortly after her. White light burst behind my eyes as I buried myself deeper. I panted, pulling out to flip her over to capture those beautiful eyes again.

I reached down to cup her face and kiss her. She moaned into my mouth and surrendered, supported only by my arm twisting around her waist to keep her lips against mine.

I held her closer, veering back to press my forehead against hers. I forgot about everything. About the impending war. About evading death. About all my heavy responsibilities.

At that moment, it was just Mae and me. Simple. Sweet. I gazed deeply into her glassy eyes as she panted and grinned at me. Face flushed. Beautiful and happy.

You don't deserve this.

My haze of bliss shattered.

All those awful thoughts came flooding back, filling my head with everything I hated. My heart pounded, a wave of panic clouding the passion we just shared. I clenched my hands into fists to quell how they shook.

I didn't want this to end. I didn't want to get back to the world.

To get back to everyone depending on me.

I wanted to hang on to the perfect moment. Pretend that there was a happy ending for me. That I wasn't injured.

Wasn't unbalanced.

Wasn't…

Broken.

But I am. And no one has the power to fix me.

"I need you to leave," I said, unease tensing in my belly. Her touch overwhelmed me, all my nerve endings firing off. I pulled away completely, averting my eyes.

Hurt her. She'll be safe if you hurt her.

"Wh… what?"

I grabbed the front table as I struggled to my feet, then tucked myself back into my trousers. She watched me, and I didn't miss the absolute *pain* filling her eyes. It killed me, but I didn't have enough control over myself to stop the hurtful words from thickening in my throat. Lashing out because it didn't matter what I wanted.

I wanted Mae.

I wanted to have her by my side as we stormed the seas together.

I wanted a *future*.

But men like me didn't get a future.

We end up dead.

I was no different.

Mae would wind up broken for loving someone destined for a violent end. I had to save her the heartache of loving someone as pathetic as I was.

There was *no future* for fools like us.

"Are you kicking me out?"

"I have what I want. You're not dull, Maeve."

Why in the Hells am I saying this?

Get out.

Don't leave me.

You don't deserve her.

I didn't.

"Don't make me fucking repeat myself. I can't do this." Nausea welled in my belly.

She got to her feet, crossing her arms over her chest to cover her nakedness. Her eyes were all glassy, tears welling in their corners. "Can't do *what*, Ronin?"

I couldn't look at her. "We had our fun, Maeve. But I can't do this anymore."

Those tears streamed down her cheeks. "Why not? What are you so afraid of?"

I was fucking *terrified*. "I said, *get out*."

With a stiff lip, she looked away from me. "Fuck you."

"Already did that."

I left her in the front room, completely naked. I opened the door to the head and shut it behind me before sinking to the floor. I buried my face in my hands, unable to stop them from shaking.

I heard her cry. The loud sniffles as she tried to quell it. The way her breath warbled when a sob broke out of her chest before she could swallow it down.

I did that.

I ruined this.

A few minutes later, my front door opened and then slammed closed.

The sickness welled in my throat, the bout of rage disappearing as I knelt over the chamber pot and retched. It was better this way.

She won't have to die for me if she hates me.

10

MAEVE CROSS

MY CLOTHES WERE DISHEVELED and my hair was a mess when I walked to Isa and Wesley's house.

Twenty-five minutes of wondering what I did wrong.

Of scrubbing my nose until it was red.

Of nonstop tears falling from my eyes and soft, painful sobs that hurt so badly, I was giving myself a headache.

What did I do wrong?

What did I do wrong!

I thought he loved me.

When I arrived, both feet on the mat and one hand poised to knock, I debated sinking down to the dirt so they wouldn't see me like this. Where else could I go? Maybe Siggi's tailor shop, but the walk in the morning would be awful.

Do I even want to go on the expedition? Do I want to see Ronin and burst into tears again? Do I want to be stuck with him while he stomps all over my bruised heart?

No. I didn't.

But I wasn't doing this *for* him. This wasn't even *about* him.

This was more important than loving a man who clearly

didn't feel the same way about me. My insides stirred, tangling and jumbling. I wanted to run. I wanted to turn my back and get the fuck out of here—

I don't fucking run.

A sense of duty enveloped me, because it didn't matter how badly it was going to hurt. I'd grin and bear it, swallowing down the pain if it meant protecting them.

My crew.

The innocents in Algar.

The people chewed up and spat out by Varric.

The women Nathaniel bruised and battered.

Even the man I foolishly fell in love with. He may not want my protection, may not want my help, but he was going to get it anyway. Even if he never loved me, I would do everything in my power to spare him the fate Varric intended for his bloodline.

Taking a deep breath, I knocked.

It wasn't long before Wesley opened the door, bare chested and with a silk bandana wrapped around his head. "Mae? What're you doing here?" he slurred, half asleep.

Don't cry.

Don't cry.

Be strong, Mae. You can do this.

I gulped hard, trying to form words, but my lower lip trembled and a sob broke from my chest. The tears came back full force, and I didn't have time to feel embarrassed as my hands flew up to my face and I tried to quell my cries. I couldn't stop crying long enough to give him an answer.

"Oh, Mae," he said softly, looping an arm around me to pull me into a warm hug. "Come here, lass."

My shoulders trembled with every powerful cry, and my tears moistened Wesley's bare shoulder. "He… he…," I whispered, but I couldn't get anything out.

A big palm patted me on the back, and it felt every bit like how I imagined a father would soothe his child. Or maybe how a big brother would comfort his foolish little sister.

"What's going on, love?" Isa's voice came from inside.

I burrowed deeper into his embrace, needing to hide. Wesley sighed, gently stroking my hair down my back. "Mae will be staying the night with us. Could you get her a blanket?"

"Of course." Footsteps receded and then returned moments later.

"Okay, Mae, let's get you inside. I have a nice comfortable lounge chair for you to sleep in. All right?" Wesley coaxed.

I nodded. Hesitantly, I pulled away, rubbing my face with the back of my hand. I couldn't meet Wesley's eyes, my tears glistening against his ocher-brown skin. My heart galloped in my chest, ripe with mortification. I wanted to disappear, but then Isa wrapped a blanket around my shoulders and guided me away toward the living area. I collapsed into the chair, curling up against the armrest.

Isa knelt next to me, rubbing comforting circles on my back. "Do you want to talk about it?"

I shook my head. I didn't trust my voice. Gods, I couldn't look her in the eye either, but her plush two-toned lips pulled into an understanding smile. Gentle hands stroked my hair until my chest stopped shaking.

"Wraith, with me. We're paying Levi a visit," Wesley said from down the hall. I heard his footsteps in the kitchen and then Luella's voice.

"What happened?" Luella asked, but then she trailed off, and I could only assume she noticed me. I could feel her signature scrutinizing stare anywhere. "He *didn't*. Don't tell me he fucked up again."

"She won't say anything, but judging by the utter *heartbreak* on her face, I'm going to guess yes." Wesley sounded angrier than I'd ever heard him before.

"That's a bad idea." Andra's voice.

"We just want to talk to him, love. Just talk," Luella said, but I was certain she wanted to kill him.

"You say talk, but I know you better than that," Andra replied. "Let's all get some sleep. There's plenty of time to *talk* to him during the trip."

Luella only growled in response. Thank the Gods that Andra talked them out of it. A fight between the captain and his mates was the last thing we needed.

The longer Isa stroked my hair, the lower my eyelids drooped.

"Do you think Mae will even want to go?" Wesley asked. "She could stay with Isa and me."

"That's sweet, Howler, but we all know that Mae is as stubborn as they come. We aren't going to kick her off the trip because our mate is a fucking prick," Luella said with an air of finality.

As always, she had my back.

At some point, I heard Enya pop out of her room to ask what happened, but I fell asleep before I heard the answer.

THE KIDS WOKE me up with breakfast and cheerful conversation, seemingly *thrilled* that I was visiting with them before I left. As sweet as it was, it didn't erase the bitter taste in my mouth. Thankfully, the mates didn't ask what happened. How would I explain that Ronin and I had a fight, had sex, and then he kicked me out and broke my heart?

Again.

I had seen all the signs. Each of them telling me not to give him another piece of my body. Not when we were avoiding what had happened to us. We couldn't talk about it.

Even when next to me physically, Ronin was a million miles away.

Using me as a coping mechanism.

And I let him. Because it felt good. It made me feel wanted. *Alive.*

The ketch, stocked with our bags and gear when we supplied it a few days ago, was waiting for us when we got to the dock. Ronin's back was to me where he stood by the helm, going over what looked like a route. Gunny was eating breakfast nearby, giving me a friendly wave that I returned, but I didn't have the heart to fake a smile.

Enya carried a few extra supplies on board, namely some produce we'd have to eat quickly before it spoiled.

Andra and Luella walked in front of me, and I took a deep breath, preparing myself for the most exhausting trip of my life.

Before I could climb the gangway, Wesley clapped a hand on my shoulder. "Are you positive that you want to go?"

It wasn't a matter of *want.* It was a matter of responsibility. "Want is a strong word, but I'm going."

He crooked an eyebrow into his bandana. "You can stay with me and Isa. Help me handle things here."

"Thank you, Howler, but I'll be okay."

With a nod, he removed his hand. "Good luck out there, lass. The Isles can be a mighty dangerous place."

"Good thing I'm going, then. Someone has to bring them back safely," I countered, gesturing to our friends aboard the ketch.

He chuckled, but then he replied with conviction, "Don't forget to take care of yourself, too, yeah?"

"I'll try."

We shared a look of kindred understanding as I turned away and boarded the ship. Wesley shot Ronin a nasty glare, not even waving goodbye at him when we set sail.

Ronin ignored him and *me,* giving orders to Luella and Andra. I would've thought last night hurt the most, but the cold shoulder definitely hurt more.

Luella squeezed my shoulder, and Andra whisked me

away to help her set the sails so they'd crack against the wind.

My throat thickened every single time I gazed at Ronin leaning over the railing, lost deep in thought. All those emotions from last night came back to the surface, and I practically swam in my own feelings of worthlessness.

The pit in my stomach grew deeper and deeper.

Whenever Ronin and I were together, we were in the eye of the storm. I could forget about the destruction for our moment of peace. But the storm never stopped. It kept whirling and crashing, booming and heaving as it tore through everything, leaving only devastation in its wake.

With Ronin, the peace *only* lasted a moment. As soon as it was over, he retreated. Heat rose to my cheeks as I thought about how vulnerable I was with him. Purely naked down to my core. I reveled in his touch. Delight had lightened my head, and I let myself succumb to love.

I forgot everything else. The fight. My death. The war.

When we were together, I searched his eyes for proof that he felt as *connected* as I did. Hoping to have more than a moment.

Hurt clenched inside my chest. Yet again, I had given myself to him, only to be left in the cold. Naked and *humiliated.*

I twisted my fingers together, feeling foolish that I was naive enough to think our moment of peace could stretch out forever. Perhaps I really was just a dull, foolish girl. Maybe Ronin was just using my body, and nothing had changed.

Every time I thought we were getting closer, we only drifted further apart. But instead of it being a crack in the ground, it was a chasm, and I didn't know how to close it.

I wanted Ronin.

Gods, I wanted him more than anything, but I sure as the Hells wouldn't be his blasted coping mechanism.

"Aye, birdie," Gunny greeted me, announcing his presence before slapping a hand on my shoulder. "A coin for your thoughts?"

"Oh, hello, Gunny," I answered stiffly, looking away from Ronin completely. *Gods, I hope no one noticed me staring at him like a kicked puppy.*

How pathetic.

Gunny crooked a split brow, too perceptive for his own good, but he didn't touch the topic he wanted to inquire about. Instead, he asked, "Want to go to the lower deck for a game of bones?"

Thank the Gods, a distraction. "Let me see if Boats needs anything first."

He clapped me on the shoulder again, turning on his heel to lift the hatch and descend the ladder below.

Andra was wearing a tricorn cap, eyeing the sails to make sure they pulled taut. Enya stood nearby, engaging in a hushed conversation with Ronin. Discomfort was apparent all over Andra's face at Enya's proximity. Ronin clearly didn't like it either.

I strode toward her, catching her attention. Relief swam across her features, and she waved me over.

Enya glanced my way, frowning deeply but overall ignoring me as she set her eyes on her son. For so much of my life, I didn't have a mother figure. I daydreamed about having one when I was a little girl. A guiding light who took care of me while giving me the skills to be strong.

I wished on the stars for a mother to replace the drunken woman who pretended to be mine.

But right then, with Enya glaring daggers at her son and demanding things of him, I didn't envy Ronin.

"Need anything?"

Andra flashed me a nervous smile. "We're set here. It's not a long journey to the other side of the island."

"Are you all right?" I asked, casting Enya a wayward glance.

The smile briefly fell from Andra's face, but she shook it off. "I'm fine. It's just been a little tense. Are you all right?"

"I'd rather not talk about it."

Ronin glanced at his mother and frowned. They were far enough away that I couldn't hear their discussion over the crashing waves. Exhaustion pinched his brows, and his mouth was pursed in a deep frown.

Andra tipped her hat back. "She's always been bad about boundaries. Ever since we were little. I suppose losing your children can make you extra protective."

Protectiveness vibrated in my own muscles and hummed in my sinews. I wouldn't let Enya drive him into slamming that door.

It would crack that fragile trust he maintained with his crew right in half.

My eyes flickered over to Ronin again. If I had to intervene, I would.

Andra stopped me before I could make a move to interrupt. "Don't. This is between them. Go take a load off. I'll keep an eye out."

I shoved all those emotions deep down into my belly and clenched my fists. She was right. Getting between Ronin and his mother wouldn't help anyone. "Okay. Let me know if you need anything."

I cast Ronin one last glance, my heart *aching* as I lifted the hatch and joined Gunny in the cramped lower deck.

With hammocks swinging near the stowed cannons, the ketch wasn't nearly as spacious as *The Ollipheist*. The chairs and barrels were nailed down, keeping them from knocking over as the boat hit several rough waves. *The Ollipheist* was a smoother ride, but I'd get used to this swaying eventually.

I had to catch myself a few times as I adjusted to this ship. I'd get my sea legs soon.

Gunny jotted something down on a piece of parchment, his thick dark brows furrowed, one of them split like he'd had a close call once upon a time. The patchiness of his beard had filled out in some places, but his hair was still short from the haircut I gave him a few weeks ago.

He hated it when it touched his ears. So much so that he asked me to cut it for him when Spider wasn't available.

I padded over to him, stepping over the bench seat to sit across from him at the dining table. His eyes darted up to me briefly in an acknowledgment of my presence before he got back to his writing.

I didn't interrupt, just watched him work. He chewed at his lip, tapping the handle of his fountain pen on the table as if trying to speed his thoughts along. Eventually, he huffed, looking up at me. "You can read, right?"

I quirked a brow. "Yes."

"Good. I didn't want to assume." Gunny turned his piece of parchment toward me. His penmanship was fairly shaky but neater than it used to be. "Can you tell me if this makes any sense?"

"Of course," I answered, looking over the paper. "What is this for?"

"Instructions for Spider." Gunny tapped the heading. "I'm giving him possession of Geoff if I die."

It took a moment for those words to sink in. "Geoff? Who's Geoff?"

"My parakeet," Gunny answered matter-of-factly, as if I should've known that already. "He gets seasick, so he stays at Anchorage."

"I didn't know you had a parakeet." *Or that parakeets even got seasick.* I looked over the writing. "Here I thought this was a love letter."

To that, Gunny laughed. "I'm not one for romance."

I paused, curiosity bringing a question to my lips as he fiddled with his pen. "Why not? Is it a commitment thing?"

He shook his head. "Not like that. Don't get me wrong, I'm happy for people like Wraith and Boats or Howler and his family, but I've never been interested in that." He put the pen down. "Not one for sex either."

"Really?" I asked. "Maybe you just haven't found the right person—"

"I've fallen in love with people, just not romantically or sexually. I've partaken in sex a handful of times, but it's not for me."

I hummed. I'd never met anyone who didn't want sex. Perhaps because it had been weaponized against me for so long.

A slow smile pulled at his lips. "I love my friends. My gunning family. And I love you, birdie."

"Aw, Gunny, I love you, too, you flirt," I teased, kicking him under the table.

His smile stretched into a full ear-to-ear grin. "In general, I don't feel like I need anything else. I'm happy with everything I have."

"Then that's all that matters," I replied, turning my attention back to the paper. There was a clear improvement since he'd started practicing after Enya's lessons.

Whatever my problem with Enya was, I was thankful she used her expertise to help teach the sailors how to read and write and to clean and suture wounds. I knew her heart was in the right place. I just wished she didn't come down on everyone so hard.

But I supposed that once a captain, always a captain.

I read the notes Gunny had written, notating them for spelling or grammar errors that would confuse Spider. "Looks good for the most part," I said, sliding the notes back over.

"I appreciate this."

"Anytime." I frowned, taking a moment too long to ask him, "Do you really think we'll die out there?"

Gunny looked me directly in the eye, then flicked his gaze down to my shaking hands before meeting mine again. "It's a possibility. From what I hear, we don't have the best reputation with the monarchs, so I want to cover all my bases."

He said it so plainly, as if he had already come to terms with it.

I gulped thickly, a feeling of dread spreading through my belly at the thought of anyone on this ship dying.

He reached out his hand, patting mine. "I'm sure we'll be fine, Mae. If we go out, we'll go out together."

No, we won't.

The dread cooled my fingers, ice injected through my veins. My spine went stiff, lip trembling.

Gunny tried to cheer me up, clearly struggling with how to do so. "Chin up, lass! Let's play some bones. I'm sure we'll be fine."

I forced a smile, realizing the awfulness of what would happen if this all went to shit. I tried to shove the thoughts down, but they wouldn't leave.

The dark mouth of the ocean opened up beneath me, threatening to swallow me.

I'd survive.

I'd be fine.

But they wouldn't.

And that terrified me more than anything. My friends would suffer and die like the merrow had all those years ago.

A whisper tickled my mind, as if I'd forgotten something.

Something *older*.

The cold feeling spread through my chest. I'd lost something else, but I didn't know what it was. No matter how hard I racked my brain, I couldn't place it.

I squared my shoulders, determination swelling in my belly, shutting that awful abyss beneath me.

I wouldn't let that happen. Not while I still breathed.

I'll protect them the way that I couldn't protect the merrow.

11

RONIN MURDOCH

SEEING MAE AGAIN *HURT*. I'd driven her away, but she still came back. Upon departure, Wesley refused to look at me. Isa too. I knew I was pushing *everyone* away.

But I couldn't stop myself. They were better off without me. I'd suffer for as long as it took to ensure their safety.

It's not important now. I need to be sharp for my contact with Lucky.

Lucky Bartram had been in my life as long as I could remember, either as a mate to Albatross or as his rival. It was dizzying to keep up with which one. One second he would betray my father, and the next he would make it up to him.

An odd relationship unique to Albatross and Lucky. Their respect for each other never waned no matter which way the needle fell.

But no amount of respect in the world could outweigh the jealousy Lucky carried. I didn't think he'd ever stopped loving my mother. The closer we got to the Outpost, the more I thought about it. For such a long time, I didn't understand how Lucky could hold so much jealousy in his heart.

I understood it now. Imagining my girl with someone else left a bitter taste in my mouth. If I ever saw Mae with anyone else, I didn't think I'd recover. I'd be bitter and jealous until the day I died, and it would all be *my fault*.

Because she wasn't *my* Mae. I fucked it up all on my own without the help of another person.

I frowned, feeling more and more disgusted with myself for kicking her out of my cabana after she gave me her body. Every time I caught a glimpse of her, I felt sick to my stomach with the hot feeling of shame. Even when I didn't see her or catch a whiff of her hair, Luella and Andra gave me plenty of reminders with their glares.

I'd never been so alone in my life, and I'd done it to myself. Everything inside me wanted to take me down the path of self-destruction.

What use would I be if I was half the man I was a few months ago?

Everyone is relying on me, and I'm not worthy to lead.

But here I was, sitting at a desk in the tiny separate cabin while everyone else ate dinner, played cards, and passed the time. It wouldn't be long before we came upon Lucky's Outpost.

We'd anticipated arriving early in the morning, but it was now late at night the same day. The shores were uncharacteristically smooth. The nausea and withdrawal symptoms had thankfully subsided, but I still couldn't sleep. I couldn't stop visualizing Mae's death and my dragon abandoning me, every horrible thing personified in my subconscious, and I couldn't get away from it. My body ached, and I wasn't able to keep putting on a brave face and pretending that I wasn't deeply traumatized by my capture.

My shoulders sagged. In an ideal world, I'd take the time to heal properly, coax my dragon back to the surface again, and let my mates take care of me.

But I needed the alliance. Anything else could wait.

If I wasn't so godsdamn stressed, I could even let Mae in, but I'd made my choice and slammed that door. I listened to her cry and broke her heart right after she gave it to me. I had to live with it. If she hated me enough, she wouldn't lay down her life for me.

Painful or not, my distance would keep her alive.

The world wasn't fucking fair, and there wasn't a gods-damn thing I could do about it.

I poured another glass of bourbon and brought it to my lips. A thick swallow did nothing to rattle loose the lump in my throat.

It didn't help that the mere idea of someone touching me made me flinch, no matter what I wanted. How badly I yearned for all my afflictions to be soothed away with gentle strokes of fingertips that only Mae was capable of.

Never once had I ever ached for intimacy the way I ached for hers. The way she looked at me as if I wasn't a fucking prick.

But it doesn't matter what I want. The damage is done. I ended it.

I'd never been in a complicated relationship before. One I wanted to get right even though I intentionally destroyed it.

Like mother, like son.

My mother never talked about her relationships.

Not once.

The twins and I had to guess that she was involved with their father. We caught them kissing only once in the entirety of our lives, and that was the night my mother up and left for the entire week without warning.

After waiting for her to come back to no avail, Lucky and Albatross left us to watch ourselves one night while they hunted her down. The twins and I stayed up waiting all evening, terrified that our only mother had abandoned us. I couldn't have been older than ten at the time, prepared to protect the lives of my siblings if our parents were to never return.

At the break of dawn, a stormy horizon behind them, my

mother returned with Lucky and Albatross at her back, the red glow of the sky illuminating her white-blonde hair. They never told us where they found her. But that day was forever chiseled into my memory—not because she left, but because she came back.

A few years later, Albatross died and Lucky left.

My life had been a never-ending wheel of death and abandonment. Even into my adulthood, my lovers left and people died. I had one fucking job now, and that was to keep my people alive. My comfort was secondary.

It had to be.

Lucky Bartram was the first step to getting the monarchs to side with us. Sure, they all hated one another and tried to kill each other *numerous* times, but if we didn't stand together, we'd fall apart.

There was a rap at my door. The sound made my belly turn uncomfortably.

It wasn't too long ago that my mates wouldn't knock. They'd just stride in like they owned the place, but after my capture, they started knocking.

I'd complained about them barging in time and time again, so why did it hurt so much that they no longer did? It was just another reminder that I was different now. *Everything* was different. That it wasn't just the boundaries I threw up. There were also physical boundaries everywhere. It added to my isolation, but I wasn't capable of tearing them down. Not when those barriers protected them from me.

"Come in," I called out.

The door opened, and Andra peeked her head in. She closed a spyglass, tucked it into her pocket, and said, "We're closing in on the Outpost. Lucky's men are lining the docks."

"Armed?"

"I'd be concerned if they weren't."

The corner of my mouth crooked upward. "That would be odd, wouldn't it? Be on your guard. I'll be out shortly."

"Aye, aye." She paused before adding, "There is something odd about the Outpost, though."

I perked up. "What do you mean?"

"It's too quiet, Levi. Something is wrong here." She turned and closed my door behind her, clearly not wanting to be in my cabin longer than necessary.

With a deep breath, I got to my feet. My legs whined with exhaustion, and my head throbbed painfully. I shoved all the discomfort down. *Too fucking bad.* This war wasn't going to wait for me to piece myself together again.

Everyone is relying on you.

I mustered all the energy I could and marched myself to the door before flinging it open to greet my crew. The absolute silence engulfed me, making all the hair stand up on the back of my neck.

Andra was right. Something felt *wrong*, even if I couldn't place it.

The only noise was the sound of our ketch gliding through the water. No waves. No insects. No birds. Even late at night, the silence was unnerving. Eerie emptiness.

My crew stood along the side of the boat. All were accounted for except my mother, who was likely still on the lower deck. They watched the lights from the pier get closer and closer.

Huge shadows of trees fell over the island. Trees that wouldn't exist if it weren't for Lucky's lineage. Being a dryad's son offered several benefits, like natural wild magic. He could also sense illness in plants, using his own magic to strengthen crops. There was a time that he helped the twins and me plant our first garden before we took to the sea.

Not only was he deeply in-tune with the ground, but he had the mind for business.

Lucky used to be a boatmaker, catering to the fishermen before he became a pirate. Now he had land and influence, literally growing and nourishing the trees that gave him the lumber to craft his fleet and sell quality products.

But in the dark, the massive trees looked eerie, especially with the silence. Not a word was spoken as Luella brought us in along the pier. The hull of the ship knocked into the wood slats with a clapping sound, waves gurgling around us.

The only noises were the ones we were making.

But occasionally, I'd catch something that sounded like the wind howling… but I knew *it wasn't the wind.*

A few of Lucky's sailors met us on the pier. The atmosphere felt uneasy, and I noticed a few of the men looking out to the water, then back at us. As if they heard something we didn't.

I followed their line of sight to a ship turned on its side, washed ashore not far from the pier. In the darkness, I caught a flicker of light casting a shadow along the bow of the ship—a fishing barge.

A maximum crew of fifteen sailors.

Could that be a ghost ship?

I don't like this.

Lucky's Outpost was off a ship graveyard, so it wasn't unusual for there to be boats washed up on shore, but only when something truly awful happened did a shipwreck *become* a ghost ship.

"Good evening. I'm First Mate Ethan. We were expecting you tomorrow morning," a redheaded officer said at the front. His mouth was set in a grim line, and scars decorated his forearms. Brown sunspots betrayed his age near his hairline. Curved ears unlike Lucky's extended ones.

"The waters were smooth tonight." I looked past him at a few of the other sailors staring anxiously out at the bay. "Is it a bad time for an audience with Captain Lucky?"

"The *commander* is indisposed at the moment," Ethan replied. "But we do have sleeping arrangements for you. Come. *Quickly.* The sea isn't forgiving at this hour."

I crossed my arms, peering out into the inky darkness. Anxiety welled under my skin. Something akin to fear lumped in my throat. Never once had I been afraid of the ocean.

I *was* what the sea beasts feared.

But I wasn't a leviathan. I was painfully *vulnerable,* trapped in my human form.

This was *why* leviathans had sentries on land.

"What do you mean?" Mae asked from behind me. "If something threatens our safety, we have the right to know it."

She took a few steps forward, and I could practically feel the anxiety in my chest starting to ebb away. I glanced down at her. She didn't need to touch me to soothe me. Her presence was enough. I squared my shoulders, strength weaving its way through my limbs again.

At that exact moment, I was thankful she was here with me.

Why do I keep pushing her away?

"Answer her," I insisted.

Ethan bowed his head in a deep nod before meeting my gaze. "A ghost ship washed ashore a few nights ago, but it's nothing Commander Bartram can't handle. You'll fare fine for the night. You lot may not be a favorite of the commander, but you are guests, and he ensures the safety of his guests."

"That doesn't answer my question," Mae pressed. The whispers reverberated through the wind again. There was a sound so soft, I almost couldn't place it.

Crying.

Followed by a *scream.*

Ethan flinched, gathering his wits before addressing Mae. "If the commander wishes for you to know, then you will know. But I do not and will not answer to you."

From the corner of my eye, I could see Mae bristle. Her

back straightened, and she stared Ethan down with a deep concern for our crew.

Once upon a time, I thought that Mae would demand I pick her over the crew just as my previous lovers had. Then I realized just how wrong I was to think her priorities were any different from mine.

My chest squeezed. *Gods, I'm a fucking fool.*

Subtly, I reached over to pull on the back of her blouse. I tugged on the material once before releasing her. I hadn't earned the right to touch her. Her eyes shot up to mine, and I raised a brow, peering down my nose at her, silently willing her to drop it. *We're not getting anything out of him.*

Pinkness dusted her cheeks, but she relented. The fresh hurt glimmered in her eyes, but she pushed it down. I'd been observing her the entire trip, not least of all the glossiness in her eyes every time she looked in my direction.

Guilt churned in my belly.

I'm sorry, Mae.

Doesn't matter. She'll never forgive you.

I ached to say the words to her. Even if it wasn't enough, she deserved an apology.

Her nose crinkled, and her spiteful little mouth screwed to the side as she stopped herself.

"We'll let the matter rest," I decided.

Ethan nodded once. "Then follow me."

The men behind him fell into formation, still on guard, eyes on the ever-mysterious sea.

With one last glance, I finally saw the sea the same way the land dwellers did. A vast emptiness of mystery. It called to me, but I was in no place to answer. An integral part of me had been broken off like brittle glass.

Too many shards to piece it together again.

We followed Ethan to a tent off the main beach large enough to fit all of us, complete with bedrolls and a few supply items, like sea biscuits and water to tide us over until the meeting with Lucky in the morning. A fire flickered in front of it. The windless night seemed even eerier on land, nearly silent except for the sand crunching beneath our feet and the roaring of the campfire.

"I implore you to stay put until sunrise," Ethan said. "A few guards will be posted nearby, but make our job easier and stay put."

I glanced over at Luella. She was watching me, likely thinking the same thing I was.

We need someone on watch.

She might be angry at me, but this was work. We could fight later.

Ethan left, and I could hear him barking out a few orders in the distance as well as an occasional low whine in the wind. A distant wail of agony.

"Well, I don't like this at all," Andra said, sitting down on a bedroll.

"No," Luella agreed, crossing her arms and leaning against a metal support in the tent. "It's too quiet... aside from the exceptionally off-putting screams."

Gunny was quiet, mirroring Andra by sitting on his own bedroll. Despite the circumstances, he didn't seem remotely concerned. Of course. No matter what, Gunny kept a cool head. I was beginning to think nothing ever spooked him.

It's what made him such a good head gunner in the throes of battle.

"Well, I'm off to bed. Keep it down, will ya?" Gunny said, lying flat on the roll.

"Really? Now?" Mae asked, smacking her hand into her face.

He made himself comfortable. "It's been a long night. What else am I gonna do?"

"You're not the least bit concerned about—"

"If I get eaten, I get eaten. It is what it is."

"Gunny! I don't think so!" Mae gasped before kicking the lump of Gunny's body in the bedroll. "Get up, you madman!"

I stifled a chuckle. "Stop kicking the poor man, Mae. One of us needs to sleep."

Gunny shot me a toothy grin, twisted canine on display, before looking back at Mae. "See? Cap gets it." He pulled a woolen blanket over his head. "Good night."

Mae looked between the gunner and me, mouth agape.

"As much as I'd like to be as comfortable as our gunner, I think we should have someone on watch," Luella said. "If it's a ghost ship, we could be dealing with echoes."

I nodded in agreement.

"Echoes?" Mae asked.

Everyone was quiet for a moment, and that was when I remembered that Mae hadn't been at sea as long as the rest of us. The only sea beastie she'd ever dealt with was a siren.

And technically, me.

I settled my chin in my hand before answering. "You've heard ghost stories, right?"

Both her eyebrows shot up. "Yes. What does that have to do with anything?"

"Then you know what an echo is."

"But why are they called echoes if they're just ghosts?" Mae continued.

Andra responded this time. "When sailors are away too long, suffer too much, sometimes they lose themselves in the bleak. The ocean takes everything, twists them into a beast until the only thing left is an echo of who they were."

"I see…," Mae trailed off, looking out the tent flap to the inky darkness of the water.

I wished I could hear her thoughts. Listen to the gears turning in her head. I knew whatever she was thinking had to be as interesting as she was.

"Echoes are fairly rare," I added. "But they are incredibly hard to get rid of. Lucky has his work cut out for him."

Mae's round eyes met mine, her bottom lip getting hooked between her teeth. "Then why don't we lend a hand?"

My mother scoffed, "Help Lucky? Please. He'd sooner get his head bitten off by a shark." She picked at her cuticles, mouth curved into a deep frown.

"Why do you sound so bitter?" Andra demanded, crossing her arms.

I raised both my eyebrows, and I caught the rare visual of Mama seething at Andra. I didn't intervene, wanting to hear her answer. She couldn't avoid us this time. Couldn't turn tail and run into the horizon or slip down to the lower decks.

"Every single time Lucky comes up in conversation, you snap tighter than a clam," Andra added.

"Why in the Hells do you think? He got your father killed." The retort came out like a hiss. She straightened up. "I'm going outside."

"Mama," I warned. *Don't run away from this conversation.*

She raised one hand, silencing me. "Not far. Just outside. Don't follow me." Before anyone could argue, she tucked her hands in her jacket and stepped outside.

"Every time," Andra sighed. "Every single fucking time."

I cast her a sidelong glance. "I know."

Luella reached out and stroked Andra's forearm in a gentle show of support. My sister rewarded her with a smile that didn't reach her eyes. Our mother had always been a private woman, and it was tenfold worse with Lucky Bartram.

"I can take the first watch," Mae offered, breaking the awkward silence.

"You get some sleep, lass," Luella argued. "I'll keep watch."

Mae opened her mouth in opposition, but Luella silenced her.

"Don't worry. I'll wake you if anything fun happens."

Luella looked over at me, taking her role as my second-in-command. "What are the orders, Cap?"

"Wraith will take the first watch. I will handle any disturbances. Under no circumstances does anyone go out to the beach alone. We will stick together," I ordered.

MAEVE CROSS

"Wake up." The voice was accompanied with a kick to the side.

"Go away," I grunted and flopped over onto my stomach.

"Seabird is gone."

That was enough to jostle me awake, and I sat straight up on my bedroll. I rubbed my eyes, loosening the grit that had collected in the corners. Luella stood over me, blurry until I blinked away the sleepiness. She frowned deeply, a crease in her forehead.

"What?" I asked, voice thick and groggy.

I glanced to either side, noticing that everyone else was sound asleep. Even Ronin, who desperately needed the rest. For once, he finally looked at ease, one hand reached out to my bedroll, his fingers loosely gripping the fabric.

My heart squeezed, feeling awfully conflicted that he was reaching out to me when he slept but shoved me away when he was awake. It hurt too much to dwell on it.

What is he so afraid of?

"She never came back. She's gone. Get up," Luella replied tersely.

I glanced up at her and outstretched my hand.

She pulled me to my feet. "Wake Levi. I'll wake the others."

I stopped her. "No. Let them sleep."

"I'm waking them."

"And then what? We all go after Seabird?" I pointed out.

Confusion flickered across her face. "Those are the orders. I'm not leaving Seabird out there either."

I shook my head. "That's not what I mean. Everyone will be safe here with you. Let me go after Seabird." I didn't know what echoes were capable of, but I knew five people wandering in the dark was a recipe for disaster.

I'll be fine. I'll live.

"There is a thin line between bravery and foolishness, Mae," she replied.

"Think about it, Lulu." I glanced at our sleeping friends, who still weren't stirring. "You know that I can evade death. No one else here can."

Luella seemed to be considering it. "Levi will kill me if anything happens to you."

"I'll be all right."

Her piercing green eyes searched mine. "Fine." She sighed deeply. "But if you die, I'll find your corpse and kick it a few times."

A quiet laugh slipped past my lips. "I can deal with that." I leaned down and grasped my cutlass, housing it in the sash around my waist.

"Before you go," Luella said, pulling the neckline of her shirt out to retrieve what looked like a pendant made of petrified pieces of wood and various greenery. She untied it. "For good luck. I will not let you leave without it."

"Thank you," I murmured, accepting the necklace. As soon as it touched my palm, magic pulsed from the small trinket, seeping into my skin. "What is it?"

"Elven magic. A good luck charm. From my homeland...," she trailed off, clenching her teeth before she grasped my hand. "You ought to give it back when I see you again."

A warm feeling brewed in my belly. This little bauble was precious to her. I squeezed her hand back and replied, "If I lose this, I'll let you kick my corpse a few more times."

The side of her mouth quirked up. "Good. Now git before I change my mind."

I nodded once and snuck out the tent flap into the night. The fire smoldered nearby, now only red embers. Sand kicked up with my every step, dusting my trousers and getting stuck in my shoelaces.

I thought hard about where Enya could've gone.

Just a short walk away, I could hear the noise of Lucky's sailors chatting. That was enough to brush away any other nerves about leaving the crew like this. They had Luella, and now I knew they had reinforcements around the corner.

In theory, I could ask them to help me, but they would probably tell me to go back to the tent while they handled it.

I didn't trust them, but I trusted myself to get the job done. After all, I knew Enya better than they did.

With a deep sigh, I looked around, analyzing the darkness.

What in the Hells am I doing?

I knew nothing of tracking and had nothing to go on aside from pure intuition. Unconsciously, I rubbed the part of my arm that Enya had grabbed only a few days ago. It wasn't bruised or red, but I could still feel the phantom touch.

My teeth gritted together, as I loathed the feeling. Nothing I could do would make it go away. It wasn't a sickness in my belly like I felt when Nathaniel touched me, but it lingered. A reminder of the fierce woman who thought I was the reason her son had withdrawn.

I understood that protectiveness. I couldn't be angry with her, but I also couldn't cross Ronin's trust for his mother.

I *wouldn't*. I valued it too much.

I thought back to Ronin, how he unconsciously reached toward my bedroll like it was a source of comfort. Everything in me yearned to protect him. But every passing day, our relationship became more fragile.

Until it cracked.

And I didn't know if it would ever fuse together again. I didn't know if it was broken like a bone and could be nurtured to heal back stronger than before, or if it was like glass—shattered in a million pieces with no hope of coming together again.

I rubbed my arm again, but my touch couldn't wash the other one away.

Is this how Ronin feels all the time?

Phantom touches all over his body. Unable to escape them. Gods, how I ached to wash them away, but that was out of my power.

But this isn't. Seeking out Enya was something I *could* do. I was more than capable of lifting this burden. And if all went well, we'd be back before the crew woke up.

Before they can worry about me.

I can do this.

Even though I was traveling without anyone, I didn't feel alone. Eerie noises echoed through my ears, flooding down my spine like a thousand fingertips. There were massive trees all over the beach, making it look otherworldly.

A wail broke through the silence, startling me. I reached for my cutlass and stalled my steps. I clenched my eyes shut, willing the familiar stroke of fear to go away.

I would not be afraid of the whispers.

I refused to cower at the sounds of screams.

Icy tendrils of apprehension licked at the back of my neck, as if eyes were watching me, but I refused to bend to them. Like with the sirens… like with my father… *I will not be afraid.*

Slowly, I opened my eyes again, steeling myself against the worries.

The only luminance danced in the distance, drawing long shadows across an abandoned fisherman's barge. If I were Enya, I'd go toward the light.

Aside from the sounds of my walking and the occasional shout or wail, it was utterly quiet, the windless, moonless night only amplifying the surrealness of it.

It didn't feel like I was in Farlight Isles. I was in some abyss, unable to see anything but my shoes hitting the sand in front of me. I reached up to stroke Luella's pendant. Magic seeped from it, offering me a moment of soothing relief.

I heard a clapping noise, the sound of boots on wood.

The whining of something swinging back and forth.

A grunt and a soft swear.

What the Hells?

I followed the noise, the light getting brighter the closer I was to the barge. A massive bonfire brightened the abyss around it.

"Godsdamn Hells," a soft voice wheezed, followed by the grinding of a foothold trap holding something heavier than intended. "*Oof.*"

It sounded like that time Isa's rabbit trap caught a massive wild cat. The poor thing was exhausted when we set it free, but it sprinted up the hills, far away from any of the other houses. A nice reminder that even if I didn't see many big predators, we shared Anchorage Cove with them all the same.

"Seabird?" I asked, rounding the thicket to see her hanging there. Upside down. Her hat and gear on the ground. Blonde hair swooping and brushing the tree.

"What are you doing here?" she hissed, hiding the embarrassment that mottled her cheeks. Or maybe that was just all the blood rushing to her head.

I sheathed my cutlass and crossed my arms. "Looking for you."

She wriggled harder in an attempt to loosen the knot around her ankle. "Well, you found me." Enya tried to reach up to grasp her ankle, tugging at the rope. "Hells."

I tried to repress a smile at the hilarity of the situation. Enya swinging upside down in a trap. "Need some help?"

"Piss off," she growled. She grunted and yanked at the loop to no avail. "I can—oof—do this myself!"

"If you insist," I replied, leaning against a tree to watch her struggle. "How long have you been dangling there?"

If the blood pooling in her head was any indication, she'd been here for a while. "Not—" She huffed. "—long."

"*Right*. Whatever you say."

She let go of her ankle and hung there for a moment in defeat. "Well, if you're going to be so godsdamn cheeky about it, then make yourself useful and cut me down."

I straightened up and replied with mock innocence. "Oh! Why didn't you just say so? Of course." I drew my cutlass and cut the rope easily.

Enya crashed into the sand. "I don't know why my son likes you," she gasped heavily.

Her words felt sharp, a cruel poke in the ribs. "He doesn't."

"Whatever," she grumbled. She lay there for a few more moments to catch her breath. "Does he know I'm missing?"

"No. I snuck out."

I sheathed my sword again. Ronin was so much of a wild card lately that I didn't know if he'd be relieved that someone whisked me away or if he'd raise all Nine Hells to hunt me down.

I reached out a hand, but Enya smacked it away. She got to her feet, then grabbed her hat and her gear.

"I see the lack of *thank you* runs in the family," I uttered under my breath. "What are you doing out here anyway?"

Enya averted her eyes and said, "I needed some fresh air."

"You couldn't have waited for a less perilous time for a nighttime stroll?"

She didn't reply right away, gazing out toward the bonfire. "I don't expect you to understand."

There was only one person by the barge that we knew of. *Lucky Bartram.* My eyes darted back to Enya, and I caught a wistful regret flickering across her face. I watched utter *longing* unfold in her eyes.

Oh.

When Ronin said that Lucky was in love with his mother, he never mentioned that she returned the feelings. Or at least a fraction of them.

"You're coming out here to help him, aren't you?" I asked.

The guilt in Enya's blue gaze was unmistakable. As soon as I noticed it, she threw up her defenses. "Like I said… you wouldn't understand."

"If there is one thing I *do* understand, it's wanting to protect the ones you love." I sighed, squaring my shoulders. "You don't have to explain anything to me, okay?"

Her gaze softened again, a flash of relief.

I gave her a nod and placed one hand on my cutlass, preparing myself to wander closer to the bonfire. An answering wail echoed around us. "Well, let's go, then. We've already come out so far."

"You want to help me?"

I shrugged. "I can't go back empty-handed, and if you're anything like me, you're not leaving either."

The corner of Enya's mouth curved. "All right, lass. But I'm still suspicious of you."

"Fair. I get it, but one of these days, you'll have to accept that I'm not going anywhere."

Enya narrowed her eyes, pressing her tongue against the inside of her cheek. "And one of these days, I will."

13

MAEVE CROSS

Antediluvian incantations echoed around us as we got closer to the ghost ship. I identified Lucky's voice as he commanded the spirits away. I didn't know exactly what he was saying, but I recognized the dialect that Varric used whenever he conjured magic.

I'd heard it plenty when he used his magic to shatter my belongings. Erase the few friends I had. When I was twelve, there had been a mouse that crawled through the cracks in the walls. When Varric locked my doors and forbid me from leaving, I looked forward to seeing the little creature.

I named it Crumb because I always saved my crumbs for it.

Where I saw a friend, Varric saw vermin. Everything I liked was *vermin* or a *useless hobby*. He taught me—his *petulant daughter*—a lesson learned when he caught me giggling while it nibbled on my leftovers. The sound that mouse made when Varric disposed of it gave me nightmares for weeks. If any other mouse came into my chambers, I did my best to scare it away.

He hadn't needed to use the magic on me to hurt me. Varric was more creative than that.

Lucky's voice wasn't as forceful. He didn't have to try as hard to summon magic. The light flickered and danced across the sand. The disembodied wails softened, more akin to weeping than screams.

Enya and I walked around the corner to see Lucky in front of a glowing mass of echoes, his back to us as numerous spirits vanished, disappearing into the darkness and taking their cries with them.

Except for one.

"*I will not leave!*" it screamed, a powerful wave of energy rippling off it that was strong enough to knock Lucky back onto the sand, his tricorn cap flying off into the distance and grit kicking up.

The barge shuddered, and it looked as if the entity was splitting the wood and metal with incredible strength.

"Your time is over here, spirit!" Lucky shouted back in Common. "You must move on."

The shapeless mass flung itself forward. It was pure malice and utter torment vibrating into the air. I gasped as the wave of suffering flowed forward, washing over me completely. My heart squeezed, and a sense of loss gripped me.

I didn't even realize I was crying until I felt the tears stream down my cheeks.

Lucky's violet eyes darted over to me, now realizing he had an audience. Sweat clung to his dark brows, adding a sheen to his burnt umber skin. Grit dusted over his thick braids, a different hairstyle than the last time I saw him.

Surprise pulled his brows up, but then his face fell when he saw Enya standing next to me. In a split second, Lucky vanished before appearing right in front of me.

A shout of surprise left my lips as he grabbed my arm and Enya's before teleporting us away from the remaining echo. The world swirled, my stomach rising to my throat as I fought a potent rush of nausea.

I occasionally got nauseous, but not on sea, not from spinning in circles, and rarely from food. Teleporting, however, was *rough*.

"Ugh," I moaned before falling headfirst into the ground.

I blinked, trying to focus my gaze as Lucky grasped Enya by the arms and pushed her into the trunk of a tree. Even though the gesture seemed aggressive, I noticed the care he took in not hurting her three-fingered hand.

We were just far enough from the fishing barge that the echo couldn't hurt us directly. It seemed bound to the vessel, pulling on invisible chains. An enraged howl crackled through the air with pure energy.

"What are you doing here?" he demanded. His uniquely violet eyes danced with magic and authority.

Enya didn't back down. Not once. "Some way to thank the people coming to help you." Her own influence permeated the air, reminding me that she used to be a captain and had never forgotten that fact. "Now let me go."

He hesitated, a frown creasing his forehead deeply before he released her and took a full step away. "I don't need your help. I have this under control."

While that seemed true to an extent, one of the echoes was clearly intent on remaining. I grunted and rose to my feet, shaking sand from my hair. "What about that last one?"

Lucky hit me with a withering stare. "Resistant. Nothing I haven't dealt with before. While the others have found peace, this one is full of suffering. Whatever happened to it was so awful that it won't listen to reason."

"Do you know what happened?" Enya asked.

"I don't. But it's angry with me. Perhaps a fresh face would help." Lucky looked between Enya and me. "Besides, I exhausted the rest of my reserves teleporting away from the barge."

Magic was finite, only able to stretch as far as the user. From what Ronin had told me, it was like training a muscle. Anyone could learn it, but it came easier to fae and elves.

Enya crossed her arms as the sounds of horrible, heart-wrenching sobbing filled the night air. "It may not listen to reason, but it might listen to empathy. Something is tying it here. We just need to cut the tether."

Cutting that restraint was an awful idea. "What if it escapes? Wreaks havoc?"

"Doesn't work like that, lassie." Lucky's violet eyes found mine, curiosity swirling and dancing within them as much as authority did. "I didn't expect to see you again, Maeve." He eyed me intensely as if trying to dissect me. "Captain Leviathan loosened his leash, hm?"

I gulped down the sinking feeling in my gut along with how badly everything hurt. But if I knew anything about Lucky from our brief spar outside the tavern, he was trying to get a rise out of me. "Someone sounds bitter."

The older man laughed at my response. "I'm always bitter." He cast Enya a sideways glance before saying, "I'll stay back. The echo will get aggressive if it sees me again. But I'll be close enough to hear what happens."

"All right," I replied.

I stepped in front of him, and while I didn't like the idea of Lucky behind me, he wasn't a threat. Even when he fought Ronin and me all those months ago, I didn't think his intention was to hurt me.

Enya and I approached the barge again. A wave of despair washed over me just as it had the first time.

"*I will find you! I will find you!*" the echo wailed, sobbing as the shapeless mass charged at the barge. The ship shuddered, but never enough to move. "*Where are you?*"

The crackling energy almost overwhelmed me, as if a fist gripped my heart and was squeezing and squeezing. Weakness weighed down my hands and my feet as if I were trudging through tar. I rubbed at my chest, swallowing thick tears. I glanced over at Enya, and she seemed to feel it, too, but it didn't affect her as potently.

Maybe she's already suffered like this before? This feeling of grief isn't new to her.

The echo froze, and the shapeless light flickered, shrinking down to become the body of a woman. She was nearly transparent and wearing a sailor's garments, a wool coat and a scarf around her head. Trousers tied off at the knee. Void of all color.

Her fingernails were broken, as if she had tried to dig underneath the barge. A crystalline chain looped around her ankles and wrists, tying her to the ship. Her strife became her own chains.

A panicked voice resonated through the air. *"You! Help me, please. He's under the ship!"*

Without thinking, I went to help, digging through the sand at the base of the ship. Enya didn't move. She remained over by the fire, watching. I didn't know if this was the best course of action, but if anyone asked me for help, I'd jump at the opportunity.

Maybe it was my own naivety, but I rather liked this about myself. For better or worse, at least I knew that I tried.

"What happened?" I asked.

The spirit sobbed, a ripple of that despair washing over me again. I was drowning in it. The sadness filled my lungs, gripping my throat with viselike strength.

"He shouldn't have been here. I shouldn't have let him come."

"Who?"

"My son," the echo whimpered. *"My son. I need to find him. He's only six."*

Oh.

Dread came over me as I realized what had happened. I glanced at the hull of the ship and saw a hole where it had sprung a leak. There were claw marks along the wood. Gouges several inches thick.

I'd seen scratches just like those after the sirens attacked us, only *The Ollipheist* was a massive ship with layers of wood and tar along the hull. It could handle a few scratches from sea beasties. This barge was only built for a few people.

The spirit seemed to become more panicked, the wooden planks on the barge shuddering and snapping as tormented energy pulled at the nails. The grip on my throat got tighter, and tears streamed down my cheeks from how potent it all felt.

It was *agony*. A type of loss I'd never truly experienced.

"We can try to find him," I whispered, digging into the sand. Her son wasn't there. I knew it, but I didn't know what else to do. "We have to try."

Enya stood back, watching, but from the corner of my eye, I could see tears streaming down the sides of her face.

The more I dug, the more hopeless it seemed, until the echo became angry. *"You aren't helping me. My son will die, and it will be your fault!"* it roared, shoving me backward.

A vision flitted across my mind.

The echo, only a woman at the time, playing with her six-year-old son, who held a small wooden horse in his hands as he giggled.

Her smile was warm and full of love.

Then a siren song vibrated through the waves. Her body contorted while her son cried out for her. She stepped over the guardrail into the big blue.

It felt like acrid seawater flowed down my throat, burst after burst. Water coated my eyelashes. I could feel the ocean envelop my body, filling my lungs. I could *feel* it knock me back and forth as if I were lost under the surface.

I can't breathe.

Everything burns.

"Mae!" Enya shouted as I grabbed my throat. She grasped my arm with both hands, but my vision was blurry as every breath was stolen from me.

"My death will be yours. Everything is your fault," the echo hissed.

I heard it as if I were underwater, my ears clogged with brine. I could only scream as I felt teeth sink into my flesh, phantom sensations of sirens frenzying over my body, tearing chunks of me away with violent bites.

I could smell blood and seawater, even if my body remained intact. I could feel every moment of her *agony*. But that wasn't the worst part.

Her pain.

Her stolen breaths.

Her body being torn apart.

It was *nothing* compared to the fear of knowing she couldn't save her son.

Panicked, I gazed up at Enya's face as she shook me, trying to snap me out of the spell. I couldn't see Lucky, but a powerful aura of magic enveloped us, fighting the death spell the echo had cast on me.

A hand grasped my ankle, dragging me through the sand as I limply succumbed to it.

Darkness stole my vision as pain ripped through my chest, followed by unmistakable peace. The lull of calm replaced the panic.

"You're safe, child," another voice whispered through my mind.

A shadowy figure floated nearby. Close, but never close enough to claim me.

Then I wasn't there anymore. I was somewhere else.

I sank into the deep abyss beneath me, never seeing the bottom as my own deaths came for me. The memories of when I'd drowned.

The first one, I remembered. The time Ronin saved me. Though now I realized that he never saved me. Death merely let me go.

Why?

But there was something else.

Something *older.*

A baby shoved through the waves, crying, and with every cry, it inhaled more awful water again and again. Dragged away from death over and over again until the waves brought that baby to the shore of Fisherman's Gully.

The merrow thought I was a miracle.

But instead, I only brought death to them.

Enya's voice flooded my ears as the darkness ebbed away. "Your son is dead," she declared, addressing the echo.

Tired. I'm so tired.

An unfamiliar hand cupped my shoulder as I sleepily looked up at Lucky. Astonishment flickered over his expression as a sly smile swept across his mouth. "Full of surprises, aren't you?"

I only groaned, head lolling over to watch Enya face off against the echo. She bristled, visibly angry but not letting it break her concentration. My death wouldn't be the only one if she lost control of the situation.

Her back was to me as she stood in front of the echo that was growing larger and larger with impending rage. The wood of the hull splintered and cracked, tearing clear off the ship.

Suspending the debris over her, the echo screamed, *"You lie! I will find him!"*

"It hurts, doesn't it?" Enya asked, not unkindly, her voice quaking as she barely controlled her shakiness. "I know that pain."

The nails on the wooden planks stopped trembling as the echo replied with *"You know nothing of this pain."*

Enya slowly knelt down, maintaining eye contact with the echo's transparent gaze. "Like a piece of you is gone. Like you'll never get it back."

The debris slowly fell to the ground, piece by piece, each

accompanied with a soft thud. *"I can't leave until I find him. I need to find my boy."*

Enya turned her head, and I got the briefest glimpse of tears glistening against her cheeks. "I had two boys taken from me. I never got to lay them to rest. They weren't much older than yours. Stolen too soon."

The echo's massive shape shrank down to the size she was before. *"I... I can't leave without him."*

"He's already gone," Enya whispered. "You're the one holding on so tightly."

"I don't know how to let go," the echo admitted as the glow around it slowly dissipated, becoming more and more like how she had been in life. *"How... how did you?"*

"I didn't. I don't think I'd ever be able to. A mother's grief is something you never let go, but I know that the day I die, I'll get to see my boys again."

The agony was split in two, replaced by the smallest bout of *hope. "Do you think my son is waiting for me?"*

"There's only one way to find out, isn't there?" Enya asked.

The glow ebbed entirely, leaving just the woman behind. *"Then... why am I still here?"*

"You're tied to something you had in life," Enya explained gently. "Do you know what that could be?"

I glanced up at Lucky. "A wooden horse," I answered, my voice scratchy. "I saw it."

Lucky dipped his head into a deep nod and rose to his feet. He approached them as I lay there. The echo bristled again, a renewed glow showing from inside it. He reached into a pocket inside his jacket and retrieved a small water-logged horse. "Is this it?"

The echo softened completely, floating toward him. It reached forward and touched the toy. *"Yes."* Then she turned around to face Enya. *"Thank you."*

She dissipated into nothing, the toy vanishing with her.

At once, the tormented energy disappeared. The sound of insects and birds returned. The clouds that shrouded the moon dissolved, and the moon lit up the sky again.

A heavy weight slid right off my shoulders.

Lucky released a deep breath, staring up at the sky.

Enya hung her head, burying her face in her hands. Shakily, she cried, "Dear Gods, *Mae*."

Lucky glanced over at me before laying a hand on Enya's shoulder. "Your girl is more resilient than you think."

Her eyes were glistening, nose red and irritated. Distress colored her tone as she hissed, "Now is not the time for your jokes. That *girl* came out here to help you, and you make a mockery of her death. That *girl* risked her own hide to save my son from death, and that *demands respect*." Her words spat fire, daring Lucky to say something else.

I was out of the light, too exhausted to get up.

"Seabird—"

"And it was *my fault*. Gods, how could I be so blinded by my feelings for you that I allowed that brave girl to *die*." Each word was shriller than the last.

I didn't think she even liked me.

My chest twisted with a complicated feeling.

Lucky stuck his tongue in his cheek, repressing a grin.

"And you have the fucking stones to stand there and *grin*."

He shook his head. "Look, Seabird." He pointed over to me, and I had to use all my strength to push myself into a sitting position.

Enya's eyes grew into round saucers, and she darted through the sand. She dove in front of me and onto her knees. "Let me look at you." Her hand snapped out to grab my face, jerking it back and forth, up and down.

Ugh. I'm too weak to be jostled around like this, Enya.

Then she slapped both hands on my cheeks to hold me still. Her eyes were still wet, wrapped up in a cocktail of grief and relief. "How? I saw you go pale. I saw the life leave you."

"Death didn't claim her," Lucky commented, stepping over to look at us. "I can't recall the last time I saw an immortal. If ever."

Enya stared me down. "What is going on, Mae? How are you—" She stopped to sniffle and wipe away another tear. "I need to hear your pulse. Now." Two fingers thwacked against my wrist that she held in a vise grip.

The fact that she was fussing over me brought suppressed tears to my eyes again. The woman who had questioned me and backed me into a corner was gone. She became the mother that I needed.

I slowly grabbed her hands and brought them up to my ears. "They're tipped."

Her gentle fingers caressed the scars, eyes widening more when she came to a quick realization. "You're not Varric's daughter."

I shook my head.

Lucky raised one hand. "Back up. Varric *Cross*?"

Enya glanced at him and gave him a brief explanation. "Runaway princess. Stowaway. Helped us commit high treason. Long story that I'll get into later."

He tapped his chin and nodded. Then he winked at me and repeated, *"Full of surprises."*

"How are you alive?" Enya demanded, continuing her interrogation. "Fae aren't immortal. Not even the Gods. Only Death is."

"I don't know. All I know is that I come back every time I die." The cat was out of the bag, so there was no point in hiding my identity from Lucky either. "You said you met an immortal before?"

Lucky shook his head. "No. I haven't met anyone with unnatural healing either."

How did he know that? I parted my lips to ask, but he beat me to it.

"You got a little beat up when I dragged you away. In my

defense, I thought you were a corpse. But look at you now. No bruises. No cuts. Only a little dirty." He gestured to my filthy hands that were splattered with blood but no lesions.

Enya asked the next question. "Do you think Violetta could help?"

Violetta? Ronin's ex-lover Violetta? The third monarch?

Lucky sucked his teeth. "I suppose. Not for free. She deals in blood." He paused, deep in thought. "I wish I could help you more, kid, but I'm at a loss."

My gut twisted, but I also felt somewhat relieved that someone else could help me. "Thank you," I said, earning a pleasant smile from Lucky.

Enya was still gripping my hands as if I'd suddenly die if she let go.

"I'm okay," I whispered.

She released me as soon as she realized how tight her grip was. She swallowed and stood up, dragging me with her by my shirt. My legs were a little wobbly, but I felt steady enough to walk.

Lucky looked between us and said, "I appreciate the assistance. Don't worry about the meeting with Leviathan in the morning. If nothing else, your help has more than earned my audience for the alliance."

I grinned, the weight in my chest lifting. But then Lucky turned his attention to Enya and brushed his braids out of his face as if tidying himself up. "Do the kids know?"

I had no idea what he was talking about, but Enya did. "No."

"Still ashamed of me, hm?" he sighed. He didn't give her a chance to reply. "This has gone on long enough. I'm not keeping your secrets anymore."

Enya sucked on her teeth and replied, "I will see you in the morning, Lucky."

What happened between them?

"Aye. You will." He glanced at me. "Good night, Maeve."

"Good night," I offered, leaning on Enya for support.

She wrapped an arm around my shoulder as Lucky left, disappearing into the thick throng of trees.

Then she asked, "Now that we don't have an audience, will you tell me what happened at the prison?"

I nodded. "I'll tell you my side. Not Ronin's. That's his story to tell."

She made a throaty noise. "All right."

14

RONIN MURDOCH

THE SAME DREAMS assaulted me like some eternal purgatory. A layer of my own personal Hells. It was as if the Gods chiseled away a piece of the Great Tree just for me, under the massive root system down to the worms that squirmed in the dirt beneath. I was separated from the life that thrived above in the green. I couldn't escape the weight of the dark, and my subconscious reminded me of it each time I closed my eyes.

Mae died.

My leviathan abandoned me.

The tar swallowed me.

I unconsciously reached out for Mae in her bedroll barely a few feet from me. I had no right seeking her out for a moment of comfort. But in my state of half-asleep exhaustion, I wasn't thinking clearly.

I fucking *ached* for her. My fingers sought the warm skin of her arm, even just the cool fabric of her shirt. Not enough to wake her, just enough to reassure me that she was there. Considering the echoes in the darkness, I needed to know that she was all right.

That she wasn't one of the bodies underneath Farlight Castle.

That she didn't disappear into nothing.

Why is her bedroll cold?

My eyes snapped open, and I bolted upright, much to the complaint of my stiff back. I groaned, barely awake as I searched for her. A bout of fear bubbled up in my belly when I didn't find her.

I didn't see my mother either.

What the fuck?

Who I did see, however, was Luella leaning against a post, still on watch. Did she not realize they were missing?

"Wraith."

"Shit," she muttered under her breath before glancing over at me. She straightened up. "Go back to sleep, Levi. Everything is under control."

Like fuck that was going to happen. "Bull-fucking-shit. Where are they?"

"Seabird was missing. I sent Mae after her."

"You *what?*" I nearly shouted, not giving a shit if I woke Andra or Gunny. I got up, now violently pissed off. "You sent Mae out into the woods in the middle of the night?"

Worry plagued my gut, my face creasing into a deep frown. The explanation only made me feel worse. All I could think about was Mae lying face down in a pool of her own blood. Me not knowing if she'd ever get up again.

If that was the extent of her abilities.

If that death would be the final one.

And that scared the shit out of me.

"Get up," I commanded, giving Andra a soft kick to wake her. "We're going after them."

My sister grunted, uttering, "What?"

I didn't answer. My legs ached as I knelt down to grab my gear, and then I charged toward the tent flap. I wasn't leaving Mae and my mother out there alone. *Fuck no.* Aches and exhaustion be damned. All that mattered was their safety.

"Slow down, Ronin," Luella snapped, but I didn't. "Fuck, mate, slow down!"

"No," I hissed. "My girl and my mother have been out there for Gods know how long." I threw the tent open, expecting to be met by an eerie silence, but instead, it was the sound of insects.

Birds.

Wind.

The moon was silver and large in the sky.

I stopped in my tracks. Andra sleepily got up and stumbled around behind me.

"I told you everything was under control, mate." Luella hadn't moved from her spot, the corner of her mouth turned down as she growled, "*Your* girl, huh? Was she *your girl* when she showed up at Howler and Isa's with tears running down her face?"

A spike of guilt ignited in my belly and bubbled up to my chest. I rubbed at it as if that would take it away, but it only added to the roaring cacophony within me. Another layer of noise on top of the intrusive thoughts and swirling cocktail of self-hatred.

"I'm not in the fucking mood," I nearly snarled. "This is not the time to question me on personal matters."

"I never knew you to be a worrywart," Luella commented, no trace of concern in her voice. But I did catch the disdain for me coming through in her eyes, like flickering flames threatening to devour anything that spited her. She slowly straightened, her body language altering from relaxed to aggressive, and made her way toward me. "However, I think it's the perfect time to question you."

I glared, trying to sidestep her as she came for me. "Drop it."

Luella was faster, getting right in front of me. "I was going to march my way over to your cabana and stab you in the belly for making Mae cry. Howler was going to be my witness."

Our eyes caught, and my upper lip curled. "Then why didn't you?"

She gestured over to Andra, who was now wide awake and watching us both. Gunny, somehow, was still asleep. "Her. And it seemed unfair to kill you when I didn't hear your side of the story."

"You're losing your edge. You've stabbed me for less."

"Fuck you," Luella replied before grabbing my collar and jerking my entire body down a few inches to her level. "Talk. Now. Mae isn't here to stop me. She's too fucking nice to you, but I'm not going to let it go."

My gaze bounced between Andra and Luella. "Fine. Let me the fuck go."

"Not until you tell me, pretty boy. Before I make you not so pretty."

Clearly not a bluff.

"We fought, we fucked, and then I kicked her out after." I knew how awful it sounded, but that was the reality of it. I *was awful* to her.

"You're a real piece of shit, Levi." Luella let me go but never averted her eyes from me.

I couldn't keep her gaze anymore, however.

Andra shook her head. "*Seriously?* How could you do that to Mae?"

"I can't—" I paused to collect my thoughts, feeling more and more like a fool by the moment. "Why can't I stop myself?"

Luella gave me the most incredulous expression. "Get the fuck over yourself. I'd start there."

"Lu—" Andra started, pinching her nose between her fingers. "That's not helpful."

"I think it's plenty helpful." Luella turned away from me

to go back to her previous spot. "I think I could charge good coin for my advice."

I can't do this right now. I took in a deep breath of night-time air and asked, "Why didn't you wake me?"

"I may think you're being an insufferable prick, but we already almost lost you once. You needed your rest."

Even if a part of me was softened by her comment, it didn't wash away the thickness in my throat. "I am your captain. That was not your decision."

Luella knew fair and well that she went against my orders, but I didn't have it in me to keep up with the anger anymore.

"Captain is a title of respect, and you're going to have to work really fucking hard to get that back. When I dueled you all those years ago, I agreed to serve under the man you were then, not the man who's so afraid of his own fucking feelings that he'd push away everyone who cares about him."

I couldn't even be upset with her. Not when I barely recognized myself in the mirror. I swallowed down the bitter bile that threatened to spill over. "I'm not having this conversation right now."

"Oh, get over yourself, dipshit." Luella jabbed me in the chest with her pointer finger again. "We have your back. We already swore ourselves to this cause for better or worse. Whether or not you like it, we're here for you, you fucking cunt."

Andra glanced over at her wife, agreeing with everything she said. Then her dark eyes came back over to me, relenting. "I don't know what's going on with you, but you need to figure it out, or we're destined to fail."

They were right. I *knew* they were right. If I kept going down this path, I was only going to break whatever was left of my friendships, my family. I'd never be able to pick up the pieces of Mae's broken heart and salvage what we had.

Mae....

I was so fucking worried about her.

Everything in me wanted to find her, drag her into my arms, and breathe in the scent of her hair so I knew she was all right. Then I wanted to bend her over my knee for making me worry.

I thought back to the other night, the raw wound of breaking things off with the one person I wanted more than anything else. I hated the way Mae looked at me like she wanted to feel connected to me and I severed the link because I didn't want her to *see* me.

It was selfish for me to push her away, then feel entitled to her attention. But I couldn't help myself from wanting her even if I hated that she wanted me too.

Contradictions warred inside me, but it boiled down to one thing.

I couldn't keep lying to her.

I need to fucking apologize.

Across the sand, I heard footsteps in the distance, and a wave of relief cascaded over me when Mae and my mother crested a hill.

Mae was leaning heavily on her, and my heart squeezed tightly. *Is she hurt?* Then she pulled away from my mother to walk on her own with only a slight wobble to her stride.

"I told you. Have a little faith," Luella said matter-of-factly, as if she'd had no doubt that Mae would get back safely.

I briefly wondered if Luella knew Mae's secrets.

But all that speculation vanished when Mae looked at me. My reaction was completely involuntary. My heart pounded, my breath caught, and a swarm of butterflies erupted in my belly.

I pushed down the nerves pattering across my skin like little bouts of tingly light. My entire body *craved* her touch. Ached for the tenderness in her eyes that was only for me.

I don't deserve it.

As Mae approached me, she rubbed her arm, flushing deeply. I noticed the sand in her hair. The dirt caked on her arms. Old blood that had stopped running a while ago splattered across her skin.

What the fuck happened?

My teeth clenched.

"Hey…." Mae tucked a stray piece of hair behind her ear. "I see you're awake."

I frowned, crossing my arms, staring down at her from the bridge of my nose. "You went against my orders." My voice was full of authority, because the fact of the matter was that a sailor under my charge overtly disobeyed me.

"It's my fault," Mama said. "She wouldn't have gone out there if it wasn't for me."

A tic formed in my jaw. "You put yourselves in danger." I was too fucking tired for this. "I'll deal with you later, Mama."

My mother sighed and said, "No. We're doing this now."

"Are we now?" I asked dryly. "Fine. What the fuck happened?"

She looked down at her feet, clearly uncomfortable. Andra and Luella waited by the tent flap, both listening intently. I could barely make out the sound of Gunny snoring the night away.

Mama had never been a shy woman. Callous and authoritative, yes, but never shy. It was completely out of character for her to twist her fingers together, her face flushed. She gulped several times. She looked downright *guilty.*

Mae's mouth scrunched to the side as she looked between me and Mama. "I wanted to help!" Mae blurted suddenly. "So… I, uh, went out into the woods. Seabird followed me…."

I raised both eyebrows and waited, expecting her to fold because I knew she was lying. *Why is she protecting my mother?* "Yeah? And then what?"

"And then we helped Lucky banish the echoes." Mae

jutted her hip out, crossing her arms. "You should be thanking us for doing what was necessary to solidify an alliance."

I narrowed my eyes and shot Mama a warning glance. "Go. We'll talk later."

Mama released a nervous breath and brushed past me to go into the tent. I glared at Luella, and she rolled her eyes before closing the tent flap so I could put all my attention on the infuriating woman in front of me.

"Don't fucking lie to me, Mae," I demanded.

"You're one to talk," she replied, keeping my gaze, not backing down. "Why can't you trust me, Ronin?"

"I do trust you."

Mae looked away from me, all that hurt coming back to the surface.

I did that. She's hurting because of me.

"Then why are you lying to me? Why are you keeping secrets? It doesn't feel like you trust me when you push me away after everything we've been through together."

I can't tell her. She can't know how pathetic I've become.
Coward.

Several moments of silence passed, and then she softened. "Look, I can't tell you everything because it's not my story to tell, but I can tell you that Seabird and I helped Lucky."

"You disobeyed me," I said. "You can't keep challenging my authority."

She rubbed her hands together, cheeks pinkened to that hue I liked. "You were finally sleeping. I wanted you to rest."

My Mae....

Her statement alleviated the godsdamn pressure in my chest. I couldn't be angry anymore. I stepped toward her and brushed her jaw with my fingertips. She looked up at me, pressing her face into my palm as if she couldn't get enough of how my touch felt. Like everything else didn't matter.

I gulped, lost in her expression.

It fucking melted me.

"I was worried about you," I said, wanting to pull her into an embrace. "If you do this again, I'll be forced to reprimand you for disobeying a direct order."

Her eyes snapped to mine. "Maybe I wouldn't disobey if I thought you were remotely receptive to anything."

"What do you—"

Then her eyes hardened, and she pulled away from me. My hands ached to hold her, to press her against me and inhale the scent of her hair.

"You know *exactly* what I mean. You think that it's *you* against the world, but it's not. It's *us*." She shook her head. "But you're not going to listen to me. You made that abundantly clear when you used me and shoved me away."

Every word was a strike to the chest, but I deserved it. I wanted to mend this. I reached out, wanting to soothe myself with her touch, only proving just how right she was. "Mae."

She sidestepped me, glaring up at me with barely veiled hurt. "I didn't give you permission to touch me."

I dropped my hand. "Heard."

She stepped around me and headed directly to the tent.

"I'm sorry, Mae," I whispered, unable to bring myself to say it louder. "I'm so fucking sorry."

15

MAEVE CROSS

WHEN I DUCKED into the tent, I made sure to give Luella back her pendant, which she tucked away just as quickly. The warm sensation of magic ebbed away, and I missed its presence almost immediately.

It felt good to give Ronin a piece of my mind, even if I felt a little guilty about it. I wasn't going to be an item for him to take comfort in and soothe him when he did something wrong. That wasn't my job.

If he wanted to make it up to me, then I needed to be a partner. An equal. Not a pawn. Not a plaything. But the way it was, he seemed more than content to lock himself away behind some invisible wall, making me miss him even when he was right next to me.

BEFORE THE MEETING, and after a few decent hours of sleep, I washed up and changed into my first set of fresh clothes so I could wash the other set when we got back to the ketch. I only had two sets of casual clothes and one set of nicer ones for the voyage.

Still, it was nice to feel clean for the morning.

Among the tents and supply caches, we could see one large beach house shadowed by the giant trees. I noticed boatmakers along the beach, processing lumber and crafting new ships. It was quite fascinating to see firsthand.

But most of the sailors were entering and exiting the beach house all morning, going back and forth with supplies for ships. Occasionally, various other sailors docked in prospect of purchasing one of the ships.

In the middle of the night, I couldn't pick out the house, but in broad daylight, it was quite charming. It had a wrap-around porch with freshly painted panels and was well taken care of. This was a *home*. Several of the younger recruits swept the wooden planks, dusted the lighting fixtures, and weeded an ample garden.

Lucky's men had brought us breakfast to enjoy at our leisure before the meeting, so we walked inside the beach house with full bellies and a pleasant attitude. I took in the surroundings as we followed Ethan to the study.

Bunks. A mess hall. A common area where sailors read or played games in their free time. It reminded me of *The Ollipheist* during those long stretches without work. The energy was so familiar to me that I instantly felt at ease.

Ethan guided us to an open suite.

Gunny and Luella broke away from us to keep on schedule. We were leaving the next morning, so there wasn't a ton of time to restock. At this port, Luella and Gunny were in charge of the restock, but that could change depending on what we needed.

"Please sit. Get comfortable. Commander Bartram will be here shortly," Ethan assured us before closing the suite behind us. Aside from two sailors by the doors, we were alone.

I took a seat when everyone else did, trying not to absorb Enya's nervous energy.

She took a deep breath. "Before Lucky gets here, I need you to know something."

The doors opened, and Enya's mouth snapped closed. Lucky came in, dressed in an expensive leather coat and a feathered hat. He looked incredibly put together considering how late we all stayed up to get rid of the echo situation. No speck of sand in his locs or sheen to his skin.

We all stood up, and Ronin outstretched his hand to shake Lucky's. "Good morning," he greeted.

Lucky raised both eyebrows as if Ronin's civility amused him. "You look like shit, Captain Leviathan. What can I do for you?"

Ronin frowned but decided to let the jab go. "I'm here to invite you to join the first ever pirate council."

"*Invite?*" Lucky pinpointed the word. He chuckled. "Why should I accept your invitation, then?" I didn't miss the way his violet eyes flashed over to Enya before going back to Ronin.

Enya and I already knew Lucky had no intention of denying the invitation, but he was playing with Ronin, not unlike how a cat toys around with a mouse.

"Make it worth my while, Levi."

Ronin squared his shoulders, standing tall. "Varric Cross is plotting a siege on Shipwreck Bay. He's planning to dismantle and draft all the pirate colonies. The only way to combat this is to forge a council and offer protections to all the colonies."

We hadn't told Lucky that. The smile left his face. "I can't say I'm surprised. Sit." We obeyed. "I'm guessing you learned this information from the princess here?" He gestured to me.

"Guilty." I offered him a hesitant smile, but I could see an unspoken question in Ronin's eyes.

"How much did you tell him last night?"

Lucky's eyes darted over to Ronin again. "But *why* should I put my colors behind you? You told me that not everyone wants to rule the world, so why did you change your mind? I can only assume that you plan to unseat Cross."

Ronin exhaled heavily from his nose. It was one thing to reveal his identity to his crew, and another thing altogether to share that with an adversary. "My name is Ronin Murdoch. I'm the rightful heir to the throne. I'm asking you to follow me to unseat the usurper."

There was a lilt to his tone. I didn't know if I believed him. If *he* believed himself.

A grin swept across Lucky's face as he stood up, downright beaming as he looked between Enya and Ronin. He slapped his fist against his desk. "About fucking time, kid."

Shock painted Ronin's features.

Andra spoke next. "You knew?"

The grin fell as he made direct eye contact with Enya. "I think it's time they know. About me and Albatross." Disappointment fell across his face as he pressed his tongue against the inside of his cheek.

Enya remained silent, but that was revealing enough.

"Told us what?" Ronin asked.

"You know, I understood not telling the kids when they were kids, but they're adults now, Enya," Lucky said, using her birth name. That wasn't lost on me or anyone else. "All this time, and you're still ashamed of me."

"Did you… *cheat* on Dad?" Andra demanded, anger flaring in her eyes. She looked completely flabbergasted, glancing back and forth between them.

Still, Enya didn't say a word.

"You're really going to sit there and let them hate me?" Lucky sighed.

All eyes fell on Enya, but she kept her mouth shut. She tilted her head back, lips drawn into a grimace.

Lucky addressed Andra's question. "No. You misunderstand. Your father and I loved each other the same way we loved Enya. We were a unit. All three of us."

"What?" Ronin asked. "This whole time… you knew who we were… but you still got Albatross killed."

Lucky stiffened. "That's *not* what happened," he retorted, hitting Enya with a withering stare, the unique violet irises swirling with buried contempt. "She just needed someone to blame."

Finally, Enya spoke. "It was *your* fault Albatross died."

Lucky released a bitter laugh. "All right. If that's what you want to believe. Easier to do that than to face the reality that you *forced* your children to continue life at sea when you had someone who loved you and was more than eager to take care of you and the kids."

Enya wasn't looking at him, her eyes filling with unshed tears. "Cross would've come, Lucky. He would've killed you and taken everything."

"Speculation," Lucky objected. "You didn't know that." Then he turned his gaze back to Andra and Ronin. "Eighteen years ago, our captain was a paranoid bastard. He thought I stole from him, which I didn't. Albatross took the blame. And he died for it. He died for me."

Enya made a strangled noise, and wetness streamed down her cheeks.

Lucky continued the story, visibly bitter. "I was marooned on an island where I found treasure. When I found a way back to Shipwreck Bay, I searched for you, Enya. I was ready to be a father to the kids. I loved them and wanted to take care of them. And *you*, but I guess you were too ashamed of me to even return my letters."

"I was never ashamed of you, Lucky," Enya murmured. "I was ashamed that I was too broken by his death to love you."

Lucky softened. "I lost him too. And the only other person I had abandoned me."

"I'm sorry," she whispered.

"An apology that comes too late. I can't forgive you for abandoning me when I needed you," Lucky replied before he turned his attention back to Ronin. "But my quarrel is not with you, kid. I will help you. I owe Albatross that much."

"This is a lot to process," Ronin admitted.

Andra glanced over at Enya. *How could you?*

"A life at sea, on the move, was the only way I could keep you safe," Enya answered, voice audibly thick.

Andra scoffed, her eyes locked on her mother. "I spent my entire youth hating him." She waved a hand in Lucky's direction. "He was family, and we kicked him out of our lives because of *you*."

Enya's baby blues were shining when she gazed at Lucky, a million emotions washing ashore in the oceans of her eyes. "I regret hurting you, but I would do it again."

"I can't believe you." Andra ground her teeth together. "I'm sorry, Lucky. I'm sorry."

Before he could respond, Andra got up from her seat and left, closing the door softly behind her.

Enya winced, taking a deep breath, and buried her face in her hands. "I hope you're happy."

"I am. You had no right to take the kids from me when I played a part in raising them." He paused, clicking his fingernails against the desk. "I'll be talking to you later, Ronin. We have some private matters to discuss."

Ronin's expression was unreadable. "Aye."

I felt like a fly on the wall, trapped between Ronin and Enya. At least until Lucky addressed me again. "With those echoes gone, we can finally host our nightly cookout again. That brave lassie there gets the first drink. Consider it a proper thanks."

My cheeks warmed, but I nodded. "I look forward to it."

16

RONIN MURDOCH

After such a long day, I leaned against the banister on the porch and watched my crew socialize during the cookout. It was exhausting to listen to my mother and sister fight, the pair of them constantly going back and forth about how Mama had taken the choice away from us.

I couldn't do it anymore.

Andra maintained that it didn't matter that we were children at the time. We deserved a say. That Lucky didn't deserve to be cut out by his family.

Family was deeply important to Andra. Abandoning anyone considered such was out of the question, so she wanted to know why it was all right to make Lucky a scapegoat.

It wasn't.

Mama seemed to disagree.

The meeting with Lucky only gave me more questions. I couldn't help glancing in my mother's direction, equally angry and betrayed by her secrets. With Andra laying into her through one ear, I didn't want to add to it.

I'd get my answers later.

The heat from the fire warmed me but did nothing to

melt the icy guilt in my chest. Not far from me, Mae was stretched out in the sand, her brown ringlets cascading down her back, slightly frizzy from the humidity. She had that first promised drink in the sand next to her. She stared up at the sky, and all I wanted to do was talk to her.

Gulp down all my pride and apologize.

But at this rate, I'd have to get down to my knees and beg her forgiveness.

I gazed longingly at her, my fingertips aching for her. I knew I'd pushed her away, but I didn't know how to stop myself or bring her back. Everything she told me was valid, but there was no point in apologizing if I kept repeating the behavior.

An apology had to mean something. Not a bandage. A promise to be better.

I have to be better.

Lucky's voice disrupted my train of thought. "I know that look."

I glanced over at him. "Do you?"

"It's the exact same way Albatross used to look at your mother. Don't get me wrong, he was a mean motherfucker most of the time, but he liked her. And he liked you." Lucky sighed. "I still miss him, you know. He understood me like no one else."

His body language had changed. He wasn't standing tall. He wasn't wearing expensive leathers or a feathered hat. Without the hat, I could pinpoint the grayed hairs twisted in his locs. For the first time, I saw him as a man. Not an adversary or someone I had to fight, but just a man. As simple as I was.

"I have to admit," I mused, "I'm having a hard time wrapping my head around you three. I had no idea."

He shrugged. "You were a kid. And I was just your dad's friend."

"So, were you in a relationship with Albatross before my mother and I came into the picture?" I asked.

"I would say yes. Albatross would've said no." Lucky waved his hand, dismissing the thought. "It was complicated. But that didn't matter. I just wanted to be there for the twins after their mother died. Then you came along, and I wanted to be there for you too. It takes a village, you know." He was quiet for a moment, staring at the fire that danced in his purple irises. "I'm sorry."

I raised my eyebrows. "Why are you sorry?"

"My folks were never there for me. I'm sorry I wasn't there after he died."

"You don't have to apologize for that. It wasn't your decision."

Lucky looked at me long and hard for a moment before he said, "Kids don't know the difference. Just that one day you're there and the next you're not. For that, I'm sorry."

"Well, thank you. I appreciate that."

He nodded before changing the subject. "How's Howler? I was expecting to see him here."

"He stayed back to be with his wife and kids."

"Good man," Lucky commented. "It's still hard not to see you as kids, but considering the adults you became, I can't help but feel a touch of pride that I contributed to that."

The secret I'd been keeping got heavier and heavier. But Lucky had kept my identity a secret for twenty-five years. He knew who I was this whole time and never betrayed me, not once. Maybe he could keep this one too.

"I can't shift," I said.

Lucky's gaze darted over to me again. "What?"

"Pike and Cross did a number on me when I was captured. I haven't been able to shift since." The weight of a thousand bricks lifted off my shoulders.

"Captured? They got you?" His concern was apparent, as

was the knowledge of what that meant. He knew more than I gave him credit for.

The information wasn't stuck in my throat like a lump I couldn't swallow. Lucky felt safe. He wasn't connected to my crew. He wasn't connected to my birth father. And now I knew that he wouldn't open his mouth to tell anyone else.

When he wasn't sizing me up, Lucky seemed to genuinely care. Underneath all those layers of bravado, he was exactly how I remembered him from when I was a child. How, with a drink in his hand, he'd listen to me practice piano, puff a cigar, and applaud my progress. When my mother or my stepfather was busy with the twins, Lucky would be there with me.

I told him about my forced bedrest. How I put *The Ollipheist* between Pike's man-o'-war and Shipwreck Bay. I didn't give him the details, but I told him that Pike tormented me before handing me over to Cross.

"And how did you get out of Farlight Prison?"

I gave Mae another yearning glance. "She came after me."

He clapped his hands together. "That explains the stolen sloop."

"She said she paid for it," I interjected.

Lucky chuckled. "Oh, she did. That hideous ring was worth three of them."

We shared a laugh.

"She's worth her weight in gold, Levi. Brave. Proved that to me last night. You're fortunate to have her at your back."

"I don't know how long that'll last. I'm really fucking it up." I sighed and scrubbed my beard before taking another gulp of bourbon.

Lucky tilted his head to the side. "They don't know, do they?"

I only looked at him.

"You are your mother's son, aren't you?" He sighed. "It's sweet that I'm the first you let in on this little secret, but you need to tell them. That princess of yours has her own secrets to boot."

"How much do you know?"

He tapped his nose. "A killing spell should claim any soul it's cast on. Fae, elf, human—it doesn't matter. She's something else, and she is going to play a vital role in this war. There is one thing certain in this world, kid. The dead stay dead, so why is she any different?"

Mae died last night.

A tic formed in my jaw as I watched her again. I glanced at her, looking for the signs of her chest rising and falling with her breath. The hue of life pinkened her cheeks. Luella joined her, the two immediately becoming embroiled in their own conversation.

Mae's alive. She's right there.

"We don't know the source of her vitality."

Lucky blew a breath from his nose. "Then *find* it. You *need* her. You need her loyalty. That power could turn the tide of this war."

"Speak plainly."

"Everyone wants to rule the world, just like everyone wants to be immortal."

"You think someone could strip that from her?"

"We didn't know Cross could strip the power from the leviathans until he did. He razes villages. He murders innocents and bypasses the natural limits of magic. I believe he would do anything to steal her gift like he's stolen the gifts from your people." He paused, a serious gleam in his eye. "Especially since she betrayed him."

Jagged ice flooded my veins, painfully sliding through them until it chilled my heart. "I don't like the fact that I don't know what Cross is doing. I don't know who his allies are. I don't know what he's planning."

"Me neither, but we can't dwell on it. We need action. We also need to be alert. You slipped Cross's leash, but he never lets anyone escape for long. Cross has powerful people working for him behind the scenes. They will do anything they can to keep the iron grip they've maintained over the past two decades. And they will come for you."

He was right. It was only a matter of time until Cross sent either Pike or someone else he had under his thumb after Mae and me.

"You also need to stay vigilant," I advised. "If any of our plans get out there, Cross is going to come down even harder."

"You'll be the first to know if any of his allies come into my crosshairs." Lucky gestured toward me with his glass. "You have me, for what it's worth. I'll be at your back."

"And I at yours."

"But you'll need more. Why haven't you told your crew about your affliction?"

That was a great question, and the only answer I could give him was "They're relying on me. I can't be weak."

"Weakness isn't a bad thing." He tapped his lips, thinking of a proper allegory. "A ship is at its weakest on land when we careen it. But that moment of weakness weeds out the shipworms. Parasites rear their heads when their host is vulnerable."

I sighed. "Exactly."

"You miss the point." Lucky gestured to my various crewmembers around the bonfire. Gunny grinning and playing bones with sailors. Luella and Mae chatting. Andra and our mother on opposite sides of the beach from each other. "When you're vulnerable, you know who's at your back and who wants to put a knife in it."

I didn't reply, mulling over his advice.

"This is an opportunity to clean house, Levi. This is too important to let the shipworms sink the ship. I've dealt with a few broken bones and cleaned out mutineers more than once, but your crew is some of the most loyal I've ever met."

Mae stole a glance at me, and when our eyes met, her cheeks darkened before she looked away.

"I'm not saying you should tell everyone you can't shift. In fact, don't. But your crew?" Lucky gestured toward Mae. "Especially that lass. She stole a sloop and risked her hide for you."

"I do trust them," I said.

"Then tell them. You'll feel better. And you can come back to good ol' Uncle Lucky for more advice."

I stole another glance at Mae, wanting to mend all the pain I'd caused her. Maybe I had broken us, but even glass tumbled in the waves could become something precious. "Thank you, Lucky. If I'd known you were this wise, maybe I wouldn't have started all those fights."

He chuckled, showing off his elongated canines. "By all means, keep challenging me. It keeps me sharp. An old sea dog needs the reminder that he can still go toe to toe with a spring chicken." He winked and snatched my empty glass. "Talk to your lass, kid. You'll either fuck it up or you won't."

The duality of his statement gave me a sense of peace I hadn't expected. Right or wrong, I had to give it a chance.

17

MAEVE CROSS

THE FIRST TASTE of success was sweet. There was no promise that the next monarch would be as willing to help as Lucky was, so I'd enjoy it while it lasted. The next day we would sail off to Bliss's Colony, and I'd see Fisherman's Gully for the first time since I was stolen.

I didn't know how to process that, but I'd cross that bridge when I got there.

While my friends were enjoying dinner, I lay out on the sand, staring up at the sky. I could hear Ethan in a conversation with Gunny, the sound of rolling bones and boisterous laughter. Of course. Gunny was a lot of fun to be around.

Meanwhile, Enya and Andra were sitting on opposite sides of the beach, drinks in hand and scowls on their faces. I could only imagine how they were feeling.

Not only had Enya lied about Lucky's role in Albatross's death, but also about keeping the kids out at sea when Lucky was willing to give them the means to stop pirating.

What would that have looked like?

Would they have had a little farm on the far islands?

Or perhaps they would've been merchants or tradesmen. A quiet life like the one Isa and Wesley's kids had. As much as

Wesley loved the open sea, it spoke volumes that he didn't let his kids or Isa work on the ship like he was forced to as a child.

"I take the risks so they don't have to."

His family seemed content with their little slice of heaven. He and Isa were in love and happy. The home life looked good on him. Being a present, loving father suited him more than being Ronin's first mate. That was a job, secondary to who he was. Wesley was a father, a husband, and a brother first.

Andra and Luella? They *were* pirates. Through and through. I couldn't imagine either of them giving up the sea. I think they enjoyed the challenges and loved the ship and their roles.

That's why they worked so well together. They loved the sea the same way they loved each other. Being on land was a vacation. The ship was *home*.

I turned my head to see Ronin by the fire, away from everyone else. Lucky was beside him, the two of them seemingly in friendly conversation. They were sharing a bottle of bourbon, refilling the glasses as they talked.

It looked so vastly different from when I'd met Lucky in Shipwreck Bay.

At the time, I would've fought Lucky just to taste what it was like to battle. Now it was apparent that he had never intended to hurt us. He arrogantly put up this facade of violence, but he'd merely been baiting us to see what Ronin was made of. Considering that Lucky *knew everything*, his actions made more sense.

Everything Lucky did was a challenge. A *lesson*, even.

The older man's guard was down as he listened intently to what Ronin had to say, almost as if a long-lost relationship was rising to the surface.

Ronin looked better than he had, clearly getting his strength back. Similar to Luella and Andra, the sea suited

Ronin. And while I'd love him on land or sea, I preferred the ship.

The freedom this lifestyle gave me.

But I couldn't help but wonder if he felt trapped by it. If my freedom was his cage.

Gods, I just wish he would talk to me.

Come back to me.

Give us a chance.

The sand kicked up next to me as Luella sat down. She didn't say anything, just gave me her company. She drank a golden cocktail of bourbon and an herb that smelled like licorice while I sat up to sip on the drink Lucky had poured for me.

"How's Andra doing?" I asked.

Luella sighed. "She's usually forthright with her feelings, but she's mixed up right now."

"I understand that. I've been rather mixed up myself."

"I imagine so." She took another sip before making direct eye contact with me. "Especially since you died again last night."

"How did you know that? I was trying to keep it quiet."

"After everyone went to bed, Seabird was in a state of panic. She kept staring at you like she didn't believe you were there. I talked her through it, and we had a good little chat. Did you learn anything?"

I glanced around, briefly catching eyes with Ronin before I blushed and looked away. Then I told her about the memory where I drowned. When I was at sea until I washed up on the shore of Fisherman's Gully.

"Most people don't remember things from when they were a babe. Maybe someone is trying to tell you something."

I thought back to the dark figure that was always nearby when I died but never close enough to claim me.

Whenever I died, I remembered something similar that happened in a previous death.

Would each death reveal the secrets of my life to me?

"Maybe," I concurred. "We'll see if I'm unfortunate enough to die again to prove that theory."

She nudged my shoulder with hers and said, "Or maybe we'll get answers at Fisherman's Gully. I'd rather you not suffer for the sake of knowledge."

"'Knowledge is everything to the powerful,'" I recited under my breath. I tipped my glass back, downing the rest of my bourbon.

Luella sighed and said, "You're not wrong, but I—" Her eyes darted up to someone approaching us. I could hear the sand crunch under their feet. "What the fuck do you want?"

I didn't need to look to feel Ronin's presence. But I turned to peer up at him anyway, flushing deeply. I couldn't help it. My knees felt weak as his gaze pierced me. The way my mouth watered and drank him up—it was involuntary.

I crave him. I miss him. I want him.

But I couldn't have him. I loved him, and I didn't think that would ever change, but I refused to be part of a one-sided relationship.

"Can we talk, Mae? Privately."

That doesn't sound good.

That had to be hands down the *worst* thing a man could ever say to a woman who loved him as painfully as I did.

I narrowed my eyes and retorted, "We *can.* But should we? That's a whole other question."

Ronin looked over at Luella, a surprisingly unguarded expression in his eyes as he wordlessly asked her to leave.

She crossed her arms. "I'm not leaving *my girl* here with you so you can continue to be a fucking prick."

I *adored* Luella. But I said, "It's all right, Lulu. We do need to talk."

"If she comes back with tears in her eyes, you're not going to live through the night."

She got up from her spot, taking the remainder of her drink, and left to watch Gunny play bones.

Hesitantly, I looked up at him, taking a deep breath to lay down my boundaries. "If you think you can use me again, Ronin, then you can forget it. I'm not going to be your plaything."

"I know." His eyes captured mine, intensely filled with fondness. "Please."

I never thought a single word could melt me so completely, but the *way* he said it…. My heart thundered in my chest, and I could only reply with "Okay."

We didn't say anything as we headed toward the ocean bank. The moonlight glimmered off the water, dancing across Ronin's face as I walked beside him. Even from right next to him, I felt the chasm between us.

I love you.

You're not alone.

Come back to me.

When we were far enough from the bonfire, he stopped, shoulders bent forward as if he was tired of carrying their weight. His eyes met mine, and I could see through them to the pain he'd been too afraid to show.

He took a deep breath and slowly sank to his knees in front of me. His face darkened, a flush starting at his cheeks. He couldn't meet my gaze. Unlike the last time he was on his knees in front of me, there was nothing erotic about it.

I tilted my head in confusion. "What are you doing?"

He dipped his head, the hollows beneath his cheeks deepening under the moonlight. The flush spread to his ears. He looked down, and all I could see was the crown of his head, his dark hair tied up. I noticed that the haircut I'd given him was starting to grow out.

He tapped his fingers on his thighs and said, "I don't know how else I'm supposed to beg for your forgiveness unless I'm on my knees."

My throat felt thick. I'd never been in this type of situation before. I knew how badly he needed control after Farlight Prison. He wouldn't even let me take charge in bed. Everything he did was to ensure that he kept all the power in every encounter.

It was a surprise that he hadn't asked to tie me up yet.

Ronin never talked about what happened to him on the ship. All I knew was that he bristled every time anyone touched him, snuck up on him, or even asked him about it. My heart squeezed in my chest as his hands shook against his thighs.

"I'm sorry, Mae," he murmured. Slowly, his eyes climbed my body, and he captured my gaze. My heart ached at the tenderness in his eyes. It nearly took my breath away. "I'm so fucking sorry for how awful I've been to you."

My lips parted, and I had to stop myself from telling him it was fine.

It *wasn't* fine. And I wasn't going to give him a throwaway response when this was the opportunity to have a real conversation. One where he didn't lie to me and was *right here,* giving me the chance to see through the frosty layers of ice.

"And?" I pressed. "What else?"

"I know I'm pushing you away, but I can't stop myself." He stayed on his knees, his shoulders drooped. Completely at my mercy. "I *love you,* Mae. I trust you more than anyone else in the whole fucking Isles, but I keep *hurting* you."

His throat bobbed a few times as I let his words hang there in silence.

"I…," he trailed off, clearly trying to find the right way to say it. "I thought that if I pushed you away far enough, then you'd be safe. From me. From Cross. From this whole world. I didn't want you to get hurt."

"I'm already hurt, Ronin. I love you, and every time I make myself vulnerable for you, you say something awful or slam the door in my face. Do you know how much that *hurts*? You're supposed to be the person I confide in. My *partner*. But instead, you… you treat me like I'm just a *thing to use*."

He flinched. "I'm sorry."

"I'm not your godsdamn pawn." I took a deep breath. "I'm not someone to take your frustration out on. I'm not someone to fuck when you need a coping mechanism."

"I know. And I *will* fix this. I'm not going to fill your ears with empty apologies." Shame filled his eyes, and with another shaky breath, he said, "Here's the truth. I'm not okay, Mae. I haven't been since Pike captured me."

There it was. The first honest thing he'd said to me in months. "I don't expect you to be. I'm not okay either." I gave him a soft smile, hoping he didn't hurt me again. "But can we be… not okay together?"

"I'd like that quite a lot," he admitted. "I've just been trying so hard to pretend. Everyone is relying on me, but I'm struggling under it. But that's not all either."

He swallowed, and the shame that filled his eyes only got more apparent.

"What is it? You can tell me." *Don't shut that door. Just be here with me.*

"I can't shift, Mae."

The world went still. My eyebrows came together, and Ronin looked away from me. He wrung his hands like they were dirty, unable to look at me again.

"Then every time you said you were going out for a swim…."

"I was lying." Everything bubbled up as he continued to speak. "How am I going to fight Cross's army? How am I supposed to unite the colonies if I can't be the Royal Leviathan they need me to be? I don't know who I am anymore."

The pain in his voice was palpable. It wasn't just a matter of being vulnerable, it was a matter of losing touch with everything he was supposed to be. His family. His lineage. *Everything* that made him who he was.

"Ronin…."

"I'm weak, Mae. I'm so fucking weak. How am I supposed to—"

I fell to my knees, wrapping my arms around his shoulders, pulling him directly into my chest in the tightest hug I could manage. I froze, having completely forgotten his aversion to touch, but I just wanted so badly to comfort him in the only way I knew how.

He could've shoved me away. He could've snapped and shut me out, but I felt his arms curl around my waist, holding me even closer. His breath blew shakily out against my neck as his body molded against mine.

My heart thundered, my skin *singing* at the sensation. I missed this. I missed *him*. And finally, he wasn't a million miles away. He was right here. With me.

"Is this what you've been keeping from me?" I asked, smoothing my hands down his back.

He uttered a quiet "Yes."

"You're still healing, Ronin," I murmured into his neck, igniting goose bumps across his collarbone. He melted, holding me closer as if I was his only source of comfort.

"I'm sorry. I'm sorry," he repeated, his voice breaking just as all the walls around him crumbled. In this moment, he wasn't trying to be the strong man he thought everyone wanted. He was just Ronin, but that made him even more magnificent in my eyes.

"You don't need to pretend with me. You never have."

He slouched against me, resting his head on my shoulder. I combed my fingers through his hair. He only burrowed his face into my neck even deeper.

I didn't want to be his coping mechanism, but I wanted to be the person he could come to. The person who he felt safe with. I wanted *this*.

"Have you never been hurt this badly before?"

"Nothing I never bounced back from before," he admitted. "But that's not all. I... can't feel my spirit. It feels *gone*."

I leaned back from him, cupping his scratchy jaw. I searched his eyes, looking for anything else he was so terrified to share. He stared back, as if wondering if I was going to leave him now that I knew.

If I thought as little of him as he thought of himself.

"Nothing is ever gone," I murmured, stroking his jaw with my thumb. "Sometimes it's just lost. And you putting all this pressure on yourself is only making it harder to find."

"Gods, I feel so weak. Fucking pathetic."

"Stop it. You've never been weak. This weight is just too heavy. That's why you have friends to help you hold it. We're all here for you, Ronin," I said, pressing my lips to his forehead.

The intimacy between us closed some of the gaps, and he released another shaky breath before falling slack in my arms, accepting my touch as if he was starved of it.

"Just know that this isn't a one-sided endeavor," I added. "I need some help carrying my own weight, too, from time to time."

He nodded. "I will, sweetheart."

Sweetheart. For a pet name I used to hate, I didn't realize how much I missed it.

"I'm sorry I kept this from you. If I told you sooner, I could've saved us all this pain."

"There's no point in speculating, but thank you for telling me now." I sighed and tucked his head under my chin. "Now stay still. I'm soaking up this hug. You owe me many hugs."

He chuckled, and I could imagine the dimples puncturing his cheeks and the relief in his eyes.

I didn't know how long we stayed out there, just holding each other, curling around the other like roots of a tree spreading through the dirt to strengthen the forest. I felt stronger. More reassured. The pain wasn't gone, but this was a start.

We'd started to mend.

I leaned against him, and I could feel him inhaling deeply against my neck. He wasn't shaking anymore. His hands stroked my back as if he was reminding himself how I felt.

The trench that kept us apart was finally starting to close.

18

RONIN MURDOCH

With one final goodbye, Lucky saw us off to our next destination. He gave me a wide grin and waved us away with his loyal First Mate Ethan by his side. I returned the wave, grateful to have reconnected with family, no matter how estranged we'd become over the years.

Lucky was once at Albatross's back, and now he was at mine. As tortuous as their relationship had been, I couldn't help but feel as if my stepfather watched over me, giving me his guidance through Lucky. We weren't family by blood, but we were in spirit.

I missed Albatross more than I missed my own father—a fact that had guilted me for years—but that wasn't Raiden's fault. He never had the chance to be my parent. Albatross was the one who picked the mantle up and wore it with pride.

I glanced over at Mae, thankful that Lucky had been the one to give me the final push to apologize to her. I was my mother's son, but I wouldn't make her mistakes.

The relationship between Mae and me wasn't perfect, but I'd wrap the broken pieces in bandages. I'd nurse the wound. I'd salve the scar. I'd do whatever it took because Mae was worth it.

I thought about the way her fingers combed through my hair and how good she smelled. As we moved into the dead of summer, she felt like springtime. She wrapped her arms around my shoulders as if she could physically lift some of my burden. The relief swam in my veins, and I felt like I had weathered the storm long enough to seek shelter.

Mae was my shelter.

Fuck, she was *everything*.

Luella stood by the helm, carefully maneuvering around the choppy water that wasn't nearly as calm as it had been when the echoes dominated the skies. She was still pissed at me, as was Andra, a fact made obvious by every glare she threw in my direction.

It was different from her normal one. This was clearly a *I'll-gut-you-if-you-fuck-this-up-again* glare. Luella had become incredibly protective of Mae after their rescue mission. Honestly, I wouldn't have anyone else at Mae's back.

Even if everything went to shit with me, at least I knew she had the support of my mates. They'd take care of her if I succumbed to the dark. Not that Mae needed it. She was more courageous than we gave her credit for, but I didn't want her to be alone.

Never again.

She had *us*.

Family.

I stole an eyeful of Mae, who was tentatively looking in my direction. The hurt remained in her eyes, but not without cautious affection. As soon as she caught my gaze, she looked away, opening the hatch to go to the lower deck.

My sister and mother sat on opposite sides of the boat, not talking after their fight. I was still angry at my mother for keeping so many secrets from me, but who was I to judge? I was just as bad, if not worse.

Gunny sat on a nailed-down barrel, blissfully unaware of

everything as he chewed on an apple and read a book. Or perhaps he simply didn't care about the strife happening on board.

Either way, he was a lucky bastard.

When the Outpost was no longer in sight, I went to my cabin. My body ached from standing. Even if my endurance was better, I needed to rest whenever I could. I rolled my shoulders, rubbing the back of my neck in an attempt to work out another knot.

When did I get so old?

I used to be able to sleep flat on my back, high up in the crow's nest where my mother wouldn't find me. I'd succeeded in avoiding swabbing the deck several times simply because I could sleep *anywhere*.

As a cabin boy, I was quite the rascal, sneaking off to shift and bring back various trinkets I'd found on the seafloor. Andra and Wesley loved getting gifts from me in our youth, but after my mother became captain, she brought the hammer down on all my little excursions.

I missed my bed on *The Ollipheist*, but the captain's quarters on the ketch were homely enough. I could get some shut-eye and hope the fucking nightmares wouldn't come back.

No luck yet.

But I had some time to try and rest. Bliss's Colony was a few days' voyage at the farthest point away from Farlight Harbor.

It was the place formerly known as Fisherman's Gully.

Mae is going to need me.

Between her history and her nightmares, this wasn't going to be easy.

She'd been there for me every time I needed her. Even at my most vulnerable, she never looked at me like I was lesser for letting her in. If anything, the warmth in her eyes grew.

She made me believe that I was at my strongest when I felt my weakest.

The thought of her was a balm soothing the ragged flesh of my wounds. Even those invisible ones hiding under the surface.

I'd be okay.

Eventually.

And even if I wasn't, Mae and I would be not okay together.

With a grunt, I kicked my feet up on the small desk, wishing Lieutenant Commander Lazlo were here to keep me company, but he never liked smaller vessels. He got bored if there weren't enough mice to hunt.

A warm breeze came through the porthole that was not at all like my wall of windows on *The Ollipheist*. The smell of the sea air was welcome and familiar. But with the height of summer quickly approaching, it was way too fucking hot in here without the window open.

Part of me wished Mae was with me. That I could lie next to her in my cot and lose myself in how safe I felt around her.

However, the other part of me was more practical. The conversation between us last night was intense, and it would take time before Mae would trust me with her body again. Before *I* was ready for that intimacy again. Her body was a gift, and I had taken it for granted.

I *used* her the exact same way any other man would have, and she accepted it like it was normal. She loved me, and by the Gods, I wouldn't use that against her.

I'd sooner take Luella's knife to the gut.

A soft knock came from my door before Andra peeked her head in, interrupting my thoughts. "Are you up for company right now?" She was troubled, a hard line across her forehead where it crinkled.

"Of course. Have a seat."

Without another word, she entered, closing the door

behind her. Her boots thumped against the planks, and she found her seat at the edge of my cot. "Are you as bothered as I am about Mama? You haven't said much, and I was doing most of the yelling."

"Do you want me to be honest or agree with you?" I asked, crossing my arms.

Her dark eyes shot over to mine, and her foot tapped incessantly on the floor. *Tap. Tap. Tap.* "Obviously I want you to be honest."

I shrugged. "Never hurts to ask." I took my feet off my desk and said, "I've been too wrapped up in my own shit to even consider being angry at Mama."

She scoffed, visibly reeling back from me. "She *lied* to us. She blamed Lucky for Dad's death when it wasn't his fault."

"I'm not defending her when I say that people do bad things when they're grieving."

Andra lifted one arched brow. "It's been eighteen years."

I nodded. "And she should've told us. We shouldn't have had to hear that from Lucky."

She slouched and took a breath through her nose. "It's not even that, Levi. It's just that he… he offered to take care of us. Hells, he *wanted* to take care of us, and Mama just abandoned him. It leaves a bitter taste in my mouth."

I couldn't help thinking about the life we could've had if Mama and Lucky raised us outside of piracy, but then I wouldn't be the man I was. I could speculate all I wanted, but it wouldn't change a fucking thing.

No point getting angry over it.

She looked away from me as if trying to put her thoughts into words. "I feel fucking robbed," she admitted.

Robbed.

What a good word for it.

"We could've had a life outside of this." She tapped her fingers on her thighs. "Lucky could've been there for us."

I dipped my chin. "Yeah. We could have."

"That wasn't Mama's decision to make. Cutting him out of our lives. Sentencing us to life on the big salt." She was vocally working out some of that childhood resentment with me, and I let her.

We all had it.

I remembered being thirteen, scrubbing the deck until my fingers were numb. It was never good enough for our mother. Not until my palms were raw and my fingernails were bloody. But the twins and I had one another.

As the eldest, it was my job to protect them even then.

Though we were offered a jar of salve, I'd sneak away to shift into my leviathan form and get some of that healing silt from the bottom of the ocean. It worked better than the salve. I made sure Andra and Wesley relieved their ragged hands before I'd take care of my own. Then the next day, we'd start all over again.

When our brother was sixteen, he dislocated his shoulder on the rigging, and Mama told him to shrug it off. It was Andra and me who popped it back into place and fashioned a sling out of the shirt off my back.

I took care of them because I had to. *They relied on me.*

Our mother was always too distracted with raids to look after us. The price of being a captain. When I turned eighteen, she started preparing me to take over. I could say it was because I was the most qualified, but it could've been an excuse for her to get to know me again after being neglectful for so many years. At that point, I was no longer a boy. I'd grown into a man she didn't know anymore.

So the thought of Mama taking the hard way out when a potential life of peace was *right there* felt jarring to say the least. She was afraid to stay in one place too long, as it would only be a matter of time before Varric found us and stole everything from her again.

The safer option, in her eyes, would be to cut her ties with Lucky, take the kids, and run.

I couldn't fault her for that, but I *could* fault her for hurting Lucky when she could've spoken with him.

I gazed at my sister for a long moment. Her lip curled into a near snarl, and a vein popped in her forehead. The red hue in her skin was more prominent as anger flushed her cheeks.

"Do you remember when Howler met Isa? That shore leave?"

Her eyes snapped to me, the angry expression melting off her face for a moment. "What of it?"

"Do you remember when Mama told him to forget about her and get back on the ship, but he just couldn't do it?"

I recalled the memory perfectly.

From the first moment Wesley saw Isa, he was smitten. He was nineteen, and I hadn't taken on the mantle of captain yet. This was even before Luella came into our lives. We were at a tavern, drinking until we acted like fools. Isa was our barmaid, already pregnant with Maya, preparing to take care of her as a single mother.

During the last night of shore leave, we were incredibly rowdy. Wesley and I shoved each other around until I knocked him over the bar and into the wall of glasses.

I'd never forget the cacophony of glass shattering as Isa watched helplessly. Wesley felt so awful that he made us all stay behind to clean up the mess no matter how early we had to get up the next day.

The two of them hit it off all night, and I'd never seen him so lovestruck.

When we walked up the gangway the next morning, hungover and exhausted, Wesley stopped midstep and said, "I can't leave yet."

Mama was on a tight deadline to catch up with a merchant ship, so she shouted at him, but he still turned and ran off toward the tavern.

Isa was just as tired as we were, but Wesley ran up to her,

kissed her, and promised to write to her the next time he could. The next year of their relationship was by letter, but that never diminished their feelings for each other. She would tell him about her new baby, and he told her that he couldn't wait to meet Maya. That he bet she was as pretty as her mama.

Wesley beamed every time he got a letter, jumping into his bunk to read them out loud. He stopped reading them to us once they started getting saucy. Andra and I watched his eyes go wide and his face flush before he tucked the letter under his pillow and threatened to wring our necks if we tried to read it.

If Wesley had listened to Mama, he wouldn't have taken that shot with Isa, and he wouldn't have five kids, a wonderful wife, and a home to go back to.

"I do," Andra answered. "Why?"

"We are the people we are today *because* of Mama's choices. We aren't Mama, and we sure as Hells aren't going to make her mistakes. What she did was fucking awful, but I'm not going to dwell on it, and neither should you," I replied.

She gave me a firm look, crossing her arms over her chest. "We're not going to make her mistakes, huh? What about you? You're *just like her.*"

"Don't compare me to Mama."

She raised both eyebrows and said, "You're just as high-strung. Just as quiet. Just as quick to cut someone out if they make you uncomfortable."

Fuck, you didn't have to call me out like that. "You've made your point. I'm working on it."

"We aren't young little shits anymore, Levi. You don't get the benefit of the doubt any longer. You sure as shit *better* be working on it, because I'm not going to pick up the pieces if you treat Mae the same way Mama treated Lucky."

Ouch.

I gulped thickly, the lingering feeling of guilt welling in my belly again. "I came clean to her last night," I said softly. It was just as difficult to say this time as it was last time. "I can't shift. I've been trying to deal with it, but I just can't."

"Oh fuck." Andra paused, her expression morphing to one of sympathy instead of frustration. "That explains why you've been such an ass lately."

"Thanks," I replied dryly before adding, "Lucky and I actually had a good talk—"

"You told *Lucky?*"

"He kept my identity a secret for twenty-odd years, and I wasn't ready to tell anyone close to me yet," I said with a shrug.

"Fair. All right. Well, what're you going to do about it?" Andra demanded, ever the practical one.

That was pretty funny considering she was rather impulsive in her youth. A whirlwind of irrational glee. Always starting fights she never intended to finish. That recklessness was unsustainable, and this lifestyle has a way of teaching the most painful lessons.

As an adult, she was the one I went to for personal advice. I never went to Luella or Wesley if I was overstimulated. They weren't equipped to help. Andra, on the other hand, had a calmer cadence, easily laying out a plan in a way I could digest.

"How do you eat an elephant, Levi? One bite at a time. What do you eat first?"

So, what was I going to do first?

"I'm going to heal," I decided.

Mae was right when she told me that I hadn't given myself time to heal. And this expedition to each of the monarchs was a good opportunity for it. I didn't have a whole ship of sailors or an endless sea to navigate. I had my most trusted friends and the gentle waves of shoreline sailing.

"That's a good start," Andra agreed. "I hate to see you so miserable. Promise me you'll make time during these next few weeks to take a load off."

I couldn't promise that, so I said, "I'll try. I'm not ready for everyone to know my affliction—"

"I'll keep it quiet, but don't take forever. We're here for you. All of us. You know that, right?"

The corner of my mouth tilted up, and my chest felt lighter. "I do. Thanks, Boats."

She threw me a wink. "Thanks for the chat."

"And as for Mama, I'm not defending her when I say that, while shitty, she did what she thought was best for us. We were kids."

She dipped her head, locs and braids falling in front of her face. "I know, but that doesn't make it feel like less of a betrayal." She sighed. "I don't forgive her, and I don't think I will for a while."

I nodded, trying to offer a little piece of support. My family was there for me, so I'd be there for them. "I get that. You don't owe her forgiveness, but don't let that be all you think about. You tend to dwell when you're upset."

She scoffed. "I don't dwell."

"Yes, you do. Do I need to remind you what happened with that one barmaid—"

She got up from my cot and fixed her hat on her head. "Fuck off, Levi. At least I wasn't so desperate for a fuck that I got robbed."

I'm never going to live down my relationship with Violetta, am I?

"Low blow."

Andra gave me a cheeky smile before ducking out of the cabin.

19

MAEVE CROSS

I ADMIRED THE SCENERY. When we were on the open ocean, it was blue. All blue as far as I could see. The ocean was all-consuming. But sailing shorelines granted me more of an opportunity to adore the islands. I watched fishes swim in the shallows. Interesting foliage and tropical flowers decorated the shores. It wasn't always sand and beaches. Occasionally, I'd stare up at cliff faces and catch the wildlife looking down at us curiously.

When I wasn't distracted by the sights, my days were filled with work. Even if the ketch was considerably smaller than *The Ollipheist*, with a crew of only six, there was always something to do.

Gunny maintained the five cannons on board.

Luella stood by the helm, adjusting to keep us on route. When she wasn't, Ronin took over. Considering our proximity to land, it was easy to hit a sandbank or a reef, so someone had to be on the helm at all times.

Andra adjusted the sails or took inventory of supplies. Meanwhile, I'd handle the leftover duties—swabbing the deck, cleaning, cooking, and being the extra pair of hands to float between positions.

I didn't mind. The busier I was with my hands, the less I thought about Fisherman's Gully. I even threw out a net to catch some fish for dinner. Shallows were lush with catch, and it was easier to keep up with nutrition after finishing our produce right before hitting our next destination.

Enya slept during the day to take over the helm in the evenings. Not only was she the night helmsman, but she also kept watch in case sirens, beasties, unaligned pirates, or even military personnel decided to attack us. Not as big a risk as on the open seas, but still a concern. She'd wake up to prepare dinner for us before starting her shift.

While our days were filled with work, our nights were filled with games, stories, and drinks before bed. Because what else would we do in the dark? Gunny, Andra, Luella, and I had a good time.

Ever since we left Lucky's Outpost, Ronin joined us more often. He seemed to be taking my advice to heart and letting himself enjoy our company.

I missed his smile.

I'd catch his gaze every once in a while, but he'd been giving me space. Though even with the physical distance, he didn't feel so far away anymore.

He didn't flinch as often if I brushed by him. In fact, if he did, he'd reach out and stroke my arm in an almost reassuring gesture.

He was trying.

In the small moments, it meant the world to me.

WITH THE MOON high in the sky, it was another night of friendly conversation. We were on deck. Enya steered the ship and watched us fondly. I knew Andra and Ronin were still angry with her for keeping such a big secret, but their mother was letting them come to their own conclusions.

But I didn't miss the pain in her eyes. The regret. I was sure she'd had her reasons, but that didn't make the aftermath any easier.

Luella leaned back on Andra as she combed through Luella's red hair, redoing some of her braids. Her hair didn't have the right texture to lock, so the comb went through easily, brushing out any knots into a waterfall of crimson across Andra's lap. Usually, I'd catch Luella kissing Andra's forehead as she picked out her locs to refresh them. They'd even talk about taking her hair out of the protective hairstyle next time they were at Anchorage Cove just to change it up a bit.

Seeing Luella on the receiving end was a nice change.

It amused me to watch her staring up at Andra with wide eyes, looking more like a lovesick puppy than a cutthroat pirate. Her eyes shone, and she might as well be offering Andra her belly for rubs.

I sat on a barrel near the bow, enjoying the breeze in my hair. Next to me, Gunny carved a new knucklebone set from hooves and ankle bones he'd bought from Lucky's Outpost. It was nothing more than scrap after they butchered livestock, but every piece of the animal went to use, whether the skin was tanned into leather, the bones used to make broth, cartilage pieces for the dogs to chew on, or hooves and horns used as material for knives or, in Gunny's case, game pieces.

He whittled the sharp sides down so they were all relatively the same size. Then he took his knife and scraped pips into each of the six sides. On opposite sides, the number of dots had to add up to seven. Aside from that, every knucklebone piece was completely unique to the player.

"Almost done," he mumbled.

The oil lamp between us flickered amber flames across everyone's face, bathing my friends in a warm yellow light. The captain's cabin hatch door creaked open as Ronin poked his head out. His eyes caught mine, and I gave him a soft smile.

He returned it, dimples puncturing his cheeks. He climbed up the few steps to the main deck to join us, receiving a glare from Luella.

He had to make it up to her too.

"Carving bones, Gunny?" Ronin asked, taking a seat on the deck between Gunny and Andra.

"Gotta do something," Gunny replied. "You lot won't play cards with me." As soon as the words came past his lips, the corner of his mouth turned up, revealing his twisted tooth.

Luella laughed loudly. "I learned my lesson with you."

"They won't even let you play cards at the tavern," Andra added playfully.

I hadn't heard this story before. "Is that why you only play bones?" I asked.

Ronin leaned back on his elbows. "Correction. He is only *allowed* to play bones."

Gunny rolled his eyes and gestured to our captain. "He's no fun."

"How about I play you, then?" I offered. "They don't like when I win either."

Ronin chuckled, knowing how good I was at cards. "Don't say we didn't warn you, sweetheart."

Sweetheart. My cheeks darkened as a helpless smile curved one side of my mouth. "You need to have more faith in me."

"Faith has nothing to do with it," Luella commented, so amused that she finally stopped glaring at Ronin for a moment.

Gunny's half smile turned into a full-blown grin as he pulled a deck of cards out of his jacket pocket as if he'd been waiting for this moment. "Let's play, birdie."

"All right," I decided, getting off my barrel to sit across from Gunny on the deck. "Give me your worst."

"I'll deal," Andra said as Luella got off her lap. "Gotta give you a decent shot."

"For the last time, I'm not cheating," Gunny stated.

"Sounds like something a cheat would say," I teased as he gave Andra the cards.

Gunny stuck his tongue out at me, and I returned the childish gesture, crinkling my nose. His eagerness to play cards should've been a warning, but he looked so thrilled that I couldn't back out.

As Andra dealt out the first round, Gunny procured a single coin and said, "I never play for free."

"Oh? Neither do I," I replied.

The way Ronin and Luella shared a look should've told me to back out, but I didn't.

"Mae…," Ronin trailed off with a sigh when I stubbornly ramped it up tenfold.

I pulled ten coins from my pocket and dropped them next to the oil lamp between us. Gunny matched my bet and picked up his cards.

"She never listens, does she?" Ronin asked.

Luella laughed. "No, she doesn't."

I laid down a card, and Gunny laid down his.

"Ha!" I said as I took the first round.

I don't know what they're on about.

Then Gunny took the next round, but I ultimately took the hand and the coin.

"Aw, I normally play better than this," Gunny said, but there was something insincere about how he said it, a coy grin lingering on his lips accompanying a devious glimmer in his eyes.

"Maybe you're just out of practice," I jested, gathering the coin.

"Another round?" Gunny asked.

What harm could that do? "All right. But we're doubling the bet."

"Of course," he agreed.

Andra bit back a smile. *Did they know something I didn't?*

Too late now. I had a taste of winning, so I didn't want to back down.

She dealt out the next hand, and I laid out the coins. Gunny laid the first card, and I won the round.

He's terrible at this. I almost feel bad winning.

Then I won the second hand. "Better luck next time, Gunny."

"One more," he insisted. "We can even *triple* the bet."

"Oh, sure," I chuckled. "If you want to keep losing coin."

Andra laid out the next hand. I flipped the first card, and Gunny played his, losing the first round. I laughed and took the round.

"Oh, Mae…." Gunny shook his head. "You're making this too easy."

My eyes darted up, and I noticed that his smile didn't go away. "What do you mean?"

I played my next card, but this time, Gunny took the round easily. I laid down the next card, but again, Gunny took it.

He won each round of the hand, and it finally dawned on me that he'd lost *on purpose.* My mouth fell open as everyone across from me laughed.

I glanced over at Ronin, and he chuckled, shaking his head as Gunny merrily took all the coin. "That was mean, Gunny."

The gunner hummed and plopped the coin into his pocket. "It's not my fault that birdie here didn't listen to you."

"How did you…?" I was flabbergasted that he'd taken all my coin in one fell swoop.

"He counts cards, Mae," Andra explained.

"You didn't stand a chance," Luella added, deeply amused that I got swindled.

That was clearly why he was only allowed to play bones. *Can't cheat at that.*

But then it dawned on me that he was carving his own set.

"You hustler!" I gaped, only half serious.

Ronin stretched out on the deck, looking unbearably attractive as he said, "How about you tell Mae how you ended up on my crew, Gunny?"

He gave me a nervous smile, rubbing the back of his neck, cheeks brightening the tawny hue of his skin a dusty pink. "I was a stowaway."

"What?" I asked. "You *must* tell me that story."

Ronin gave Gunny a friendly smile, urging him to continue. "It's a good story."

"I grew up in Farlight, on the docks. I always caused problems for the orphanage, so they kicked me out early. I liked to swindle the guards when I could, which was all the time because they were in rotation. It was good money for a few years, as I never went after the same guard twice. But apparently they talked about the kid at the docks who robbed them."

Gunny twisted his fingers together, the smile growing on his face until it was blinding. "One day, I was ambushed by a bunch of guards." He used his hands while he talked, really regaling me with the tale. "I ran away and sprinted down the gangway of the first ship I saw and dove behind a load of crates. It was a miracle no one saw me and turned me over to the guards."

Luella smirked and added, "I was already on board at this point, so when I saw a bunch of guards coming toward the ship, I distracted them, not knowing I was letting a little stowaway find a hiding place behind me."

"I was real good at hiding, so no one found me on board for a few weeks," Gunny said. "Except for Spider. He was a cabin boy at the time, so he'd sneak me grub while I hid."

"I didn't even know we had a stowaway until we were attacked by a rogue pirate ship and Gunny came up from the bilge to fight them off with us." Ronin glanced over at Luella. "Little did we know we were about to hire the best head gunner this side of the Algarian Sea."

Gunny shrugged, grinning from ear to ear and showing off his twisted tooth. "And the rest is history."

His smile was so infectious, all of us were soon beaming.

"That is a good story," I said before adding, "but I'm never playing cards with you again."

Gunny kicked me playfully. "It was worth it. I'll buy you drinks next time we dock."

"You better."

20

MAEVE CROSS

Unlike at Lucky's Outpost, we arrived at Bliss's Colony in the afternoon. The sun was high in the sky, and the water glittered with picturesque sunshine. The pier was full of boats—small five-person vessels used for fishing or short trips to a nearby island.

No sailors in sight.

Nerves sat heavily in my stomach.

It looked different than I remembered it from my nightmares.

Smoke didn't blot out the sun. I couldn't smell the charred flesh from the pyres. No screams drowning out the sounds of the world. The rapid splashing of predators feasting on merrow.

A jagged rock on the coastline decorated with colorful flowers drew my attention.

Ice slid down my spine.

I knew that rock.

A memory flashed over my eyes, and I remembered seeing one of the other children draped over it. Sinews twisting around their ankles and wrists. Lifeless eyes.

Usually deeply tanned skin void of all color... except for *crimson.*

Crimson everywhere.

My hands shook as that memory anchored me there. It didn't matter how much time had passed. I was a child again, leaning against Varric's chest as he swept me away, the cool crystal of his amulet making bile rise in my throat.

I felt sick... so *sick.*

"You're something special. I won't waste you."

His words echoed in my ears as I shut my eyes, but the visual of the mutilated child remained. My caretaker's blood splattered on my face. My own saturated my skin, clotting around my ears.

My ears hurt.

"Muirgen! Muirgen!" The roared name was cut short. The sound of splashing followed. Gurgling cries of agony. Conway.

That was Conway's voice.

"Muirgen doesn't fit such a fine creature," Varric mused. "Nor her beauty."

"What about Morgana, my liege?" one of his guards offered.

His chest vibrated as he hummed, but I couldn't bear to open my eyes. The darkness swam in front of my vision, but his voice screwed its way into my ears. "No. Not quite right."

"Margaret?" another asked.

They were discussing what to change my name to moments after murdering those who took care of me. Moments after killing and stealing me.

"Maeve," Varric decided. "One of intoxicating beauty. The name is rightful for my daughter. Maeve Cross."

He gripped my chin, jolting my head up with force. His fingers were so slippery with blood that it felt like oil. "Open your eyes, child."

Fear puffed down the back of my neck as I slowly opened them, meeting the eyes of my murderer. All at once, he'd stolen my family, my life, and my identity.

"I can see your use already—"

I blinked hard, trying to come back to the present. But I was drowning in dark water, clawing to the surface, and the memory repeated, the visual of death burned into my eyes. Chills swept over my arms, my heart throbbing so hard that I could hear it pounding in my ears.

The abyss beneath me opened its mouth wide, and I plummeted into the trenches.

I glanced at my hands to see crimson staining my fingertips. My mouth tasted of metal as I reached up to touch my ears. The tips of them felt wet and raw.

My entire body trembled, shaking as if I was cold in the tropical heat.

Wetness spilled down my neck, and I reached for my throat. All I could think about was the slick red between my toes, saturating my shirt.

I need to stop the bleeding.

I need to stop the bleeding.

I need to—

"Mae." Two firm hands grasped my arms like twin lifelines extended into the sea, pulling me out of the dark and into the sun. "Hey. Hey. Breathe."

Ronin's voice snapped me out of my spiral. He pulled me directly into his chest, then began combing my hair down my back. Instantly, I was surrounded by the scent of cedar and the briny sea. I inhaled deeply, finding comfort in it.

Peering around his arm, I could see the rest of the crew staring at me.

Andra and Gunny didn't know why I'd had such a big reaction, but Enya and Luella did. They understood, as did Ronin.

My face was wet, and I realized what I thought was blood were my tears. I shook violently in the aftermath of my panic attack, grabbing handfuls of his shirt to anchor myself into the present. To not slip down into the trenches again.

"It's okay, sweetheart. I'm here. I have you. Come back to me," Ronin murmured into the crown of my head.

Come back to me.

Something I'd begged time and time again, praying for him to escape the depths of his own mind, and now here he was. Fulfilling his promise of being present when I needed him.

I inhaled the comforting smell of his shirt again, calming my racing pulse. I slunk down, burying deeper to escape the concerned eyes of everyone on board. "I know that rock...."

I felt him look toward the shore to the massive rock I referenced. "The one with the flowers on it?"

With a sniffle, I nodded. "There was another child, maybe ten, *displayed* there."

Ronin made a noise, nothing more than a deep rumble in his chest, but I could tell that my statement disgusted him. "If this is too much for you, I won't think any less of you if you want to stay in my cabin. I can handle this."

I shook my head. "I can do this. I just didn't think I'd react so strongly."

"Trauma can be unpredictable. It doesn't care where you are or what's going on around you," Ronin answered. "But you don't have to face it alone, sweetheart. Just breathe right now. We can stay like this as long as you need to."

His words warmed me as I leaned in, his arms forming a protective barrier around me. "Are they still staring at me?" Shame heated my cheeks as I fought the urge to look back at the crew.

"They're worried about you too," he said. "I just got to you first."

I soaked up the embrace until I stopped trembling.

Just a little longer....

I pulled back, and Ronin's big hands cupped my face. He searched my eyes intently. "Are you all right?"

He stroked my cheeks with his thumbs, wiping away any

trace of my tears. The shame in my cheeks morphed into adoration, getting even warmer as my heart fluttered helplessly. It swelled in my chest at *how* he looked at me.

Like I was everything.

"I'm better now," I answered.

The corner of his mouth turned up ever so slightly as he brushed my cheeks one more time before letting me go.

I'm okay. I'm alive.

Luella's concerned voice carried over to me. "You good there, lass?"

I looked over at her, broad-brimmed hat shadowing her eyes. In response, I gave her a weak smile. "I'm all right."

Andra, Gunny, and Enya were all on deck. All three of them had noticed what happened. I could see it all over their faces, but they didn't say anything.

But then something drew all the eyes to the ocean.

There was a splashing noise several feet away, and my heart rate kicked up again, but I held on to the present.

I held on to the fact that I was surrounded by my friends. People I loved. I *wasn't* alone. Admittedly, I was still trying to get used to it, considering I'd spent most of my life isolated from everything.

Ronin's eyebrows scrunched together as he looked behind me, which told me that this noise wasn't in my head. Luella put her hand up as she watched glittering bodies cut through the clear water.

On either side of our ketch, I caught glimpses of multicolored scales.

Flowing hair.

Webbed hands curled around spears and tridents.

Fabric dancing in the water around their bodies in colors complementary to their tails.

Were those… *merrow?*

I thought all the merrow here were killed or displaced.

Does Conway know? My mind went to him, to the grief he

still carried after all these years. The guilt of running while his kin were slaughtered. Someone had to tell him that his family might have survived.

I ignored my inner turmoil, pushing it all down. It was in the past. I could forget about my trauma if that meant finding Conway's family.

My mouth dropped open in awe as the merrow came to shore. They shifted, finned tails splitting and scales dissolving into ink under their skin similar to how Ronin's leviathan form did. Like how Conway's scales imprinted the skin on his arms.

Six of them strode down the pier to where Andra had dropped anchor.

Enya opened the small side door and dropped a short gangway as the merrow approached, giving them the unsaid invitation to come aboard. Only the lead merrow and two of their companions boarded, offering their hand to Ronin.

He took it and gave it a shake.

When he was initiating the touch, it was easier to hide his aversion, and I noticed how his muscles didn't bunch together as tightly as they used to. He was growing comfortable in his skin again.

Fabric clung to the merrow, lightweight and brightly colored. A few of them wore mesh across their chests, serving to house supplies and small tools. Shells and sea kelp were threaded through their hair. Some of them wore their hair in braids, some loose so it plastered wet against their shoulders.

Each of them had tresses that hung down their backs, but Conway's was still trimmed short.

In mourning.

Another memory came to me. When death took someone, it wasn't uncommon for those left behind to cut their hair as part of their grieving process, usually after their dead had been brought to their final resting place, deep in the ocean trenches. They would only let their hair grow back when they *chose* to move past their mourning.

Choice was deeply personal to the merrow. They were inherently androgynous, so they had the choice of love, career, and gender. They even had a naming ceremony when they came of age to embrace the person they decided to become. I remembered how much fun they were.

Conway's naming ceremony included carving toys from driftwood to give to the children. Sweets that we never indulged in otherwise. That was when he chose the name *Conway* to replace his juvenile name *Oisín*.

Just being in the presence of the merrow made memories flare up left and right as more of my youth came back to me. It became harder and harder to stay present.

"We've been expecting you," the merrow at the front stated, releasing Ronin's hand.

They wore orange fabric, draping their shoulders and body and tied to them with twine. Their status was boasted by the frosted-glass armor dangling and clasped under the orange fabric, resembling fine jewels that I could only see when they moved. Their strawberry blonde hair caught the sunlight, framing incredibly angular features.

Scars accentuated their face, just as faded as the hash marks that decorated their arms. The scars were an angry red color, standing out against their deep olive complexion. Unique orange irises curled around their large crescent-shaped pupils, matching the color of their dressing. While Conway's eyes were completely milky, most of the merrow didn't seem to have any whites to their eyes at all.

"Captain Bliss has requested that Captain Leviathan meet with them alone for lunch."

I don't like that.

A wave of protective energy came over me as I crossed my arms, stepping closer to Ronin. He noticed, taking a deep breath and replying, "Of course."

"But—" I started.

Ronin pinned me with that authoritative gaze. "Whatever Bliss Thatcher wants, they will get."

The lead merrow dipped their head. "Glorious. As for the rest of your crew, they're welcome into the colony as well, as long as your weapons are left either on your ship or with the guards at the gateway of the grove. We're having a ceremony at the temple."

"Thank you…," he trailed off, letting the merrow introduce themselves.

"Udine. Refer to me as *she*. Matriarch of the merrow and lieutenant under Captain Thatcher."

Ronin bowed his head in a show of respect. "Thank you, Matriarch Udine." He turned his head to look down at me. "Are you sure that you're all right?"

I gave him a soft smile and nodded. "I will be."

"I'll take good care of her, Levi," Luella offered, leaving the helm to take long strides up to my side. She placed a hand on my shoulder, and I took another deep breath.

Then she turned to Ronin. "Stay safe, aye?"

Luella and Ronin shared a look of understanding. One that they only gave each other. He didn't say anything else, just dipped his tricorn hat and walked toward the gangway, but before he stepped onto it, he grabbed his jacket with the long tails, a sign of status. He shrugged it over his shoulders and went on his way. The farther away he got, the more nerves puddled in my stomach.

But when Luella nudged me with her elbow, it helped wash all the anxiety away. "Gunny and Seabird are restocking, and Boats is going to check out our accommodation. How about you come with me?"

It was a good suggestion. A walk around would do me some good. "Where are we going?"

She looked over my shoulder and gave whoever was looking at us a reassuring nod. "I would like to join the merrow for their ceremony. I've heard it's similar to my Rite of Land."

I blinked. Luella usually did her prayers in privacy, even from her wife. "Your rite? You want me to come?"

"I wouldn't invite you if I didn't."

I glanced over at the merrow as they walked through the tree line. Attending the ceremony would give me a great opportunity to talk to them. I gulped down all my nerves, preparing myself for going down the gangway.

"It'll be good for me," I replied. "I'd like to know if anyone knows Conway."

Luella nodded, a pleased smile lingering on her lips. "Plus, even if you're not merrow, it'll also be good for you to surround yourself with other fae. Who knows, it might trigger something."

It already has.

21

MAEVE CROSS

LUELLA and I followed the sandy path to the tree line. On either side of the trail, trimmed bushes and tropical flowers guided us toward the grove. Blossoms fully unfurled for the sun, revealing lovely cerulean and ivory petals. Their sweet scent permeated the air, complementing the salty ocean breeze.

The flowers climbed the ivy gates, curving along a gated archway where a merrow and human stood guard. They were in a friendly conversation before they saw us and instantly fell into formation. Both of them wielded halberds —long metal poles with what looked like thick sea-glass daggers bound to the end.

The archway was surrounded by thick foliage and vividly colored flowers, giving the impression that this was the only way to enter the colony.

The human gave us a sharp look as we approached and said, "Outsiders are welcome into the grove as long as you relinquish all your weapons."

Luella nodded. "Of course," she said as she reached for her sash. She unfastened her gear and dropped it into the barrel.

I narrowed my eyes, a little surprised that she didn't put up more of a fight. Luella lifted her hat slightly to pin me with a stare that demanded I follow her example.

The idea of not having my cutlass made my belly roll uncomfortably. Especially because the creeping sensation of panic wasn't too far away. But I obeyed nonetheless. This wasn't my home. I would respect their rules.

Even if I didn't want to.

The guards lifted their halberds, and the merrow said, "Please be respectful during the ceremony. It will begin shortly in the temple."

Temple?

A modest building of wood and stone where the orphans slept and the merrow paid respect to their gods. Mostly one goddess in particular—Cliohde. It was the warmest place to sleep during cold nights, and the entire shoal would lay down bedrolls to wait out winter.

The matriarch told us that the temple was another way Cliohde protected them.

It was the first building to burn when Varric razed the shoal to the ground.

"Mae," Luella murmured calmly, setting a hand on my shoulder.

I blinked a few times, gulping down the memories of fire and blood. "Sorry."

Neither of the guards said anything as Luella guided me inside. Under her breath, she asked, "What's going on, love?"

"I'm remembering," I answered. My throat felt thick. "I'm remembering *everything.*"

"Explain," she ordered, her voice still softer than she'd ever used with me before.

"Not from my own eyes," I said. "It's as if I'm a fly on the wall. An outsider looking in. But these are my memories. Like someone or some*thing* is showing them to me."

Luella nodded. "Were the other flashbacks like this?"

"Some, but not all of them. It feels like I'm being dragged away, Lu."

She reached over and squeezed my hand. "Even if they take you away, Mae, I've got you. You're not alone. All right?"

My gaze grew watery. *I'm not alone. I'll never be alone again.*

"I know," I said softly, squeezing her hand back.

Luella didn't smile—she rarely did—but I knew by the fierceness in her eyes that I'd have her unrelenting support. I couldn't have asked for a better friend. Truly.

With a deep breath, I looked away, drawn to all the greenery. Rich brown soil at the base of crops. Flowers and trees. The panicky feeling in my belly slowly subsided as I took in the beauty. It looked as if the attack never happened.

As if the land was never salted.

The houses had never burned.

The reefs were never bloodied.

Ash had never rained from the sky.

Merrow and sailors worked alongside each other effortlessly. Some were farming in the field, some sold food at a canopied market, and some were even combat training at the base of a hill. I was amazed at how lively it was.

A group of adolescents and young adults came barreling through the walkway with fish speared on their harpoons. They were chattering and grinning, teasing one another like they didn't know what happened all those years ago.

"Did you see what I caught?"

"I caught more!"

"You're a merrow! Of course you caught more—" They sidestepped me. "Oh, excuse us!"

Could that have been me if I'd stayed? If I'd woken up long after Varric and his soldiers left? Would I be happy and fishing without a care in the world?

I didn't know what to expect. That the pyre still shrouded the blue in the sky with smoke? That I could still smell blood and burnt flesh? That the houses and temple would be nothing but a pile of ash?

The temple.

I spun around toward the sea and stared up at it. The temple was bigger than I remembered it but just as grand, with hand-carved banisters and depictions of Cliohde sculpted into the doors and walls.

Before the massacre, I remembered the shoal being full of life, thriving with energy and the promise of tomorrow. But now the sounds of children laughing and the scent of fresh fish from the market made its bustle even louder. There were more little ones running around and kicking sand on the beach. Adolescents picked purple flowers and presented them in a show of young love.

My heart ached from how full it felt.

Merrow, humans, and a handful of elves alike walked through the massive temple doors open to all.

"They rebuilt," I uttered softly. But they didn't just rebuild —they *grew*.

Luella watched me intently, trying to read me. I couldn't hide my expressions even if I tried. My eyes pricked with tears.

They're okay.

Maybe I could be too.

The girl who Varric stole awoke within me, full of child-like joy. Even if I had grown up, Muirgen was still alive inside me. It wasn't her fault that Varric came to raise all Nine Hells on the merrow. She couldn't protect them, but *I could.*

I would preserve what they'd built from the ashes.

"Come now, lass," Luella said, walking toward the temple, her hand leaving mine after another supportive squeeze.

The sunlight danced and sparkled off the domed glass roof. Stained glass windows crafted from frosty sea glass.

Text and prayers carved into the banisters. Freshly sanded steps. Colored glass doorknobs.

It was even more magnificent within. As soon as Luella stepped inside, she removed her hat, then guided me to the seats. The sun came through the ceiling, red, orange, and blue, reflecting off a glimmering pool of water at the front.

We climbed a few steps and took a seat closer to the back. The chatter from other people died down as the water rippled, the strawberry blonde hair of the matriarch breaching the surface. As she rose on two legs instead of a golden tail, two merrow joined behind her.

Udine pulled the orange fabric from around her neck and tied it at her waist, showing off a magnificent breastplate. Sea glass of a variety of colors hung from her shoulders, each piece frosted and tied together with golden wire.

The armor was clasped at her back, mesmerizing me as it dangled just above her abdomen where a belly button would be if she were warm-blooded.

She placed both of her hands together in prayer and extended both arms up. "While I worship Cliohde, you are welcome to pray as you see fit." She tilted her head toward the water. "We have a few new faces, so I will talk through the ceremony out loud. To begin the service, we offer thanks."

Udine spoke firmly, her voice washing over everyone in attendance.

"We are still here. I thank my goddess Cliohde for watching over us. Even in darkness, she gives us hope."

I followed Luella's example as she knelt in the aisle in front of the seat, her eyes closed and lips fluttering in silent prayer. I watched everyone as they worshipped; each of their chants was personal, not meant to be heard by prying ears.

Part of me felt I should pray too. But to who? I didn't know who was pulling the strings. I didn't know who or what was delaying my death. So, I decided not to join the prayer and just patiently be present in the moment.

"After thanks, we offer tribute. To those we lost and to those we found."

The merrow in attendance began to hum, the noise melding with my blood. It vibrated in my veins, soothing the pain in my heart with every beat. I closed my eyes, letting the familiar sound take me away to a simpler time, when a man with cloudy eyes gave me a toy carved from driftwood and made me laugh.

Conway would be so happy to see this.

"We accept tribute at the end by monetary means, food, and clothing, or even taking the time to pay respect to the dead. Whatever you can spare."

The humming got louder, the merrow in the stands adding to the harmony with various timbres.

"To finish, we offer prayer to those in need. To the sick, the injured, or the alone. To those still suffering under the Besieger. May he die bloody." Udine lifted her head, her orange eyes running across the crowd.

Varric Cross—the Usurper and the Besieger. No king of mine.

The crowd muttered their agreement, followed by silence. Everyone remained silent for several minutes, lost in their own prayers. When it was over, Luella got back to her seat, and several attendees greeted Udine and paid their tribute before leaving.

"What do you think? Was it similar to your rite?" I asked.

Her green eyes flashed over to me. "It was. The main difference is that I fast before the rite, and at the end, I feast with the other elves. A way to celebrate the return to land."

"Oh? Are you hungry now? We can get some food from the market," I offered.

Luella smiled but shook her head. "I only do the Rite of Land when I return home, so I wouldn't partake in fasting until the morning we return to Anchorage."

Another question swam in my head. "Do you worship Cliohde?"

"Zerenyth." She felt for the necklace under her collar. "God of Port and Sea. I hail from the Kingdom of Edessa. We'd pray for a good catch and for good weather." She shrugged. "Seems foolish to think he'd listen to me out here, but it reminds me of home."

"It's not foolish," I said, shaking my head intently.

Her gaze softened.

"Is that why you don't let Andra join you? Because you think it's foolish?" I asked.

Luella waved my statement off. "That's a little personal, Mae."

I gulped, cheeks feeling hot. "Oh. Sorry." *Boundaries, Mae. Boundaries.*

"Don't look at me like that. I'm not opposed to telling you one day, but right now, the mental load would be heavier than I want to carry." Luella glanced over at the podium and tilted her head, directing my attention to Udine.

"Thank you for remaining respectful for the ceremony, but it's customary not to loiter. And if you do, at least donate," Udine said. The corner of her mouth twitched, revealing pointed teeth. But something about her mouth was shaped similarly to Conway's. Even if they had different colors of hair and eyes, even skin, there was something familiar in her facial structure.

"Oh, I'm sorry," I replied, getting up from my seat. "I just wanted to speak to you."

Udine raised a skeptical brow before waving us forward to the side of the pool. I walked down the steps to the water.

"You're the girl who objected to your captain meeting with Bliss."

"That's me," I said, outstretching my hand now that I was closer. "I'm Mae."

The merrow behind Udine watched me carefully, as if expecting me to try something with the matriarch.

Did that happen often?

Is that why we had to turn over our weapons at the gate?

Luella's presence loomed behind me, granting me some comfort while I traversed this unfamiliar situation.

Udine glanced at my hand, then back up at my eyes. "What is it, then?"

I brushed some rogue hair back, feeling nervous under her crescent-pupiled gaze. "I was wondering if you happened to know a... erm... Conway?"

Udine straightened up, expression becoming suspicious instead of scrutinizing. "What of him?"

"He was from Fisherman's Gully—"

"Yes," she spat sharply. "He *was*. Like so many, there wasn't anything left of him to bury in the trenches." Pain flitted in her voice before it became hard again. "What's your point? Aside from prodding old wounds."

"You don't know?" I wondered. "You've never been to Shipwreck Bay?"

Udine waved her hand dismissively. "We protect our home. Bliss handles outside matters."

They really don't know. "He's alive," I said, twisting my fingers together.

"Wh... what?" The water swished as Udine stepped out of the pool and came right toward me. I didn't move as she closed in, barely a foot away as she searched my eyes. "Liars lose their tongue."

Luella cleared her throat, making both Udine and me glance back at her. "Dark hair, pale eyes, blind? He's also very good at growing fruit."

The matriarch blinked.

"He's married to the cook on my ship, *The Ollipheist*." Luella crossed her arms and watched the shock unfold on Udine's face.

"My brother… is alive?" Her throat bobbed a few times as if she was gulping down thick tears. "I thought he was dead."

"He thinks the same about the shoal," I said quietly.

Udine's orange eyes became glossy. "I must go." She turned to the other merrow, who seemed just as shocked as she was. "*We* must see him." She grasped my arms. "Thank you. Thank you."

"I have another question for you," I said.

"Anything you want to know," Udine answered.

"There was a girl… Muirgen…. Do you know what happened to her?"

She looked up as if recounting the memory. "How do you know that name?"

I didn't answer, and the matriarch looked at me closely, stroking my cheek tenderly now. I couldn't keep her gaze as I looked away.

"The Besieger struck her down, but then she rose up. He stole the Blessing from us when the shoal was in shambles." Udine sought out my eyes. "Did the Blessing come back to us?"

Hesitantly, I met her gaze. "Blessing?"

"Blessed to survive. You survived the sea, you survived death, and now you've survived the tyrant."

I didn't deny it. I couldn't anymore. "My name is Mae now—Maeve."

"Maeve," she hummed. "I remember hiding in the bushes, listening to them name you. I wasn't a warrior then. I couldn't save you, and for that, I'm sorry. If that name is what you chose, then I'm pleased to call you Maeve. If only we had a naming ceremony for you first."

The merrow warriors behind Udine watched me with their eyes wide.

"Mae or Muirgen, welcome back, sister."

"Thank you." My voice was barely audible, but I felt this

churning in my stomach. Now I knew my past, but I only had more questions. "Do you… know how I survived?"

Udine shook her head. "I don't. Just that you are neither human nor elf. I don't even believe you're fae. Everything beyond that is yours to find out."

I didn't know what I was, and maybe I never would. I had to be at peace with that.

Udine straightened up. "Now, come, Mae and Mae's friend—"

"Luella," the red-haired woman corrected. "You might know me as *Wraith o' the Sea*."

A grin broke across the matriarch's face. "Oh, indeed I do. Forgive me for not addressing you properly. It is a pleasure." Udine reached to where Luella stood next to me and shook her hand, but still not mine. "Shame Captain Bliss wasn't able to recruit you from that Captain Leviathan. You would've made quite the first mate."

Luella returned the grin, looking downright terrifying. "I'm nothing if not loyal. Even if Cap is a prick, he's our prick. Ain't that right, Mae?"

I choked down a laugh and shook my head. "Let's keep that between us until he solidifies that deal with Bliss."

Udine tilted her head to the side. "Deal?"

I nodded. "To join the council. We're on a mission to unite the colonies to strengthen us against Varric Cross."

"*May his death be bloody,*" Udine murmured to herself. She looked back at the two merrow behind her, and they all shared a knowing look. "Come with us. Let's talk to Captain Bliss together. Consider it a favor for delivering the news about my brother."

"Together?" I inquired.

Udine turned on her heel, beckoning us to follow. "Bliss respects our input, not only for the colony but the shoal. If for nothing else, I will see my brother, but if we're lucky, we'll have the opportunity to bleed the Besieger like the pig he is."

"Then lead the way," Luella encouraged, that grin becoming more and more smug by the moment.

22

RONIN MURDOCH

THANK the Gods Luella jumped in to look after Mae.

After promising that she wouldn't be alone, going to see Bliss felt bitter. Mae belonged at my side. Not only because she made me feel stronger with her presence, but because I valued her.

My beautiful, tenacious Mae.

Seeing her uncharacteristically wide-eyed and terrified, pupils contracted with the primal urge to fight, flee, or freeze, broke something inside me.

I knew she was having a panic attack. I'd had my share over the years, and more frequently the past few months. Always triggered by something that seemed mundane, but that was all it took.

She would've lost herself in the tar as I had.

It would've dragged her under, thrashed her until she lost sight of the light.

Every step of the way, she'd been there for me, for better or worse. It didn't matter if I didn't deserve it. She saw past that. I grasped her arm, and when she saw me, her eyes dilated and softened.

She came back to me.

It had taken me months to drag myself out of the dark, and it only took her minutes.

Gods, Mae was so much stronger than I was, and the fact that she was willing to share that strength with me was a testament to it. She didn't need to hoard power. Not like Varric Cross or the monsters in the monarchy.

A trap many men had fallen victim to until they became what they hated. One that I could've easily fallen into if I didn't have the people who loved me at my back.

After being led through the colony, it was hard to imagine how it looked after Cross destroyed it twenty years ago. The merrow were clearly doing very well for themselves. Lush fields of crops. Rich soil and plentiful fish in the small bay.

The houses and structures were built for the climate with wood and thick straw. Some of the larger buildings were reinforced with stone, similar to my cabana back at Anchorage Cove. They were built to withstand the test of time.

A feeling of unease licked at my spine.

If I wasn't able to get Bliss to join the alliance, then there was no telling how long it would be until Cross came back— or sent someone else to do his dirty work.

Considering what happened at Farlight Harbor, I doubt he'd leave the castle. Not until he got me out of the picture. He didn't know that I couldn't shift, and if I could keep it that way, then he'd stay in Farlight Castle until it was necessary for him to leave.

There was a cabin at the top of a hill overlooking the bay, a great vantage point for the captain to see into the distance. Near the cabin was what looked like a bell tower, modest in size, but it would be loud enough to reach the people living below.

Not only useful for warning others of an incoming attack but also if the ocean brought in unsavory weather.

When I reached the base, I was met by a few sailors. The

merrow passed me off and went to partake in their ceremony. I wasn't particularly religious, but I respected those who were and their beliefs.

There were several occasions on *The Ollipheist* when crew members would abstain from work in observance of a certain holiday or another.

Butcher would even make something special for them if requested.

It was never a problem as long as they had someone fill their boots, but if no one was around, either the mates or I would handle it. As the captain, I wasn't thrilled to take to the rigging or record the inventory, but I'd make an exception if I needed to.

I always did what needed to get done. Meeting with Bliss was no different.

My legs ached as I climbed the steep pathway up the hill, but I didn't let it show. They were slowly getting their strength back, but endurance was another issue altogether. There was no way I'd have been able to make this climb a month ago, but now, I could tolerate it.

A warm feeling swelled in my chest because this was proof that I was healing. Not as fast as I wanted, but *I was healing*.

We crested the top of the hill, and as we stepped up the stairs of the porch, both of the sailors moved to either side of the door.

One of the sailors opened the door outward, allowing me to walk into the darkened space. I nodded respectfully at them and strode inside. A few oil lamps lit spots where the natural sunlight wasn't enough.

I'd only met Bliss a handful of times, but I'd heard their reputation, and reputation was *everything* to a pirate. The more cutthroat, the better. And the more likely they were to be left the fuck alone.

Each time I'd met Bliss was under the glower of their

sailors and always surrounded by an entourage of equally intimidating mates. I supposed I was the same, my mates always close by.

Bliss and I never talked directly. No reason to. We stayed out of each other's way, and that was enough to remain amicable. But because of that, I had no idea what I was walking into.

Bliss had the reputation of stabbing first and asking questions later, but I knew firsthand how stories were exaggerated by crewmates to make their captain seem larger than life. In my case, most of the rumors were true, but I doubted Bliss was *actually* half ram, half demon—though stranger things had happened.

"Captain Leviathan," a smooth, deep voice greeted me through the top of a double-hung door split in the middle. "Come to the kitchen." The sound of running water soon followed.

I unlatched the bottom half of the door to walk into the well-ventilated kitchen. Large bay windows opened to the cliff face, adding the familiar scent of seawater to the rich smells of vegetables and meat.

Bliss stood in front of a sink, their curly hair cropped just short enough at the base of their neck to expose the nape. An apron was tied around their neck and waist, hanging off their stout physique. Bliss was noticeably shorter than I was, but the air of authority coming off them was enough to give me pause.

Bliss turned around, knife in hand. They dried the wet metal with their apron, and I instantly grew rigid.

Their golden eyes met mine, and Bliss threw their head back in rich laughter. "If I was going to stab you, Captain Leviathan, I wouldn't have washed my knife first."

"I suppose you would've wanted me to die from infection if the stab wound didn't do me in."

Bliss clicked their tongue. "Precisely. Now sit." They slid

their knife into the block, then grabbed a sizzling cast iron pan to lay it on a pot holder on the dining table, its wood sanded and stained to perfection.

Like with the rest of the colony, I noticed the fantastic craftsmanship.

"Aye," I answered, pulling a chair out and taking a seat at my place setting. I glanced around, half expecting to see guards or mates, but there didn't seem to be anyone else in the cabin.

Glossy wood caught my eye as I looked up at the top of the cabinets where several violins were on display, the wood freshly oiled and free of any rosin dust. More of them were mounted on the wall behind me. There had to be at least twelve pristine violins. I hadn't noticed them given my focus on Bliss.

My mouth grew dry, my fingers itching to press a violin under my chin, to draw the bow across the strings, to make it sing. I used to hate it when my fingers and hair were coated in rosin specks after playing a vigorous melody, but now I missed it.

"Do you collect?" I asked, gesturing to the instruments.

Bliss turned, glancing over their shoulder. A contented smile swept over their face, showcasing a great pride in their collection. "I play and collect where I can. Udine is quite a craftswoman. She carved my favorite."

"That's incredible," I said.

"Do you play?" Bliss wondered.

A moment passed, and then I replied, "I used to."

"Pity" was all Bliss said before getting back to what they were doing.

"Why did you want to speak to me alone?"

Bliss untied their apron and hung it neatly on a coatrack before joining me. Their curls bounced around, framing a round face. Their eyes were sharp, trained to cut through lies and intimidation. They weren't softened by the circular glasses perched on top of their curved nose either.

"People are more honest when they're alone," they replied.

Bliss rested their elbows on the table, watching me closely. They were waiting for me to serve myself from the fragrant meal, but I didn't trust Bliss. We sat for a few moments, and Bliss's eyes darted from the food back to me.

They released an amused huff. Bliss kept direct eye contact as they skewered a piece of meat with their fork and brought it to their lips. "At least I know you're not foolish enough to accept food before it's been sampled by the one preparing it. And if I wanted to kill you, it wouldn't be poison."

"I'd hope it'd be more creative," I replied, earning another short laugh. I served myself, then took a bite of lunch. "Thank you. It's lovely."

Bliss shrugged. "I enjoy feeding my people when I have the time. A way to show my appreciation."

"I'm pleased to see the merrow thriving here," I said. "I heard it was carnage."

With a deep intake of breath, they replied, "It was." After another pause, they added, "This gully was still occupied when I came across it. My ship was sunk by pirate hunters, and we washed ashore."

I hummed, listening intently to Bliss's story.

"Udine saved my life. In return, I got rid of the military problem." Bliss put down their fork and clasped their hands together. "We fought tooth and nail for what we have, so I want to know why in the Nine fucking Hells you think I'd risk that for an alliance."

I narrowed my eyes, now understanding Bliss's intention. This wasn't a friendly lunch. This was Bliss sizing me up. I straightened my shoulders, sitting tall in my seat. "It would be a bigger risk not to join us. Varric Cross is planning a full-scale invasion to force all the colonies to join his army."

"And why the fuck would he do that?"

"Because he needs numbers to attack Algar. That and to get the pirates out of the way," I answered.

Bliss glared at me, not hiding their suspicion. "How would *you* know that?"

"For one, I have his daughter under my charge. For two, my name is Ronin Murdoch, and I recently broke out of Farlight Prison. Varric told me his plan himself."

A mocking laugh spilled from their lips. "*Ronin?* Long-lost Prince Ronin? Well, fuck me sideways. *And* you happen to have the princess under your charge? *And* you broke out of prison? What? Are you going to tell me you're *actually* a leviathan too?"

My tongue pressed into my cheek. It *did* sound absolutely ludicrous. "Everything you stated is a fact."

Bliss rose up from their seat, slamming both palms onto the table. "You come into my home and mock me like a fool?" They grasped a knife from their belt and thrust it toward my throat. "Perhaps I should take you prisoner? Hm? I'd get my weight in gold out of you."

I bared my teeth, not moving an inch or I'd be risking the kiss of Bliss's blade. "Believe me or not, but when Varric comes sniffing at your door, you won't have anyone to save you."

One hand came for my place setting, and they swiped it off the table. It clattered loudly against the floor. "I don't need saving." The tip of the dagger brushed my chin, just barely grazing me. "I won't join your pathetic alliance. We don't need you. If Varric comes, I'll deal with him the same way I deal with his mercenaries."

"We already have Lucky Bartram at our back."

Bliss laughed again. "Ah yes, the *lecher*. That man broke

my heart two times over. I would never allow myself to serve his flag. He can burn in Varric's next raid."

I knew the rumors surrounding their relationship, but it would've been really helpful if Lucky had told me that. "See reason, Bliss."

Their eyelids lowered, and I could tell they wanted to slit my throat. "There was a lass on your ketch as you came inland. I saw you from up here. I bet she'd be real heart-broken if you bled out on my floor."

I ground my teeth together, cursing the guards who took my weapons. I also cursed the leviathan spirit that refused to come to the surface. Most of all, I cursed Cross for even putting me in this situation.

"I'm not a monster," Bliss sighed. Slowly, they lowered their dagger. "I want you to take your ketch and sail away. After everything my people have lost, I'm not risking their happiness and safety to go after Varric Cross."

I veered back, the chair scraping behind me as I stood. "After the regency gets rid of the rest of us, they will come for you, and then you'll be alone."

"Then I die among friends and not from seeking an unwinnable fight."

I stood tall, looking down at Bliss from the bridge of my nose. "It's only unwinnable if we don't stand together."

"Get out," Bliss hissed with finality.

Right then, the cabin door opened, the sound of boots hitting the wood and bare feet padding in the entryway following. We watched, the tension so thick I could cut it with the knife Bliss was threatening me with, as Matriarch Udine stepped through the half-hung door.

"I hope we're not interrupting," Udine said, and that was when I noticed Mae and Luella standing behind her. Mae caught my eye and offered me a soft smile that almost soothed away the ache of failure.

What are they doing here?

"Not at all. I was bidding our guests farewell. They can take their ridiculous proposition with them," Bliss answered without an ounce of friendliness in their voice.

"Oh, I disagree," Udine replied. "These lassies here have filled me in on the situation, and I think it's very worth our time to hear out the alliance."

Bliss recoiled, shock coloring their golden skin a shade of pink. "What are you talking about?"

Udine stood there, full of regality. "It has come to my attention that my brother lives, and he's in Shipwreck Bay."

"Conway?" I asked.

She gave me a broad grin. "The only one I have." She tapped her clawed fingers together. "Now, I will be going to Shipwreck Bay, and I would like you to come, Bliss. And while we're there, we might as well meet with the other monarchs."

Bliss's jaw ticked as they uttered, "You know what you're suggesting?"

"All I care about is the survival of our colony, and I think there is no such thing as too many friends. Why not make the most powerful friends this side of the Algarian Sea?" Udine drove a hard bargain. I wished I were as eloquent as she was.

I cleared my throat. "I don't need an answer now, but I do invite you to come to the council meeting with the other monarchs. Then you can decide if it's worth it."

A low growl bubbled up from Bliss's throat as they looked from Udine to me to Mae to Luella.

"You wouldn't deny Udine's chance to see her brother, would you?" Mae asked innocently.

"And who are you?" Bliss hissed.

Mae outstretched her hand. "Maeve Cross."

Udine smiled fondly, patting Mae on the shoulder. "Muirgen has returned home."

Mae makes friends wherever she goes, doesn't she? The corner of my mouth drew up as Bliss made an expression of utter disbelief.

"Then… you…?" They paused. "You're an actual *leviathan?*"

"I didn't lie to you, Bliss," I reaffirmed. "Come to Shipwreck Bay. Give it a chance. The only thing you have to lose is your time."

Bliss's back became ramrod straight. "Show me. Show me now. Your form."

I bit down the chill that swept my spine. "I—"

"No," Udine interrupted. "I will not have a leviathan damage our reefs. The form of a Royal Leviathan especially is too large for the bay."

"Then in a clearing. I need proof," Bliss insisted.

I shook my head. "Shifting on land is too draining. I *am* still recovering from breaking out of Farlight Prison."

I surprised myself when I admitted that out loud. Even more so that no one batted an eye and just accepted that fact. *I've never needed to pretend that I was okay.*

Mae sidestepped Udine to stand next to me, and her presence soothed me more than anything else. My *magnificent* girl. It felt so good to be standing next to her. Not hiding. Not pretending. I began to feel more like myself. Like he had never disappeared, just got lost for a little while.

Bliss narrowed their eyes, more suspicious than ever, but then they relented. "Fine. I will hear you out, but I will not promise anything."

"I respect that," I said.

"Good, and because I'm so *hospitable*, you may stay the night, but I want you gone by tomorrow afternoon." Bliss waved their hand and shooed us.

Udine nodded in confirmation of Bliss's dismissal before her eyes settled on Mae. "It was lovely to see you again."

Mae squeezed the matriarch's arm. "Thank you." Then Mae looked up at me and gave me the most disarming smile that my heart slammed against my ribs, nearly knocking the breath out of me.

Luella, Mae, and I left the cabin. When the door closed, I looked over at them and said, "You saved my hide. Again. How'd you pull that off?"

Luella answered, "With our sparkling personalities."

Mae laughed. A glorious sound. "How about we tell you over lunch?"

I agreed. After all, I hadn't eaten much of what Bliss made.

While it wasn't the victory I'd anticipated, it tasted just as sweet.

23

MAEVE CROSS

"A BOOKSHOP? WHERE?" Ronin asked when we passed Andra in the town center.

During lunch, Luella and I told Ronin all about what we'd learned from Udine. Then we spent the afternoon basking in the sunlight, enjoying the warmth of victory.

The sun was getting low, casting the entire horizon in a multihued warm light.

Fisherman's Gully didn't sit so heavily in my stomach anymore as little pieces of who I had been came back to me. The floodgates were open now, but every moment of pain was dulled by memories of happiness.

The excitement in Ronin's voice wasn't lost on me when Andra grinned and said, "Next to the temple on the other side of the fruit stand."

He bounced on his heels as this boyish charm overtook his face, a grin dimpling his cheeks.

"Leave some books for the rest of the colony, you bookworm!" Andra teased.

Bookworm? Ronin? Well, if I thought about it, his shelves at his cabana and in his cabin on *The Ollipheist* were full of books, or at least they had been before Nathaniel destroyed a significant part of Ronin's collection.

"I'm merely investing in their town," he returned. "Don't wait for me."

Luella rolled her eyes, stepping beside her wife. "We won't." She met Andra's eyes as a wolfish smile tugged on her lips. "We haven't had time alone in quite some time, have we, love?"

The next words she said weren't meant for my ears as Luella leaned in, walking her fingers up Andra's arm before a blush bloomed on Andra's ocher cheeks, deepening her warm undertone.

"We'll catch up with you two later," Andra said quickly, grasping Luella's hand.

Ronin shook his head. "Just keep it down. I'd like to be able to sleep tonight."

"It's not my fault that I have a talented tongue," Luella shot back, making Andra's cheeks darken even more as her eyelids drooped in half-lidded longing.

"Ugh. That's my sister," he retorted, lip curling with disgust.

"Gunny is in a tavern, and Seabird is off at the market. You make yourself scarce," Andra ordered.

Luella turned around, tossing her hair over one shoulder, her hand clasped tightly around Andra's.

Ronin sighed as the two women ran off toward our accommodation. To be fair, they lived with Wesley and Isa when we were at Anchorage Cove. The officers' quarters weren't built for privacy either.

Of course they'd take the first opportunity to be alone.

I glanced up at him as he rubbed the back of his neck. "Would you like to join me?"

"I didn't know you were such a voracious reader," I commented, shifting from foot to foot. My heart pitter-pattered in my chest as I was reminded that this was one of the few times I'd been alone with him on this trip.

Something occurred to me as I stood there. Now that the lies were behind us, I didn't think I knew much about Ronin.

Sure, I knew the big things. The secrets and the wounds.

But I didn't know what his favorite color was.

I didn't know his hobbies or his favorite thing to cook. I didn't know if he liked music or if he was partial to painting.

"There's not much else to do on the ship when it gets dark aside from reading or drinking," he commented almost sheepishly.

I took a tentative step closer to him as we walked side by side down the path. I stole little glances at him, enjoying the subtle curve of his mouth and his relaxed steps. "What do you like to read?"

That dimple punctured his cheek again.

I would do anything to keep it there.

"Adventure maybe. But I'm also really partial to horror."

"Horror, huh?"

"There's nothing quite like clutching the pages of a thrilling book in the middle of the night with a bottle of rum to keep me company," he answered fondly, his voice lighting up and eyes sparkling. "What about you? Any preferences?"

I shrugged. "To be honest, there wasn't anything to read at the castle aside from history books or these giant tomes about flora and fauna. My fa—Varric," I corrected myself. It was still difficult to look back to when Varric *was* my father and not refer to him as such. "Varric thought fiction was for the dull minded, so I never had the opportunity to lose myself in a good book." I paused, grinning. "At least not ones I didn't hide under my bed."

Fondness shone in his eyes as he cast me a sideways glance. "That's my girl."

My cheeks flushed, pride swelling in my chest. "He caught

me eventually, but it was nice while it lasted." I looked away, a piece of hair falling into my face.

My lips screwed downward as that piece of hair shrouded my vision.

My steps stalled as the oil lamps illuminating the bookstore came into sight.

Ronin stopped next to me, reaching a hesitant hand out to tuck that tendril of hair behind my ear. "Nonfiction has its place, but in my opinion, it's not superior to fiction. How about we get you a good book, hm? One you don't have to hide."

My cheeks heated as our eyes locked together. The flecks of blue glimmered in the deep, dark depths. I couldn't help my smile from tugging on either side of my mouth. "I'd like that."

His returning smile was blinding, both dimples proudly on display. "I'll get you something good, I promise."

"I thought you never promised anything," I teased.

"If there is one thing I can promise, it's a good book. I have exceptional taste." He winked, making me smile broader.

"You're awfully full of yourself."

"Part of my charm." He stroked my cheek with his thumb before he pulled away and got the door for me.

The bell above the wooden door dinged, and I was enveloped in the smell of parchment and ink. Dust lined the stacks, adding to the musty smell, but there was something comforting about it.

I noticed Ronin inhaling deeply when he stepped into the store, a smile playing on his lips like it was his favorite scent. There were a few people browsing the stacks and a merchant at the front desk chatting happily with one of the patrons.

Ronin stepped beside me, keeping his voice low but loud enough that I could hear him. "My mother used to take me and the twins into a bookstore every time we docked. She got us each one book. We couldn't keep much because it would take up space in our racks, but we could always make room for a book."

It sounded like a simpler time, reminding me of when Varric would encourage me to go to the castle library with him. But those memories were never warm. At the time, I was happy he wanted to spend time with me, but he always did something to tarnish those moments.

I tried not to frown as I thought about Varric calling me a foolish, dull-minded girl when he found my stash of stories under my bed. Tears would stream down my cheeks each time as he took all the items I liked and made me kneel in front of the fireplace to watch them burn. Books. My journals. Even my paints and my half-finished painting of the harbor.

It was devastating. I never painted again. Never read. Never wrote. But in that devastation, I grew resentful. That festering seed of spite blossomed.

What else could he take from me?

Varric seized many things over the years. Friends. Hobbies. Keepsakes. Anything to keep me where he wanted me, isolated and subservient. He never was a father, was he? He'd viewed me as property from the very beginning.

As I watched Ronin smile, I forgot about everything behind me and focused on the man in front of me. I wasn't locked away in my chambers. I was free. More so than I'd ever been before.

I was making new memories now, and those were brighter than the dark ones behind me.

I shook away the negative thoughts and approached a bookshelf where the covers looked like unique shades of leather. A few of them had distinct paper covers sewn into the leather. Some red, some blue, some patterned with foliage.

All of them were more interesting than the beige-bound books Varric had shoved into my hands.

"Knowledge is power, Maeve. Don't waste your time on hobbies that don't serve you."

Ronin stepped beside me, leaving barely a foot between us. I could feel his presence swallow me. He stroked the spines of several books with his broad-tipped finger, humming contently deep in his chest. "What type of book do you want to read?"

"How about one of your favorites? Surprise me."

He nudged me playfully with his elbow. "All right, sweetheart. I need a new copy of it anyway."

"What happened to the old copy?" I wondered.

For a split second, the smile fell off his face before he shook it off. "Pike happened to it." He shrugged, trying to hide how much it bothered him. "It was an old copy. A comfort read. It would've fallen apart at my fingertips any day."

I tilted my head to the side, watching him as his thick eyebrows furrowed, a tic in his jaw. After a moment, I said, "Then we just have to wear this one in as much as the old one, right?"

His eyes flickered over to me, and they softened, a genuine affection in them as they held mine. "Right. Shouldn't be too difficult with you sharing a copy."

I balked playfully. "Whatever do you mean?"

Ronin gestured at my shoes, my trousers, and my blouse. All were a little worn despite the fact that I hadn't gotten any of them too long ago. "You're rough on everything, sweetheart. I bet your ball gowns had frayed hems from you dragging your dresses through mud."

He wasn't wrong. I'd earned many scoldings from my handmaidens for roughing up my dresses before events. "I get your point," I said, blushing deeply. "But I'll be gentle with this."

I'll be gentle with you.

"I'm only teasing, baby," he murmured. "You're gentle when it matters."

The soft pink rising to his cheeks under his beard wasn't lost on me. The moment felt so incredibly tender that I reached over and stroked the back of his hand as he gently rifled through the books.

He didn't flinch or move away from me.

He embraced the moment as fully as I did.

And *Gods*, it made my heart positively soar.

For the next hour or so, we browsed the stacks. Occasionally, Ronin would comment about a book he liked or didn't like.

"Well-written action. The descriptions were so vivid. Perfect for escapism."

"The main character was a prick who never changed. But fuck, the dialogue was hilarious."

"My mother surprised me with a copy of this for my thirteenth birthday. It's still on *The Ollipheist*. I didn't have the heart to tell her that I hated it."

Eventually, we found the book he was looking for. His eyes lit up when he reached for it. The yellowing parchment looked like it had been loved by someone before they donated it. He leaned back, opening it to read the dedication.

The stamped ink was smudged in some places, but the imperfections were what made each copy unique. It wouldn't be the same as his copy, but this one would come with new memories. Maybe better ones.

"So, what is it about?" I asked.

The excitement in his voice was palpable and, frankly, *adorable*. "Well, it's a story about betrayal, revenge, and sex. The main character, Gerard, is perceived dead, and his best friend, Victor, makes himself at home with Gerard's fortune and his wife."

I wasn't sure what was more exciting, Ronin's enthusiasm or the plot. "I can't wait to read it."

"Does anything else catch your eye?" he asked as we headed toward the merchant.

Just you....

I gulped, my throat bobbing as I cast my gaze toward my boots. "No. Maybe we can get another book at Violetta's Haven. Or when we get back to Shipwreck Bay."

His shoulders drew up at the mention of Violetta, and he bypassed the mention of her completely. "I know a good shop at Shipwreck's port."

I'll let that go... for now.

According to Lucky, she dealt in blood. I didn't know what that meant, exactly, but if my blood was special, maybe she could uncover something else. As curious as I was, I didn't want to ruin our night out with talk of his ex-lover.

After a little chitchat with the shopkeeper, we were on our way. This time, I rushed ahead of Ronin, getting the door for him and sticking my tongue out at him when he rolled his eyes at me.

I wasn't ready to turn in for the night, and I also didn't want to interrupt Luella and Andra. They deserved some well-earned alone time. The longer we were out, the better.

Moonlight cast a silvery gleam on the pathway that was only shadowed by palm trees and tropical shrubs. The trail disappeared into the trees around the hill Bliss lived on. I'd explored Lucky's Outpost, and I hoped to explore this landscape a little before we left.

"Do you know why they call these island clusters the Gullies?" I asked as we lazily walked down the path.

Ronin paused, tucking the book into his jacket. He rubbed his jaw, and instead of telling me, he said, "How about I show you?"

I raised an eyebrow. "Have you been here before?"

"I have a great sense of direction," he stated as a nonanswer. "It'll be easier to show you."

He turned down off the main trail to a narrower, less beaten path. The idea of getting a little lost appealed to me. The tall palm trees obscured the path, sand melding with rich dirt. I stepped over foliage and tree roots that grew into the trail.

The only light was the moon, but it was enough for us.

He looked up at the stars every once in a while, using the brightest ones to make sure we were going the right way. I noticed how he moved less rigidly than he did at Shipwreck Bay. He was clearly making progress, but every few steps, he'd take in a ragged breath.

I hoped I wasn't pushing him too hard.

"We don't have to go any farther if you don't want to," I said.

He waved a hand over his head, dismissing my comment. "We won't have time for this tomorrow. I've only ever seen the Gullies on maps. I want to see it for myself."

"Really? You've never been to these islands?" I asked, stepping over another tree branch.

He paused, taking a few breaths. "I only ever targeted merchant ships in the main channels and then traded at Shipwreck Bay. They were never en route. *And* most of them are still military occupied."

"That's fair." I strode beside him, harmlessly letting my arm brush his. Unconsciously, he leaned into it. "Is it much farther?" I asked as I looked up at him, eyes becoming all the more half lidded the longer I gazed at him bathed in moonlight.

The light reflected off his eyes, reminding me of when we first met and I'd been enthralled by how unique his eyes were. I still was. The side of his mouth curled up, dimples denting either side of his face.

I'd become so fond of his dimpled smile that my knees

wobbled, and I had to fight the urge to get up onto my toes to kiss him. My heart squeezed as I realized how badly I missed this closeness. How easy it felt.

Everything I took for granted before.

This time I wasn't in the eye of the storm but relieved that I'd survived the aftermath. Calm, cloudless skies. No wind. We were gifted peace, and it would last longer than a moment.

His calloused fingers left pleasant scratches on my chin as he pinched it between his thumb and pointer finger. He wriggled my chin teasingly and said, "You're not getting tired already, are you? I'm supposed to be the recovering one. You're Miss Death-Can't-Keep-Me-Down."

My cheeks flushed, and I couldn't help returning the playful grin. "*Psh*, no. I just want to know how much longer I have to wait before kissing you."

The delightful mauve of his lips enticed me more than his smile. "Why wait?"

I wiggled my eyebrows and pulled away from his inviting grip. "I've had a lot of fun with you tonight, Ronin. I'd like to cap it off with a sightseeing kiss."

His hand fell to his side as his smile became softer, almost shy. "I've quite enjoyed myself tonight as well." He turned away from me and gestured for me to follow. "It's not far. Assuming the map in my head is correct."

"And how often is it correct?" I asked, trying not to get too distracted by his glorious back.

He shrugged. "Eh… about 60 percent of the time."

I bit back a laugh. "Better than 50 percent, I guess."

"Exactly."

The playful banter kept the energy between us alive. We'd shoot half-hearted insults at each other and receive them in kind.

The sound of rushing water joined the cacophony of insects and wildlife. It grew louder and louder as Ronin guided me along the trail, careful not to trip in the dark. And just as we walked over a hill, I could see the handrail of a wooden bridge atop a waterfall that spilled into a massive split in the ground where white water roared.

Ronin stepped over to the bridge and stared down at the waterfall, inhaling the scent of brackish water. I stepped beside him and felt him slowly wind his arm around my waist.

"The Gullies are called that because of how the water collected between the hills in the rainy season. Over time, it eroded a massive gully that overflows into the sea. Each of the gullies is unique to the island's landscape. This one is the biggest. In the dry season, they're shallow. Even bone dry. But now, when it's wettest, they're in their full glory."

I leaned into his chest, the smell of cedar and seawater making my heart pound harder. "It's beautiful."

"It is… but even this view pales next to you, Mae."

Heat flushed my cheeks, and my eyes darted up to him. *Did I hear him correctly?* The pink in his face deepened, the blush spreading to his ears. I watched his throat work as he swallowed, not looking away as he stroked my face with his thumb.

"I can't tell you how happy I am that you're here with me." His voice deepened as he murmured the words, as if making sure they were only for me to hear. Even though we were already alone, this was a moment *only* for us.

Warmth filled my chest. "I'm happy to be here." I got up on my toes, pressing my face into the crook of his neck. "*Gods*, I missed you." I didn't mean to say the second part out loud, but he knew what I meant.

"Me, too, sweetheart," he replied softly.

I drew back, staring up at him, searching his eyes to find them as full of affection as I felt for him. And finally, I ran my hand up the back of his neck and drew him into a soft, passionate kiss.

24

RONIN MURDOCH

THE NAPE of my neck tingled as Mae's slender fingers curled through my hair. Happiness swelled in my chest when she canted her head toward me, parting her lips to capture mine in an unbelievably tender kiss.

I missed her. How natural it felt with Mae. How easily she saw through me. How she always knew what to say. I'd never had anything like this before.

I pulled her in closer, cupping her silky jaw and feeling how perfectly her body molded into mine, always so soft and pliant in my hands.

But I liked her softness just as much as I liked her abrasiveness. Two sides of the coin that made her who she was, perfect with all her imperfections. Her hopeful heart melted away the wall of ice I'd thrown up around myself.

I could tell myself that I did it for protection, but all it did was make me cold. Unable to accept warmth from anyone else.

At that moment, holding Mae in my arms with nothing but the sound of a waterfall underneath us, I believed in a future.

And even if it all went to shit, I had to *believe* it was worth it.

Because these little moments meant something. All the pain and cold was worth it for a second of her warmth.

My arm curled tighter around her waist, earning a quiet, giggly squeak when I hauled her right up against me. Her tongue swiped at my bottom lip, and I let her take control of the kiss.

I gave her the control I was terrified of giving up.

But I wasn't afraid now… I was *safe*.

I kissed her like I'd never kissed her before. I savored the taste of her lips and the way she slid her hands down to tighten her fists around my collar, the excitement in how she twisted and writhed in my arms as if she wanted to climb under my skin.

She drank up the sensation of my touch like she was parched. Devoured my mouth like she was *starving*. Instead of a ball of anxiety tightening in my chest with every stroke of her fingertips, I was overcome with an overwhelming sense of relief.

I sighed blissfully, growing lightheaded because kissing her was more important than breathing.

Gods, she tasted like the sun cresting over the horizon on a freezing morning. The delightful moment when a cat curled up under the window just to sunbathe once the sun broke through the clouds. A promise that I'd survive this winter and I could do it again.

Springtime.

She was my springtime.

My heart raced so hard, I could hear it pounding in my ears. But despite how loudly it pulsed, I could still hear Mae moan against my lips, a sound that vibrated directly down to my cock. Her tongue slid across my lips, battling mine for domination.

She can have it. She can have anything she wants.

Mae threw her head back, gasping. I blinked slowly, not realizing I'd closed my eyes. I panted, a smile stretching across my face. Her pupils were blown to the Hells, nothing but a thin ring of honey brown around inky, dark desire.

Her lips were swollen, bitten and red. As much as I wanted to push that boundary and kiss her until neither of us could take it anymore, her foolish grin satisfied me more than enough.

"I love your smile," she said, mirroring my thoughts as her fingers loosened from my shirt to trace one of my dimples. "I'd make you smile all the time if I could."

My face got warmer, and I leaned close to rest my forehead against hers. I wasn't ready to untangle myself. Not when the moment felt so tooth-achingly sweet. Yet I still craved more sweetness. "I love you, sweetheart. The words don't feel like enough."

A little giggle slipped past her lips, making me smile so wide that my face hurt. "Say it again. Pretty please."

I leaned down and pressed a kiss on the tip of her nose. "I love you."

She giggled again, and the sound was music. A pure, untainted melody for my ears only. Mae stared up at me, her eyes full of unadulterated affection, and I imagined mine looked the same. "I happen to love you too. Very much so."

I captured her lips again, unable to help myself. She sighed against me, stroking one finger along my collarbone while the fingers of her other hand tangled in my hair. My own hands roamed the curve of her waist, the softness of her stomach, the delicious handfuls of her ass.

A filthy groan spilled from my throat when she arched into me, her stomach pressing hard against my cock that was now fucking *aching* like I'd been punishing it the most by keeping my distance from Mae.

My hands glided up her body, moving on their own to

her pretty tits. The silky swells of her breasts molded into my palms, her nipples hard and beaded against my thumbs.

I had half a mind to tear her fucking shirt open and take what I wanted, her thighs wrapped around my head while I drove my tongue into her until she screamed my name. I'd deny her each orgasm until she begged me to bend her over the railing, and then she'd fall apart around my cock.

I need to stop.

I couldn't be completely sure that we'd be having sex to enjoy ourselves, or if I'd be using her to distract myself again.

From what? I wasn't sure, but I wasn't going to fuck this up. Not again.

Mae cried out, throwing her head back and exposing the tempting column of her neck. Gods, what I wouldn't do just to leave bites up and down her peachy skin for the sole purpose of soothing the sting with kisses.

Her fingers were still tangled in my hair, and each time she pulled, a zap of pleasurable electricity shot right down my body. "Mae," I groaned when her leg pressed between mine, that fucking thigh rubbing me up and down.

Up and fucking down.

"Keep touching me. *Oh Gods, please,*" Mae panted, goose bumps rising along her arms as her nipples strained against the fabric of her shirt, enticing me to rub harder.

The sound of her begging will be the fucking death of me.

I devoured the image of her flushed cheeks and her lip sandwiched between her teeth. The soft cries as she searched for pleasure. And I wanted to give it to her. I *really* wanted to. But not now. Not when everything was still so delicate.

I clamped one of my hands on Mae's thigh, stopping her before that last sliver of control snapped and I did something I'd regret. "Sweetheart," I urged gently, sliding my other hand down to her waist before I was tempted to see if she could come from nipple stimulation alone.

Lust drunk, she blinked slowly, chest heaving with every labored breath. "Wh… what?"

"Not tonight."

I didn't miss the hurt flash across her eyes. She tore herself from me, looking away. The last thing I wanted to do was hurt her again. It felt like a wet blanket had been thrown over me.

Why does it feel like every answer is the wrong one? Have sex and regret taking her on a whim when I inevitably push her away, or deny sex and make her feel like I don't want her?

"Did I do something wrong?" she asked, her voice meek as if she was anticipating rejection.

No. I reached out and grasped her arm. "Look me in the eye, Mae."

Slowly, she turned back, looking up at me with vulnerability glimmering in her eyes.

"You're everything I want, baby," I told her intently. "But you know just as much as I do that having sex right now is a bad idea. It's not that I don't want to, because I do." I took a deep breath. "*Fuck*, I do. But look, we started our relationship with casual sex, and I fucked that up. Then we picked it back up, and I fucked it up again. This is the third time, and I don't think I'll be lucky enough for a fourth—"

A finger pressed against my lips, silencing the never-ending garble of words falling from them. "You babble when you feel vulnerable."

Embarrassment mottled my cheeks. My eyes widened as I realized that every time I felt like I had to explain myself to her, I couldn't shut myself up.

I rubbed the back of my neck, releasing her arm. "I'm not used to justifying my actions."

"What? The Big Bad Captain Leviathan has never had to answer to anyone?" Mae teased.

"No. Not really." *Except my mother, but I'm not vying for her approval like I am for Mae's.*

She tilted her head to the side, a smile playing on her lips. The hurt in her eyes melted away. "You're right. It's not a good idea. But you didn't have to wind me up like that either."

"I may have gotten a little carried away." I swallowed, unable to help myself from committing her flushed cheeks to memory. Those perky nipples asking for attention. "One thing would've led to another, and before we knew it, I would've had you bent over the railing, doing absolutely *filthy* things to you."

A full-body shudder ran rampant all over her body as she released a pent-up groan. She shifted from foot to foot, thighs pressed together. "Scoundrel."

She turned away from me to step toward the railing of the bridge and looked down into the rushing water. The mist spat up from the gully, offering a little cooling relief.

I laughed and followed her example, stepping behind her. She leaned her back against my chest as I wound my arms around her waist, resting my chin on the top of her head as we enjoyed the view.

"You better finish the job next time," Mae demanded. "I might die otherwise."

"I'll make you forget your own name."

She was drawn taut like a bowstring. A well-placed touch or a filthy word could make her snap. But I wouldn't give it to her. I liked teasing her. Torture for us both, but it would be worth it.

"Is that a promise?" she breathed.

"This time, it *is* a promise."

"You're making a lot of promises tonight."

"Tonight is worth the promises."

Mae sighed, leaning farther back into my chest as her shoulders relaxed. We stared out at the breathtaking view that was second only to my girl. The moon was high in the sky and the warm breeze on our faces. I felt elated, so fucking happy.

It was the perfect end to the day.

A mist swept over the bridge, puffing around my ankles like a winter fog. The scent of smoke rose around us. Not like a campfire but like a hearth. Hair pricked the back of my neck, and I got the distinct feeling that...

Someone is watching us.

I whipped my head around, drawing Mae behind me as the fog spilled over the bridge into the rushing water. My legs ached as my survival instincts kicked in. I became vastly aware that Mae and I were nowhere near the town, and our weapons had been taken at the blasted gate.

In an instant, the fog settled, revealing a masked figure standing at the edge of the bridge, clad in black and armed to the teeth. They were rather slender, built more for speed than strength.

Yellow eyes caught the light, narrowed at the pupils and so stark in color that they almost seemed to glow.

My heart dropped into my stomach as they drew a broadsword from their back and flicked it around in the moonlight. The black-and-blue crystal was different from Nathaniel's sword, but the material was the same.

Draconite.

Oh, fuck me.

MAEVE CROSS

I COULD FEEL the draconite before I saw it—the sickly feeling of stolen power. The nearly silent cries for freedom. The cries were louder than before, igniting a primordial power inside me. It moved through me—guiding me.

That power isn't yours.

It's *mine.*

Mine to protect.

Mine to wield.

Mine to *free.*

A seething anger welled in my belly. A white-hot froth boiled in my bones.

Who died for your weapon? How many souls are shackled within it for you to use?

Use....

People are not items to use.

My eyes darted around Ronin's shoulder. The rage within me grew when the twinkling of a broadsword in the light caught my eye, wielded by gloved hands. A figure stood there cloaked in black with a fabric mask pulled over its face.

My instincts pulled me to the side, and I wrapped myself around Ronin.

Get between them.

Get between them now.

"Mae," he warned, but I wasn't listening.

My body drew taut, adrenaline kicking my heart into a roaring beat. I didn't think, just acted. The broadsword whistled as it cut through the air. The figure oozed raw power, not just from the weapon they wielded but also by the way they swung it like it weighed nothing.

I'd never seen anyone use a broadsword. Not the guards at the castle or any of the pirates I'd met. This style of swordsmanship was something I was unprepared to deal with.

An ominous *woosh* of heavy metal was barely perceivable over the roaring water beneath us, but with every swing, I could *hear* the draconite. The souls within screaming and begging for liberation.

It made me angrier and angrier every time.

They are a thief.

A thick fog chilled the air as they vanished within it. It disoriented me as Ronin's hand closed over my arm. His touch broke the spiral of wrath before I could succumb to it. When I looked up at him, the boiling anger grew cold.

I was *afraid.*

We raced across the bridge to the other side, but Ronin could barely keep up with me.

"Run. You need to run," he panted as the fog grew closer.

You need to run. Not *we.*

You.

Ronin wasn't in any shape for a chase through the trees. He knew that, and so did I. A flare of indignance fired through my belly. If he thought I was going to leave him here to get assassinated, then he didn't know the first thing about me.

Before I could reply, the fog got thicker, and I could hear the draconite screaming. I grabbed Ronin's arm and jerked him to the side just as a broadsword clipped the air where he had been standing.

Ronin crumpled to the ground, grunting like his legs were giving out on him. I didn't want him to overexert himself, but it wasn't like we had much of a choice.

"Mae," he gasped, fear coloring his tone as I dodged another swipe. I could barely see the assailant through the fog, but I could hear the leviathans within the sword, giving me an edge I wouldn't have had otherwise.

"*It's not yours!*" I shouted, kicking one foot out blindly into the fog. Satisfaction curled in my belly as the fog fizzled out, and my boot collided with their leg. Goose bumps prickled down my arms as if a winter chill had devoured the summer air around me.

The yellow eyes under the mask looked past me at Ronin, and a protective energy swam over me. No way in the Nine Hells was I going to let this assassin get any closer to him.

He's mine to protect.

Mine.

The broadsword came toward me again, but this time a familiar hand grabbed me, tossing me behind them. As I collided with the wooden slats of the bridge, splinters cutting into my palms, I couldn't find it in me to be angry or even feel the pain.

I was *terrified.*

My heart squeezed, a tremor of dread raising the hair on the back of my neck. It froze me. I became afraid of looking up and seeing the man I loved spread out into a puddle of viscera on the ground because he foolishly pulled me behind him when I would've survived.

I knew how easily that sword could've cut into him. He wouldn't have had time to shout. The only noise I'd hear would be a thud when he hit the ground.

Not him. Gods, not him. Take me.

Hot tears streamed down my face as my heart raced viciously in my chest.

Fight the fear.

I will not be afraid!

A pained shout drew my head up, and I refused to let that fear paralyze me. Ronin barely dodged the next attack, grasping his arm as crimson dripped along the wooden boards.

The assassin was poised to strike again, not looking at me, only their target.

I moved faster than I thought possible, throwing myself between the two of them. My hands flew up in a weak attempt to stop the heavy blade.

"*Sentry.*"

The blade sliced into my hands, but before it could cleave fingers or bury itself into my chest, the draconite *shattered.*

From the tip to the hilt, something from the sword fused to me, crying out in salvation as the energy rippled, crunching the crystal into powder. Glowing blue light exploded from the sword, the force of it erupting to thrust the assassin down into the rushing white water.

Immense power flew *through me* just as it had in Varric's chamber. But this time it was so fast that my vision spotted. My mouth became dry, my palms aching as the glowing spirit wrapped around me before flitting toward the ocean… to go home.

The trenches. The final resting place for merrow, sirens, and leviathan alike.

I crumpled to the ground, completely overwhelmed.

Ronin fell to his knees next to me, the book we had gotten earlier falling out of his jacket and onto the planks. He gasped as he clutched at his chest. Through his shirt, the outline of his tattoo glowed just for a moment before disappearing again.

"Your tattoo," I murmured.

"I feel it…." He tilted his head back, looking up at the sky to relish the feeling. He closed his eyes, overcome with emotion. *"It's still there."* He shook his head, reaching for my hands.

I didn't even notice the blood on them. The slashes weren't incredibly deep, but my hands were numb, so that wasn't good.

"Are you all right?" he asked, looking intensely at my hands and rubbing my wrists like that would take the injuries away.

The adrenaline left my system, making my shoulders slouch as exhaustion took over. If I felt this worn out, I could only imagine how he felt. "I'm tired."

He brushed rogue tendrils of hair from my face, touching my skin as if making sure I was still there. "Me too. But we can't rest yet. Come on. Get up."

He grabbed the book before he pushed himself to his feet, groaning and grasping at his arm. "Fuck, that hurts." He tucked the book away and rolled his shoulder, reaching out with his undamaged arm to pull me up.

"Are *you* all right?" I asked, taking his hand to stand on wobbly legs.

"I'll be much better when we get back to town. There's no telling if there are more out there."

He stepped over to the railing. I followed him, but there was no sign of the assassin aside from a sword hilt resting on one of the rocks.

The mist at the base of the waterfall looked thicker than usual, and an awful sensation churned in my stomach. Bile rose to my throat at the thought that I'd… *murdered* someone. "Do you think I killed them?"

"Maybe. Wouldn't that be a good thing?" He wasn't looking at me, only gazing over the edge into the water.

A soft noise bubbled up from my throat, my hands

shaking violently. My cheeks were suddenly wet. "I... I've never killed anyone before."

It felt foolish. The assassin had been sent after us, so why did the prospect of killing them feel so awful?

I looked down at my feet, my hands. *Did Ronin ever think that my soft hands could be the hands of a killer?* The blood was mine, but it didn't feel like mine.

"Oh, sweetheart," Ronin murmured, his comforting body closing around me like a warm blanket.

I accepted the embrace, the tears rolling down my cheeks more freely.

"Does it get easier?" I asked, voice warbling.

I felt him shake his head. "No. And it shouldn't." He pulled away, looking deeply into my eyes. "But you did what you had to. You saved my life... again... for the hundredth fucking time."

I smiled weakly, but everything was heavy.

"Come on. We need to go." He sighed and hesitantly added, "You're going to have to help me. My legs feel like lead."

I blinked away my tears, taking his good arm to drape it over my shoulders. "Look at you. Asking for help."

Ronin grunted in mock annoyance as he walked in step with me. "Don't get used to it."

We were on edge the entire walk back, eyes darting toward each crunching leaf or shaking shrub. But we encountered nothing else aside from rabbits and massive grasshoppers. Before we even made it back to town, Luella and Andra were rushing onto the trail with oil lanterns in hand.

"I thought you two needed some alone time," Ronin commented, grunting in pain.

Luella scoffed. "We saw this blue light and—" Her eyes dropped to the bloodstains on our clothes. "What the fuck happened?"

"Assassin in the woods," he answered. "I wouldn't say no to a little help. Mae's been pulling my heavy ass along for almost a mile."

Instantly, they got to either side of him, giving me a moment to catch my breath as we continued toward the town.

26

MAEVE CROSS

With Luella and Andra's help, we hauled Ronin to the cabin we were staying in for the night. A few of the locals stopped to look at us, at which Luella demanded an audience with Bliss or Udine immediately.

I opened the door to the cabin, a humble house with six bunks nailed to the walls and a bench table for meals. It reminded me a little of the officers' quarters, especially with the big bay window next to the table.

Ronin grunted a few curses as Luella and Andra helped him to one of the bunks. He fell back onto the pillow, huffing and puffing with exhaustion. I was tired, too, but I knew he had it worse.

"I'm going to go get Mama, all right?" Andra said, backing away with blood staining her jacket.

Ronin's arm still bled steadily from a sizable gash adorning his bicep. I could breathe a sigh of relief because it wasn't bleeding heavily enough for the blade to have nicked anything vital.

"Thanks," Ronin muttered, sweat beading profusely along his forehead.

"You." Luella pointed at me. "Let me look at those hands."

I hesitantly looked down, realizing now how much blood coated them. They felt crusty and gummy, but they didn't hurt or feel numb. But under the light of oil lamps in the cabin, my hands looked considerably worse than they did in the dark.

"I'm fine," I said, clutching them into fists. No pain. No fresh blood. My hands had healed, while Ronin still bled. My heart squeezed in my chest as the awful reality of his near death permeated my mind.

"Listen to her, Mae," Ronin ordered.

My eyes darted over to him. His gaze met mine, and I debated whether or not to listen. A flicker of anger welled in my belly, getting larger by the second.

My anger was unreasonable. I knew that. But I didn't know how else to interpret the feeling of being so *infuriated* that Ronin had put himself in danger when we both knew I could handle it.

Does he not think I can handle it? Does he view me as this delicate little thing who can't hold my own in a fight?

I sucked my teeth, trying to push it down but failing.

"That's a fucking order," he grumbled, pissing me off even more.

Stop telling me what to do.

"You heard Cap. Get your ass over here," Luella tacked on, sitting on the bench with a bowl of water at the ready. She took her hat off, intensifying her gaze, concern pulling at the corners of her mouth.

I hesitated but ultimately sighed, relenting. I stepped toward her and held out my palms.

"Gods, that's a nasty gash," Luella commented, examining one of them. "It'll leave a fantastic scar." She took a rag and dipped it in water before placing it to where the blood was the thickest.

"I doubt it," I murmured as she wiped the blood away, revealing a narrow pink line where my hand had been cut open an hour ago.

"Whose blood is this, Mae?" Luella demanded, eyes shooting to mine. She dunked the cloth again and rubbed it over the other hand, uncovering the same little pink line.

"Mine."

"Bullshit. You don't heal *that fast*, do you?"

I shrugged. "I guess I do."

"Come here," Ronin ordered.

"I'm fine," I said, stepping over to him to hold my hands out. "See? Fine."

He took my hands in his and brushed the healed injuries affectionately with his thumbs. But even with the tenderness of the gesture, anger roared within me.

Luella's eyes were on my back. I tried to shove those emotions down.

I tried so hard, but I couldn't. The anger within me grew to the point that I ground my teeth together, my shoulders quaking.

"Well, all right, then," she said. "We just have to wait for Seabird to look at you, mate."

With a subtle look over my shoulder and a thin voice, I asked Luella, "Could you give us a few minutes?"

She cocked a brow but didn't object. "Aye. I'll be outside."

I waited until the door closed to say, "You didn't have to protect me." I didn't even bother to hide the bite in my tone.

He dragged his eyes away from my hands and looked up at me, but he didn't look remotely sorry for putting himself in that position. "Yes, I did," he replied, letting my hands fall to my sides.

"I can't die, Ronin. You *know* that."

"I don't give a fuck that you can't die. I'd take a stab wound before I let anyone harm a hair on your head." His eyes never left mine as he said every word with pure conviction.

Gods, he's infuriating. "I don't want you getting hurt, you fool!"

"Then it shouldn't be a big fucking surprise that I *don't* want you to get between me and a giant *fucking* broadsword." He threw his legs over the side of the cot and got up to stare down at me. "I *never* want you to put yourself in that position."

"I get back up, Ronin! I heal! *I can take it!*" I threw my hands up to prove my point. "Why do you treat me like I can't handle it? I can!"

His eyes softened, and he exhaled heavily while anger blazed in my eyes. Heat bloomed in my cheeks as fire spilled over in my chest.

I'm not weak! I'm not afraid! I don't need you to take care of me!

"You shouldn't have to."

Heat simmered in my belly as if a pot of water had been thrown over my fire. It smoldered and glowed as the embers cooled. Smoke smothered the blaze, as if all the oxygen feeding it had been exhausted.

The argument died in my throat. My shoulders slackened, and all my strength left me. I didn't have the energy to be angry anymore.

A moment of silence passed, and then he reached down to take my hand, drawing it up to press a tender kiss against my palm. "In Farlight, I watched Varric slice your throat open. I watched you convulse as the light left your eyes." He paused, bringing my hand to his chest to cradle it. "You felt every moment of it, didn't you?"

I did. The ghost of a steel scalpel kissed my throat, and I had to look away. "It certainly didn't feel good."

"Look at me, sweetheart. *Tell me,*" he urged.

I obeyed, feeling vulnerable and tender. Tears welled in the corners of my eyes as I gazed up at him. Those dark eyes searched mine, aching for the connection I'd also been waiting for. "I did," I uttered, barely audible.

"I would die a thousand times to save you *one* death."

My heart stuttered in my chest. "That's foolish. I... I get back up." I could barely get the words out, not when he was looking at me like that.

"*We don't know that.* We don't know if the next death will be the final one. We don't know if there's a limit, and I sure as fuck don't want to test that. I will not take that risk. Do you understand me?"

My throat felt thick, and I couldn't keep his gaze. "I do, but I don't agree."

"I don't like to repeat myself."

There was so much we each wanted to say. So much floating in the air between us, but all of those unspoken words were cut off when we heard a knock at the door. We stared at each other for another moment or two, and all I wanted to do was call him a brute, throttle him, and kiss his foolish mouth for making me feel...

Angry and loved.

Special.

And I hated the fact that I understood exactly how he felt because he was just as special to me.

Love made us into fools, but I wouldn't trade it for anything.

"Come in," Ronin called out, sitting back down on the cot. He stared me down, silently telling me to *sit the fuck down* before he made me.

I rolled my eyes and sat on the bench table as the door opened, and Enya quickly entered with Udine and Bliss behind her. Several sailors and a few merrow warriors lingered by the door, sharing a few quiet words with Luella.

"Where was the attack?" Bliss asked sharply, their golden eyes darting to Ronin's wound to investigate the severity of it.

"On the gully bridge," he reported. "The assassin had a draconite broadsword. They were one of Cross's."

Bliss nodded, their eyes shooting over to Udine, who glanced between me and Ronin before saying, "I'll sweep the area with my warriors. Did you see where they went?"

"I knocked them off the bridge," I answered, rubbing my hands together, feeling sour. I didn't know if the fall killed the assassin, but I also didn't like the idea that it was *me* who sent them to their doom.

Udine dipped her head and turned around completely to face her warriors. "Patrol the waters and the wooded areas. In pairs."

The warriors obeyed and left immediately.

Enya put a bag down on the table next to me. I recognized it as her suture case from the ship. She unzipped the top, revealing needles and fiber for stitching, bandages, and high-percentage alcohol for sterilization.

The concern was obvious in her voice as she asked, "How bad is it?"

"Missed anything important, but still hurts like a mother-fucker," Ronin answered.

Enya looked at her son, alcohol and cloth poised in her hands, but before she acted, she asked, "Is it all right if I treat you? If you don't want me to touch you, I can sterilize the needle and thread for you."

Ronin's eyebrows shot up to his hairline, pleasant surprise puncturing a dimple on the side of his face. "Thanks, Mama. I appreciate the ask. It's all right. Go ahead."

His mother tilted her head to the side and returned the soft smile, and when she leaned in to clean up the wound, he didn't flinch. Warmth filled my chest as I glanced at Enya. I was proud of her.

He winced as the alcohol stung his arm, revealing the gash before it bled again, mucking up visibility.

"Do you need some help?" I asked.

"If you don't mind," Enya replied, handing me the cloth.

I paused, waiting for him to give me the go-ahead. I didn't want my touch to be too much.

Silently, Ronin nodded, moving his arm so I could wipe the blood away with every stitch his mother made.

"There shouldn't have been anyone on the island," Bliss said. "You were under my protection. This shouldn't have happened."

Ronin shrugged his good shoulder as his mother and I continued to treat his wound. "Cross has wanted a piece of me since I was born. Though I'm surprised he opted for assassination rather than capture."

That was true. It was odd that Varric would rather kill Ronin than harvest the draconite.

Great, another variable. We didn't know what Varric was planning. We didn't know where Nathaniel was. And *now* we didn't know if an assassin had been following us and giving Varric all our secrets.

I didn't think it was anyone I'd met yet. I'd recognize that build and their other traits. Tall and slender with piercing yellow eyes. Not to mention, I'd definitely recognize anyone who wielded a broadsword. That was unusual in Farlight.

Even when I'd get a drink with Siggi, he'd comment that he wished sailors used gambesons here so he could make them for some variety in his designs, but those were only worn in cold climates like Skadi's, where they frequently used heavy armor and broadswords. But they were too bulky to be applied practically on a ship. Even castle guards preferred infantry swords.

There was no real use for broadswords in the Isles except as collector's items.

Bliss sighed. "I will leave you to it, but I expect to have a word with you before you depart tomorrow."

"Aye, aye," Ronin concurred as both Udine and Bliss turned and left.

27

RONIN MURDOCH

My arm ached all night. While I appreciated both Mae and my mother helping me with my wound, I was too touched out to invite Mae to my bunk for the chance to hold her before we disembarked.

Next stop: my former… lover?

That wasn't the right word for Violetta. Hells, no word was right for Violetta. The woman used me, drugged me, and then hung me out to dry at a local inn where I was expected to foot the bill for our tryst.

But I *couldn't* pay the fucking innkeeper. She made off with my coin and my weapons. The clothes off my back. Even my fucking boots.

Violetta left a note thanking me for the coin and the sex and broke off our fling. Not that it was ever serious, but that was a truly awful way to end it. I had to get Wesley and Isa to bail me out and bring me a pair of trousers. He never let me live that one down. Luella either.

And now Mae…

My Mae…

Was about to meet the woman who'd *fucked me over.*

I didn't know how to prepare her for that encounter. Or

the fact that Violetta and I weren't just a fling. We'd been seeing each other off and on for years. She never knew my name, and I didn't know hers either, but it sure as fuck wasn't *Violetta.*

We never talked like Mae and I did. I hadn't wanted a future with Violetta, and she didn't want one with me either. There couldn't be lost love between us if there wasn't any to begin with.

But Mae didn't know that. And I was so fucking worried this fragile, delicate, *perfect* relationship between us would suffer because Violetta liked to fuck around. She was the type of woman to mess with someone's head just for shits and giggles.

Violetta *lived* for the mind games. Her and her partner in crime, Pinky. It didn't help that she was blood-cursed and always seeking new ways to profit from it. I never let her feed off me, much to her disappointment. If she had, then she'd *know* who I was.

I'd seen her use blood memories to blackmail sailors.

I hated the prospect of navigating that with Mae.

Then something occurred to me.

If Violetta drank from Mae, would she be able to find the answers we were looking for? Maybe. But I'd need to ask Mae first.

With my good arm folded under my head, I lay in my cot. Mae was off eating breakfast with Gunny. My mother was getting the ketch ready with Andra and Luella, and I was able to snatch a few extra minutes of sleep.

Honestly, I needed it. And with the extra rest, the leviathan spirit coiled under my skin like a preening feline. Kneading paws against my chest, rolled belly up to bask under the sun. It felt like when Lazlo would weave between my legs and purr after he knocked a trinket off my desk.

Like it was asking forgiveness after misbehaving.

After being gone for so long, it felt like an intrusion. The spirit crawled up from the depths of my being, as if it had scratched its way up from a grave. The neat and packed dirt was now disturbed, the headstone in disarray.

Last night was incredible, even with the assassin. I watched Mae shatter draconite, releasing the spirits within. Blue streaks of light exploded, shooting across the sky like stars to return to the water.

When we died, we returned home, to the trenches, to Cliohde's embrace. The final resting place for merrow and leviathans alike.

My own spirit reacted, and I felt a wave of relief and... shame.

I never wanted to be a leviathan.

Without it, I could entertain the idea of just being a man. Not hunted for the magic behind my eyes. Not in hiding. I could just... *be.*

How selfish was that?

I couldn't turn my back on my father, my brothers, and everyone who came before.

But I wanted to. That stone of shame in my chest grew when I realized the disappointment that swam in my head that my leviathan was still there.

And the weight that came with it.

So much *fucking weight.*

I didn't ask for this. I didn't want this.

Too fucking bad.

Before I could let those thoughts take me on an exhausting journey of guilt, there was a knock at the door. Bliss had guards posted outside the cabin all night just in case more assassins roamed the woods, but there was no sign of any others.

No sign of the one who'd been knocked into the gully either.

"Come in," I answered and then grunted as I sat up, my muscles whining from overexertion.

"Greetings, Captain," Bliss said as they strode into the

main area of the cabin to set a large canvas bag on the counter.

"Good morning, Captain Bliss. What can I do for you?" I asked.

"You? Nothing," they answered. "I merely wanted a private word before you embarked."

Their demeanor was different from yesterday. Bliss was no longer sizing me up and threatening me. They no longer saw me as someone waiting for the opportunity to strike.

"You said you used to play, yes?"

I furrowed my brows. "The violin? Aye."

"Have you always been partial to stringed instruments?" Bliss continued, no trace of a smile on their face. They oozed pure intensity, but I actually liked that about them. No bullshit. If Luella had taken Bliss up on their offer to join their crew, I think they would've gotten along well.

"I suppose," I answered. "I'm quite fond of piano, but the violin is more portable."

Quietly, Bliss released a chuckle. "Sorry to disappoint, but I couldn't fit a piano in this bag."

I blinked. "What?"

They reached for the beige canvas and unzipped it, opening the mouth wide to pull a small, elegant violin from it. I noticed wrapping and padding inside the bag, as well as a bow delicately nestled among the lining.

They didn't say anything, just held the instrument out.

I couldn't control my reaction. My fingers ached. My heart pitter-pattered at the thought of releasing the tension inside me with music. Every note would banish a new stroke of pain.

Sweet, sweet relief in the form of a melody.

"What is this?" I asked, my throat feeling thick.

"It's customary in merrow culture to offer a gift as an apology. Forgiveness is given when it's accepted," Bliss explained. They handled the curves of the instrument with affection, stroking its glorious amber varnish with an intricate scroll carved into it. The strings were made from wound sheep gut, a much warmer sound than unwound strings.

I knew it cost a fucking fortune. Even with all the coin I made in my career, I couldn't justify buying an instrument that was so lovely. "You have nothing to apologize for."

"I disagree," Bliss stated. "I should've swept the island. I should've made sure it was safe for you and your crew. The sheer fact that it wasn't and you could've lost your life is worth an apology."

I shook my head. "I accept your apology, but I can't accept this—"

"Take the fucking violin."

The abruptness of the statement took me off guard.

"I don't want to owe you a favor. Take the fucking violin so I can get on with my life."

I put both my hands up. "All right. All right." I accepted the instrument, feeling the weight of it in my hands. A mixture of awe and disbelief came over me. "Thank you."

"Thank me by bleeding Varric Cross like a stuck pig," Bliss retorted. "I hope you can pull this off."

You and me both. "With your help, we can."

They nodded. "I suppose your chances of success go up significantly with me and my people involved. Safe travels."

Bliss turned their entire body toward the door, leaving me and my new violin alone. I marveled at the craftsmanship. I knew I'd be able to draw out a beautiful melody the next chance I got, and it reinvigorated this sense of excitement that I'd forgotten.

But not now. The ketch would be ready any moment. I rose up from my seat to tuck the violin safely back in the bag and zip it closed.

A smile tugged at the corners of my mouth, and I *couldn't wait* to revisit my music. Now I had both a book and a violin to fill my nights with comfort.

But something was still missing.

I didn't want to spend those nights alone.

For the first time in my life, I wanted to *share* it. I wanted Mae to rest her head in my lap when I read my favorite excerpts of my books to her. I could imagine her smiling at me with those wide doe eyes as I played her a tune.

Those moments would be *everything*.

The tight band in my chest that liked to squeeze and contract with guilt loosened as if it had been softened by thoughts of Mae. The wounds deep and violent, long and wide, never healing, always festering within me, felt like they'd been glossed over with a soothing balm.

I am going to be okay.

For now, I could push away those thoughts of shame and let myself enjoy the happiness.

WHEN I MADE it back to the ketch, Gunny and Mae had yet to return. Luella and Andra were restocking the shelves on the lower deck.

And I was alone on the main deck with my mother.

She stood beside the helm, dragging her finger along the woodgrain as if debating whether or not she needed to sand it down. She scratched at a splinter and frowned. When she was captain, she ran a tight ship. All sailors were expected to dust their racks. No splinter or stain in sight.

As tough as I was on my crew, I ran the ship for efficiency. We were always doing one thing or another under Mama, and it never left a lot of time for the in-between. She thought that if we could sit, we could clean.

For me, the in-between was just as important as the hunt for merchant ships. I ensured that we always had time for the bonding moments at the end of the day. I valued the relationship between the crew.

"The blood of the covenant runs thicker than the water from the womb." A piece of advice I lived by. Having a tight-knit crew meant that they protected one anotherwhen I couldn't. There were times during my youth when a handful of scorned crew members mutinied against my mother for one reason or another.

Mutinies meant a painful death. I'd be damned if it was my mother and not the mutineer. At the age of thirteen, I wet my cutlass with blood for the first time. I wasn't the same after that.

I did what I had to do. *Always.*

But as tough as my childhood was, I wouldn't be the man I was without it.

I knew my mother pushed because she loved me.

I knew she pried and walked over boundaries because she wanted to protect me. She couldn't protect my brothers, and she was too late to save my father, so she held on too tight.

I was all she had left of our family, but I'd spent too much time trying to be the man he was and not the man *I* was.

It was time to get this off my chest. She had to know I couldn't shift. She would understand more than anyone what that *meant.*

"Mama," I said, getting her attention as she looked up from the helm at me.

She raised both blonde eyebrows.

"Can we talk?" I asked, gesturing to my cabin.

Her eyes lit up. "Of course we can."

This awkward silence settled over us as we walked into the cabin. I set the bag Bliss had given me on my desk, still excited to play it later. Silence filled the air, almost louder than the sound of the ketch rocking against the pier.

"What's in the bag?" Mama asked, thankfully severing the silence.

"A gift from Bliss," I replied, the corner of my lip curling up when I added, "It's one of their violins."

Mama looked away, her eyes lingering on the bag. "Oh, that's nice. I've missed listening to you play." She rubbed her hands together. "Your father used to play, too, you know. At dinner, your brothers would serenade me, and you'd jam your fingers on the keys of a piano. The sentries had to plug their ears."

A fond smile curved her lips before it was washed away by a wave of sadness.

"Well, I hope I'm a better musician now than I was then," I said, hoping to lift the mood a little bit.

She laughed softly. "You are. It's nice to see you getting back to your hobbies." After a clearing of her throat, she asked, "What did you want to talk about?"

Just tell her. But the words got stuck in my throat. I truly didn't know how she'd react. But I knew that I'd have both Andra and Mae at my back if she took the news poorly.

"I can't shift, Mama." I couldn't look at her. "I haven't been able to after Farlight Prison."

She didn't respond for a long time while I let the shame wash over me again. Her silence made my mind race. What was she thinking? How could I tell her that I wasn't turning my back on our family?

"Hey, look at me," she ordered.

I couldn't.

"Don't make me repeat myself."

Slowly, I tore my eyes away from the dust in the corners of the room. The swirl of woodgrain in the walls. My clothesline with a fresh shirt still hanging on it. My chest squeezed as my heart pounded. At that moment, I didn't feel like a captain. I felt like a child again, about to be reprimanded by their mother.

After all, parents were gods in the eyes of a child.

Maybe that was why I was so afraid to tell her. *I do want my mother's approval. I want to be as great as my father or grandparents. I want to be the man she sees me as.*

"It's okay, Ronin."

Time stood still. "What?"

"I understand why you kept this from me," she said, lowering herself to sit at my desk. "It's a heavy thing to deal with."

Maybe she didn't understand what I'd told her. "Mama, *I can't shift*. These monarchs are expecting to follow a Royal Leviathan. They're expecting to follow a *king*."

"And you are."

My eyebrows came together. "Do you not understand me? I can't be a king like my father or grandfather. I'm not like the rest of the line of Royal Leviathans. I never *wanted* this."

"Thank the Gods for that."

I stood there, completely baffled. "I don't understand."

She leaned forward, propping her elbows up on my desk. Her eyes bored into mine. "Do you think the dragon makes the king, Ronin?"

I remained silent.

"I didn't raise you to be a leviathan. I raised you to be a good man. That is *enough*. That is what everyone needs." She tapped her chin. "The Royal Leviathans weren't perfect. Your grandfather was a real prick with how he treated the hungry. The class system failed many, many people. Raiden worked to fix that, but when you're born into a system of privilege, you just don't see the world the same way."

This was a story I'd never heard. Then something occurred to me. "The coup…. Was that the reason so many nobles turned against my father? Not the bloodline, but because he was changing how they made profit?"

"There were many layers to it, and that was one of them. The sentries didn't trust Varric, but Raiden saw the good everywhere he looked. Idealistic." She leaned back as if recounting a fond memory. "I liked that about him, but we were young and foolish with dreams of changing the world.

Of uniting Algar and Farlight Isles again. You know how that story ended. It could've been worse."

I sat down on the edge of the cot, just listening.

"A sentry saved me when the nobles turned on us. She was the only reason I was able to get down to the dungeons. Her life for mine. It had to mean something…," she trailed off. "She was young. She had just taken her oath at nineteen, earlier than most of the sentries did. Mouthy. I liked her."

She waved the memory off, dismissing it altogether before she got too upset.

"The point I'm trying to make is that it takes more than blood to make a king. It takes heart and desire to do the right thing. The fact that you don't *want* power is a good thing. Those who hunt for power abuse it."

The ball of shame in my throat suddenly knocked free.

"I love you, Ronin. You're my boy. Right here, right now, you're everything you're supposed to be. A king is only as good as their advisers, and you have a godsdamn good roster."

"I love you, too, Mama." My shoulders slouched as if the weight I'd been struggling to carry slid right off their slopes. "I needed to hear that."

She gave me a smile and waved her hand. "Now that that's out of the way, let's chat. We have much to catch up on."

The corner of my mouth twitched. The awkward, heavy atmosphere dissipated, and I finally felt comfortable in my mother's presence again. "We do. Did you find anything good at the market?"

MAEVE CROSS

Now that we were en route to the third monarch, we developed a routine for dinnertime.

Enya would wake up from the hammocks on the lower deck and start cooking dinner for the rest of us. The galley itself could barely fit two people at once, so she would hand me dirty dishes and cookware out the pass-through window after dinner, and I'd take the dishes and two buckets to the mess.

Gunny and I had a system.

I did the cookware, and he did the dinnerware. It was on a much smaller scale than *The Ollipheist*, where there were hundreds of dishes that needed to be scrubbed every night. This voyage certainly felt like a vacation next to that.

While Gunny and I were elbow-deep in soapy water after dinner one evening, Andra stood next to me. She shrugged her jacket off and rolled her sleeves up. Enya and Andra shared a look, but they still weren't talking.

"Need some help?" Andra asked when Enya climbed the hatch to relieve Luella from her post.

"I won't say no," I answered, scooting over so she could help.

She immediately took a clean rag to dry the stacks of dishes. Above us, I could hear the pitter-patter of rain colliding with the deck. While it never stormed much at Shipwreck Bay, the Gullies were considerably wetter.

I wouldn't want to be rained on all night, but I also knew Enya wouldn't complain about it. She and Ronin shared an ironclad work ethic. If it needed to get done, they would do it. No complaining, no avoiding, just got it done.

It wasn't long before Luella joined us, sighing as she sat on the bench. She dropped her dinner bowl into Gunny's bucket and kicked her feet up on the other bench. Another happy noise of relief left her lips.

She took her hat off and shook droplets off the points.

"How long until we get to Violetta's Haven?" I asked, scrubbing a stubborn stain on the bottom of a pot. I wasn't completely thrilled about meeting one of Ronin's casual partners, but there wasn't much I could do about it.

The newness of the situation churned in my belly, making the stew I ate for dinner feel heavy.

"Another few days or so. Depends on the rain. If it gets too heavy, we're close enough to a sandbank to drop anchor until it passes," Luella said.

"Ah," I murmured.

"I heard Violetta has the best blacksmiths under her charge," Gunny mused.

"Oh yeah? Want to get a fresh piece?" Andra wondered.

Gunny smiled, showing off his twisted tooth. "I've maintained weapons as long as I can remember, but I'd love to learn how to *make* them." He paused, dunking a dish into the clean bucket. "Just for fun."

"What's wrong with Ingrid?" Luella interjected, referencing the blacksmith from Shipwreck Bay.

I'd never met her in person, but I had noticed sailors toting around new swords or a fresh satchel of bullets from her shop.

"Ingrid doesn't take students. I've asked. She told me she'd teach me if I give her Geoff, and there is no blazing way I'd hand him off."

Both Andra and Luella looked at each other. "Is this the same Geoff you've talked about? Your... friend Geoff?" Andra asked hesitantly.

His eyebrows furrowed in confusion. "I guess Geoff is my friend, yes."

Andra hesitated. "What do you mean, Gun? Why is Ingrid trying to take your friend?"

"He has a great singing voice."

"So, she wants to *hire* Geoff?" Luella probed.

"That's ridiculous. He has no concept of money."

Looking between Andra, Luella, and Gunny, it became increasingly difficult to bite back a laugh. Andra and Luella had this horrified expression over their faces, while Gunny seemed genuinely confused. I pressed my fingers against my lips, waiting for Gunny to clear it up, but he didn't. The three of them just stared at one another for a solid few moments before I couldn't hold it back anymore.

An uncontrollable laugh spilled past my lips before I slapped my hand over my mouth to stifle it. I rubbed my eyes as tears of amusement ran from the corners. "Gunny is talking about his parakeet. Geoff is a parakeet."

Gunny gave them the most incredulous expression. "Obviously. Who else would I be talking about?"

Oh, Gunny....

Relief washed over Andra and Luella's faces, and they looked at each other and laughed. "Thank the Gods," Andra sighed. "I didn't know you had a parakeet. Geoff is just such a... *human* name."

Gunny's eyes went wide. "I should lead with the parakeet part, shouldn't I?"

Andra nodded. "That would be smart. I was really concerned for a moment."

Luella didn't stop laughing as she gathered the clean dishes. "You lot are hilarious." She took them into the galley, and we could hear them clacking together as she put them away.

"Sorry about that," Gunny apologized sheepishly.

Andra chuckled and shook her head. "That's fine, Gunny. At least now I know you're talking about a parakeet and not a partner."

"So, every time I brought my parakeet up in conversation…."

"Yes. You, not once, ever said that Geoff was *not* a person." She pinched the bridge of her nose.

"Oh no."

I laughed under my breath, shaking my head.

Suddenly, a melody permeated the lower deck, the sound of a violin in a gentle rhythm.

The first thought that crossed my mind was that the beautiful song had to be from somewhere else. A trick or a warning, like a siren song.

My eyes darted to both Gunny and Andra, wondering if they heard it too.

"He's playing again," Andra said softly.

After another moment, I recognized the melody. The sound was richer, a warmer tone than on *The Ollipheist*, but it was the same song I'd hear echoing into the officers' quarters after I'd gone to bed. I would stare up at the mattress above me and wonder where it was coming from.

Ronin. How did I not know it was him playing?

He never talked about music or reading. He didn't talk much about himself at all.

But I never asked.

I *never* asked.

I scratched the back of my hand, mouth turning downward. I claimed that I loved him, but I never asked about his hobbies? With a hard swallow, I straightened up, pushing the gnawing guilt down. Me feeling sorry for myself wouldn't fix anything.

Andra chuckled quietly next to me, the noise full of a fond memory. "He used to practice every night when we were kids. It sounded like a dying animal half the time, but he kept at it. I'm glad he didn't listen to me when I told him a yowling cat sounded prettier than his music."

"I had no idea he played," I admitted, standing up, overcome with the desire to see him with a bow in his hand, forehead pinched in focus. I wanted to see him lost in something he enjoyed. "Do you think he'd be angry with me if I popped in on him?"

Andra hummed, tapping her chin. "A few weeks ago, I'd say yes. But now, I don't think he'd mind if it's you. He's nicer to you lately."

Warmth rose to my cheeks. "Do you mind—"

"Finishing up? No. But don't be too upset if he tells you to leave."

I nodded. "Thanks. I'll talk to you later."

She gave me a warm smile. "Good luck with my brother, Mae."

With a final wave at Gunny, I ducked to climb up to the hatch and pushed it open to follow the music as rain glossed over my cheeks. It wasn't raining very hard, but I felt every drop soak into my blouse, plastering it to my skin.

Enya whistled, getting my attention.

I looked over my shoulder, and she offered me a polite wave. I smiled at her and stepped under the narrow overhang by the captain's quarters. My heart thudded harder. Hesitantly, I poised my hand to knock.

The rhythm of the music picked up into a captivating crescendo. My hand fell to my side. I wouldn't barge in and break the magnificent harmony. Slowly, I sank down outside his door, listening to it. My eyelids fluttered closed as I let the melody cascade over me like the water.

Gods, I could listen to him all night.

I couldn't care less about the rain. Getting drenched was worth it.

Suddenly, the music came to a stop, and I didn't have time to get to my feet before his door flew open. I yelped and fell backward into the doorway.

Heat rose over my face as I stared up at him from the floor. "Hi."

Both his eyebrows came together as he repressed a smile fighting to take over his face. "What are you doing?"

"Eavesdropping."

"You're soaking wet," he observed, tilting his head to the side.

My face was hot, while my translucent white blouse was cold and wet where it was plastered to my skin. "I didn't want to interrupt. It was lovely."

He pressed his tongue to the inside of his cheek, unable to hide one of those disarming dimples from puncturing the other side. "Thank you, sweetheart."

I grinned, still flat on my back. Water cascaded from the overhang, clinging to my eyelashes. From this angle, I noticed the instrument and bow in one of his large hands, looking comically dainty in his grasp.

He rolled his eyes. "Stop lying in my doorway and get up."

"Right." I rolled over onto my knees, and Ronin held out his hand to pull me to my feet.

A full smile had taken the place of the half one. "Unless you'd prefer to lie in my doorway all night."

"It's a little cold down there, but I should probably get back to my hammock and some fresh clothes," I said. I doubted he wanted me to get his cot all wet.

"Don't be ridiculous. Come in. You can wear something of mine until yours dry," he offered, stepping to the side so I could squeeze in beside him.

"My things are right down—"

"Mae," he interrupted. "Maybe I don't want you to leave just yet. Do you *want* to come in?"

I blushed. "Yes."

"Then come in and stop fussing about your clothes. I prefer you in mine anyway."

My cheeks darkened further as I stepped into his cabin and was immediately surrounded by a scent so recognizably *Ronin* that it made my belly tighten with delight. I'd only been in this cabin once or twice, and always with another crewmember for something business related.

I watched him place the violin and bow into a padded canvas bag. The same bag he left Bliss's Colony with.

"Did Bliss give that to you?"

He hummed. "Mm-hmm. A little apology for my injury."

"That's nice. I didn't know you played."

"I never played for anyone but myself. Performing music helps me think through things if I'm having a hard time processing them."

I tucked a wet tendril of hair behind my ear. "I understand why. When you played, everyone started drumming along and singing. I felt so connected to the crew when I heard it."

He ran his hand through his hair. He usually wore it up to keep it out of his eyes, and even around friends, he kept his appearance fairly neat. But I rather liked seeing it unkempt and ruffled.

"Even if I couldn't see them, they were there. I didn't realize I took it for granted until Pike smashed my fucking violin."

My mouth dropped open as a fizzle of anger spat in my belly. "That prick!"

Ronin nodded, but I didn't miss how his shoulders drew up like he was starting to get uneasy. He'd never told me what happened during that month of forced bedrest.

He zipped the bag and looked at me, his throat bobbing

like he was swallowing down his discomfort. "He said some disturbing things to me."

I thought about my next words. The last thing I wanted to do was push, but Ronin was clearly willing to talk. He wouldn't have brought it up if he wasn't. "Like what?"

"How he treated his wives." The shadows of the oil lamp flickered across his face. "How he had the heads of captains stuffed on display at his estate. What he was going to do to me. Over the entire trip, he warned me about what his men would do to me if I tried to fight." He took a deep breath, but he wasn't able to keep my gaze. "Fighting was pointless."

"You don't have to tell me anything, you know?" I said softly.

When his eyes met mine again, they were tender. Beautifully unguarded. I could see the slightest hint of fear, something he was working past. "I know. I trust you, Mae."

Hesitantly, I reached over, my heart feeling unbearably full as I squeezed his hand where it rested on top of his desk.

"Most days I wished they'd overdose the vitrophine so I'd sleep through it. When they did, I'd only be vaguely aware of what was happening."

The fizzle of anger grew, heating my blood and boiling my bones. "Did they hurt you?" I asked, keeping my voice as smooth and even as possible. I thought about how I stood over Nathaniel's unconscious body back at Farlight Castle. How I was tempted to kill him right then and there.

I wished I had.

But I didn't, and now whatever came after that would be partially my fault. I'd have to live with it, knowing I could've killed him before he hurt anyone else.

"They'd either let me lie in my filth or wash me. I didn't know what was worse. Then there were the crude comments and unwanted touches. It was fucking humiliating, but that was the point. They *wanted* to humiliate me."

I squeezed his hand, forgetting my wet clothes clinging to

me. I wanted to hold him. Shield him as he shared these vulnerable moments with me. "I'm sorry."

He ran his thumb over the backs of my knuckles. "It happened. I survived. You survived. I'm getting through it." His gaze was fixated on my hands, shoulders still tight. "I'm done with the secrets, Mae. I'm done with fucking everything up and shutting everyone out."

I reached over with my other hand to cup the bottom of his chin. Those intense eyes met mine, his hair mussed across his forehead. I caressed his cheek with my fingertips, trailing them up to brush his hair out of his eyes in a motion that was all affection. "I'm here for you if you ever want to talk about it more. Or not. You don't have to suffer in silence. I love you, and nothing will change that, all right?"

His shoulders sloped downward, and he brought my hand up to his lips. He laid a tender kiss on my palm. "I love you, too, sweetheart."

We shared a warm moment just looking at each other. His eyes glimmered with unbelievable warmth. I absorbed the interlude, letting it wash over me.

The tether that bound us together strengthened.

Even if he never fully told me what happened to him, it wouldn't change the reality that he was still the man who'd enamored me from the very first time I saw him.

He shook his head. "Enough about me. Let's get you changed."

Right. I shivered as a breeze from his open window blew over me, emphasizing the wet clothing clinging to my body.

His broad form shadowed mine as he stood between me and the oil lamp. "Do you mind if I unbutton this for you?" he asked, gesturing to my blouse.

I glanced down, now completely aware of the pink buds poking through the translucent fabric. I was tempted to arch my back to offer myself to him, but neither of us was ready for that. Not after that conversation. We needed to sit in it, not distract ourselves.

"How about you just pass me one of your shirts while I fiddle with it?" I asked before tacking on, "You're always too impatient with my buttons."

A warm chuckle bubbled up from his throat. "I *do* like the noise they make when they ping off everything."

"I only have three shirts for this trip, and I'm not spending the evening trying to find buttons and sew them back on," I retorted, poking fun at him as I unbuttoned the wet cloth from my chest, getting chillier by the moment.

"I can thread a needle," he teased back, pulling his shirt up and over his head to offer it to me.

My eyes dropped helplessly to his chest and the narrow dip of his waist. The dragon tattoo still wove around his body, even if it wasn't as vibrant as it once was, only slightly hidden in coarse chest hair. And now that I was shrugging my shirt off, my nipples tightened even more, nearly buzzing with the desire to feel his calloused hands scratching up my skin.

I gulped, a whorl of lust coiling in my belly like leaves in the wind.

Damn him and his magnificent body.

"My eyes are up here, Mae," he said playfully.

My own eyes climbed his body until they eventually made it to his intense gaze. "Are you trying to tempt me? Hm?"

"Do you want me to?"

Yes. "This isn't the time or place, and you know it."

"All right, sweetheart. Heard loud and clear, but you should put those tits away before *I'm* tempted to play with them."

"You're not already?" I took his shirt and reached up in an exaggerated stretch.

The growly noise he made was incredibly gratifying.

Ronin's gaze dropped down to my waistband, and he

eyed me up thoroughly before answering. "Of course I am, but you said no. So put me out of my misery."

I giggled and pulled the shirt over my head, letting it fall to midthigh. Ronin took my shirt and clipped it onto the clothesline across the side of the room before grabbing himself a new shirt while I unlaced my damp breeches for him to hang up too.

I sat in his chair, pulling my knees up so they disappeared into the shirt. It smelled so much like him that I happily rested my head on my knees, tucking my face into the fabric.

"What would you like to do while we wait for the clothes to dry?" he asked, his cot creaking under him when he sat.

I popped my head up, crooking an eyebrow. Now that I was wrapped up in his clothes and he couldn't tell me to leave, he couldn't get out of this conversation. "You could tell me about Violetta so I know what we're walking into," I commented. "I know she's blood-cursed and also deals in blood, but that's about it."

He groaned, also aware that he couldn't run away. "Yeah. Right. Okay. Listen, not many blood-cursed elves learn to live with the affliction. Many of them become beasts in the shallows, feasting on fishermen and tormenting small communities. Doomed to live short, hungry lives."

"But she's different?"

"She… well…." He scratched the back of his neck. "She's learned to sustain herself by offering her services. She was a seer before she was cursed, so now she can learn about bloodlines through tasting blood. Essentially tasting the history of your family tree as an added benefit to her gift of *sight*."

Then what if…?

He continued, "I wanted to ask you if I could talk to Violetta about you. In theory, she could tell you about your parents. Where you come from."

"That… could tell me *everything*." It took me a few

moments to absorb the information. "Has she ever—Gods, this *phrasing*—tasted you?"

He cracked a smile. "If she tasted my blood, she'd know my history, so no. Too risky. Though she was always disappointed when I said no. She was so interested in my personal life."

"What does it entail?" I wondered. "Would she bite into my throat or… what?"

"Travelers bring vials of blood or offer a wrist." He tapped his chin. "Honestly, it's a clever way to get the blood she needs."

I nodded in agreement, especially since this service could grant me the final piece of my puzzle. It could finally unravel the cipher of my past. "I want to do it, then."

"Yeah?" he asked. "I have your consent to bring this up to Violetta?"

"You do. I'm ready to know."

He offered me a soft smile. "Then I'll be with you when you do."

We settled into a comfortable silence as something caught my eye.

The book we got from Bliss's Colony was perched on his desk. I reached out and ran my finger along the cover. "How about we crack into this book, hm? Could you read a little to me?"

"You want me to read to you?" Ronin clarified.

Heat spread over my cheeks as I tucked my hair behind my ears, looking over at him from under my lashes. "I like your voice."

I didn't expect to see a beaming smile broaden across his face. Excitement lit up his eyes. "You want me to read you my favorite book?" He laughed under his breath and patted the cot next to him. "Get over here."

His smile was infectious, as one of my own took root. I

jumped to my feet with the book in hand, chewing on my lower lip. "Scoot over, you big brute."

Ronin raised his eyebrows and moved over so I could wriggle myself between him and the wall. I made a noise of contentment as I pressed against his side, pulling his blanket over my legs.

"Comfortable?" he asked, plucking the book from my hands to flip to the dedication.

"Very."

"Good," he murmured, pressing a kiss to the top of my head before leaning against the headboard. After clearing his throat, he read, "'Dedicated to all the scoundrels of Farlight Isles who smuggle my books into stores they shouldn't be in. Never stop being a thorn in that slimy bastard's side.'"

I chuckled. "I like that."

He gave me a devious smile and turned to the first chapter.

Each passing sentence became page after page, chapter after chapter.

I'd ask questions about the plot, and Ronin would tell me to stop being so impatient. We'd laugh and have little side conversations about the characters, eventually settling deeper and deeper in the cot. At some point we settled in so deep, the book rolled onto the bed, and I fell asleep against his shoulder.

THE NEXT FEW days were filled with nonsense. The fun kind. After work, the crew and I would enjoy drinks and play bones. There was no way I'd play cards with Gunny again, so bones had to suffice.

Over those games, I finally told him about my vitality. Andra too. Gunny was surprised to say the least, but he was equally thrilled to be let in on our secrets. Ronin had been more open about his struggles to shift, even around the crew.

We both shed that weight because it was so much lighter in good company.

After that first night when Ronin read parts of his book and we fell asleep together, I found myself coming back to stay up far too late just to spend some time with him.

His favorite color was blue. Like the glimmering water at Anchorage Cove.

He loved the smell of freshly baked bread just as much as he liked making it.

He used to let Andra braid his hair when they were kids and secretly missed bonding with her when he helped her change her hairstyle between voyages.

When the twins got into fights with other teenagers, he was the one who got them out of it. Funnily enough, it was usually Andra who started it. According to Ronin, she was quite a troublemaker.

I wondered what happened to make her so responsible now.

We would lie in his cot and talk for hours. He'd comb his fingers through my hair and ask me what I liked to do for fun at the castle. Mainly, I'd cause trouble for the guards. Sneak about the castle before they tossed me back into my chambers with the doors locked.

I only became more spiteful, but the most complicated part of it was that even if I did everything I could to get under Varric's skin, I still wanted his approval.

The chasm that used to separate Ronin and me closed in, leaving only a scar. Maybe one day it would fade altogether. Or maybe it would be painted over with gold like those shiny handmade plates I'd see at the market. The scars highlighted what made it so beautiful.

MAEVE CROSS

Violetta's Haven was the farthest from the dwellings of the other monarchs. Nearly a week away from Bliss's Colony and two weeks away from Anchorage Cove. It was on the far side of the main island and the opposite side of Farlight Harbor.

Instead of being sunny, a gloomy cloudiness shrouded the sky. It was not unlike the foggy environment from my childhood, but the air was thicker, hotter, and muggier. A sheen of sweat perpetually beaded along my forehead from the humidity. My hair stuck up in different directions, making me feel sticky and uncomfortable.

With every rise and fall of my chest, it felt like I was breathing in soup.

Thick clouds loomed over the canopies of sprawling greenery with trunks sticking out of the treacherous water, which was an opaque muddy color from the sediment constantly kicked up by wildlife.

Varric's soldiers never went to this side of the island, which was commonly referred to as the Wilds, a wetland hard to maneuver by foot with shallow rivers and massive roots connecting a network of cypress trees. They considered it a no-man's-land, home to outlaws and maneaters.

After a sixth scout never returned, Varric had decided it wasn't worth it to explore and simply turned his efforts to other things. But eventually, he'd return to pick it apart. He always did.

I couldn't help but wonder if Violetta was responsible for the missing scouts. If she was the maneater they spoke of.

"Careful at the edge of the boat, lass," Luella warned me, shouting from the helm. I snapped out of my thoughts. "These are different beasties than the sea."

To aid her point, the water splashed not too far from us, a leathery tail crashing into the murky surface before disappearing altogether.

What in the Nine Hells was that?

I straightened up and moved back from the rippling water before whatever it was jumped up and pulled me into the deep. Would I come back if I got eaten? How would that work?

Let's not find out.

Ronin exited his cabin to stride across the ketch to Luella and Andra. I watched him out of the corner of my eye, feeling awfully fuzzy at the sight of him. He wore a tricorn cap and tipped it up to shoot me a playful wink before asking Andra something I couldn't hear.

Luella nodded and stepped away from the helm so Ronin could take over. She reached into her coat and pulled out a rolled map. She scribbled something on it.

Curiosity encouraged me to walk over to them and eavesdrop.

"There should be a dock around here," Luella muttered, tracing a line with her finger.

"How old is that map?" Ronin asked, steering us carefully around woody debris floating in the water.

It isn't woody debris.

As soon as the ketch floated by, the creature sank into the water, the leathery tail I'd mistaken for flotsam splashing the surface as if it was trying to lure prey. I gulped, startled as a shiver of fear ran down my spine. This was different from the sirens or the echoes.

This creature was *hunting*.

"It's a saltie." Andra's voice startled me even more than the creature did. "A saltwater reptile. You don't see them east of the Gullies." She hummed, scanning the swampy water before pointing in the distance. "There's another one. They look like floating logs."

I followed her gesture, and the only reason I even saw it was because of its big round eyes peering at us with interest above a long, thick muzzle lined with teeth.

"Have you seen them before?" I asked.

"Wraith and I had our honeymoon out here," Andra answered offhandedly. "Levi never liked leaving the main routes at work, so we spent our honeymoon exploring."

Luella smiled, glancing up from the map to look at her wife adoringly. "Best three weeks of my life."

Another saltie dove into the water, and my belly jumped into my throat. "That's nice…. Uh… do we have to worry about being eaten?"

Andra laughed. "Just try not to fall overboard."

Thanks, Andra. That makes me feel so much better.

The expression I gave her was enough for her smile to grow, and she nudged me in the ribs before stepping past me to the sails to twist the ropes, bringing the canvas down.

"There," Ronin announced, pointing at a wooden platform beneath a canopy. It was hard to see under the tree shadows, but several skiffs were pulled up along the sides, and sailors were waiting nearby, tossing fish into the water.

The salties dove for the food, moving out of the way for our ketch.

Luella made an adjustment on her map, then rolled it up

and tucked it into her pocket before taking over the helm to bring us to the platform.

"Aye," Ronin greeted, stepping over to the side of the boat where the welcoming party was.

"Captain Leviathan," the tallest one said, outstretching a lanky arm to greet Ronin. He had long pointed ears decorated with numerous piercings. The silver jewelry glimmered against deep blue skin. "Nice to see you again."

Ronin grasped the man's forearm, dipping it down in a firm shake. "Pinky. It's been a while."

So that's Pinky....

"Violetta is expecting you. She sent me to bring you in on a skiff," Pinky explained.

"We can't sail any closer?"

"Too shallow. How many men you got? I can fit two in each skiff."

"There are six."

Pinky nodded, gesturing for the sailors to get back into their boats, one at the bow and the other at the stern, a bucket of fish in each. "Grab your things. We won't be coming back out here until first light the day after tomorrow. We have the summer festival tomorrow night."

"Heard," Ronin said, glancing over at me when Pinky hopped into one of the boats. "Mae, do you want to come with me?"

I glanced over at Luella and Andra to see if they needed anything.

"We'll finish up here and get Gunny and Seabird at the ready," Andra offered. "You two go ahead."

Gunny had been meticulously carving a new set of bones pieces all day, this time from calcified coral. I doubted he even knew we'd docked. Once he got focused on something, nothing could snap him out of it. And Enya was still sleeping from her night shift.

"Git." Luella waved her hand dismissively, but then she

seemed to change her mind about letting us go quite yet, looking over at Ronin and squinting those intense eyes, her lips in a thin line.

She let go of the helm and stepped over to him, barely making any noise. Ronin stood perfectly still, not remotely surprised at Luella's advancement. She glared at him as they held each other's gaze intently.

"If you fuck with her feelings again, I'll kill you," she threatened, her voice incredibly low. "I don't let *anyone* fuck with Mae. Not even you. Do you understand?"

Embarrassment pinkened my cheeks as my eyes darted over to Violetta's sailors, hoping they didn't hear anything. "That's really not necessary—" I tried to interject.

Luella put one finger up to silence me, still staring Ronin down. "Do you understand?"

"I do," he answered, looking past her at me. He tilted his head toward the skiffs, encouraging me to join him.

She stared him down for a moment or two longer before turning on her heel and walking straight over to me. She didn't even say anything, just picked up my bag from where it was sitting next to the mast, dropped it into my hands, and pinched my cheek. Then she patted the top of my head before leaving my side to help Andra lock down the boat.

My face boiled. *Luella always knows how to make a statement, doesn't she?*

I waved them goodbye and stepped over to the edge of the boat. Ronin got out first, reaching out to help me onto the platform. The pier wriggled on the water, but his grip kept me steady so I didn't fall into whatever jaws were awaiting me beneath the murky surface.

We got into the skiff behind Pinky, another sailor at the rear to be on saltie watch. Nerves ran rampant in my belly, not only over the reptiles but also Violetta.

Ronin didn't talk about her much, and I didn't know if

that should bother me or not. *Should I be concerned about a former lover?*

I think the worst part of it was that I didn't know what to expect. I mulled over possible conversations, internally practicing what I was going to say. Every new thought I had seemed more ridiculous than the previous one.

What in the Hells am I supposed to say to her?

The sailor at the rear used a long oar to push the shallow boat through the wetlands.

"I haven't seen you before," Pinky commented, which, thankfully, shook me out of whatever ridiculous scenario I would've imagined next. His light-colored eyes met mine. "I'm familiar with several of Levi's mates, but not you."

"This is Mae," Ronin answered. "She's my partner. Wherever I go, she goes with me."

Warmth flooded my face. He didn't say it like he expected me to follow him around. I was beside him, an equal. Not a lost puppy waiting behind him for a pat on the head.

"Does she now?" Pinky chuckled, then remained quiet for a few moments while they navigated around the interlocking tree roots. "That's not going to work for Vee, Levi. You know that."

"Then she has the wrong impression," he replied.

"I only repeat orders I'm given. I don't make them," the lanky man replied, waving his hand in the air. "Vee wants to see you at sundown, alone, for whatever terms you want to outline in this allyship."

Bliss had wanted to see him privately, too, but this felt different. The plan was to go there together, discuss the alliance, and then ask her about my bloodline. So that threw a kink into our strategy.

"Whatever she wants, she gets, hm?" Ronin sucked his teeth, looking downright pissed off now.

Pinky glanced back at Ronin, a devious gleam in his eye. "She always does."

After gliding along the river for what felt like forever, on edge from numerous salties watching us from boulders and debris, I saw the first glimpse of a floating town.

It seemed like the piers where skiffs docked were anchored to the river floor with stilts, and most of the community consisted of wooden platforms connecting each of the houses and shops for a sprawling water town. As waves licked at the walkways, the paths moved with them.

Oil lamps decorated every house and tree, dangling over townspeople as they went about their day. My eyes rounded as I marveled at it, completely different from anything I'd ever seen before. It was just as unique as each gully and beach.

No wonder Andra and Luella had their honeymoon here. It was ripe for exploring.

Pinky directed us to a platform at the base of an inn near the town center. Above the main entrance was what looked like a wraparound balcony. I could imagine sitting out there, staring at the sky. It was so different from the other seaside towns, but it was connected to the ocean like we all were.

"We booked out the inn for you. Every person gets their own room," Pinky said, kicking his foot out to stop the skiff from bumping into the docking area. He got out and held his hand out to me, helping me onto the platform. "The rest of your crew should be here shortly. Once everyone is accounted for, I'll take you to Vee, all right?"

"All right" was all Ronin said as he turned his back on Pinky. I noticed the hard line of his back and how his shoulders stiffened like they did when he was uncomfortable. He didn't say anything to me as he walked up the steps toward the entrance.

Does he want me to follow him?

Before I could, Pinky cleared his throat, capturing my attention.

"He shouldn't have brought you here, little lady," he commented. "Vee isn't going to be happy about it."

A spiteful bout of heat simmered in my belly. "Why not?" I asked sharply, crossing my arms. I didn't like that Ronin looked so uncomfortable, and I certainly didn't like Pinky stirring the pot either.

"Vee and Levi have a rather tortuous relationship. On again, off again. She gets what she wants—even if she has to steal it." He laughed a little under his breath. "And she loves to steal."

My mouth opened, a petty retort on the tip of my tongue.

But I stopped myself. *I'm not doing this. Too many things are at stake to indulge a petty hypothetical.* "If she can steal him, then he's not the man I thought he was. She can have him," I decided. "Good day."

"Good day," Pinky replied, the corner of his mouth twitching up. His eyes flashed again with that devious gleam.

That was when it hit me.

He was sizing me up. Poking at me to see if I'd bite back. *Why?*

"Mae, come on," Ronin called from the double doors.

I looked up to see him glaring daggers at Pinky, who only seemed amused by it.

I turned around and walked up the steps with my bag in hand. Ronin moved slightly so I could pass by him, and then the double doors clanked closed behind us.

The main floor was a tavern, smelling like rich herbs and meat.

Dinner would be excellent here later.

The innkeeper noticed us from the bar. Ronin was perfectly polite to them as he gathered the keys, and then we headed toward the stairs. We didn't say anything until we got to the second floor and stood in the hallway between several rooms.

"Fucking Pinky. I'm sorry you had to deal with him. He's

just as troublesome as his cousin." He released an exhausted sigh before opening the door to his room to toss his bag inside.

"Violetta?" I wondered.

My room was right next to Ronin's, and I unlocked the door to check it out. Nothing special. A nice enough bed, a little desk, and a rocking chair. I put my bag on the bed, careful because I had Ronin's book inside. I promised him I'd be gentle with it, and I intended on upholding that promise.

Ronin followed me inside. "Mm-hmm. Thick as thieves. Literally."

"I can handle it," I replied.

He smiled, leaning against the desk. "I know you can." He looked away again, his shoulders drooping. "I just don't like it."

"Will you be okay?" I asked as I brushed his stiff back with my fingertips. "You're tense."

He flinched for a moment before relaxing. "I'm not exactly thrilled about this situation, but yes, I'll be fine."

"I can't imagine why. It's not every day you have the opportunity to introduce your current lover to your former lover. I, for one, am so *excited*," I stated teasingly, hoping to lighten the mood a little.

"Ha. Ha. Very funny." He turned around, looking down at me with that all-too-familiar adoration that I couldn't get enough of. He grazed my jaw with his fingertips, guiding my face up. "I'm glad you're so enthusiastic about it."

"It's a nice way to hide all the dread," I replied.

He stroked my cheek with his thumb, making me blush. "There's nothing to dread, sweetheart. I'll convince Violetta to come to Shipwreck Bay for the alliance, and then we'll be on our merry way."

"And ask her about me," I reminded him.

"Yes, and ask her about you." His eyes danced with nerves,

a tic embedded in his jaw. But that wasn't all. There was fear lingering in his expression as well.

"What're you so afraid of?" I asked before I could stop myself.

Silence followed, and I was worried he'd withdraw and bury himself in that wall of ice he used to throw up. But he didn't. He released my jaw, and those big hands cupped mine instead.

He released a sharp breath through his nose. "She's handsy, Mae. Violetta is really fucking handsy."

Oh.

"Whenever we were together, she could never keep her fucking hands to herself. Of course, at the time, I didn't mind, but now, just the thought of her touching me makes me want to puke my fucking guts out."

His shoulders stiffened again as he looked away from me, shame darkening his cheeks.

"I know this is probably the last thing you want to hear right now, but I know what she's going to do the second she gets me alone."

"You think she's going to jump you?" I inquired.

"That was our *thing*. Pretend to be on business and fuck when no one was looking." He couldn't meet my eyes.

I gulped. "Oh. Well, I definitely don't like the sound of that." My belly turned uncomfortably, but not because I thought Ronin would betray me. His distraught demeanor was what worried me. "Are you sure I can't go with you?"

He shook his head, still not looking at me. "Not for this first meeting. Violetta is incredibly guarded. Pinky won't take me to her with you by my side. He made that clear."

"Look at me, Ronin," I said, brushing my fingers along his stubbly jaw.

Slowly, he met my gaze.

"I trust you, all right?" I murmured.

His eyes softened, and he cupped the hand holding his face. "I trust you too."

We stayed like that for a moment, and then I said, "Well, I'm going to catch up on some reading while you're away. It'll give us something new to talk about."

He grinned and said, "I doubt we'll ever run out of things to talk about."

My cheeks heated, and my lips parted to say something, but then there was a knock at my door.

"Change of plans, Leviathan. Let's go." It was Pinky's voice.

Ronin tilted his head back and sighed, but before he could pull away, I got up on my toes to peck him on the cheek, loving the feel of his scratchy stubble against my lips. "See you later. Good luck."

He squeezed my hand, then veered back to my room door and disappeared down the hallway with Pinky.

RONIN MURDOCH

My cheek tingled from Mae's kiss as I left with Pinky, a helpless half smile curling the side of my mouth. But as soon as she was out of sight, it vanished. Without her by my side, I was on edge.

I had to be.

I'd never been to Violetta's Haven before, and I couldn't let my guard down around Pinky.

He was the type of man to take advantage of a doe-eyed sailor the second they took their hand off their coin pouch. I'd seen it. I'd even participated in pickpocketing before I climbed the ship ranks.

Over the past several years, I'd become quite aware of his habits. He liked to fuck around with *fresh meat,* and Mae was as fresh as it came.

I assumed my relationship with Mae was all the more enticing to him for that same reason. Just as cutthroat and cunning as Violetta, it was no surprise that she became a monarch with her loyal cousin by her side. Pinky didn't like the heat that came with being a captain. He preferred to lurk and give Violetta any advantage she needed to get ahead.

Blackmail.

Thieving.

Mercenary work.

Kidnapping for ransom.

Dirty work.

The uglier side of pirating.

But it existed all the same, like the dark, rat-infested corners of the bilge. It didn't take away from the joys and freedoms I'd gained through this lifestyle, but I'd be a fool to pretend pirates like Pinky didn't exist.

I also couldn't deny that Violetta's Haven was like something out of a children's book. Visitors and pirates wandered along the busy corridors, in and out of taverns and storefronts. Oil lamps lit up the entire settlement, making it seem like a twinkling paradise in the heart of the swamp.

Scents of fresh food wafted from a few taverns, and all I could think about was going to one of them with my crew for food and drink.

I may not like how they gained their fortune, but they were thriving. People from all over came here to start over and were welcomed with open arms. That in and of itself was worth respect.

It wasn't unlike Shipwreck Bay in that sense. A home to society's rejects or those fleeing a war. No one got turned away, and everyone got something to eat.

"I've gotta ask, Levi," Pinky started, his voice taking on that lilt that told me he was about to push my buttons. "When you fuck over that freshie, do you think she'd take me for a ride?"

I don't think so, you fucking prick.

I clenched my fists, but I didn't punch him in the face. "Fuck off, Pinky."

He didn't fuck off. *Of course not.* "It's a serious question. I've got a thing for those big round eyes. I bet they get all wide when—"

I tensed, a tic forming in my jaw. I kept reminding myself

not to split his lip. I knew he'd been waiting for an opportunity to fuck me over even before I started seeing Violetta. "I'll repeat myself only once. *Fuck off.*"

"How about when you're busy with Vee, I go check in on her? Hm? It gets cold at night. I bet I could keep her warm."

A white-hot flare of rage spat up into my chest, fizzling my blood. I knew what he was doing, but that didn't keep me from stopping in my tracks and grabbing him by the collar. "I'll rip your fucking hands off," I growled.

His eyes went wide before he frowned. "Aw, Levi. I'm just fucking around. Let go."

"Stay away from Mae. Fuck with her and you're fucking with me."

Pinky put up both hands. "Fine. Fine. Testy. I didn't think you were so opposed to sharing." His lips tilted into a wry smile. "That freshie certainly doesn't mind sharing *you* with Vee."

"She's not sharing me with anyone."

I let him go, and he continued guiding me to a large house in the center of town.

He barked a mocking laugh. "You seem so sure of yourself. That's fine. I'll just make myself available if that freshie goes looking for a revenge fuck."

Before I could reply, he stopped, pointing up the steps to a wraparound porch that had Violetta written all over it with the expensive window dressings. She always did have a taste for luxury.

"I'll wait out here, but not all night."

I didn't reply, tossing him a scathing glare before climbing the steps. The door had a knocker made of fine metal with a matching doorknob. Embedded stained glass that shone every time light hit it.

Even something as plain as an entryway door was adorned with upscale finishings.

I really didn't want to do this.

Too fucking bad.

I used the knocker to announce my presence, enjoying the warm, full sound of it hitting the wood. Quality metal.

Violetta's voice carried through the door. "Come in."

I entered, closing the door behind me. I didn't see Violetta right away, but there was no shortage of lavish paintings and sculptures lining the walls. Leather embossed furniture and fur rugs. Just as plush as her cabin on *The Lilac Queen*.

"Lock the door, would you? I'd hate to have any strays pop in," she called out.

I looked up the stairs where her voice came from, but I didn't see her.

"Unless you don't mind an audience."

I pinched the bridge of my nose with my thumb and index finger, quelling my annoyance before asking, "Did you get my letter, Violetta?"

"A little elaborate for a rendezvous, but I was too intrigued to decline." Her voice got closer, and a shadow appeared at the top of the stairs.

I wasn't surprised to see her dressed in a feathered floor-length wine-red robe.

I could also make out her long dark hair, peachy skin, pointed, pierced ears, and the scar that split her eyebrow down to the bow of her lips. Not many people were taller than me, but Violetta was one of the few I had to glance up at to look in the eye. She looked nothing like Pinky despite being related to him.

Her glossy blue eyes dropped down to my boots and climbed the entire way back up again.

Once upon a time, I'd be incredibly flattered, but she was taking up my time. Time I could be spending with Mae and my mates. I wanted to know if Mae had gotten to my favorite chapter of our book yet.

My indifference caused Violetta to step down the stairs,

playing with the tie on her robe. She was devastatingly pretty, but I wasn't remotely interested.

"I was wondering when you'd be back. I hoped you wouldn't be too broken up after our... split."

"Listen, Violetta—" I tried to say, but she grabbed me by my jacket, knocking me down on top of a plush armchair.

My eyes went wide as she pounced onto my lap, though I should've seen it coming.

My entire body grew rigid, and I could feel hands *everywhere*. Sickly, overwhelming fingertips that made me want to expel the contents of my stomach.

"I missed your body, but you're thinner," she hummed, not noticing my discomfort as her hands drifted down my chest. "Did something happen?"

Overstimulation ran rampant all over me, and it took everything I had not to knock her onto the floor, because it would piss her off and she wouldn't agree to the alliance or help Mae.

Her hands drifted farther down, and it felt like I swallowed my tongue. I couldn't speak past my rigid shoulders. Every muscle grew stiff as if I'd been subjected to another dose of vitrophine.

She pouted. "You're not...."

I grabbed her hand before she could fondle me through my trousers.

"Get the fuck off me," I uttered from between my teeth. "*Please.*"

Violetta drew back completely. "What? You're not here for—" Her eyes went wide. "Oh shit. How embarrassing."

My jaw was locked, and I glared her down as she got off me, tightening her robe. "No. I'm actually here for business."

She fluffed her hair and sighed, not hiding the utter annoyance in her tone. "Forgive me. That was how we usually conducted business."

"I remember." I got up from the armchair and smoothed

my trousers, then adjusted my jacket, brushing the sensation of her touch off me. "But what we have to discuss is more imperative than sex."

"Nothing is more imperative than sex," she chuckled. "How disappointing. I've been looking forward to this all week. Surely this can wait until after."

"I'm spoken for, Violetta. It's not going to happen."

"Oh?" Surprise colored her tone. "Good for you. And here I was, hoping you were here to revisit our old habits."

I couldn't stop myself from rolling my eyes. "Last time we were together, you robbed me. Another tumble in the sheets wouldn't be enough to forget that."

She tsked, waving her hand dismissively. "You're still upset about that? It was your fault you had your coin satchel with you. I couldn't resist."

I gave her another eye roll. "I'm not here to talk about you fucking me over."

She turned around to her massive bookshelf, where there was an expensive-looking decanter with fine liquor. She grabbed two crystal glasses and filled them. "Well, out with it."

She offered me a glass, and I took it as I advised, "You're going to want to sit down for this."

Her split eyebrow canted upward. "If you insist." Violetta stretched out on a leather chair, kicking her legs up.

"Cross is on the hunt for pirates."

She tossed her head back with a long, drawn-out groan. "Gods. Not Cross. Does the man sleep? How does he have all the time in the day to muck around with us? I thought I ate enough of his soldiers for him to give it a rest."

Yet another way Violetta secured her influence across the pirate colonies. Everyone was eager to put their colors behind the captain who *ate* the same soldiers who terrorized them.

Once upon a time, before being blood-cursed, Violetta

was from Farlight Harbor. She knew what happened to kids who ended up on the streets, especially poor kids. The guards considered them vermin, and the ones they caught would go missing. Like many of us in the lifestyle, she knew the cruelty Varric could inflict.

I explained, "To make a long story short, I ended up at Farlight Prison after I was captured by Nathaniel Pike—"

"The prison? Captains don't make it that far. Pike kills captains. I've heard stories of heads mounted at his estate. How'd you escape?" Violetta's eyes were wide.

"He was under orders not to kill me. But while I was there—"

"Under orders? How fucking special could you be—"

I pinched the bridge of my nose. "Can I fucking get to that part without you interrupting me?"

She put both hands up. "Fine."

"Cross wants to go to war with Algar, and he wants to recruit pirates. This shouldn't be a surprise, considering he's drafted rebels before. He's going to pick us off one by one unless we band together. I'm proposing the formation of a council—"

"You learned this in prison?" She leaned forward and rested her chin on her palm. "And *how* did you end up in prison, exactly?"

Will it kill her to stop interrupting me? Even when we were in bed together, she was impatient. "My name is Ronin Murdoch. Cross can't harvest my draconite if I'm already dead."

She recoiled in her seat. "*You're* Ronin Murdoch?" She barked a laugh. "Sure you are."

When I didn't reply, she took a big gulp of her bourbon.

"Fucking Hells." She paused, finishing her glass. "Well, I don't believe you." She tapped her chin, thinking deeply about her next words. "Wait. Is that why you never let me have a bite?" Her eyes lit up. "I've never tasted a leviathan before."

I don't want to do this. "Would that be enough for you to believe me?"

She leaned forward, darkness swirling in the blues of her eyes. "It would be."

My heart pounded hard. I didn't want her to *touch* me, much less *bite* me. But I would do what I had to. "Fine. Take a nibble." I outstretched a wrist.

"It would be," she repeated before releasing an annoyed groan. "If you were consenting. But you're not."

My hand fell to my side, the band in my chest incredibly tight. I frowned.

"As much as I would *love* to take a bite out of you, I won't do it if you don't want me to. Coercion is not consent. I won't do that to you. I know you. You're enthusiastic when you want something." She paused, tapping her chin before placing her glass on the side table. "I'll tell you what. I've got a prize east of Shipwreck Bay. I'll stop by your little council meeting on the way back."

I nodded. "That's all I'm asking."

"You're fortunate that I like you," Violetta commented. "And it's a shame you won't be coming to bed with me, but I'm glad you found someone. I hope they're as honorable as you are."

She is. "She's too good for me, Violetta."

"Pishposh," she laughed, waving her hand back and forth. "That's the real reason we'd never work out. Honorable people tend to bunch together. Is there anything else you wanted before I kick you out and scratch my own itch?"

I nodded. "Actually, I have another favor to ask you."

"More favors? As long as I get to meet your new lover, I'll help you with whatever you want." She grinned, eyes dancing with excitement.

Violetta had always been incredibly interested in my

personal life. Probably because I never gave her anything to go on.

"Funny you say that. My girl needs your services. It's a delicate matter, so don't go fucking around with her."

There was a glimmer of deviousness in her gaze that rivaled Pinky's. "You're no fun, but I'd love to get a taste of her if I can't get a taste of you."

I did *not like* how she phrased that, but I chose to ignore it. She was just trying to press my buttons. "How's tomorrow night?"

"That's perfect." Her red lips pulled into a smirk. "Bring her to me during the festivities. Don't worry, it'll be perfectly private."

"All right. How much do I owe you?"

"Consider it paid in advance." She winked.

A short laugh fell from my lips. "I'll take it."

She pulled her lower lip between her teeth, fluttering her lashes longingly. "If you and your lover ever want another playmate, all you have to do is ask. After all, readings make me incredibly *thirsty*."

That's enough of that. I rolled my eyes and turned toward the door to leave. "Good night, Violetta. I'll see you tomorrow night."

She chuckled and walked me over to the door. "Good night, Levi. Or I suppose it's Ronin now?"

"Either, really." I didn't have a preference. Except when it came to Mae. I much preferred the way my birth name sounded on her lips.

She opened the door for me and said, "I like Ronin. It suits you."

I smiled and walked outside, hearing her close the door behind me. And thank the Gods, Pinky was still waiting, seemingly deep in conversation with one of the locals, or I might have knocked a few of his teeth out.

MAEVE CROSS

WHILE RONIN WAS AWAY with Violetta, the crew and I had dinner in the tavern. I had a big bowl of stew in front of me and was dunking crusty bread in it to sop up the flavorful broth. We sat around a table, chatting about what we were going to do during the summer festival.

Gunny wanted to get a few weapon blueprints to practice crafting when he got back to Anchorage Cove. Enya was looking to buy bits and bobs from the market. Luella and Andra planned to dance the night away.

I didn't have any plans, and I wasn't much of a dancer, but I wanted to dance with Ronin. I wanted to laugh with him under the warm light from oil lamps and maybe share a few romantic kisses. Not that I *told* the crew any of that, because that would make me sound incredibly pitiful.

I just told them I'd eat every tiny bit of food served on a platter.

When Ronin walked in, I turned my head to say something to him, but the first thing he did was cup my face in his hands and press a kiss to my lips in front of everyone. Nothing but pure, tender affection.

My cheeks grew hot, and my eyelashes fluttered.

The kiss wasn't anything spectacular, barely more than a peck, but it still made my pulse soar because every time we kissed or shared any type of touch, we'd been alone. Our relationship wasn't a secret, but sometimes I felt like he wanted to hide me just in case it fell apart.

Like he was afraid of what our future would look like, or he didn't want one to begin with.

Now, there was no question about it. He wanted me, and doubt had no place between us.

Luella whistled, and I knew my cheeks turned several more shades of red.

Ronin smiled down at me, and I couldn't help but return it, feeling awfully nervous about his mother standing across the room from us.

I could've sworn she stifled an amused smile with her gloved hand.

Ronin scooted onto the bench next to me and ordered himself dinner. After it arrived, we discussed our day between bites. Then we listened to Gunny talk about a blacksmith he'd popped in on who was crafting a broadsword and let him fan the flames for the molten metal.

Enya commented on the craftsmanship of the pipe system and how she wanted to implement aspects of it on *The Ollipheist.*

Meanwhile, Andra and Luella kept themselves busy by feeding salties with the other sailors.

These were the dinners that I'd remember on cold nights. A big pot of stew and hearty bread shared between the six of us as we talked about our interests. Moments I'd look back on if anything went to shit.

The small things would keep me warm.

This was what we were fighting for.

THE NEXT NIGHT, we were greeted with live music. Lutes and drums. Singing and dancing. Every corner of the town had food stands and vendors. The sounds of shoes clapping against the wooden deck added to the cacophony.

There was so much excitement in the air that it felt wrong to go to Violetta's home and miss out on the festivities. But learning about my history was more important than drinking and dancing.

Ronin tried to warn me about Violetta as we got closer to her house.

But I didn't think *anything* would actually prepare me for her.

Before we even knocked on the door, it flew open, and I was met face-to-breasts with an incredibly tall—taller than Ronin *tall*—dark-haired woman with bright blue eyes. I tilted my head back, my eyes wide as I gazed up at her.

Every greeting I'd rehearsed in my head left me. My mouth fell open, and I stood there like a fool, trying to think of something. *Anything.* But I had nothing.

Her eyes darted from Ronin to me, a big grin plastered across her face.

"Is this her?" she asked, looking directly at Ronin while her eyes danced with inky darkness.

"Mae, meet Violetta." He gestured to the tall elven woman. "Violetta, this is Mae."

"Oh, she is *adorable*!" she squealed, reaching over to pinch my cheeks like an overly touchy relative.

I recoiled in shock and said, without thinking, "You *are* handsy."

Good job, Mae. Way to make a first impression.

Violetta chuckled, revealing elongated teeth that seemed to get longer as the moments passed. Uneasiness tightened in my belly. I became vastly aware of the predatory way she looked at me. "Come in, darling," she finally said and invited us in.

A firm hand found my waist as she went back into her home, clearly expecting us to follow. "We can leave." Ronin squeezed, and my heart thudded hard at the protective way he held me.

The sentiment was sweet, but I wasn't going to turn around. Not when I was so close to my answers. "I'll be okay. You're here."

The corner of his mouth turned up and dented his cheek on one side. He squeezed my waist again before he released me. We both stepped inside and closed the door behind us.

I gazed around at the lavish furniture and window dressings as Violetta settled on a chaise lounge.

She was dressed in expensive leathers and a corset emphasizing her curvy form. She crossed her legs, patting the seat next to her. The motion felt incredibly suggestive, as was the way she looked me up and down.

Everything about Violetta screamed sex appeal, and she knew how to use it. I had mixed feelings about that. For one, I had never met a woman so comfortable with their sexuality. I grew up in an environment where that was considered *wrong.* Lewd. Scandalous. Women like Violetta were called nasty things.

But look at the power she holds... how she's not viewed as lesser because of it....

I felt a sort of empowerment just being near her, even if she intimidated me.

"Would you like a drink?" Violetta asked, stretching out against her seat. Despite her relaxed form, she put off this air of *owning* the room and *everyone* in it.

"No," Ronin answered. "Not for me."

As tempting as it was to dull my nerves, I also denied her offer. When I sat beside her, I felt distinctly like a prey animal, and she was all predator. But this felt entirely different from when I'd once felt like a bunny before Nathaniel's jaws.

The air around Violetta was dangerous, but only if *I* wanted it to be.

I put my hands on my thighs, twisting my fingers together as heat warmed my face. "So, you just need to bite my wrist, right? Not my throat?"

"Do you *want* me to bite your throat?" she asked, eyes flickering across the place in my throat that was absolutely *pounding*. "There's nothing like the hammering of a heart. I could grant you sensations you've *never* felt before."

My face boiled. I couldn't keep her gaze as I looked across the rug at the upholstered seat where Ronin sat. He didn't seem remotely surprised by her comment, even if he was grumpy as all Hells.

"Stop trying to seduce my girl, Violetta."

My girl?

I'd be his, but only if he agreed to be mine too. I chewed my lower lip, my eyes locking with his.

"Aw," she pouted, sticking her lower lip out, painted with a red stain. "But just *look* at her pink face! How can I not? She's just so charming. And do you see how she's looking at you? If you ever want an audience, I could—"

My cheeks got hotter as I just barely realized what she was asking. My eyes grew all wide, and I lost track of what I wanted to say as I glanced between Ronin and Violetta.

"Fuck no," Ronin said with finality. "That's off the table."

"Oh, fine. Spoilsport." Violetta returned her gaze to me, and the atmosphere changed, as did the tone of her voice. "He's so serious."

She straightened up, all business now. "To read your bloodline, I only need a few drops. Your wrist, or even a little prick of your finger would do just fine. Depends how much you want to know."

My throat bobbed as I outstretched my arm to her. "My wrist."

A long fingernail stroked the pulse point there. "Blood is

infinite, full of memories and ancestral trees, but my magic isn't. What do you want to know? I can only look where you want me to."

"I want to know where I come from," I said.

"More specific, darling. Do you want to know the land from which you hail? Do you want to know who your parents were? Do you want to know if you're royalty?"

I nodded. "I want to know about my parents. What happened to them? What… *were* they?"

Violetta tapped her chin. "All right. Now, I've been told that this isn't too painful, but it will not be comfortable. Just try to relax and open your mind."

"Open my mind?" I repeated.

"If you don't, this will be incredibly exhausting for the both of us. Do I have your consent? I will not do this without it," Violetta said firmly.

"You do," I replied wholeheartedly.

"Good," she decided, bringing my wrist to her lips.

My heart pounded harder and harder, throbbing against the pulse point. I took a deep breath and tried to relax, but it was difficult with Violetta blowing air against my skin.

I glanced over at Ronin, and he gave me his full attention, reminding me that I was safe. I knew that if anything happened, he would step in. I trusted him with everything I had.

My heart, my body, all of it.

Violetta's teeth brushed my wrist right before she bit down. The oil lamps flickered off and on as a wave of magical energy flooded the room. Her eyes filled with inky darkness before the irises flashed completely red.

I winced at the fresh stab of pain, but it didn't last long.

The pale veins under her skin bulged slightly as she filled her mouth with my blood. She pulled away a moment later, tilting her head back. Her pupils darted back and forth as if she was dreaming with her eyes open.

She released my wrist, and I instantly clamped my hand over it to quell the bleeding, but like before, my skin stitched up right before my eyes, leaving nothing but blood as an indication of the injury.

"Are you all right?" Ronin asked, voice low but tight.

I nodded, lifting my wrist to show him my lack of an injury. He released his breath, settling back in his seat.

Violetta's head turned back and forth rapidly. "That's not right. That can't be right." The red ebbed out of her eyes, followed by the black until the magic dissipated completely. Her blue eyes flashed over to me, the most perplexed expression on her face.

"What did you see?" I asked.

"Nothing," she replied.

I sat up straight. "What?"

"No, that can't be right," Ronin repeated. "What did you see?"

She looked between us. "*Nothing*. I saw absolutely nothing." Her eyes fixed on me. "What *are* you? You *tasted* like fae, but you aren't fae."

Her words startled me. What did that mean?

"I'm sorry. I wish I could help you, but I saw nothing." Violetta stood up, obviously put off. "I think you should leave. Go enjoy the festival."

Ronin agreed, grasping my hand to pull me out the door. I didn't know what to feel or how to fill the emptiness growing inside.

I will never get my answers, will I?

The music and ruckus outside seemed so out of place. I frowned deeply, tears welling in my eyes at the knowledge that I may never know who I am or where I came from. Just a whole load of nothing, like Violetta said.

We started going toward the main walkway, and every step made my heart feel heavier and heavier. I could've handled grieving parents I never knew. I could've handled being the last of whatever I was. I could've absorbed that to move on.

But the fact that there was *nothing* to grieve made everything feel so much worse.

All I could see was emptiness. A cast of blue crashing waves with darkness beneath it. A darkness I'd never see into. I'd never see the bottom.

Why does that feel so unbearable?

"Hey, hey." Ronin's voice pulled me out of my thoughts. "Look at me, sweetheart."

I looked up at him, at an utter loss.

His fingers wove between mine. "Let's go to the festival."

"What? How can we go to the festival right now after that?"

"Because I want to dance with you," he said, intense eyes capturing mine.

Confusion tightened the crease between my eyebrows. "You want to dance with me?"

He nodded, his hands coming up to cup my face, thumbs stroking away my frown. "Listen, we don't know what any of this means, but I sure as the Hells am not going to let you suffer in your own thoughts."

Emotion welled in my eyes and spilled over. Even in the emptiness of the sea, Ronin was still there like a beaming light, reminding me that I didn't have to sink. I could swim to the surface.

"Fuck," he groaned, pulling away to rub at the back of his neck. He scrubbed at his face as if desperately seeking the right thing to say.

I didn't understand his reaction until I felt the tears streaming down my face. "These aren't because of you."

He sighed. "I just want to make you feel better, sweetheart."

He can be sweet when he wants to be.

I sniffled, rubbing my nose. "Thank you." I took a deep,

wavering breath. "You know what? You're right. Everything is a big question mark, but I'm not going to learn anything new by moping around."

He showed off his dimples. "The night is young. Let's have some fun before we ask the big questions in the morning."

I threaded my fingers through his, rocking our hands together. "What a marvelous plan."

There was no point in dwelling, so I decided to have a good night. Not a distraction. Not a coping mechanism. I didn't need to escape the uncertainty of the present. I was choosing to let myself be happy for a change.

With every new step, the dread steadily melted away. We wandered the stalls of the market, finding Enya chatting with a merchant. Gunny was wide-eyed at the blacksmithing demonstration. And among the wiggling, dancing bodies, Luella and Andra were spinning and laughing with the music.

Ronin caught me staring longingly at the dance floor. "Do you want to dance?"

"Yes," I answered too quickly.

He grinned at me, pulling me with him over into the heart of the music. Then it occurred to me that I had no idea how to dance. I would purposefully step on the foot of every tutor at the castle. Eventually Varric stopped ordering the lessons. Unfortunately, that meant that I never learned how to dance properly.

What if I stepped on his foot?

Or tripped?

Or—

"Come here," he rumbled, winding an arm around my waist and pulling me into his chest. I gasped when he spun me around.

I lost my balance, face burning up completely when I fell into his arms like a dead fish.

He chuckled, and I was so relieved he found my clumsiness endearing and not embarrassing. The melody rang through my bones, and I steadied myself. I threw my arms around his neck and tried to sway along with the music.

Dear Gods, I have absolutely no rhythm.

"You're so charming," he murmured. "But we're not two virgins at our first festival." He gripped my hips with either hand, pulling me so close that I could feel his breath against my lips.

My mouth watered, and my mind turned fuzzy for a moment before I responded, "This is my first festival, and I've never danced without the intention of stomping on my partner's foot."

He laughed. "That sounds like something you'd do."

The music picked up, and he spun me again. My eyes went wide, but I didn't trip over my own two feet this time.

"But you dance like this all the time. You just don't realize it." He turned me around, arm flat against my waist as my back collided with his chest.

I couldn't dance… but he *definitely* could. He was a musician, great with a sword, and he knew exactly what rhythm I liked when he had me sprawled out underneath him.

My belly tightened with a flush of heat. Lust coiled there, a dull ache starting to throb between my legs. *It's been so long.*

My eyelashes fluttered, tingles shooting up my spine. He'd wound me up several times over the past week, but it had never been the right time. He wouldn't initiate anything despite those eyes raking me up and down every time he saw me.

"Dancing isn't too different from sparring." His hands slid up my waist, even more maddening since I wasn't looking at him. My nipples tightened in anticipation, but I knew he wasn't going to touch me like that here. Especially not when anyone else could see us.

I knew how possessive he was when it came to intimacy.

I gulped, trying to swallow down all the desire trapping the words in my throat. "How so?"

"I move, *you react.*"

Before I could think about what he'd said, he spun me back to face him and dipped me backward. A giggle left my lips as he held me there. The music hummed through me as I hooked one of my legs around his hip, finding the right movement to complement the melody.

"Attagirl," he said as I moved with him, winding around him in time with the music.

It was just like how we'd spar, only this time I didn't have a cutlass. I beamed, laughing again as we danced. It felt so good to touch him like this, to *move* like this.

This was a type of intimacy we hadn't experienced yet, and I drank up every second of it.

He returned my smile with a blinding one of his own. My heart hammered as his hands grazed my hips again, and I arched my back, needing to be closer.

Excitement thrummed inside me. My pulse roared in my ears, hands buzzing with the desire to feel the heat of his skin. My mouth went dry, as all I could think about was dragging him into a kiss.

I felt my eyelids droop, my lips parting in a clear invitation.

Ronin's eyes dropped to my mouth, and he drew his lower lip between his teeth. His pupils were blown to the Hells, nothing but a thin thread of dark brown around them, blue crystal sparkling in their depths.

The song slowed, and I wasn't sure how many of them we danced through, but I knew I didn't want to dance anymore. That, and we were wearing far too many clothes and there were far too many eyes around for me to do what I wanted.

"I'm tired," I said, my gaze darting between his mouth and his eyes.

"Tired?" His throat worked down a swallow, and I wanted to sink my teeth into that strained tendon.

"Exhausted." I kept staring at his neck, a bead of sweat welling in the hollow between his collarbones. It captured my attention, and my tongue darted out to swipe my lower lip. "Would you take me back?"

He knew *exactly* what I was asking.

"Are you sure that's what you want?" His voice came out incredibly low.

My scalp tightened with delight.

Yes. "I am. I want you."

He closed his eyes as a blissful sigh crawled up his throat to puff across my face. It was as if he had been craving those words. He pulled me deeper into his arms, breathing in the scent of my hair. "I'll wait as long as I need to."

I veered back, stretching my arm to curl my fingers into the hair at the nape of his neck. "I'm done waiting. Are you?"

He melted into my touch, leaning down to press his forehead against mine. "Yes."

One of his hands left my hip to pinch my chin between his thumb and index finger. Without another word, he captured my lips in a tender kiss.

MAEVE CROSS

Back at the inn, we stumbled up the stairs, grinning like fools.

Ronin pinned me against the door to his room and kissed me like his life depended on it. I sighed against his lips and got up on my toes, giving back as much as I was given. Lust flared in my belly, welling between my legs as I devoured him.

Never stop kissing me.

He moaned when my fingernails bit into his shoulders, the thick column of his cock pressing against my stomach. I slid one of my hands up the back of his neck, pulling and scratching at his scalp.

He groaned in response, kicking my legs apart to notch himself right where I ached for him. A mutual noise of desperation left our lips as I arched my back, meeting each grind of his hips. He grumbled with annoyance as he reached for the doorknob, struggling with the room key.

I whined when he pulled away to open the door, hooking one of my legs around his hip.

"Be fucking patient, Mae," he groaned, even if he wasn't much better. He shuddered, getting thicker against me.

"I've been fucking patient," I retorted, soaking wet between my legs. "If you can't open the door, I'm having you in the hallway."

"Absolutely fucking not." He glared at me, nearly growling. "I'll be damned if anyone else sees you like this."

"Then open the blasted door, or I will not be held responsible for my actions."

His hand fell to my leg, unwinding me from him briefly as he unlocked the door. "Fucking door."

He grasped my shirt with his other big hand, guiding me backward into the room. My nipples beaded underneath the fabric, and I secretly wanted him to rip the damn thing open even if I'd have to spend the morning repairing it.

He slammed the door closed and locked it before pulling me roughly back into him.

Our lips crashed back together. I melted into him as his hands roamed up and down my sides. I missed how he tasted. How he felt against me. Tingles ran across my skin. My belly tightened, thighs smashing together to quell the tension rising within me.

I pulled back and delighted in the sight of his swollen lips. The inky desire threaded through his pupils. He stared at my lips as if it physically pained him not to kiss me. His breath came out in ragged gasps.

"Someone is desperate," I teased, raising my pointer finger to run it across his lips. He shuddered, his mouth falling open as he thrust his hips forward. His body betrayed how badly he craved me, and I wasn't above drawing it out.

If he could toy with me, I could toy with him.

"Damn it. Don't play with me, sweetheart," he muttered, gritting his teeth as he tried to capture my lips.

I evaded him.

He gripped my hips even harder as he tried to kiss me again, and I moved at the last moment so he only kissed my cheek. He groaned, making all sorts of needy noises that I'd never heard from him before.

But I need more.

Whenever he took me to bed, he was in control. Completely. Deciding the positions. Bending me whichever way he wanted. It was what he needed, so I let him take it. I never complained, but tonight would be different.

He wasn't trying to distract himself with intimacy tonight. And neither was I. We were both so incredibly present in that moment that I noticed things I wouldn't have otherwise.

I noted the tremor in his shoulders. He held me closer as if he couldn't stand the thought of being any farther away. His eyes were dark and hooded, that tendon in his neck strained from how hard he clenched his jaw.

He was desperately holding himself back.

His hands are shaking.

"You're shaking," I murmured, cupping his hands with mine.

As soon as I pointed it out, his eyes flared open, glossy and full of helplessness. A soft, tender expression took over his face. "I am. Fucking Hells." He drew back, that thick throat of his working down a swallow.

His hands left my hips, and he rubbed the back of his neck. For a split second, I was worried I'd spoiled the moment, but he still strained against the front of his trousers, aching to be set free.

"I'm a little overwhelmed," he admitted, a pink hue deepening his already flushed face.

I tilted my head to the side, loving how I affected him. I stepped forward, drawing my hands down his arms with featherlight touches to test how he tolerated it.

Is this too much, too fast? I stared into his eyes, searching for any sign that he didn't want this. I played with the buttons of his shirt, and he tossed his head back, groaning deeply.

"We can stop anytime you want," I offered seriously.

Ronin objected with a harsh nip on the soft place under my ear. "You might as well just fucking kill me."

That elicited a giggle from me. Newly emboldened, I slid my fingers between the slats of his shirt, unbuttoning it one by one. Painfully slowly.

It was easy to lose myself when I was with him, get swept up into a violent current and ride the wave too quickly. I had no intention of rushing this. With every new strip of skin revealed, I got on my toes to kiss it, sliding my tongue teasingly down his chest. I'd occasionally nip, sucking hard enough to leave a mark.

Ronin rewarded me with a throaty noise of surrender each time, which only made me want to do it again. "So godsdamn cheeky," he hissed.

"It's your favorite thing about me," I replied, pushing his shirt off his shoulders. I grabbed his belt, jerking him against me.

The minor act of aggression blew his eyes wide, heart thrumming with excitement as his cock twitched against my stomach.

"How do you want me, baby?" I asked.

Ronin swallowed, his chest rising and falling rapidly. He tilted his head back when I slid my tongue along his nipple, making his hips bump hard against my stomach. "What kind of question is that? You could get away with just about anything right now."

"*Anything?*"

"Anything that involves you sinking down on my cock," he clarified. "I need to remind myself how fucking good your sweet cunt feels around me."

His filthy mouth.

I missed it. A full-body shiver ran rampant, and I moaned, pressing my thighs together. His words alone could push me to the edge of oblivion. "*Ronin*," I complained.

"Do you want me to remind you how full my cock makes you feel, baby? Hm?"

He grasped my throat, not squeezing, just demanding my attention while my knees shook. My insides clenched around nothing, molten honey flowing through my veins.

"I... I...," I stammered, trying to speak, but my mouth wouldn't let me.

"Words, Mae. Use your words."

That condescending tone added to my torment. I gulped, feeling a surge of wetness dampen my undergarments. My nipples tightened to the point of pain and pressed against my blouse. I ached to feel his mouth *everywhere*.

I grasped the hand that wasn't around my throat and brought it down to the laces of my breeches. "Do you want to see for yourself?"

He looked like he wanted to devour me entirely. He released me, taking a full step back. "Show me."

Ronin's attention never left me as he sat on his bed, still unmade from that morning, his hands fisted at his sides. His legs wide so I could see his cock tenting his trousers.

My confidence soared as I pulled my blouse over my head, hearing his breath catch as he made a noise of agony. My nipples ached, my breasts feeling heavy as I yearned for him to touch them.

Instead, I cupped them, moaning softly as I pinched my nipples, sliding my hands down my soft stomach to undo the laces. The various expressions of anguish crossing his face made me feel greedy. I wasn't ready to climb on top of him just yet.

I wanted to tease.

I wanted to give him a taste of torment.

Before he could object, I slipped my hand into my breeches, gasping as my fingertips slicked along my swollen clit. My eyelashes fluttered closed as I embraced the pleasure. My belly tightened more, heat welling at the base of my spine.

"Look at me." Ronin's voice cut through the haze. "Right fucking *now*."

When I opened my eyes, delight rushed through me at the sight of his cock in his fist. Everything tightened, my inner walls fluttering around nothing. Pearlescent arousal beaded at the crown of his cock as he stroked himself.

Even though he wasn't touching me, I could feel him *everywhere*. His eyes hungered for me, devouring me as ravenously as his hands would. The longer I teased him, the more completely I ruined my breeches, fully saturating the fabric with every glide of my fingertips.

He groaned, tilting his head back as if all he could imagine was how good it would feel when he had me. When the teasing was over, and we could lose ourselves. I'd drink him in as if he were the last taste I'd ever have, and I knew he'd return the sentiment in full.

"*Gods*, look at you," he panted, barely stringing words together as lust flushed his face. "Those fucking tits. Take your fucking trousers off so I can see how fucking wet you are."

His cock swelled even more as he stroked himself. Every filthy thing he said turned him on, his fist gripping harder, rubbing faster. I got so wrapped up in watching that I wasn't even touching myself anymore. Instead, I listened to him groan and huff and make all sorts of noises.

Ronin was relatively quiet with his pleasure. He always had been, but like this, all pent up and impatient, he was deliciously vocal.

I ached to touch him and feel that velvety smooth skin in

my hands, throbbing and hard. So swollen that he'd burst any moment. I ached to watch him groan in agony, a type of pain only I could soothe.

And I would.

But he would have to beg me for it first.

I had no plans of giving myself over easily.

"Mae," he ground out between his teeth, leaning back on one of his thick arms while he gave me a show of his pleasure. "Get your fucking ass over here."

A mischievous grin pulled at my lips. I liked him like this. Achy and desperate. "Why would I do that when you look like this?" I finished unlacing my breeches and pinched my fingers around the waistband but didn't pull them down. "I'd rather you sit and watch like a good boy."

Oh, he doesn't like that.

He made this deep growly noise, looking more tormented than angry. He released his cock, breathing heavily as it slapped against his stomach. "When I get my hands on you—"

"Uh, uh, uh." I wagged my finger. "You touch me, I stop. Do you want me to stop?"

With narrowed eyes, he retorted, "I *want* to bend you over every fucking surface in this room until you can't use your legs anymore."

He could threaten me all he wanted, but they were empty. The second I told him to stop, he would, no matter how badly he didn't want to. I could be on my knees, but I still had power over him.

This magnificent man could easily overpower me in any situation. But I had him ready to bend over backward for me. This man was *mine* in every sense of the word.

I wanted to push him to the edge.

I'd lost myself every time we were together. Once upon a time, he used to lose himself with me, but I hadn't seen that side of him since I got him back from Farlight Prison.

"Yes or no, Ronin."

He huffed in pure carnal frustration. "No. Okay? No. Now get over here and fuck me."

Not good enough. "Say please."

"*Please*, you fucking brat."

I tsked. "So rude."

He released a noise of exasperation and said the next statement with exaggerated niceties, as if he'd dipped his tongue in sugar. "Please, my darling Mae, get over here and fuck me like you mean it before all my blood goes to my cock and *I fucking die.*"

A smile curled the corners of my mouth as I wiggled my breeches down and kicked them into a corner of the room. I was drenched from all the teasing. He hadn't even touched me yet. Because I couldn't get enough of his torment, I slipped my hand back down to my clit.

My hips bucked when I touched myself, a startled cry leaving my lips at how sensitive it was. I rubbed gentle circles around myself, whimpering at the pleasure while Ronin watched patiently.

Well, patiently for him.

He glared at me, hissing expletives. Surprisingly, he remained still, even though he looked like he wanted to bend me over his knee and spank me until my ass was red.

"Mae," he growled, "if you keep doing that, I'm not going to be able to stop from finishing all over myself, and I'd much rather do that when you're choking the life from my cock."

I whimpered, slipping my clit between two soaking wet fingers. Ronin looked wild, like he became more beast than man the longer I denied him. I preferred him like this. Through lowered lashes, I watched his hands tighten into white-knuckled fists. The crown of his cock made a mess against his stomach, so swollen it looked like it hurt.

"*Fucking Hells, Mae.* Please." He watched me through half-lidded eyes, his face completely flushed, rocking his hips unconsciously as if trying to take the pressure away. *"Shit."*

His eyes fell closed, his teeth sinking into his lower lip.

I'm going to remember this visual of him to keep me warm at night if we're ever apart.

I couldn't take it anymore. My legs moved without my approval, my core clenching over and over again. My entire body cried out for him. I stopped myself, pressing my thighs together. I denied myself until I got what I wanted.

"Beg."

I didn't even realize I'd said it out loud until Ronin's eyes flew open. He panted, pupils completely dilated.

"Baby," he murmured, all breathy. That alone made my knees weaken. *"Please.* I want you so fucking badly, I can't think of anything else. Everything *hurts* for you. Please take it away, sweetheart. Put me out of my misery."

With every word, I inched closer toward him until my knees brushed his and he released the most guttural noise. It all felt like too much. My chest was too tight. The scent of cedar and sea air was too intense. He shuddered when I draped one leg over him, straddling his lap as he sat on the edge of the bed.

"Can I touch you now?" he panted.

I stared into his eyes, cupping his face with both hands. "Yes," I murmured before I captured his lips in a soft kiss.

Both of his arms tightened around me instantly as he reciprocated the kiss, nipping my bottom lip and diving his tongue into my mouth. I moaned softly, rising up onto my knees.

One of my hands left his face to grasp his cock. He groaned, and his hips bucked wildly as I touched him. I notched him right against where I was drenched, rubbing him back and forth.

"Shit. Fucking—" His curses got lost as I rocked myself against him, moaning as I saturated him with my desire.

Every other word out of him was a curse, but I loved him for it. His filthy mouth and unabashed appetite for me.

We were panting against each other, my belly growing tighter as heat bunched at the base of my spine. My core clenched around nothing, aching so badly for him that I thought I'd die if I didn't take him.

He grasped my hips hard, as if he, too, couldn't take much more.

My clit swelled with every nudge of his cock until I positioned him at my slit, then sank down slowly.

"*Fuck. Fuck. Fuck,*" Ronin swore into my mouth as I released a noise of mutual pleasure. He pulled back, jaw slack as sweat beaded along the thick cords of his neck.

The tense muscle of his throat was so enticing that I leaned in and slid my tongue across it, nibbling and kissing as I rolled my hips, taking more of him deep inside. "*Ronin,*" I moaned. "You feel so *good.*"

"Sweetheart," he uttered, barely able to speak past his clenched teeth. "You're perfect. So fucking perfect."

I sank down farther, engulfing him entirely. His arms shook around me, and he pressed his forehead against mine. I felt so full, so *connected.* Goose bumps rose across my arms, lust coiling hotter in my belly. My walls fluttered around him, and he moaned loudly. He ground his hips upward, the head of his cock rubbing a sensitive soft spot deep inside me.

It'd been a while since we had sex, and despite my mind and heart crying out in relief, my body objected. Discomfort pinched my spine, and I couldn't help the little whine from falling from my lips. The slow grinding of our hips stopped.

Ronin's hand curled in my hair, and he pulled my head back gently. He definitely heard me. "Are you all right?"

I released a shuddering breath. "I just need a moment to get used to you."

He pressed a kiss against my forehead. "We don't have to do this."

So sweet. Even as his brows pinched together and his hips stuttered in desperation, he cared about my comfort first.

"I must've not made myself clear," I stated, staring deeply into his eyes.

Confusion danced across his face, as if he was having a hard time focusing on anything but the way I was squeezing his cock. "What's not clear?"

I rocked my hips hard, winding up to swallow him entirely. The discomfort was gone, replaced by molten desire.

He barked a curse, grasping my hips to slow me down. His eyes rolled back for a moment, and he panted heavily. *"Fucking Hells."*

"You can be really sweet when you're not being rude, but I want this." I rose and sank down again slowly, enjoying every inch. I tilted my head back and moaned, vocally showing him how I craved him. *"Gods,* I want you."

He groaned my name when he loosened his grip on my hips, letting me churn my body against him, rising and sinking on his cock. Stars flitted across my vision when I rose all the way up to slam back down. Ronin's hands tensed on my hips, bouncing me on his cock while he released a slew of curses.

We held each other tight, me rocking up and down while he thrust up to spear me deeply. I could feel him getting thicker and thicker while my body fluttered.

A give and take.

I wrapped my arms around his neck, panting and moaning his name. He stared into my eyes, forehead resting against mine as we lost ourselves in each other. His glorious body propelled me higher and higher toward the clouds.

Sweat ran down the nape of his neck, and mine beaded across my chest. He leaned down to lick a line across my throat, sucking on an especially tender spot that had me making all sorts of indiscernible noises.

I bowed my back, pressing my breasts into his chest. He groaned and slid his tongue across any patch of skin he could reach.

"Mae…. Fuck, *Mae*." He hummed my name repeatedly.

Our bodies moved on their own, perfectly coordinated with the other. I could feel my body getting more sensitive, more swollen as my clit bumped into his pelvis, grinding against his stomach.

So…

So close…

Oh Gods….

All the tension inside me came to a blistering head, exploding with a potent sensation of relief. I tilted my head back and cried out, tears slipping down my cheeks as he held me close, my orgasm lightening my head into a hazy blissfulness.

A rapturous warmth slid up my skin, ebbing all over my body as I tightened around him. I felt him get thicker, adding a new wave of euphoria to my orgasm.

He swore, punching his hips up as his thrusts lost their rhythm. He pressed his face into the crook of my neck, panting as his cock swelled and spilled inside me.

We gasped, sweating profusely. He murmured something against my throat, peppering soft kisses there. I fell slack in his arms, no energy left to keep myself upright. Ronin groaned again and flopped onto his back with me on top of him.

"Gods, we're filthy," I said, burying my face in his chest.

He didn't say anything, so I leaned back to look at him. His eyes looked all sleepy, as if he was ready to curl up with me and never let me go. My heart knocked against my ribs, aching for the same thing.

But he loosened his grip. "Go hit the head, and then we'll clean up."

"Together?"

"Together."

I nuzzled the side of his face before getting up. I glanced over my shoulder at Ronin. He was watching me like I was *everything* to him.

And he was everything to me.

"I love you, you know."

"I love you, too, sweetheart."

33

RONIN MURDOCH

I WOKE up to the view of a golden halo surrounding Mae's head. The sun had finally burst through the rolling clouds, sending a column of light around the woman in my arms.

She had a magnetic quality, even in her sleep. And I was helplessly drawn in by every detail. Her hair mussed against the pillows. Her soft breathing as she nuzzled my chest. Her skin soothed mine, her body perfectly molded against me.

Before I did anything else, I pressed a kiss against her tempting mouth. She hummed in her sleep, those pink lips falling open. Her eyes crinkled as she rolled over, fitting her ass against my cock.

She wriggled happily, making a little noise of contentment before her sleepy wheezes filled the room again. The scent of her hair kicked up my pulse, making my heart hammer against her back as warmth spilled into my chest.

I had settled into a slice of paradise.

My beautiful girl....

"I love you," I murmured, kissing her soft neck.

Half asleep, she muttered something, pressing her back against me. A tremor ran across her shoulders, the bare skin prickling as my breath tickled her. Under the blanket, she stretched. Her breath shallowed as she stirred awake.

"Good morning," I said. I brushed my lips against the nape of her neck.

She sighed, throwing her head to the side in an offering. I could only give her what she wanted, sampling the soft flesh with kisses and wet presses of my tongue.

"Morning," she replied, shuddering again, moving against my hands that were tracing subconscious circles on her hips.

I could feel the goose bumps rising across her hips, the bare skin of her thighs reacting to the smallest touch. "How did you sleep?" I asked against her throat, my hands roaming up to her waist, then the soft curve of her belly and up to the silky shells of her breasts.

"Well, I closed my eyes, and then I—" she teased before I nipped her shoulder.

Her answering giggle rivaled the morning music of the birds and chirping insects outside.

"Brat."

She turned her head to look over her shoulder at me. I could dive into those beautiful brown eyes, nearly honey-colored from the sun reflected in them. A rich shade of gold worth more than the coin from my years of pirating.

Her face was dusted with that pink shade I liked, and her lips pulled up in a blinding smile.

"It was everything," she answered shyly before adding, "And you?"

It was one of the few nights I hadn't been woken up by some tormented thought. I felt rested and beyond happy that I'd opened my eyes to find Mae in my arms. I wasn't over-whelmed or touched out. It felt *right*.

I didn't answer, my gaze flitting to the delicate bow of her petal-pink lips. I brought one of my hands up over the blanket to cup her face, kissing her deeply as if that would tell her everything I needed to say.

She moaned against my mouth, a rapturous noise that went right to my cock. I was already half hard from waking up next to her. But with the taste of her on my lips and the smell of her surrounding me, I stiffened painfully.

I didn't need to make the first move because Mae rocked her ass against me. A jolt of lust rang through me, from the tingling of my scalp to the tips of my toes. Her nipple hardened in my hand that cupped her breast.

I drew back, finding those wide brown eyes completely dilated. "We don't have a lot of time."

"Then let's make the most of it," Mae replied unevenly with another torturous rock of her hips.

My cock grew even harder at the breathy way she spoke, her eyelashes fluttering as she moved against me, arching deeply so I could feel how fucking slick she was. Her eyes closed, a soft whimper rumbling up her throat.

I don't think so.

My hand slipped from her face to her throat, demanding she look at me. "Eyes."

She obeyed, meeting my gaze with a ravenous one of her own. She looked as fucking hungry as I felt. But there was no mistaking the *brat* that flared in her eyes. With an exaggerated flourish, she turned around so she wasn't looking at me, neck arched toward the ceiling as she offered her throat to me.

I fucking loved it when she misbehaved.

I tightened my grasp just barely. "Show me what you want," I whispered in her ear, nipping the lobe and feeling her pulse jump.

Mae didn't speak, only reached for my hand that was pinching her nipple and brought it down between her legs.

I groaned deep in my chest. "You're always so fucking wet for me," I rumbled, my own heart rate kicking up at the mere thought of holding her against me while she broke. "Do you want me to touch you? Play with you?"

"Yes," she whimpered. "Please."

"If we weren't so pressed for time, I'd feast on you for breakfast," I said, strumming her swollen clit.

I borrowed some of her arousal to slick my fingers, moving them in circles. She shook, breath puffing out harder as she strained against my grasp on her throat.

"R... *Ronin*," she moaned, torn between grinding against my cock or my fingers.

I had her completely trapped within my arms, and I wouldn't have it any other way. The thought of releasing her or putting any sort of distance between us felt like fucking torture.

I ached for her touch, the noises only I could draw from her, the perfect feeling of her coming apart around me.

"Maybe I'd deny you until you begged for me." I blew hot air into her ear, and her thighs trembled. "Or I'd be the one begging to taste that sweet fucking cunt so I could see how many times you'd soak my face."

"*I'd.... Filthy...,*" she choked out right as I slid two fingers inside her. Her back bowed, and she cried out. "Oh *Gods.*"

"Hmm, baby? What was that?" I teased, toying with her as I curved my fingers up into a soft, spongey place behind her clit. As badly as my cock ached, I got off more on her pleasure. I could reach my end easily, but I prided myself on getting her there first.

Between desperate pants, she uttered, "I'd ride that filthy mouth." She took a deep breath. "But only if you beg for it."

I grinned, thrusting my fingers even harder as her body writhed, inner walls fluttering. Her clit swelled against my palm, the sweet spot inside her getting firmer. "You liked that last night, didn't you?"

"Uh-huh." I watched the blanket over us move as her hands came up to her nipples. I could only imagine how she was twisting them. "That was fun."

The noises falling from her lips became incoherent as I

worked her toward the pinnacle. She got wetter as my palm bumped against her clit, squeezing my fingers in little flutters. I added another, pounding against the spot that had her writhing. Goose bumps erupted across her shoulders, her head tossed back against my chest. Her mouth fell open, and I was mesmerized by it.

My cock twitched against her. Her hips punched against my hand, and her eyes rolled back. Her cunt clenched around my fingers with exquisite pulses. A rush of silky arousal saturated my hand and the bed as she cried out, falling completely slack against me.

Her muscles shuddered as aftershocks wreaked havoc through her body.

"That's my girl." Even though I hadn't found my release yet that morning, I felt rather pleased with myself.

She flopped over onto her back, tossing the covers off. "You… you…." Her pupils were blown to the Hells, a silly grin plastered all over her face. "*Scoundrel.*" She giggled, and I couldn't help but return her smile.

"And don't you forget it," I teased, sitting up in bed. My cock was still rock hard, and it didn't help that Mae was still glistening between her legs, my hand still soaking wet.

I brought my pointer finger to my lips, getting a taste of her before I got a better idea.

"You made such a mess, baby. I don't want it to go to waste."

Her eyes wide, she kept her complete attention on me as I used her spend to stroke myself. I reached between her legs, borrowing the liquid silver to slick myself up. It was absolutely filthy, the lewdness of the gesture unbelievably erotic.

I glided my hand up and down, paying special attention to the pulsing ridge on the underside of my cock. Pleasure welled in my belly with every stroke. I grew thicker, groaning deep in my throat as I put on a show for her.

Mae watched intensely, her eyes growing hooded again. It

turned me on to see how dark they got, the pink in her cheeks deepening. The honey in her gaze disappeared as inky desire blew her pupils wide, her bottom lip sandwiched between her teeth as if she wanted to swallow me instead.

She looked like she was committing every little motion to memory, learning what I liked, and had every intention of using the newfound knowledge against me later.

Any other occasion, I would encourage her to use it now. But we didn't have a lot of time, and I'd want her to suck me off for far longer than was possible at the moment. My cock swelled, growing thicker. My heart raced, and my head tilted back as my orgasm unfurled and heat pooled in the base of my spine.

I swore when I came, tightening my hand around myself to prolong it while my hips bucked. I spilled across my abdomen, groaning loudly when I finally came down from it.

My eyes squeezed closed, but when I opened them again, Mae was on her hands and knees in front of me. Her tits hung down, and I was going to fucking die from all my blood going back to my cock again.

"Mae—" I started, but she shut me up when she bent her head down and licked my own mess off me. My eyes grew wide as the filthiest noise fell from my lips. "*Mae.*"

She moaned softly, drawing her tongue across my cock and up my abdomen.

This is it.

This is how I die.

My heart is going to fucking give out.

"Can't let it go to waste, can we?" she murmured, rising onto her knees when she was finished.

Without thinking, I grasped the back of her head, tangling my fingers along the nape of her neck, and yanked her into a hard kiss. I tasted myself on her tongue, and I knew she could taste herself, too, which only made the kiss that much hotter.

We were getting all worked up again when a knock finally sounded on my door.

"We have to get going. Wrap it up," Luella yelled, probably waking up the entire inn.

I pulled away from Mae, and her face was bright red as always. "Fine," I shouted back. I turned back to Mae and kissed her again, softly this time. "She's right, you know."

Mae gave me a warm smile. "I know. I love you."

I pressed my forehead against hers. "I love you too. Let's try to get some breakfast before Pinky guides us back."

"I already had my breakfast," she replied.

An unexpected laugh spilled from my lips. "You're so fucking cheeky. Get that ass to breakfast before I give you another meal."

"Yes, *Captain.*"

I didn't reply, pinching her chin between my thumb and pointer finger. *I'm going to make her ass red the next time I have her alone.*

She stuck her tongue out, and I caught a glimpse of my spunk on the corner of her mouth. She made a move to get up, but I stopped her. "Wait, love. I can't let you go with me painted over your mouth. That's for *me* to see." I wiped it off with my thumb, and her cheeks deepened to a lovely shade of red.

I wasn't a possessive man, but when it came to our intimate moments, they were *ours.*

She slowly got out of bed.

I didn't get up right away, just watched her gather her clothes, loving the way she looked with the sunlight casting her in a glow.

34

MAEVE CROSS

WHILE RONIN, Enya, and Andra went off to the ship, I stayed with Gunny and Luella at the tavern downstairs while they retrieved our supply cache. Even in the morning, the tavern bustled with energy. Sailors and townspeople came and went.

I propped myself up on a stool, and the barmaid gave me a hot cup of tea while I waited.

"We'll be right back," Luella said, whisking Gunny away to the back room with the innkeeper.

A warm fuzziness spread in my chest, a smile fixed on my face. I sipped on my tea, humming a happy little tune to myself. I sighed, thinking about Ronin and how wonderful it felt to wake up next to him.

I felt taken care of. *Valued.* Even just the way he kissed me before he left, murmuring sweet nothings against my lips that were only meant for my ears.

How he held me close and made me feel special. My heart felt full, void of the emptiness I'd felt last night.

Even if I never discover who I was, I can be happy with who I am.

He would love me all the same. I still had my family—the crew. The people always in my corner.

My mind wandered over to Wesley and Isa, and I couldn't wait to see them again.

Dinner and the laughter of children.

Card games and drinks after the kids went to bed.

The moments of peace that felt infinite. A reminder of what all this pain was for.

I knew without a doubt that I *did* have a family, even if it was made up of all the people I met along the way. I could argue that they were the best family one could ask for.

Misfits always make the best company.

My chest got warmer as happiness flushed through me again. I was where I belonged.

"I know that look. Someone's in love," the barmaid teased, shining a glass and pouring ale for a few of the patrons. She moved effortlessly through her tasks, her eyes twinkling at me.

I couldn't help it as my smile broadened. "I am."

Out of my peripheral vision, I noticed a shadow taking a seat on the stool next to me.

"What can I get you?" the barmaid asked.

"I'll take whatever she's having," the man answered.

I know that accent. Skadian.

I glanced over at the tall, slender figure next to me, a broadsword fastened on his back. He leaned over the bar, his stark yellow eyes flashing to me and then back to the steaming mug of black tea the barmaid placed in front of him.

He scrunched his mouth to the side as if he'd been expecting something else. He raised it to his nose, giving it a curious sniff.

The barmaid raised both eyebrows before slowly asking, "Anything else?"

"No, thank you, *kona*," he replied, voice dropping several

octaves as he sipped on the drink. He had many visible pierc-ings, including at least ten on each extended ear, the silver complementing the lavender color of his skin.

I'd met several dark elves on my journey, but he stuck out far more than anyone else. It wasn't only the piercings. Or that he was clad completely in black. Or even that he had long, fine white hair woven into a neat braid, the same silver adornments he wore on his face also in his hair.

It was *how* he was behaving.

He seemed genuinely unsure how to act in a tavern. He stuck one leg out awkwardly, only to move it when he real-ized he was in the way. Even the way he sipped at the tea was odd. Black tea was a very common drink, but he looked at it like it was going to bite him.

His eyes drifted over to me, and he bluntly asked, "Why are you staring at me?"

There was something familiar about him. "Broadswords aren't common in the Isles," I commented. I'd been prac-ticing with my cutlass, and I wondered how different it would be to swing a broadsword. Would I even be able to lift it properly?

It looked incredibly heavy, and I knew firsthand how one sounded when it cut through the air.

"I've noticed." He leaned on one arm as he gave me the most incredulous expression. He had been aware of me before, but now I had all of his attention.

The man couldn't have been much older than Ronin. Maybe even a little younger. It was difficult to tell when I couldn't get a good look at him beneath all the black clothing.

"Why do you use that instead of a cutlass?" I asked.

"It's how I was trained." He paused, taking another sip of his drink, scowling at the taste. "You're new here, right?"

"I won't be here long. Just restocking before our trek back to Shipwreck Bay," I said.

He hummed. "The pirate safehold? I've never been to that port."

I raised my eyebrows. "Really? It's quite lovely if you have the chance to go. Misfits make the best company, you know."

"I see. Are you traveling alone?"

I nearly laughed out loud. "Oh, no. That's incredibly foolish. If you don't run into the navy, you still have the sirens to worry about and all sorts of other beasties."

He chuckled, waving a hand dismissively. "I've already had the pleasure."

"You must be quite the warrior to fend them off. Sirens are ruthless."

"Child's play," he replied, an arrogant smirk pulling at the side of his mouth. "I'm somewhat renowned for my prowess in battle."

"How did you manage that with the siren song?" I asked.

"Can't sing if they don't have a throat to sing from," he replied nonchalantly.

A tremor of fear licked at the back of my neck, suspicion brewing in my belly. Skadian elves weren't fae, so it made little sense to me that he'd be able to withstand the hypnotic frequency.

"Where are you from?" I wondered. "Skadian elves are rather rare in the Isles."

The arrogant smirk grew, making him look almost like a cat playing with a mouse, its tail trapped between the claws. "You're presumptuous, aren't you? Who's to say I'm from Skadi at all? Dark elves have been nomadic for centuries. Don't pretend like you know anything about us."

A shamed hue brightened my cheeks. "Oh... um—" I stammered.

"Now, where are *you* from, *kona*?" He tapped his clean-shaven jaw in mock curiosity. "If I had to guess, this is your first big trip from home, isn't it? From your sheltered little life. You look far too soft for a life on the seas. Too pretty for hard labor."

My heart kicked up, pounding hard in my chest. Whan an eerily specific comment. Then I narrowed my eyes. "Fuck off. I didn't want to deal with a prick first thing in the morning."

I watched that smirk stretch into a full-blown wolfish grin. "That bite is a welcome surprise." He muttered something in a dialect that was *obviously* Skaditung.

I became even more suspicious.

I'd spent enough time at Siggi's shop to pick out pieces of the language, even if I wasn't fluent in it. For no other reason but spite, I uttered something I often heard Siggi say to Ronin. It didn't translate exactly to Common, but it pretty much meant "You're making an ass out of yourself."

At least that's what I *thought* I'd said before the yellow-eyed man proceeded to laugh. Loudly. Obnoxiously. Honestly, for an otherwise handsome man, he had an ugly laugh. Other patrons looked at us as he doubled over, clasping one hand to his chest. He laughed so boorishly that I noticed that his tongue was a deep shade of blue.

What did I just say?

He clapped his hands together, wiping away a rogue tear. "That's good. Really good. I commend the colorful language." He laughed again. "I *think* you're trying to say—" Then he proceeded to say the exact same thing back to me, but the pronunciation was completely different. "You're lucky we're not in Skadi, or that naughty phrase would've sent you right into the stocks."

My face boiled, but I gulped the embarrassment down. "So you *are* from Skadi, then?"

His mouth curled to the side in a repressed smile, hands held up in defeat. "Fine. Fine. You called my bluff. That's all right. I needed that. I've had a rough few weeks."

"I'm sorry to hear that." I paused. "I've got a Skadian tailor back in Shipwreck Bay, and I haven't gotten the pronunciations down yet."

"No, you haven't. Skaditung is completely tonal, so you need to be careful with it." He cracked another grin, showing off elongated canines.

"If you don't mind me asking, what did I say?" I wondered.

He chuckled again. "The word *making* sounds very similar to *can have*, and *yourself* sounds like *tonight*. You pretty much told me *You can have my ass tonight*, among… other things, and that seems incredibly forward over breakfast tea."

I waved both my hands. "That's *not* what I wanted to say at all."

"Are you sure? You were quite forceful in your cadence."

"I'm very sure that I didn't mean that." My flush traveled up to my ears. "Wait a moment. Are you *coming onto me*? If you are, I'm spoken for."

He laughed, tasting the tea again before replying, "To the Gods, no. That's just my personality."

He pulled a chain up from under his collar to display the pendant dangling from it. Not unlike Luella's. And like Luella's, I could feel a little flicker of magic warping the air around it. It wasn't made of crystal and wood. Instead, it seemed to be carved from eternal ice, a coolness coming off it.

"It drives my wife up the wall." Something darkened the yellow in his eyes as he muttered, "*Drove*," under his breath so quietly that I almost didn't hear him. His smile was gone, a profound mourning deepening the creases of his frown.

"I'm sorry for your loss," I offered hesitantly, unsure if that was the right thing to say.

His eyes met mine, and I caught a spike of *rage*. I could practically taste violence in the air, as if I'd bitten my own tongue. A flicker of winter smoke flooded my nose, and he became vastly more familiar.

The broadsword.

The yellow eyes.

The rage.

I'd seen it all before.

Right before I used the draconite power to propel him off the bridge.

"You survived."

He was following us.

A cold tremor rang down my spine, and I reached to grasp the hilt of my cutlass. His eyes flickered down and then back up again before fixating on something behind me.

"I'll be seeing you, Maeve."

My lips parted to reply. To ask him what he wanted. Why was he following us? What was in this for him? But before I could ask anything, Luella shouted my name, stealing my attention for a split second.

But that was all the distraction the assassin needed to disappear before I glanced back over at him.

He was gone. Nothing left but a mostly full mug of steaming tea.

Ronin. I needed to get to the ketch. What if the assassin had made quick work of him and still had enough time to taunt me?

I rubbed at my chest, fearing that my heart would shatter just at the thought. I sprang up from my seat and made a direct line for Luella. She looked at my face, clearly seeing the fear in my eyes. Instantly, she straightened. Gunny must've felt it, too, because his eyebrows came together in worry.

"Did you see the man next to me?" I asked, my eyes darting all around the tavern in hope of finding him. But he wasn't there. He might as well have disappeared into thin air like the scent of smoke.

Just like he had appeared on the bridge with a plume of thick winter fog.

"Tall and chatty? Yes," she confirmed. "What's going on?"

I tried to quell my worry, panic rising at the thought that the longer we stood here, the less of a chance I'd have to protect Ronin. I didn't want to shout in the middle of a crowded tavern that an assassin was on the loose. That wouldn't help anyone, so instead I said, "Do you remember the Gullies? The cuts in my hands?"

"*Him?*" Luella inquired.

I nodded but didn't need to say anything else. We were on the move.

With Gunny's help, we got our supplies into a skiff and were taken back to where the ketch had been floating the past two days. I didn't have it in me to be afraid of the salties anymore.

As soon as the ketch came into view, I caught sight of Ronin, Enya, and Andra chatting, seemingly unaware of any dangers around them. A few other boats were docked, and I looked them over, trying to see if any of them seemed familiar.

How long had that assassin been following us? Was he using one of the fishing barges I'd seen at Bliss's Colony? Did he buy one of the ships Lucky had been crafting? A million questions filled my head, but I knew I had to tell Ronin and the crew *immediately*.

Ronin took the news about as well as I thought he would. He demanded to know if I'd been hurt and what the elf said to me. He practically puffed up his chest like he wanted to tuck me away in a bundle where I'd be safe.

Sweet, but ultimately unhelpful.

On the main deck, as Luella took us away from Violetta's Haven, I told them everything I knew. I tried to recount every detail from the short conversation in the tavern.

"I don't understand why he taunted you when he could've attacked me on the ketch," Ronin said. "And if he's working for Cross, why would he be trying to kill me?" He hummed, sighing as he scrubbed at his beard. "I wish Howler was here. He's so good at making sense of things."

Enya leaned against the half wall, crossing her arms in deep thought. "Me too. It's odd."

"Unless this assassin *isn't* following orders," Luella commented from the helm.

Ronin looked over at her, a perplexed expression etched across his face.

"Describe him again, Mae," Luella encouraged.

"All right," I agreed, tapping my chin to see if I remembered all the details. "Yellow eyes, lavender-hued skin, *lots* of facial piercings, and he called me *kona*. He's a dark elf but has this wintery magic around him."

"*Kona* is just a polite way to say *girl* in Skaditung," Ronin pointed out.

"Did he have a blue tongue, by chance?" Luella asked.

He did. I nodded, unsure where she was going with this.

She dipped her head, turning the helm to adjust to the wind. She tilted her head back and took a deep breath. "Listen, I'm from Edessa. Enemies of Skadi. Who you *just* described is someone of blue-blooded Skadian royalty. I didn't get a good look at him in the tavern, but no other elf or fae in Algar has a blue tongue and utilizes winter magic."

She had to be right.

Enya shook her head. "Why in the Nine blazing Hells would a Skadian heir be working for Cross?"

Luella shrugged. "I don't know, but that could explain why he isn't following orders."

Gunny chimed in. "You lot aren't even asking the biggest question." We all looked over at him. "How did he get here?"

How did *he get here?*

35

MAEVE CROSS

THE NEXT FEW days were infused with an air of dread. We couldn't get back to Anchorage Cove fast enough. Varric's plan had more moving pieces than we originally thought, and now there was the possibility that the Kingdom of Skadi had allied with him.

We kept an eye on all the horizons, making sure we weren't being followed by some unmarked ship. While we were stressed and exhausted, Ronin did his best to keep his walls down, reassuring everyone that he wouldn't cut us out again.

During the night, I'd catch him on the main deck, his shirt discarded to the side, and I'd watch his tattoo flicker and glow before it ebbed away. He told me that it was getting stronger, but he hadn't found a way to bring his leviathan back to the surface completely.

I believed him.

With the lies behind us, this new channel of communication had opened up between us. The crew and I also had a stronger bond than ever before.

Gunny frequently thought of new ways to exploit my healing, even if Ronin was adamantly against it.

"No one knows, Cap! Think of the deception," Gunny would argue. "Mae could get into places that we could never infiltrate and survive."

I'd be lying if I said I wasn't interested in testing the boundaries. With each new death came a new memory.

But Ronin said, "Over my fucking dead body, Gunny."

He'd be damned if I so much as pricked my finger.

Most of the crew sat somewhere on that spectrum between taking advantage of my gifts or protecting me from them, with Gunny and Ronin punctuating each side.

When we weren't talking or going about our daily duties, Ronin loved to spar. I used to think it was because he needed to be sharp, but he enjoyed the art of a good fight. Sometimes he'd hand me my ass, or he'd lay Gunny out on his back. Occasionally, he'd duel Enya or Andra, but he was noticeably nicer when it came to them.

But Ronin never *ever* sparred with Luella in the company of the crew.

And now I knew why.

"Hit me again!" Ronin demanded, extending a dull sparring cutlass toward Luella.

I leaned against the mast, watching Luella and Ronin duel while Andra acted as the helmsman. Sparks flew as they jumped back and forth, striking each other with wild abandon. I'd never seen either of them so thrilled to fight.

Both of them held back with me.

I hadn't noticed it because of how often they would knock me down and help me up to knock me down again. But neither of them ever struck me with *that much vigor*.

Not to mention, the amount of shit talk bouncing between them was enough to pinken my cheeks.

"You can't take another hit, you fucking cunt," Luella spat back, kicking her leg out to trip him. "I don't want to kill you."

Ronin snorted and dodged her foot. "If you wanted me

dead, I'd be dead." He turned with a flourish, reacting to Luella's attack. "Now hit me like you mean it." The next attack wasn't enough for him, apparently, as he retorted, "Fuck, you've gotten soft."

"Fuck you, you prick! The only thing soft about me are my tits."

"Tell that to your striking arm, fucker."

"Fuck you!"

"No, fuck *you!*"

"That's what I have your sister for!"

Oh my Gods...

Is this what they're like all the time when the rest of the crew isn't around?

Watching them exchange strike after strike, I started to worry that this was in fact a duel to the death and I hadn't noticed. I glanced over at Andra, who shook her head and adjusted the helm to glide along the shallow waves.

Every other word out of their mouths was a curse punctuated by the clash of dulled cutlasses.

I stepped over next to Andra and asked, "Are they always like this during sparring matches?"

She repressed a laugh and replied, "We had to ban them from fighting each other during the brawls on *The Ollipheist.*"

"I take it this is why Howler and Ronin usually train together."

Andra nodded. "Mm-hmm. Don't be concerned, though. This is just how they've always trained together."

We looked over at our partners, who remained in the midst of a vicious sparring session that had me genuinely concerned until they paused their battle when the dull cutlass Luella was using broke off at the hilt.

They looked at each other before laughing.

"Even your cutlass can't hold up to my strikes," Ronin gasped out between fits of laughter. Gods, the sound of his rumbling laughter brought even more warmth to my face.

Luella grinned from ear to ear, shaking her hilt at him wildly. "Piss off. I can take you down with my bare hands, *Captain.*"

Ronin dropped his sword into the barrel of training weapons. "Then come at me, *Lulu.*"

Luella frowned and tackled him as if they were two siblings fighting over the last pastry on a baking tray. Their friendship made more sense to me. Just old friends mucking around because it was how they had fun.

"Did you know that the *first* thing Wraith did when we saved her almost thirteen years ago was deck Levi in the face?" Andra asked, trying hard not to laugh at the childish display in front of us. "He sported a black eye for a week."

I chuckled. "That doesn't surprise me."

"Gods, I remember when the two of them would get into fisticuffs over who would be captain. It didn't help that I egged them on," she admitted, a new expression taking over her features. The corner of her mouth tilted downward.

I couldn't tell what it was.

Regret?

Sadness?

Grief?

Whatever it was, it was incredibly complicated.

What's bothering her?

Perhaps she noticed me looking at her, eyebrows knit together as if trying to search for the right thing to say.

"I favored chaos in my youth," Andra continued. "I enjoyed pressing buttons. Pushing boundaries. The strife between Wraith and Levi was no different. They hated each other, so it was easy."

"What changed?" I asked.

She waved her hand, dismissing the mourning that lingered in her eyes. "Seabird made them duel. Levi won, and by winning, he finally earned Wraith's respect. The rest is history."

I shook my head. "No. With you. I can't imagine you stir-ring up trouble."

That look was back. "I grew up, Mae." The words were sharp and bitter, different from the soft tone Andra usually used when she spoke. She released a sigh, glancing at me. I could see the painful memories washing to the surface. An old scar that reminded her it was there when it started to feel too tight.

"You don't have to tell me anything you don't want to."

"I know that, Mae, but you're such a good listener," she said, reaching over to squeeze my shoulder. "When I was younger, I liked a little chaos. Too much sometimes. And when you're young, you think you're immortal." She cast me a sideways glance, knowing the statement didn't apply to me, but we glossed over it.

I nodded, urging her to continue.

"Shortly after Wraith joined the crew, I thought I was hot shit. I was careless. When we were careening, I didn't choose the right trees. I just wanted it to be over with so I could go to the tavern...."

Oh.

"The line uprooted the trees. The ship crushed three sailors. It was my fault." This was something she'd clearly come to terms with, but that didn't make it hurt any less.

"That's awful. I'm sorry, Andra."

"I learned an important lesson that day. *Safety is every-thing.* Fool around with it and someone will wind up dead. I'll never make that mistake again." She moved the helm. "Wraith was the one who helped me move past it. Levi was training to be captain, and Howler was off writing love letters to Isa. Wraith was there when I needed it."

Andra looked over at her wife, eyes full of fondness. Her face practically glowed with love rivaling the warmth of the breeze. Meanwhile, Luella wrestled Ronin to the ground as if they were just overgrown children.

It was nice to see him open to touch, especially playful ones with his mates. I understood that this might mean that he'd be touched out later, but it'd be worth it.

"Rough around the edges, but she has a heart of gold. Falling in love was the easy part. Admitting it was everything but." She turned her head to cast me a beaming smile, and I couldn't help but return it.

A few feet away, the hatch to the lower deck opened, and Enya popped her head up. I was half expecting Gunny, since it was still a little early for Enya, but he was probably working on his weapon designs.

Meeting with the blacksmiths at Violetta's Haven inspired him, so he spent much of the day deciding what metal to use for weapons and coming up with various cannon and projectile designs to implement on *The Ollipheist.* We could use all the help we could get for the battle to come.

"Like children," Enya commented, laughing under her breath as she watched Ronin and Luella fight. "Do you mind if I steal Mae for a moment?"

"Go ahead. I'm just enjoying the entertainment," Andra said.

I looked at Enya, and she gestured to the quiet side of the ship. We walked to the barrels and sat across from each other. Her pale hair was tied up and tucked under her hat, and she wasn't wearing the three-fingered glove she usually did.

The skin where her fingers had been torn from her was thick, silver, and uneven, but otherwise, it had healed well.

"What did you want to talk about?" I asked.

"I had an interesting discussion with my son when we were preparing the ship after Bliss's Colony. I wanted to sit on it for a while before I talked to you. He opened up to me, and I think I have you to thank for that."

"You're welcome," I said softly, still not sure where this was going.

"I am protective of my kin, and in being that way, I was complicating things. It hasn't been easy, not since I lost my other sons to Cross. Ronin has a lot of weight on his shoulders, and he doesn't need me adding to it with this."

Nerves bloomed in my belly, fluttering around.

"But you can handle this, and I need to get it off my chest…." Enya trailed off as if gauging whether or not I *could* handle this conversation.

"What's going on?"

"I can see why he likes you so much." She crossed her legs, eyeing my face tentatively. "I've grown quite fond of you too. I don't want to see either of you get hurt."

She was beating around the bush, and we both knew it. "Just say what you need to say."

Enya sighed. "All right. For all we know right now, you're fae, Mae. And if you choose each other, Ronin *will* be the last of his kind."

My cheeks flared as I thought back to Violetta's reading. My lack of parentage. "That is turning out to be more complicated than you think."

Confusion flickered across her face. "Are you pregnant?"

I almost laughed at the expression on her face. She clearly wasn't sure if she'd be thrilled or devastated. "Gods, no."

Now it seemed like she wasn't sure whether to be disappointed or relieved.

After sitting on the news Violetta had saddled me with, I was more comfortable with it. My lineage was a big question mark, but I'd also concluded that it didn't change who I was. Enya listened as I recounted what Violetta had told me.

"She couldn't tell you?" she asked as if she couldn't wrap her head around it. "I was certain she'd know."

I shook my head.

Enya tapped her lips. "That doesn't make any sense. Unless something is blocking it."

That was a big possibility. Luella said the same thing

when Ronin and I told her about it over a few drinks after everyone else went to bed. If something so powerful could give me vitality, then it could warp magic too. "In all honesty, I'm trying not to lose sleep over it. But I'd be lying if I said it wasn't on my mind."

"I understand." She sighed. "I *really* do."

How could she possibly understand that? When I gave her a perplexed look, she smiled at me.

"I don't know who my parents are either," Enya explained. "Ronin's father, Raiden, and I created quite the stir with our affair."

My eyes grew wide. I didn't know much about the Royal Leviathan family tree. Only in passing did I discover that Enya and Raiden's marriage was not well received. Varric would only vaguely say that the leviathans didn't want to sully the bloodline. Oddly enough, Varric seemed to only have good things to say about Enya. He valued ambition, but even that hadn't saved her from the coup.

During my youth, Varric kept all the details under lock and key. To the point that he blacked out the history books and destroyed all catalog of the Royal Leviathan family tree.

I wanted to know more. "Do tell. I'm curious."

Enya's eyes softened with fondness. "I adore that you ask questions, Mae. For a long time, I was afraid to." She leaned back, looking up at the sky as the clouds ebbed away into the blue and red of sundown. "I grew up in Farlight Orphanage, teaching myself how to read because I was too poor to afford a proper education. When I aged out, the royal tutor found me scrounging through trash outside bookstores, piecing together tomes and scrolls that were damaged because I believed that knowledge should never be wasted."

Her smile lines deepened.

What happened to that tutor? I wondered but didn't interrupt.

"I guess I charmed her, and she took me in. The king at

the time, Raiden's father, didn't want a street rat in the castle, but the tutor defended me, and I got to study and train under her in the library."

The stories danced in her eyes. Fond and easy.

"Imagine that. Food and knowledge galore. A place to sleep. A dream come true." Her eyes became sad. "Then I met Raiden. He was… so full of himself. Such an arrogant prick."

I laughed, and Enya released a soft one of her own.

"We couldn't stand each other… but then something changed. We no longer saw each other as the spoiled prince and the uptight tutor apprentice." Pinkness dusted her face. "We saw each other in secret for quite some time. It wasn't until a wedding was arranged that he refused to keep me a secret. He was going to marry me, and all the nobles could piss off."

I know how this story ends.

"Together, we started to change things. The kingdom was transforming and… Gods, we were so, *so* in love. Raiden's father *hated* me, but he protected the bloodline, and shortly after I became pregnant with my first son, he hired a sorcerer to join the sentries in palace defense."

"Varric," I said out loud.

She dipped her head. "*Varric.* Raiden's father died mysteriously in his sleep, and I believe Varric had everything to do with it. Around the same time, I was pregnant with my second son…," she trailed off, deep in thought. "Gods, it feels so long ago and hurts like it was yesterday."

She was finished talking about it, gulping down the pain.

"I'm sorry, Enya," I said, but it didn't feel like enough.

"All I'm trying to say is that Raiden and I knew what we wanted. Children are always a part of the royal game. Times have changed, and I'm not at all saying you *need* to have them. But you need to assess if that is what you want. If that is an immovable part of your future." She didn't say it in a cruel way.

I rubbed the back of my neck, deeply uncomfortable. No one wants to talk to their lover's mother about the possibility of having children, especially the uncertainty surrounding that. "I haven't given it much thought. I don't even think it's possible."

My voice came out all squeaky because it was a lie. I'd often wonder what the future would hold, after all this was over. Would we settle in his cabana? Storm the seas? Get a little farm or maybe a bookshop?

Ronin would love a bookshop.

Would our children have his dimples when they smiled?

Maybe his eyes?

Would their ears be pointed like mine were before the tips were taken?

I wondered if I'd meet the children we were before our childhoods were stolen from us.

Enya's left hand came over to mine, those three fingers curling around my hand. I hadn't realized I'd looked away until I glanced up at her, the scarred hand offering a connection I'd never had with her before.

"My son loves you, Mae, and I know you're in love with him too. I saw how broken you two became when he shut you out." Her gaze was soft and tender, resembling the caress of a loving mother. "I don't want to see either of you so distraught again. And wanting a different future than your lover *will* end your relationship. Just give it some thought, all right?"

She wasn't wrong, and I couldn't help but ask, "Is that what happened with you and Lucky? The real reason you didn't work out?"

Enya seemed taken aback by my question. "You and your questions, lass…."

Boundaries, Mae.

I expected her to pull away and put a pin in it for later,

but she didn't. Instead, she took a deep breath. "To an extent, yes. It feels as if it was so long ago, but…."

She got really quiet before continuing.

"Lucky sent me letters. A *lot* of letters. I was so torn up over Albatross's death that I never returned them. Albatross was the tar that stuck us together. The one who smoothed over all the bumps and cracks. We would never work without him. Lucky wanted a quiet life. He wanted everything he never had. I didn't. He said he would protect us if Varric ever came, but I could *never* let that happen."

A fierceness returned to her eyes. The cutthroat captain who protected her crew with the same vigor her son did. The same way I strived to.

"Do you still love him?" I wondered.

Her cheeks flushed, and she looked away. "I miss him, and the love is still there. Lucky would never forgive me for abandoning him. I don't think I'd respect him if he did."

"The alliance will change things," I said confidently. "Maybe you two could become friends again?"

She met my eyes and tilted her head to the side. "Maybe. Only time will tell." She squeezed my hand. "Listen, I'm not telling you that you need to figure everything out right now, but I am telling you that it will hurt more if you're not honest with yourselves."

"I love Ronin. No matter what happens, I want him in my life."

Enya smiled. "All right. That's all I need to know. But just know that you're my family now too. Whatever happens between you and my son, you're one of us." She canted her head downward, pinning me with shining ocean-blue eyes. "And whatever comes of your history, you'll always have a mother to look after you. Blood or not."

RONIN MURDOCH

After dinner, Mae made a habit of coming to my cabin. Nothing satisfied me more than seeing my girl when the sun went down, resting her head against my shoulder or in my lap while we read together.

Even when I tried to shift, I didn't mind her seeing me struggle.

Sometimes, I'd go to her, and we'd stargaze on the top deck with the crew, passing around a bottle of bourbon like those late nights on *The Ollipheist*.

I combed my fingers through her hair like she often did to mine. She'd smile up at me and nuzzle my hands. Luella and Andra would join us, and we'd talk about everything. Even the hard conversations about Mae's vitality or the fact that I couldn't shift.

I wasn't keen on Gunny making jokes about Mae's unnatural healing or how we could use it to our advantage, but it was nice that our once terrifying secrets had become the subject of commonplace chatter.

I was done with the secrets, and so was Mae. *Gods*, it felt good.

So good, in fact, that the leviathan spirit was roused. A

beast awoken from a long rest. Still couldn't shift, but simply knowing it hadn't abandoned me was enough. It didn't feel like as much of an intrusion, like reconnecting a finger after it had been severed. I had to get used to it again. With each passing day, the bond between my spirit and me grew stronger.

One day I'd be strong enough to wield the leviathan again, and it would feel right.

I looked forward to seeing Wesley again, and I wondered how big his son was now. A month was a long time for an infant. I also couldn't wait to see my nieces.

I thought Wesley would be proud of me for chiseling away the ice that I'd previously put up around myself. Not to mention, I had our relationship to repair, given how I left things.

Sometimes Mae and I would lie in my cot and talk about the future.

For a conversation I used to dread, I now loved hearing about her dreams. What she wanted. And finally, after this was all over, I'd be able to give it to her. I could be the man she needed, and truly, I felt stronger now that she was in my life.

There was still uncertainty, but we wouldn't be alone. If we stormed the seas together, we'd be fucking unstoppable. If we retired on the cliffside with Wesley across the path, I'd enjoy that too.

I'd be happy regardless.

Everything was changing. I just hoped it was for the better.

THE PAST WEEK had gone by uneventfully, which was always a good thing when sailing through shallower waters. Sure, the deep oceans had sirens and devil whales to be concerned about, maybe even the kuru if we were exceptionally unlucky, but shallow waters harbored unaligned pirates, harpies, and clawed vipers.

I'd heard too many stories of crew members getting roped and dragged off the boat in shallow waters. The blood-frenzied cursed ones especially liked hunting near shallows at night. One of two things would happen to them: they either learned to live with it, like Violetta, or they succumbed to it like so many others. I'd happily go many more years without running into another cursed one.

My fingertips itched to play my violin. And instead of feeling overwhelmed with frustrations or traumas that I had to get out, I wanted to play for the fun of it.

It was no longer a coping mechanism. It was something I genuinely enjoyed.

Sure, there were things to dwell on and plenty of pits of despair to sink into, but I felt hopeful. I'd spent so much time distracted by my own toils that I put my own needs before my best friend's. Before my *family*.

I'd been such a shitty friend. A shitty lover. A shitty captain.

But that was behind me now. I would be the person they saw me as. I'd wear my flaws proudly because I knew they made me who I was. Mae loved me regardless of them, so I could learn to love them too. I couldn't wait to share a drink with Wesley while he told me about his family and I told him of my trip.

After this is all over, I think I'll take some time off. A lengthy shore leave with my mates and my girl.

Warmth filled my chest as I put my violin case on my desk and unzipped it to pull out the beautiful instrument. It was a relief that the emotion I ached to spill from myself was joy and not inner turmoil.

Perching on the edge of my bed, I held a bar of rosin with a cloth, drawing the bow across it for a few passes to get the fine hair coated evenly. I tested the bow, gliding it down the strings to make sure it was just the right level of stickiness.

Perfect.

I rested the violin under my chin and took a deep breath, gliding the bow across. But there was a knock at my door before I could get an entire note out.

My door opened, and I wasn't surprised to see Mae's head pop in, our book in her hand. I wondered if she'd finished it.

"*That* ending—" Once she saw the violin, her adorable doe eyes grew even wider. "Are you about to play?"

"No, I just sit like this in my free time," I teased, taking the violin out from under my chin. I didn't mind postponing playing if Mae would rather have my attention. "What about the ending?" I stood up to put my violin away.

"Oh no, we'll talk about that later. Don't stop on my account," she insisted. "I love listening to you play."

"I don't usually play for an audience."

She stuck her tongue out. "Stage fright?"

"No. I just don't."

Her petal-pink lips tilted downward at the corners. Disappointment was clear on her face. "Oh. Okay."

"Do you want me to play for you, sweetheart?" I asked, meeting her eyes.

She nodded excitedly, clapping her hands together. "Yes! Pretty please." She pounced onto my cot next to me, the mattress bouncing as her eyes danced with delight.

"Only because you said please," I replied, tucking the instrument back under my chin. I poised the bow against the strings, easily gliding it across to play whichever note I wanted.

Mae watched intently, her lower lip sandwiched between her teeth. Her face turned that lovely hue of pink that I liked. Her eyes were trained on my fingers on the neck of the instrument and moved down to the bow as I played a melody, an exuberant, fast-paced rhythm that had her leaning in to watch. The awe in her eyes had my heart hammering, a fuzzy warmth spreading through my chest. I noticed how her breath deepened, pupils dilating with every movement my fingers made.

Am I turning her on right now?

To test the theory, I slowed my movements, drawing out the chord a little too long before deepening the note. Her cheeks flushed even more, and I got the distinct feeling she was thinking about me playing *her* instead of my violin.

I stopped, raising an eyebrow when her breath caught. "What're you thinking about, sweetheart?"

She stumbled over her words. "Your hands." She stopped herself, flushing deeply before continuing, "Just how talented they are—" Her eyes widened. "I mean—"

I pressed a finger against her mouth before she could continue. "Does this turn you on, baby?"

Her throat bobbed, and I didn't mistake that flare of *brat* that came into her eyes. "How about you keep playing and find out?"

"All right."

"And don't stop, no matter what," she demanded. "There's something I want to try."

I raised an eyebrow. "And what do you want to try?" I was intrigued and perhaps a little wound up by how her pupils had devoured the irises. She looked like she wanted to take a bite out of me.

I'll happily wear the imprint of her teeth.

"I'm just curious how well you can focus if I'm kneeling in front of you," she said deviously, sliding off the cot to kneel between my knees. Those round hooded eyes stared up at me, and the visual was enough to make me remember how pretty she looked with my cock in her mouth.

A bolt of desire shot through me, tenting the front of my trousers. I made such a big deal of incorporating consent into our dirty talk that I thoroughly enjoyed it when Mae did the same.

"Do you want that tonight?" she asked. "Or we could talk about that book?"

"Fuck the book." Don't get me wrong, it was my favorite book, but I couldn't care less when Mae was playing with the laces of my breeches.

Deviousness was apparent in her gaze and in the way she was chewing on her lower lip. We'd created a monster when I let her take control in the bedroom at that inn, but I was *not* complaining. I rather liked switching the power dynamic.

Giving Mae control gave me liberation. She soothed the ache, but not until after she tortured me relentlessly.

But she could bet I'd get her back the moment I had her alone at Anchorage Cove. Far enough away from everyone else that we could be as loud as we wanted. Leather straps around her wrists, completely at my mercy while I took her to paradise and back. Though I'd spend just as much time kissing the red marks away as I did painting her skin pink.

I'd satisfy her, and then I'd take care of her.

"But remember, Ronin, the second you stop playing that violin, I'll stop playing you," she teased, untying the laces. "I want to listen to music while I taste you."

"You're getting so good at telling me what you want," I commented. I liked rendering her speechless whenever I could, but it was equally freeing to know exactly what she desired.

"You're still terrible at listening," she shot back with a grin. "I said, *I want to listen to music.*"

"So fucking cheeky." I tucked my violin under my chin and played a note.

Mae reached into my trousers, and the second she touched my cock, I shuddered, fucking up whatever melody I was trying to play. She looked downright smug as I gathered my wits. My cock throbbed as she stroked me once, the exact same way I did it to myself at the inn.

This woman is going to be the death of me.

The next note broke off with a squeak as her silky tongue swiped at the pearl of arousal beading at the crown of my cock.

I couldn't fucking think of anything but her mouth. My eyes rolled back as she used both hands to get me off.

Up and down.

A hot lick here and there.

The vibration of her humming around me.

Then it stopped.

"Huh?" I uttered foolishly, dark spots in my vision. My face felt hot. My hands trembled as I completely stopped my motions on the violin. My cock fucking *ached.*

I blinked, looking down at her as she raised both eyebrows expectantly at me. Why was she looking at me like that? Her mouth was swollen, my length glistening from her saliva. My mouth felt dry, and I was so strung out that my thoughts took way too long to come back to me.

Oh, right.

Focus.

I drew the bow across the strings, playing a chord that I impressed myself with. As soon as I did, I was rewarded by Mae's hot little mouth *engulfing* my cock. My note stuttered as she sucked, hollowing out her cheeks around the crown.

"*Fuck me.*"

The mind-obliterating pressure of her mouth almost threw me over the edge, but I barely held on, only staving off because I didn't want it to end just yet. It took everything in me not to put the instrument down and fist my hands in Mae's pretty brown hair to fuck her mouth.

I ground my teeth together, not even paying attention to the melody anymore. Mae seemed distracted, too, making muffled noises of delight around me while one of her hands left me to play with herself.

As badly as I wanted to encourage her and mutter filthy things to her, Mae had rendered me speechless. My mind completely hazed over with the sensation of her mouth. If only I could thread my fingers through her hair for some control, but holding the violin restricted my movement, giving Mae complete control over me.

She panted around me, gagging when she took me too deep. I swelled, and she gagged again, flexing her throat around the sensitive crown. She explored me, shuddering as her other hand rubbed wild circles over her clit.

I wanted to spread her thighs over my face and lick up the mess I *knew* she was making. I groaned, and my climax welled in my spine, heat bunching and then flooding my body.

"I'm going to—oh *fuck*—I'm… I'm—" I couldn't get the fucking words out as the song came to an end and Mae whined around my cock, the soft rumble making me go cross-eyed.

She sucked and licked, stroked, and moaned, and I couldn't *take it* anymore. I shuddered, warning her again that I was about to come, but she only took me in deeper. Her shoulders trembled the way they did when she was about to orgasm.

Is she going to finish with me in her mouth?

I dropped the bow, grasping a handful of her hair as I came, saying the filthiest things as I thrust in deeper. Her mouth fell open, eyes fluttering back. She rubbed herself eagerly with one hand while squeezing me in the other, jerking me off until I had nothing left.

I blinked blearily as she pulled off me, tilting her head back and *swallowing*. Another aftershock of my orgasm ran down my spine.

Her mouth was red and swollen, and I was so out of it

that all I could do was stare at her. I could barely function enough to rest the violin on the bedspread next to me.

She gave me a cheeky grin. "I don't hear music."

With a heavy breath, I leaned back on my cot, tucking myself back into my trousers. "You weren't complaining a moment ago."

"I suppose not," she teased, getting up from the floor.

The hand she had been using for herself caught my gaze, and I grasped her wrist, not wasting a moment to put those fingers into my mouth.

"*Oh.*" Her face got even redder as I stared into her eyes, licking them clean.

I pulled her into my lap and kissed her, tasting the combination of us on our clashing tongues. I'd always enjoyed burying my face in between a woman's legs, but aching for a kiss after being on the receiving end was new.

I quickly discovered that I enjoyed tasting myself on Mae.

She was mine just as much as I was hers.

We pulled apart, blissfully surrounded by a post-orgasm haze. I stared down at her lips, then up at her warm doe eyes. I cupped her face, stroking my thumb across her bitten lower lip. "How about you tell me what you thought of that book?"

Mae beamed, and we spent the rest of the night curled up together, talking about something unimportant that meant everything.

37

MAEVE CROSS

ANCHORAGE COVE WAS A WELCOME SIGHT.

Luella had sent out correspondence at Violetta's Haven before we left so Wesley would know when to expect us. I hoped he enjoyed the extra time with his family. We didn't know how long we'd have left before Nathaniel and Varric staged another siege.

And then there was that Skadian heir.

When we sailed up to the pier shadowed by the cove, we were greeted by familiar faces. Conway and Butcher, Spider with a parakeet on his shoulder, and of course Wesley and his family. The little boy in Wesley's arms looked bigger.

Babies always grew so fast at that age, and judging by his chubby cheeks and chunky thighs, he was eating well too. We were all on the upper deck, nearly buzzing with the excitement of greeting everyone.

It's good to be home.

As much as I enjoyed the adventure, I couldn't wait to have dinner at Isa's again. Catch up with Wesley over a drink. Hear about Ellie's chickens and Maya's writing.

Ronin stood next to me, looking so much happier than he did when we left. He waved at the welcoming party with one hand while using the other to wind his fingers through mine. Ronin didn't look down at me, his attention solely on his friend, but that didn't stop him from squeezing my hand.

Warmth found my face as I squeezed it back.

Luella pulled us aside the smaller dock near *The Ollipheist*. I stared up at the massive ship, having missed it just as much as I missed the cove. Bad memories included.

But all the bad just made our bond feel stronger.

We weren't the same people we were before. We were *better*.

Gunny looped the line to the pier, tying to the dock before he stepped off the ship and embraced Spider. His assistant grinned, and they shared some private words about the parakeet I assumed was Geoff.

"Oi, birdie, Cap!" Gunny called over to us. "I'll see you lot later, eh?"

Ronin dipped his head. "Get some rest, Gun. I'll find you if I need you."

Gunny turned around, and the bird flew over onto his shoulder before he disappeared up the stairs with Spider and Geoff in tow.

Ronin released my hand and stepped over the lip of the boat to greet Wesley. They met in a handshake, and then Ronin pulled Wesley into a friendly hug. "Hey, brother."

I watched Wesley's eyes go wide at the gesture of affection. Then he smiled and thumped Ronin on the back. "You have a lot of explaining to do."

"That I do," Ronin concurred, pulling away to slap a hand on Wesley's shoulder.

Isa and the girls ran over to the boat and climbed over to see Enya, Luella, and Andra. Isa gave all three of them a hug before her daughters disappeared with Luella under the deck. Probably for gifts.

Of course, not without saying hello to me.

I smiled and waved at them, encouraging them to go off

with their aunts. Enya stood back, watching all of us with fond eyes.

Isa glanced over at me and asked, "How're you doing, Mae?"

The last time she saw me, I was bawling my eyes out in her living room. The memory caused a little bout of embarrassment to flare in my belly. "Much better."

"Good," she decided. "You're always welcome in my home. All right?"

I appreciated that. "I know. Thank you, Isa." I looked over at Butcher and Conway where they stood on the pier. My heart tugged, as I now knew how I remembered the merrow. "If you'll excuse me," I said, ducking to the side to approach Butcher.

He gave me a broad smile. He and Conway had their arms locked and were leaning on each other. "Ahoy, lass. Bountiful excursion, I trust."

"It was successful," I said before my eyes fell on Conway. His milky eyes watched my shadow, not quite meeting my face. "There's something I need to tell you, but I'm unsure how you'll take it."

Conway perked up, silvery skin catching on the dancing sunlight reflecting off the water. His dark brows came together. "I'm blind, not delicate."

"As you know, Bliss Thatcher now controls Fisherman's Gully, but they don't rule alone." I paused, truly unsure if this information would help or hurt, but he needed to know his sister would be visiting him so he wouldn't be caught off guard. "Udine rules by Bliss's side."

His eyes went wide. "What?"

"Much of your shoal survived, Conway."

The information visibly overwhelming him, he was clearly torn between disbelief and elation. The corners of his eyes were glossy with tears. He tilted his head toward his feet, eyebrows pinched together.

"Well, we must sail there at once, then," Butcher said. "We need to see your family."

Conway turned in his husband's direction, nodding fervently.

"They'll be coming here for the council," I reported. "Udine was thrilled to hear about you, Conway. In fact, Bliss wouldn't have agreed to come if it weren't for her."

The corners of Conway's lips pulled up, revealing the row of jagged teeth. "Is she the acting matriarch now?"

"She is."

His voice became thick. "If anyone could've brought us back from the brink, it was my sister. *Gods....* Thank Cliohde. This... this is...." He took a deep breath. "This is amazing news. Thank you."

His joy was palpable, as was the way warmth beamed in Butcher's eye as if Conway was his whole world. A shrill noise of delight crawled up Conway's throat as he curled his arms around Butcher's broad chest. His husband returned the embrace, hooking an arm around Conway's narrow waist. Butcher pressed a soft kiss against his temple, relishing his lover's happiness.

"There's more," I said.

"Please, Mae, I can't take more news. My heart might burst." Conway released Butcher, wiping his streaming tears with the back of his hand.

"The girl, Muirgen...."

"Did she survive too?" Conway asked brightly, hope coloring his tone. His eyes glistened with utter elation.

I looked between Butcher and Conway. I knew Butcher could see the tears in my eyes and the way I swallowed around my overwhelming emotions. *Thank the Gods that Conway can't see how much of a mess I look.* My voice was thick when I replied, "She did. Don't be so hard on yourself."

Conway didn't need to know the details, but he did

deserve to know that the Muirgen he tortured himself over had survived.

His chin quivered. "She must be so big now. What I wouldn't do to meet the fine young lady she turned out to be."

I bit my tongue to stop the choked noise from escaping me. I cleared my throat loudly. "Well, I'll leave you to it. It's good to see you both again."

Butcher's huge hand cupped my shoulder as they turned to leave. "Thank you, lass."

My heart squeezed with a complicated emotion, as if I were laying the little girl to rest, closing that chapter of my life as I watched Conway and Butcher climb up the pier steps. I rubbed at my chest, finding no reprieve from the lingering pain.

Muirgen found peace, even if *I* still had questions in dire need of answering.

"You told him, hm?" Ronin's voice came from behind me.

I glanced over my shoulder to see Ronin and Wesley standing next to each other. A soft smile pulled at my lips. "I did. About his family, but not about me. Not yet."

Wesley's eyebrows came together in confusion. "A lot happened on that trip, huh?"

Ronin slapped him on the shoulder. "Let's catch you up over drinks tonight."

That familiar beaming smile swept Wesley's lip. "Hells yes. About time. As much as I love my babies, I couldn't help but feel like I was missing out on adventure."

"Nothing too exciting," I interjected. "I promise."

Ronin chuckled, both dimples proudly puncturing his cheeks, and Wesley pinned me with a gaze that told me he didn't believe me one bit.

38

RONIN MURDOCH

It was so good to be back home. Wesley's kids ran circles around me, and his son, Baby Brax, giggled as I bounced him on my knee. Named after Braxton "The Albatross" Rhys. He would've loved seeing his grandkids.

Albatross was so young when he was taken from us that I never found out what he looked like with wrinkles. He should've had smile lines and a home full of laughter. He would've loved Isa. He would've taken Mae under his wing.

He and Luella would've been thick as thieves.

Albatross would've loved this. Our small family that became a village.

I could even imagine Lucky puffing on a cigar, pretending to be annoyed when the kids pulled on his braids and begged to see the flowers bloom like the twins and I had in our youth.

I remembered hearing all about it during fishing trips. Those trips held some of my favorite memories. Before we took to pirating, the twins and I would go out for a good catch while Mama set up our stall at the pier. Sometimes Lucky would join us, spinning an exciting tale of Albatross's and his adventures.

We never went fishing anymore.

We should. Even if we didn't catch anything, it would be nice to remember those days when everything felt simple. To pay our respects to everyone we lost.

Inside my chest, I felt my leviathan preen and curl against my soul, a warmth spreading everywhere. *My* father would've loved to see this too. I didn't know enough about him to guess if he would've been happy for me, but something told me he'd be proud of me for finding a home after all the pain and loss.

Isa and Wesley's home always was just that—a home.

Across from me, Wesley poured us a drink.

Behind him, I caught a glimpse into the kitchen, where Mae was laughing about something with Isa, flour splotched on her cheeks. Luella poked fun at her before getting her on the nose with another bit of flour.

Mama and Andra were on the floor with Ellie and Dina climbing all over them and prattling about their hobbies, while Maya could easily be found in the corner with a fountain pen and an ink-smudged journal.

I imagined that Lissy was at the common cabana, working on her piano lessons. Sometimes she would ask me to go with her to lessons, and I would. She'd clap her hands, resembling her father when she demanded I play something else.

I rarely played for anyone, but Lissy got so excited, I couldn't say no.

The sound of Mae's giggle drew my eyes back over to her again.

I'd seen her caked in dirt. Drenched in blood. She could be covered in muck and she'd still be the loveliest woman I'd ever seen.

"You look good," Wesley commented, pushing a glass over to me.

I took a sip, still bouncing Baby Brax. He giggled, making

a face that resembled his namesake in those rare moments when my stepfather would smile. "I feel good too," I said. "This trip served me well."

He nodded as I caught him up on what happened with the monarchs. It felt odd to be on this side of the kitchen, because Isa and I usually prepared the food. But it was nice to sit down, steal glimpses at Mae, and catch up with Wesley.

I'd sent him a letter at each destination to assure him of our arrival. Wesley couldn't send me any correspondence because of how frequently we jumped from place to place. That was for the better, especially considering our letters could've been intercepted by that Skadian heir.

Thankfully, mine were vague enough that Wesley would understand them, but no one else would. No personal details. No secrets. Just business.

"Well, on this side of things, I've been keeping it ship-shape. We careened the boat, prepared the next restock, recruited a few fresh faces, and I got the portside tavern to agree to host our council meeting," he reported.

"I had no doubts, mate." Wesley was the best person to keep everyone in line while I was away. "That couldn't have been easy. What did the tavern want?"

"Gods, they were *not* happy with the suggestion. Their cook was just murdered on a fishing trip, and they were hemorrhaging coin." He took another drink. "We have to thank Butcher's apprentice, Luther, for stepping up. He offered to be their interim cook."

"Really? Well, that's splendid." Baby Brax squealed in my arms, making warmth seep into my chest. *Gods, that's fucking precious.*

A wayward thought flickered through my mind. *Do I want kids?* It startled me as I looked down at Brax, taken by how much he reminded me of both Wesley and Albatross. My eyes shot up to Mae, and my mouth went completely dry.

I don't know, but I want her and whatever comes with it.

The gears were turning in my head now as I thought about the fact that Mae *wasn't technically* fae. Did that mean—

"What's that face, mate?" Wesley commented, always too perceptive for his own good. He and Andra were alike that way.

I deflected. "Brax just looks a lot like Dad, that's all."

Wesley smiled. "He does, but you look like you just got struck in the face with baby fever."

An uncomfortable laugh built up in my chest and awkwardly spilled from my lips. "It's not a good time."

"Rarely is," he hummed. "Speaking of, I need to hear about your *personal* excursions. I'm not your first mate anymore, Levi. I'm your brother, and I nearly strangled you last time I saw you for being such a prick to that sweet girl in there." He gestured toward Mae, who was still happily chatting with Luella and Isa.

She stole a glance at me from over Isa's shoulder, and I watched her cheeks bloom with that lovely blush when I caught her. Mae tucked some hair behind her ear and got back to her conversation, but not without Isa looking over at me and teasing her about the glimmer in her eyes.

"That's putting it lightly," I admitted. "I'll be straight with you, mate. I was not in a good place last time I was here."

"No shit." Wesley arched an eyebrow, and it disappeared under his orange bandana. "Don't think I forgot about how you put me between you and Mama because you were avoiding her."

I released a breath through my nose. "I'm sorry, Howler. Truly."

"I appreciate the apology, but don't pull that shit again."

Never again. I'm not running away. I'm not avoiding it anymore. "Pike and Cross really fucked with my head. I couldn't cope, and I took it out on you and everyone. I've come to terms with it. I can't shift, mate."

His eyes went wide. "You can't?"

"I'm working through it," I said. "But no, I still can't."

"*Oh.* Gods, Levi. Why didn't you just tell me?" he asked with a little bit of exasperation in his tone.

"It was foolish, but I wrapped a lot of my self-worth up in my leviathan." I gestured toward our family. "I thought I had to bounce back immediately, but I took this time to heal. It did me good."

"Will you be all right?" Wesley tilted his head to the side.

"Yeah. I think so."

"Good. And just know that you've got me." His eyes darted over to Mae. "Not to mention, love looks good on you."

"Feels pretty good too. I'm not fucking this up again." The sides of my mouth curled up. "But we *do* have a lot more to talk about than just me."

"Such as?"

"Lucky Bartram. The Skadian heir who tried to assassinate me. Conway and the merrow."

"Nothing interesting, my ass." Wesley straightened up and took my empty glass. "Looks like we need more drinks."

By the time I finished catching him up on those details, Mae and the others brought out dinner. Between bread, roast, and alcohol, the house was filled with lively conversation. I passed Baby Brax to Mama, and he watched with wide eyes as we laughed and told stories.

Mae sat beside me, leaning on my shoulder and nudging me playfully with her hip. At some point, her vitality came up in conversation, and it was met with more questions.

"You're fae? Wait, you're *not* fae? Explain."

"Varric killed you in Farlight Prison?"

"Does that mean that when you fell off the boat, you died?"

Isa and Wesley shot off questions back and forth. The older kids littered Mae with their own curiosities, but she didn't seem bothered. In fact, she seemed happy to relieve herself of that weight. Absolving herself of the uncertainty now that she was within the safety of her family.

Because that's what we were. *Family.*

My heart felt full.

My cheeks ached from smiling.

Everything felt like it was just as it should be.

MAEVE CROSS

RONIN'S FINGERS wove through mine on the way back to his cabana. We swung our hands back and forth, enjoying the symphony of insects chirping and the occasional creak of *The Ollipheist* against the pier. Oil lamps cast the beaten path in an orange light.

A familiar sight. Nothing spectacular.

But how the moonlight danced off the ocean's surface took my breath away every time.

A dimple punctured Ronin's cheek whenever he looked down at me, a sense of peace glimmering in his dark eyes. He seemed happy, and so was I. Walls of ice had melted. The chasm gaping between us had closed, leaving a small scar where it used to be.

That fissure felt fortified, like a broken bone healing over stronger than before.

We were free of the secrets. A shared weight lifted that made everything feel so much lighter.

Down the walkway, the familiar abyssal pool beckoned me. Enticing me for a late-night dip. I felt warm and fuzzy from all the drink, and the summertime breeze licked at my cheeks. I remembered how we'd float in the water when he taught me how to swim.

He was so sure of himself back then. If he could be that confident in the face of the unknown, then I could be too. When I was with Ronin, nothing else mattered. He liked me as I was. Beaten or bruised. Nervous or confident. Though he was always that same poised man. No matter how uncertain I was, he was a constant.

I hadn't known how much he hid beneath the surface.

But everything was different now.

I'd seen him when he wasn't sure of himself.

I'd seen him broken.

I'd seen him afraid.

So when I saw him so at peace with himself, it was a victory. I wasn't only comfortable in my skin, I was no longer alone. He was no longer afraid. He gave me community, and I gave him hope.

I had mixed feelings about going back to Ronin's cabana. There were so many bad memories there. It was the place where he'd broken my heart twice. I didn't think I'd survive a third time.

But as he squeezed my hand, unconsciously rocking it back and forth while humming under his breath, I wasn't afraid of that happening. He was right here. Not far away. Not hiding.

Not *pretending*.

My chest felt full, a sensation far surpassing the fuzzy one I'd get from drinking. Especially since that hazy sensation ebbed away quickly, as if my body repaired faster than I could enjoy the effects. When we left Isa and Wesley's, everyone was drunk and giggly, and Ronin and I were not at all on the same level as them.

I knew he had an absurd tolerance for alcohol.

Probably a dragon thing.

And apparently my unnatural healing applied to poisons

as well. Luella would wake up hungover after a long night of games and brandy, and I'd be cheery as could be. That really pissed her off.

Also, when Gunny had learned about my healing, he tried to test the boundaries with alcohol. He wanted to drink me under the table, but he failed. Ronin laughed, and Luella and Andra learned to never challenge me to a drinking match.

While we walked up the hill, I took note of Ronin's stamina. He'd struggled to climb the hill before we left, but now he had little trouble. Meanwhile, I was out of breath halfway up.

Damn him.

He stopped, one dimple in his cheek deepening as a sideways smile took over his face. "Do you need me to carry you the rest of the way, sweetheart?"

My face flushed as I glared up at him. "No." I pulled my hand away playfully, and his grin stretched the rest of the way across his face.

"I don't mind. I could throw you over my shoulder. I'd get a nice handful of your ass while I'm at it," he continued, staring at me down the bridge of his nose. "And you'd get a good view of my back."

Heat rushed up to the tips of my ears. Slowly, I narrowed my eyes, a spiteful comeback filling my mouth before he cut me off.

"Don't think I don't notice every time you eye up my back." He was poking fun at me, expecting me to blabber and make a fool of myself. He thought it was charming.

But I had a better idea.

The side of my mouth curled up too. "You act like I don't notice the rest of you." I stepped closer, not breaking eye contact.

Intrigued, he tilted his head to the side. "And what about the rest of me? Go on. Don't stop while you're ahead. I might reward you for it."

A tingle ran down my spine, warmth pooling between my thighs. Slowly, I circled him, dragging my finger along the dip in his back that I liked so much. The muscle tensed under my touch, and I didn't miss the shuddering breath that Ronin drew in when I touched him.

"Sure, I enjoy this," I agreed. "It's distracted me on numerous occasions. But I also appreciate these." I walked my fingers up his spine to the long line of his broad shoulders.

A soft rumbling noise crawled up his throat.

With intention, I dragged my touch around his shoulders as I circled him to stand right in front of him again. His eyes hunted mine, pupils blown to the Hells. "I adore the way you look at me."

His cheeks pinkened, which softened his eyes. His lips parted to say something to me, but I got up on my toes and pressed a kiss against them, silencing him.

I pulled back, sliding my tongue across my lips. "I revel in the way you taste."

Every word affected him, judging by the way he clenched his fists to hold himself back from grabbing me, displaying the strained tendon in his neck I yearned to nibble. The hard column of his cock pressed against my stomach.

"But that's not what I enjoy the most," I whispered, my breath blowing against his mouth.

"And what would that be?" he murmured.

I brushed his jaw, combing my fingers through his beard, looking deeply into his eyes. "I love the noises you make the moment you slide inside me."

His throat bobbed, eyes flaring wide. "You love to torture me, don't you?"

"Then maybe you'll get a taste of how you torture me every time I look at you."

"I can show you torture, sweetheart." He grasped my hands and pinned them behind my back with one of his. His chest molded into mine as he dragged me closer. "I can show you the sweetest agony."

A spike of white-hot lust flooded my veins. "Then show me. I'm yours."

With his free hand, he brushed his thumb across my lower lip. I couldn't help myself as I nipped the tip. He groaned under his breath. "You don't realize how bad I've got it for you."

"Tell me," I urged, my mouth feeling incredibly parched with the desire to drink in his words.

"I don't think anyone has ever owned me as completely as you do." His eyes devoured mine, capturing me entirely. "You're *mine*, but I'm just as much *yours*."

My breathing became uneven. "Damn right." I struggled against his grip, aching for a kiss to remind myself how he tasted. I bet he tasted even better with all those admissions on his lips.

Mischief glimmered in his eyes, and he pressed a finger flat against my lips, preventing me from capturing his mouth and collapsing onto this hill. I wanted him right then, and I wasn't keen on waiting.

"Do you think I've forgotten how badly you tortured me at that inn? Or how you played with me while you demanded I perform for you? Or every time you teased me just because you enjoyed my desperation?"

I widened my eyes, pulse quickening delightfully as excitement cascaded down my entire body like the warm summer breeze. My hands were still behind my back, and I had no desire to break away even though I knew he'd let me if I wanted to.

"So what?" I asked, arching a defiant brow.

His cock twitched against my belly, still confined by his breeches. "So I have every intention of tying those greedy little hands above your head until *you're* the one begging *me* for rapture. I'll have your legs spread across my shoulders while I fuck your cunt with my tongue."

An uncontrollable shiver ran from the nape of my neck all the way down to my toes. "Is that your way of asking me if you can tie me up?"

"Or I can throw you over my knee and fuck you with my fingers until you make a mess of my sheets. Act like a brat and I'll fuck you like one." Ronin released my wrists, and I already wanted to feel him restraining me again.

"You'll have to tie me up to get me to behave," I replied cheekily.

The next question that left his lips was absolutely serious. "Would you want that?"

My eyelashes fluttered when I imagined it. Taking only what he was willing to give, but I knew he'd give me whatever I wanted. "Yes."

Both hands cupped my face. "I want to take care of you tonight." His eyes searched mine before he kissed me deep enough to make my belly flutter.

My hands crawled up his back to the nape of his neck. I pulled him in closer, tasting him on my lips, feeling his hands caress my face. The *connection* between us filled my chest with warmth. This invisible tether that flexed and stretched between us didn't fray or tear.

It was only us. No war. No assassins. No diplomatic bullshit.

When we pulled away, I was panting.

"Take *care* of me? No. Give me your worst," I demanded, grinning as I turned on my heel and sprinted up the hill, no longer out of breath, but my heart raced.

When I glanced over my shoulder, I saw both of Ronin's dimples fully on display as he pursued me.

MAEVE CROSS

I THREW OPEN the door to his cabana, giggling loudly as I bounded up the stairs. I untied my sash, and my gear clanked on the ground. On the way up, I discarded my boots, tossing both of them off the overlook.

One hit the floor, and the other thumped dully off something else before clattering onto the hard floor, but I didn't think much of it, distracted when Ronin closed the door, dropped his gear, and I heard his heavy footsteps come up the stairs. Another giggle of delight fell from my lips as he tackled me onto the bed, devouring my lips. My heartbeat was in my ears, muffling any other sound but Ronin's gruff throaty noises of desire.

The battle for dominance was pointless. He wasn't going to give it up tonight. The bruising kisses swelled my lips, and I kissed him back just as hard. I clawed at his shirt, trying to shove it off his shoulders.

His hands fell to my blouse, pulling it up and over my head to squeeze and knead my breasts. He paid special attention to my nipples, pinching them until they beaded into tight little peaks.

Moans spilled from my mouth as he pushed me flat onto

my back, pinning my hands over my head. "Grasp the headboard, love. Make yourself comfortable," he ordered against my lips. He got off me, and my body instantly cried out at the loss.

"What if I don't?" I asked, following his orders for now.

"Then I'll fuck you with your hands tied behind your back and your face in the pillows, but I'd much rather watch your pretty mouth make that lovely shape when I bury myself inside you."

I frowned, keeping my hands where they were. I wanted to drink up his expressions and devour his mouth. If I lost his eyes, I feared it would break our connection.

I've just gotten it back.

I reached up and gripped the headboard, finding a place that would be comfortable for me.

"Good girl," he murmured, opening a little chest he had at the foot of his bed, not unlike the one he had on *The Ollipheist.*

I caught a glimpse of a few different types of restraints next to his belts and sashes. He found the one he wanted and rose to his feet to loom over the headboard.

I gazed up at him, heart fluttering at the way he looked at me. Like I was *precious.*

Like he's afraid to break me.

That alone made my insides clench around nothing, a rush of heat saturating my breeches. I slammed my thighs together, so unbelievably worked up by just the graze of his eyes. Goose bumps pricked across my skin, the hair on my body rising in anticipation of his touch.

"I'll take these off whenever you want me to. You know that, right?"

"I know," I replied. "I trust you."

The restraints dangled from his grasp as he leaned in, buckling one wrist at a time to the notches on his wooden

headboard. The cool leather immobilized me, and another rush of excitement drenched my thighs.

"Is that what these notches are for?" I asked.

His eyes flashed between the leather cuffs to me. "If I ever trusted anyone enough to bring them here. This is the first time I've used them."

My face flushed, my lower lip catching between my teeth. I shuddered as another lustful sensation took over. My nipples tightened, the ache inside me getting worse by the moment. The fabric between my legs was absolutely soaked by my desire.

I didn't know what to do with myself.

All I could do was watch and writhe as he undressed. I ate him up with my eyes. The hard lines of his chest. The dip between his collarbones. That throbbing vein that I traced down his chest until it disappeared into the waistband of his trousers.

"Take it off." The demand sounded uneven, my breath growing heavier and heavier. "*Gods*, I need you naked."

He chuckled. "You're not in a position to make demands."

I whined, thrashing against the restraints but loving how they made me feel completely at his mercy. Adoration twinkled in his eyes. This was new for us. A new type of play that excited and terrified me.

I knew it wasn't coming from a place of control. Ronin didn't want to control me. He wasn't gripping onto every little thing because the lack of it terrified him. This was coming from a place of devotion.

Drawing out every sensation.

Praising my body.

Showing me how much he loved me.

Though I felt it every time he looked at me.

He undid the laces on his trousers and kicked them off while I watched his cock bob against his stomach, completely erect.

My mouth watered at the sight, and logic abandoned me, completely replaced by the primal need to be pinned down and fucked until I mumbled broken sentences.

"Ronin," I whimpered, parting my legs and arching my back in an unspoken demand for him to undress me.

He reached for the laces of my breeches, and my breath caught.

"Do you know what I like about you, sweetheart?"

"What?"

He climbed on top of me, shrouding my body with his. Those dark eyes traced every contour of me. Every soft curve. His blasted dimples weakened my knees, making a million flutters erupt in my belly.

I could feel his hot body through the fabric of my breeches, and I'd never hated a strip of fabric more. I spread my legs even wider, rocking my hips and seeking pressure where I *needed* it.

He didn't give it to me.

Prick.

"I enjoy how soft you are," he murmured, leaning in to kiss the tender undersides of my arms. He stroked the round, feminine curve of my belly before bracing himself on the bed, his powerful arms on either side of me.

I used to hate my belly and the way it protruded, especially after I'd eaten. I'd been told time and time again that it was undesirable, that even as slight as I was, my body wasn't good enough. But the way Ronin looked at me, the way he touched me, made all those unwelcome thoughts melt away until I felt like I was *beautiful*.

I moaned quietly, enjoying the soft presses of his mouth as he left a wet trail of kisses from my wrists to my arms quivering over my head, down my neck to my throbbing pulse.

A quick lick down my collarbone.

A nip as he trailed down my chest.

A sampling of my breasts as he took a nipple into his mouth and *pulled.*

"Ronin," I gasped, pleasure prickling my skin. My eyes rolled back as more arousal dampened my trousers.

"I adore the way you say my name. It has never sounded so divine until it spilled from your lips." He blew against the sensitive parts of my skin. The wet spots cooled while the rest felt agonizingly hot.

I whimpered, curving my throat up toward the ceiling.

Those big hands of his untied the laces of my breeches and discarded them. Now I was completely naked underneath him. His tongue darted out to lave my other nipple before he continued his descent down my body. I shivered, thighs trembling as I tried to rub myself against him.

He tasted every piece of skin available to his mouth. The soft curve of my belly and the dimples where my hips dipped in. "I love how you taste," he groaned, trailing his tongue closer to where I ached for him. "Though I prefer how we taste together."

I wriggled against the cuffs, bowing my back to get his mouth where I wanted him. Another rush of excitement saturated my thighs, and I saw Ronin's throat bob as he watched me make a mess of myself.

"You're always so fucking wet for me that I can't think straight. I ache for you all the fucking time." He groaned again when my hips bucked, unconsciously seeking him, needing him.

"And when are you going to take *my* ache away?" I mouthed off, arching my back and quivering against the sheets. "When are you going to make that sound I love?"

He veered back, eyes completely dilated. "Whenever I fucking want to, sweetheart." He grasped his cock in his hand, and I was mesmerized by it when he leaned in, rocking back and forth, sliding himself between the swollen pearl at the apex of my thighs and my slit. He watched the pleasure unfold on my face, my mouth falling open in anticipation.

Then he took it away.

I whined, starting to fight the restraints. *"Ronin... please...."*

He tsked, dipping his head down between my thighs to quickly swipe his tongue across my clit. I squealed, bucking my hips at the sudden onslaught of sensation that he took away just as quickly as he gave it.

My eyes rolled back, and I struggled harder. I tensed my legs and rotated my hips, trying to get myself closer to his mouth so I could seek oblivion against his tongue. Against his fingers. His cock. *Everything.*

"Do you want me to tie your ankles down too?" he asked.

"No," I hissed between my teeth.

"Then be a good girl and take what I give you when I give it to you."

"You're liking this too much," I complained, but even I could admit that the lack of movement amplified everything. Every touch felt so much more intense when he captured all my focus.

"You're liking it just as much as I am."

To prove his point, he stroked two fingers between the soaking wet mess between my legs. I cried out, my entire body spasming when he barely brushed my slit. My hips thrust up, desperately aching for the opportunity to take his fingers. White spots danced in my vision when he sank them inside.

His name spilled past my lips, my hips pumping up and down, needing to ride his hand as fast as possible before he snatched it away. I needed more.

More.

More.

Gods, I'm so close.

"That's enough."

My entire body *screamed* when he stopped. A sob burst through my chest. "Please. Please. *Please.*"

"You sound so fucking pretty when you beg," he growled, dropping his head between my legs.

My eyes rolled back, and my hips punched upward to his face as I released a wail of pleasure. He groaned as I soaked his face, rocking my hips up and down as he swiped his tongue in perfect circles around my clit. Everything in me swelled, pulsing a heartbeat between my legs.

He hooked an arm around my thigh, spreading me wide while he continued an unrelenting attack on my body. Two fingers replaced his tongue, driving into me again and again as he gently pursed his lips around my clit and sucked in a continuous rhythm.

My legs shook as he tucked my thigh over his shoulder. I screamed again, the restraints banging against the headboard as the fire within my body ignited, growing brighter and hotter. My heart hammered in my ears, and molten honey cascaded from me, concentrated *right* where Ronin devoured me. I ached to thread my fingers through his hair and pull just to earn those groans puffing against my skin.

I was torn between pushing him away and pulling him closer, but I didn't have a choice. With my hands pinned above my head, all I could do was sob at the torture, tears streaming down my cheeks as I shuddered.

He'd promised me the sweetest agony, and that was all I could think about as I balanced on the edge of pain and glorious pleasure.

He veered back again, chin slick from my desire.

"That's it, sweetheart. Fall apart for me."

I didn't recognize my own voice when I whimpered his name. Begging for anything and everything. His fingers hooked upward, right against that swollen bundle of nerves needing more pressure. More of this sweet agony.

My back arched toward the ceiling, stars fluttering back

and forth in front of my vision. My hair pricked on end one at a time as the orgasm unfurled inside me, leaving a trail of liberation in its wake.

"*R... Ronin. Oh Gods,*" I screamed as I crashed down onto his bedspread, completely saturated in sweat as liquid silver pooled between my legs.

I wasn't there anymore. I was floating somewhere between here and death, the pleasure so potent that it could've easily stolen my last breath. Bleariness hazed over my vision, and I didn't even come to until his lips captured mine.

It could've been the kiss of life bringing me back to the land of the living.

Soft whimpers vibrated between us, and I didn't know if they came from me or him. I could taste myself on his lips and feel his excitement as his heart hammered in his chest where he pressed it onto mine. Slowly, he pulled back, asking, "Are you all right?"

I nodded. "I am." A cheeky smile pulled up the corner of my mouth as his cock throbbed against my belly. "Are you?"

I couldn't see the flecks of blue in his eyes or the warmth of the dark brown. Drunk off me, intoxicated by how I was spread out beneath him, he mesmerized me as he propped himself up to hover over me.

A new bead of heat formed in my chest, another rush of desire in my belly. I ached all over again, and I knew that I was far from sated. One of my legs was still hiked over his shoulder, bending me at an angle that would feel divine when he finally pushed inside.

"You're fucking killing me," he answered, dilated pupils raking my entire body before he dipped down to run his deviant tongue across my neck.

I shook the cuffs, hooking my other leg over his hip and pulling him down against me. His grunt was quickly cut off by a breathless groan of desire as his cock left a wet trail down my belly.

"There are worse ways to die, Ronin," I teased, trying to trap him between my legs. My eyelashes fluttered when the crown of his cock brushed against my slit, opening it up for him easily.

His hands snapped to my hips, pinning them down so I couldn't lift them and take him. I knew I wouldn't have any trouble. "You're such a fucking brat." He was breathless, taking great pleasure in torturing himself as well as me.

I whined, wiggling under his grip but absolutely loving it at the same time. "This *fucking brat* wants you to give her another taste of agony."

He groaned again, taking his cock into his hand. I sandwiched my lip between my teeth, watching ravenously as he slicked himself back and forth again, but this time, he pressed forward. "Fuck, baby. Look at how well you take me."

My eyes rolled back and my mouth fell open at the feeling of him stretching me, filling me to the brim with his cock. His hands came down on either side of my head, caging me against his body.

Warmth swelled in my chest as words of filthy praise spilled past his lips with every thrust, and he made that tantalizing noise I *loved*. Goose bumps ran up and down my arms, that bead of heat rekindled as if it'd never been snuffed out. It was as if I'd never gotten a release.

My appetite for him would never be sated.

I'll never stop wanting him.

One of his hands cupped my face, and I opened my eyes, not realizing I'd shut them. His eyes searched mine when he pulled back to slam back in. I cried out again, rocking my hips up to meet him, the sound of slapping skin filling the room.

"You're so fucking *perfect*," Ronin declared, groaning

loudly as we moved together, both taking and giving. "*My perfect girl.*"

He thickened, and my body reacted in kind. My walls fluttered around him, a soft whimper on my lips. My breathing was uneven as my belly curled, pleasure tightening at the base of my spine, tingling my toes.

He made an indiscernible noise. Moving faster, harder, and all I could do was lie there and arch my body, taking everything he gave me. "Please," I pleaded.

"Please, what? I'll give you anything you want." He twisted my nipple, and the bite of pain sent another slurry of stars through my vision.

Nonsense words spilled forth from my lips.

He chuckled, fucking me faster. "What was that, baby? Hm? Are you so far gone, you can't speak?"

"P-*Please,*" I cried out, so close to the precipice of oblivion. Everything ached and throbbed, and I could barely hear anything but my racing pulse and the delicious noises he was making on top of me.

He groaned, tilting his head back as his eyes fluttered closed. Getting anything out of me would've been pointless, but he loved rendering me speechless. Warmth ebbed through my limbs, tightening in my chest as the ache twisted through my body.

I needed to unravel.

I needed to break.

I needed to burn and smolder.

His skin slipped along mine, a glorious bead of sweat pooling in the dip between his collarbones. His lips were swollen, face flushed. We swam in each other's eyes, and nothing else mattered. His arms shook, and I trembled uncontrollably.

"Yeah, choke my cock like that," he groaned as I clenched around him, my eyes rolling back.

Another hoarse cry fell from my lips as I tumbled over the edge, my walls fluttering and crushing him. The shaking intensified as I fell limp, blissful delight everywhere. Potent relief cascaded down my legs, flooding in my belly.

I was mesmerized by the crease between his brows and the shape his mouth made as he cursed and thickened, fucking me *hard* as he took his own pleasure. My legs fell open, sliding off his shoulders as a third orgasm swept through me. His thrusts stuttered, my name tumbling from his lips like music to my ears. I returned it in kind, whimpering his name over and over again when he finally finished, swelling and then bursting inside me.

"Fuck, Mae," he groaned, pressing a tender kiss against the throbbing pulse point in my neck. He murmured sweet nothings in my ear when he pulled out, rolling over onto his side.

A silly smile spread helplessly across my face, my head light and hazy. I couldn't feel my arms over my head anymore as I sleepily fluttered my eyelashes at him, in my own little world. He kissed me as he undid the cuffs, even if I didn't have the energy to move.

"I love you," I murmured against his lips.

He deepened the kiss before leaning back. "And I love you, my beautiful girl."

I could see it in his eyes, and it made my belly flip and flop, feeling fuzzy and satisfied.

Ronin pressed another kiss against my shoulder before grasping each wrist to kiss away the red sting left by the cuffs. "As lovely as it would be to cuddle, you need to hit the head before you fall asleep."

He was right, but I still complained. "But—"

"Don't make me repeat myself, sweetheart."

I pouted.

Dimples dented at both sides of his mouth. "And when

you're done, you better get your ass in that shower because I'm going to be joining you."

I returned his smile and cheekily replied, "Only if you carry me. I can't use my legs."

41

RONIN MURDOCH

MAE MADE all sorts of happy little noises when I soaped up her back, kneading circles on her hips where I'd left imprints of my fingers. After I kissed them away, I brought her wrists to my lips and kissed them too.

Her round eyes stared up at me in wonder as I took my time washing her. Every sigh of delight made me smile. She leaned against me as I ran my fingers through her hair, scratching her scalp. Between me and the spray of water, Mae nearly fell asleep.

She leaned into every touch with that sleepy smile on her lips as she kept telling me that she loved me.

I'd never grow tired of hearing it.

She demanded to return the favor, and I let her, basking in all the affection as she soaped me from head to toe, giggling when I kissed her nose and seated my hands on that dip above her hips that fit them perfectly.

I pressed my lips to her shoulders, down her belly, to the trembling flesh on her thighs as I dried her with a towel. We had all the time in the world, and I didn't care how late it was. The monarchs weren't coming to Shipwreck Bay for another week, and I was expecting correspondence confirming their arrival any day now.

I'd enjoy all the time we had before our lives turned upside down again.

"Are you coming to bed?" Mae asked sleepily when we went back upstairs.

"Not yet, love. I'll be in bed soon," I murmured, pressing my mouth to hers again, reveling in how she melted against me. Her pink cheeks and slackened muscles satisfied me. "Get some rest."

She sighed, nodding as she climbed into my bed, immediately settling under the covers. I smiled when she flopped over onto her stomach to curl up on my side of the bed. Her hair fanned out over the pillows, and I leaned against the wall, committing the sight of her to memory.

My beautiful girl.

After I threw on a pair of loose-fitting pants, I turned the dial down on the oil lamp, plummeting my loft into darkness. It would've been easy to crawl into bed with her, but I was wide awake. Exhilarated, even. I'd definitely toss and turn and keep her up.

Maybe after a little reading, I'd be tired enough to join her.

Even when I finished picking our gear off the floor, gathered our clothes in the basket for the wash, and put Mae's and my boots by the door, I wasn't remotely tired.

So, I picked out a book from my shelf, poured myself a glass of bourbon, and sat down on my chaise, kicking my legs up. The chirping of crickets outside seemed louder than usual, but I didn't think much of it.

Not until I heard *"Me-row"* coming from the darkness of my guest room.

What the fuck?

Instantly, I was on edge. My eyes flickered up to my loft where Mae rested, and I debated waking her *just in case*, but if it was nothing, I'd feel foolish for disrupting her when she slept so peacefully.

I snatched a dagger from my bookshelf, readying myself for anything hiding in the shadows. Making as little noise as possible, I tiptoed toward the guest room, where the noise of crickets got louder.

I don't remember closing this door.

"Me-row."

That's Lazlo's meow.

Did I leave that fucking window open?

No. I didn't.

I didn't close this door, and I sure as *fuck* didn't leave that window open.

I flung the door open. Moonlight shone in from the open bay window above the bed. The pillows were out of order. There was a gritty outline of a boot on the windowsill. A cold shiver ran down my spine when I realized that *someone had been here.*

Were they here when Mae and I were upstairs?

The thought that someone could've overheard us—*seen us* —fucking pissed me off. That intimate moment was *ours,* and I was going to *kill* whoever decided to peep in on us. I gave the room another look around, but whoever had been here earlier was long gone.

I looked down at my feet to the bright green eyes staring owlishly at me. Even with the light of the moon, I barely made out Lazlo's big, fluffy tail swishing from side to side as he nudged my leg with his nose. "Lieutenant Commander Lazlo," I greeted, dipping down to scratch his ears. "What're you doing here?"

He mewed again, purring as he wound around my legs. Then he bounded back and grasped something before coming into the light again with a small barracuda dangling in his mouth. Small for a vicious fish, but huge for Lazlo to be dragging it inside my cabana for me.

With a chirp, he laid it down in front of me, razor-sharp teeth and dead fish eyes catching the light.

"Thank you," I said, admiring his catch.

This wasn't the first time Lazlo had brought me gifts. In fact, he did it often when we were on shore leave, but this was the first time he'd gotten into my house to bring me something. I smiled, scratching his chin. "Good kitty."

Lazlo released a monstrous purr, blinking slowly as I rubbed his ears and chin to his heart's content. Then I stood up and slammed the window closed before scooping up Lazlo's kill to show him that I appreciated it even if I wasn't going to eat it.

The cat trotted into the main living area behind me, mewing and chirping.

"Hush, Lazlo. You'll wake Mae up," I murmured.

He meowed once more, following me when I washed my hands, wiggling his haunches with the intent of stretching out on my shoulder. But without a jacket or a shirt as a buffer between my skin and his claws, I'd be asking for cat scratch fever.

I sat back down on the chaise and patted the spot next to me instead. He obliged, kneading the spot on the couch before plopping down.

If I wasn't awake before, I was now.

What if the intruder came back while we slept? I didn't have locks on my doors or windows. There'd been no need for them before. And even if I *had* locks, if someone wanted to kill us, it would be relatively easy to do so while we were isolated from the rest of the crew.

I shook away the churning worry in my belly.

I sighed and petted Lazlo while I read my book and sipped on my drink. He rumbled happily, curling up next to me.

"What's the lieutenant commander doing here?" Mae asked from over the railing on the loft.

I was torn between not wanting her to worry and not wanting to keep secrets. "What are you doing up?"

"I heard meowing," she answered, a blanket draped over her shoulders as she climbed down the stairs, clutching it closed in front of her.

I shot Lazlo a knowing look. "I told you that meowing was going to wake her up." When my eyes returned to Mae, she was a vision. Hair mussed. Cheeks flushed. A sleepy smile. "You should go back to bed, love."

"Not without you. Come on, your pillow is not a good replacement."

With a deep breath, I said, "I don't think I'm coming to bed tonight. The window in my guest bedroom was open."

She sat on the other side of me. "Could Lazlo have pawed it open?"

"No," I answered. "He's never done that before, and a few things were out of place as well as a boot print on the windowsill."

She nodded, pressing a kiss to my bare shoulder. "Well, then I'll stay up with you."

"That's sweet, baby, but you don't have to."

With a yawn, she clutched the blanket closer and nuzzled the side of my neck. "No, no. I'm here. Get over it."

The scent of her hair eased the pattering in my chest. "All right."

"Now what're you reading?" she asked, making herself real comfortable in my lap.

Lazlo pressed against the other side of my leg. She reached over and scratched his ears, and he purred, also using me as a mattress.

It wasn't long before Mae fell asleep on me, and Lazlo did too. And while I was wedged between the two of them, my eyes got heavy, and I rested my cheek on the top of Mae's head, joining them in a shallow slumber.

The sleep was relatively dreamless even as I drifted between being awake and asleep. Mae slept deeper than I did, but her soft wheezes comforted me. And with Lazlo's watchful eye on us, he was a little sailor guarding us while we slept.

AFTER THE NEWS broke that someone had snuck into my cabana, the twins, Mama, and Luella all made a big fucking fuss that Mae and I should stay at Wesley's. They had a point, even if I didn't enjoy being fussed over.

I slept easier with Mae tucked into my side on Wesley's couch. Not only did I have Wesley, Mama, and Andra, but I also had Luella, who was sharp as a fucking blade. Mae and I were as safe as we were going to be.

The negatives included not being able to see Mae naked as often as I wanted to. The lack of privacy annoyed me, but I didn't mind being woken up by Wesley and Isa's kids for breakfast, Ellie and Dina standing over me at the crack of dawn. They demanded my help to gather eggs and check on tomato plants.

The first time it happened, it was terrifying. Two little girls staring at me and whispering, "Uncle Levi. Uncle Levi," with nothing but darkness behind them is enough to make any grown man's heart skip in fright. Safe to say that I wasn't used to waking up around children, especially children with no spatial awareness whatsoever.

When we'd get back inside, Mae would be helping Isa and Mama with breakfast and tea.

Considering that I'd gotten used to waking up alone and being alone most of the time during shore leave before I met Mae, this was a nice change of pace. My nieces adored that I was nearby, and I enjoyed the quality time with them. Lissy didn't have to complain or beg for me to teach her a new song on the common cabana piano.

Mae would even tag along to watch.

Honestly, the days went by too fast. Sunset came too quickly.

The long days at the beach among friends, the sea, and good drinks felt shorter and shorter the closer the council meeting came. Luella had gotten correspondence from all three monarchs. They were on time to come into port by the end of the week.

I could pretend that the blissful bubble would stretch on forever, but it wouldn't. Every day I got a little stronger, and the leviathan spirit inside me stirred as if getting impatient.

My mates, Mae, and my mother stood by while I practiced releasing it. Or *trying* to. It wasn't as easy as it used to be. And even if I could *feel* the Royal Leviathan again, I still couldn't shift. I knew I was strong enough. It was just a matter of time.

When I'd gone out for late-night swims, I could feel the leviathan testing the boundaries of my affliction, ready to release itself. Even if I wanted it to, something was in the way. I was holding myself back.

Shifting before just *happened*. Like walking or breathing. It was innate. Now I struggled to figure out *how* to let it out. It helped that my mates were so supportive.

Such a fucking relief.

Occasionally, I'd meet with the gunnery crew, and Gunny was thrilled to tell me that he'd been working on something. It wasn't ready yet, and with his perfectionism, I wasn't sure if it'd ever be ready. Nonetheless, we could use all the help we could get.

A new weapon.

A fresh bit of intel.

An edge.

The nightmares didn't plague my sleep as badly, but the uncertainty of *what* Cross and Pike were planning was never far away. I might as well be twiddling my thumbs and waiting for an attack. It didn't help that Lazlo kept bringing me more fish with razor teeth.

A school of barracudas had come to the reefs recently, devouring the native fish. It made me uneasy, but there was nothing I could do about it except prepare. And the closer the monarchs came to port, the more everyone seemed on edge.

Instead of drinking over a bonfire, all of us started preparing our weapons.

Sharpening and polishing cutlasses.

Luella would spar with anyone willing to duel with her. Usually Mae.

Andra refreshed her braids, finding the fastest way to pull a hairpin from them in defense.

Isa already knew how to fight from her years as a barmaid, but she also practiced with both Wesley and Mama.

I worked on my quickdraw with my flintlock pistol, practicing reloading between shots. I barely used it, which made it more imperative that it be battle ready. It didn't take long for several more crew members to find us on the beach, joining us in our preparations, a shipload of us working from dawn until the wee hours of the night. Including Butcher and Conway, who fed us as we worked.

Hesitantly, Conway told me he'd been nervous to see his sister and had been frantically growing more crops than he knew what to do with.

I could sense it in the air, like any experienced sailor. It felt like a distant rumble in the sky, long before the weather changed.

After spending my life at sea, it was easy to notice when the waves got choppy. The wind kicked up. A red ring circled the sun in the haze. The snails that usually clung to the tops of rocks hid beneath the surface. The clouds grew long and wispy, moving with the breeze. The smell of salt got stronger as the scent of rain weighed heavily in the air.

Sailors always know when a storm is coming.

42

MAEVE CROSS

What did Butcher always say?

"Red dawn in the morning, sailors heed the warning."

At Shipwreck Bay, as I stood on the pier, I could see the red ring around the sun. A thick haze that changed the orange sunrise to a rich crimson. Dark clouds rolled in the distance, and I knew the storm was going to hit shortly after the monarchs arrived.

We likely had a few hours before the worst of it.

I'd been on *The Ollipheist* during a rainstorm, but this was different. Not only were tensions high, but we'd be trapped in port until it passed if negotiations went sideways. It made me nervous, but at least the mates and Ronin seemed put together and determined. That was enough for me to put on a brave face.

Ronin had told me a storm was coming, but I didn't think he meant it literally. Not until I watched him give orders to crew members to throw down sandbags to prevent the winds from blowing away any gear. He diverted flood paths with Luella. Before I left for the port, Andra and the ship crew locked down the canvas and tied down *The Ollipheist* to keep it safe when the storm rolled through.

Wesley and Ronin were at the tavern, prepping the tables and making sure lodging was available at the inn. Enya would be joining me shortly to greet the monarchs as they docked, but I needed the extra time to myself.

The past week had been a nice reprieve, and I couldn't help wanting to go back to Wesley and Isa's to spend more time with the girls and Baby Brax. Who knew when I'd get time with them again? I quite enjoyed Ellie's morning chicken endeavors, and I liked listening to Maya tell me her stories. Lissy had gotten much better at the piano, and Dina's flowers were blooming.

But it was time for work, even if I ached to crawl back into my bubble of comfort.

Discomfort is a privilege.

Soon Enya joined me on the dock, dressed in her nice port clothes like I was. I rarely dressed nice, but if there was any day to wear a silken blouse and fine leathers, it was today. My cutlass rested on my hip, housed by one of Ronin's violet sashes.

The man wore *one* sash when we were at sea.

One worn-out crimson sash that he considered good luck.

But he had all sorts of colors in his cabana. Fancy jewelry and expensive fabrics. Considering none of that was missing was more of a sign that whoever snuck into his cabana wasn't there to steal from him.

It could've been the Skadian heir, but Ronin wasn't short on enemies either. He'd rubbed several dangerous people the wrong way, and if news got out that he was in recovery, that was more reason to strike.

Nonetheless, Ronin wasn't going to make use of all his embellishments, so I happily snagged a few of his accessories to look the part. A tricorn cap with a bandana layered under it so it'd fit properly. One of his golden chains around my neck that settled just under my collarbone. I doubted he'd notice with everything else going on, but if he did, I knew he found it charming when I wore a necklace because his rings were too big for my fingers.

Our mates also got a kick out of it whenever I did my best Ronin impression by the bonfire.

Enya and I made small talk while a ship crested over the horizon. As it got closer, I recognized Lucky's craftsmanship as well as the flag blowing in the wind. Ethan and Lucky were at the bow, and he waved at me as his helmsman brought them against the pier.

The gangway banged against the planks, and Lucky stepped off it, greeting me wholeheartedly. "Aye, Mae. Nice to see you again." He cast Enya a sideways glance. "Seabird."

"Lucky," she returned. It wasn't as painfully awkward as it had been back at the Outpost, but he clearly hadn't forgiven her. "I can accompany you to the tavern."

"Won't leave me halfway there?" he shot off.

"Don't tempt me," she rebutted.

He ignored the jab, glancing over at me. "Am I the first?"

A few ships were tied down at the pier, but most sailors had already prepared their ships and made their way inside except for a few of them stationed at the watchtowers and lighthouse. Behind Commander Lucky, I caught sight of Ethan ordering the crew around as they locked the ship down, tied canvases, and closed deadlights like a well-oiled machine.

I nodded. "You are. Howler and Ronin are at the tavern."

Lucky beamed. "Excellent. It'll be nice to talk to them while I wait for the others. Howler and I have a lot to talk about."

Shortly behind Lucky, Captain Bliss came into port with Udine by their side. Udine's warriors stood tall, dressed in armor embellished with sea glass, tridents and halberds in hand. Bliss obviously didn't want to be present, but Udine smiled when she saw me.

"Lock it down," Bliss ordered, stepping off the ship to pin me with a glare. "Where?"

"At the tavern."

Bliss grunted and took off with a few sailors in tow.

"Don't mind my companion, Mae. Captain Bliss hates poor weather, and it was quite the struggle to outrace the storm," Udine said calmly. "Where can I meet my brother?"

Conway was expecting Udine, and I could only imagine how nervous he was, especially considering all the years that had passed with them assuming the other was dead.

"He lives in the townhouse with the rooftop terrace garden. Across the path from the tavern." I pointed off toward town, but even from my vantage point, I could make out the greenery spilling over the edges of the roof. It wasn't far from the pier.

Udine smiled, a warmth and excitement filling her orange crescent-pupiled eyes. "He's always been partial to gardening. So gifted." She glanced at her warriors and said, "We go there immediately." Before she left, she took my hand and squeezed it. "Thank you."

I returned her smile before she left, then watched as they marched toward Conway and Butcher's house. When Conway answered the door, he cupped Udine's face. She returned the favor and touched her forehead to his. I couldn't hear what they said, but I could hear the joy in their voices.

Going from merrow to merrow, Conway pulled each of them into an embrace while Butcher watched him lovingly. I hoped their reunion would be as sweet as they deserved after so much time apart.

The wind blew harder, sending wisps of my hair lashing over my face. The storm was getting closer. I could feel it thickening the air, the scent of rain overtaking the briny sea.

While I waited for Violetta to reach the port, I caught a distant glimpse of a small sloop as it circled the port far enough away that I couldn't make anything out except for a few heads.

Just some more sailors coming in before the storm.

I didn't think about it very long once Violetta's man-o'-war came into view. Thick, fat raindrops fell from the sky as the clouds rolled in, thunder rumbling in the air. They were rolling their canvas in before they even reached the dock. The wind was strong enough that it didn't need to be at full sail.

The flame in the lighthouse ignited as the sky grew darker, the only discernible landmark now the massive golden fire above the rocky drop-off.

It was only late morning, but it was dark enough to resemble early evening. By the time Violetta's ship, *The Lilac Queen*, docked, there wasn't much visibility. Usually, we could see nearly twelve miles toward the horizon, but it was likely half that now.

Raindrops moistened my jacket, pattering off my hat. The gangway slammed down as Pinky sauntered off the ship, Violetta giving orders as the other captains had. She wore a cinched corset, with blades and a flintlock pistol buckled in her belt.

Violetta greeted me. "Apologies for the delay. Nearly got caught up in that monster." She gestured up to the clouds as it rained harder.

"It's all right," I replied. "We wouldn't have started without you."

She grinned, teeth poking out from her upper lip. "Aren't you sweet." She glanced at my outfit. "Ooh, you clean up really nice, love."

My cheeks flushed. "Thank you." I adjusted my hat.

Violetta chuckled. "You wear Levi's hat better than he does."

"I'd say," Pinky concurred. "The crew is locking it down, Vee. Let's move before we get caught in this."

A rumble of thunder shook the ground beneath my feet while an answering lightning strike cracked across the water, a single beam of light in the dark. I searched the water in the distance, but I'd lost sight of the sloop I'd seen earlier.

I hope they find some shelter.

I didn't dwell on it as I led Pinky and Violetta to the bustling tavern, the sound of yelling already permeating the entryway. As soon as we stepped into the doorway, Captain Bliss decked Lucky square in the nose.

Oh, great. This is going to be fun.

43

RONIN MURDOCH

"FUCK!" Lucky shouted, grasping his nose as Bliss knocked him onto the floor. He clattered against the table, shaking the drinks and startling the barkeep. "You still hit like shit."

As soon as Bliss walked in, they made a direct line for Lucky. Insults were hurtled back and forth. Lucky hadn't seemed surprised. Certainly didn't seem surprised that my mother didn't come to his defense either.

"Fuck you! Play with my heart again, and I'll take yours," Bliss snarled, standing above Lucky, their hands curled into white-knuckled fists. Blood dotted Bliss's knuckles, which were already bruising.

Lucky's first mate, Ethan, placed his hand on his cutlass, ready to fight the moment Lucky gave the order.

Lucky frowned, wiping the blood from his nose before he waved Ethan off. "Stand down. I deserved that."

I held out a hand, and Lucky took it, getting to his feet.

He dusted off his shoulders, looking down at Bliss, who stared up at him with all the malice they could muster. "If you want to hit me again to get it out of your system, I'll give you one more free shot."

"One was sufficient." Bliss turned on their heel and took a

seat while one of their other sailors—probably their quarter-master—came to join them with a clipboard in hand.

"Already coming to blows?" Violetta's voice came from the entryway. "But no evisceration? You've gotten soft, Bliss. Shame."

"Seems like a poor time," Bliss rebutted. "I'd hate to flee after I've already locked down the ship for the storm. The evisceration can still come later."

Violetta shrugged, seeming awfully at ease with Pinky on one side and Mae on the other. I couldn't help a half smile pulling on my lips when I noticed my hat on top of Mae's head and my violet sash around her waist. She also wore one of my golden chains around her neck. As usual, she was stunning, but even more so when she donned my accessories.

Lucky cracked a grin, walking toward Pinky and Violetta. "Captain Violetta," he greeted her with a flourish. "No blood-bath today. Sorry to disappoint."

She returned the smile and caught his hand in a firm handshake. "I'll let it go. It's nice to see you again. Without the gunpowder this time."

"Likewise," Lucky returned.

While the monarchs engaged in small talk and enjoying food that Luther whipped up in the kitchen, Mae kept them occupied. Unlike most of the people in the room, Mae had somehow gotten on the good sides of all three.

Bliss despised me for putting them in the same room with Lucky and even more for convincing them to come to Ship-wreck Bay to begin with.

Even after the disappointing results of Violetta's reading, she seemed more intrigued than anything by Mae's lineage. She listened to everything Mae said, absolutely eating it up.

Wesley and my mother stood together and prepped the visual aids.

Gunny and his gunners sealed off the entrance to the tavern to keep the meeting private.

Then Luella and Andra came in. If they were here, that told me that they'd finished the storm preparations and the meeting was ready to begin.

"Now that we're all here," my mother announced, moving toward the center of the room, demanding the attention of everyone present, "we should get started."

The small talk petered out. Of anyone, it made the most sense to have my mother lead the meeting. Former captain and former queen, she stood tall in front of the gathering, not at all shaken by the tension in the room. I followed her example, centering my presence. Mae moved closer, sitting at a nearby table adjacent to me.

Her soft smile comforted me even if my heart still slammed against my ribs. I'd never been in this position before. Sure, I captained my crew, but it was a new type of pressure to be alongside people who technically outranked me.

"Many of you know me as former Captain Seabird, but my name is Enya Murdoch. You've met my son, Ronin Murdoch, though you would likely know him as Captain Leviathan."

The monarchs knew this already, but some of their mates did not. It was imperative to get everyone on the same page if we were going to agree on anything.

My mother spoke clearly and concisely. "We've gathered you here today because we have a common enemy. Varric Cross. Nathaniel Pike. And whoever flies their colors behind them. Namely, the noble families. Likely the Kingdom of Skadi as well."

A few of the monarchs muttered among themselves. Violetta leaned over to whisper something to Pinky, and he jotted it down.

Lucky raised an eyebrow to his hairline. "Anyone with an ounce of Skadian blood could tell you that they don't ally with *anyone*. Why would Cross be the one to ally with?"

My mother tilted her head to the side and said, "Your guess is as good as mine, but we cannot deny that a Skadian heir is targeting us."

"With all due respect, Enya, what does that have to do with me?" Bliss asked. "It seems like a lot of effort to take out our colonies when he could just leave us alone."

This time, I answered. "Look at the big picture. Look at our livelihood. We stand in his way. We block his supply chain. We raid his ships. We are a thorn in his side. We hire crew he's scorned and people who have evaded his rule. He has every intention of reclaiming us and murdering everyone else."

"Captain Leviathan is right," Violetta concurred. "We caught sight of pirate hunters shortly before we left. The salties got them, but that tells me that at the very least, we're being scouted."

Lucky cleared his throat and added, "It's not just you. I've lost some of my best craftsmen to suspicious boat orders."

"Whether you like it or not, Captain Bliss, we are stronger together. At least for now. When all this is over, you can splinter off." I paused, adjusting my hat. "Or you may learn to appreciate what we build together."

Bliss huffed but didn't argue. "Fine. What's the plan, then? I'm not giving up my territory. The merrow deserve their land."

"Then let's keep our territory. Hm? Divvy it up among us?" Lucky suggested.

Violetta laughed. "What? Like little kingdoms? Would I get Farlight Bay, then? I would happily sit on that throne. Imagine all that territory, Pinky."

Her cousin grinned at her, and I could already see the gears turning in their heads.

Above us, the rain kicked up, beating the roof with deafening thuds.

"Slow down," I said, cutting off that train of thought.

"Let's not speculate on who would get what when the battle hasn't even been fought."

"Fair, fair. Then where do we start?" Violetta asked before glancing at my mother cheekily. "Hm? Former Queen Enya? You have the most experience putting laws into effect. Show us your expertise."

My mother pressed a finger to her lips. "Well, first things first. Let's decide what laws we will follow. All of us. A general rule that would be met with punishment if broken."

A moment of silence fell in the tavern.

"Well, I propose that we put those unwritten rules of the port into action," Lucky suggested. "But, before we get into war talks, we need to do our crews justice. Make their lives easier. Even influence the smaller bandits to pledge allegiance to any of us to limit the violence in port."

"And who would enforce that? You?" Pinky asked. "Why do *you* get Shipwreck Bay?"

"I happen to have the most influence here," Lucky pointed out. "And I live nearby. My crew could be enforcers."

"And who would stop all that power from getting to your head?" Bliss snipped. "I at least have the merrow to keep me in check."

It was a valid question.

Once upon a time, I viewed Lucky as a power-hungry, self-serving prick. But the picture I'd painted of him was simply his reputation, not who he was.

They bickered about the land grab. Who would get what. Why Lucky would get something they didn't.

Steadily, it got louder. Turned to shouting. Accusations. Pinky stood up, jabbing his finger into Bliss's quartermaster's chest. Bliss snarled at Lucky. The tensions only rose. My mother tried to get the meeting back on track, but the three of them were too busy yelling at one another to notice.

For fuck's sake....

I caught Mae's eyes as an idea brightened them. Wesley noticed it too.

"Eh! Quiet!" Wesley howled.

All eyes snapped over to him. He scowled and tilted his head toward me.

"You lot keep forgetting that a storm is pouring atop our heads," I stated. "If it comes to blows, we won't be able to fucking leave. Cut it out." I gestured to Mae, who had been sitting there politely, waiting for her chance to talk.

The attention shifted to Mae. Her cheeks pinkened, but she didn't buckle. Instead, she sat up, her back ramrod straight. "The biggest concern about working together is who will keep each of you in check, right?" she asked. "Is that what I'm hearing?"

The three of them looked between themselves. But the answer was clear as day. They didn't trust one another. Certainly didn't trust handing over power to anyone.

"You are captains. Who keeps you in check?" Mae asked. "Your crew. If you muck something up, your crew straightens you out. If that fails, that's what the other captains are for. It won't be perfect, but that's what we'll have to do. The Isles are just one big ship. How would you captain that ship?"

More silence. They looked between themselves again, their eyes narrowed and lips curled, each with one hand poised on their cutlass or firearm at any given moment.

The leviathan curled under my skin, rearing its head to rumble inside my chest. A haze of authority blazed behind my eyes. Just as it had in the water when I commanded sirens and kuru to leave my ship be.

I need to get control of this situation.

"You don't have to *trust* one another, but you do have to play your role. Just like on any ship." I crossed my arms, letting the influence of my dragon show itself. It emboldened my authority. While these monarchs outranked me by pirate standards, *I* outranked *them* by the order of Cliohde. The authority given to my family to rule the Isles to begin with. "This isn't a fucking land grab. This is survival. If we can't get along, Cross will have all of us dancing with Jack Ketch."

Get the fuck over yourselves.

I could feel the draconite's power reflected in my eyes, more visible now than it'd been in months. I could see the *shock* dance across Bliss's face. They didn't believe in my lineage before. With intention, they unhanded their cutlass, refusing to break eye contact with me.

With an exaggerated sigh, Bliss said, "Fuck. *Fine.* I don't like this."

"You don't have to like it, Captain Bliss, but he makes a good point," Violetta tacked on, taking her hand off her firearm. "I don't care for you lot, but I refuse to leave my haven to the mercy of pirate hunters."

Lucky slapped his hand down on the table, making a loud thud as he said, "If Farlight Isles is just an oversized ship, how would we captain that ship?"

They gave various suggestions but decided it was best to delegate. Solidify the laws that were unwritten. Control their land while taking charge of a major circuit of trade. Interlocking their ships and their roles to make them rely on one another so it was difficult to splinter off or seize too much control.

Lucky would enforce Shipwreck Bay while maintaining a neutral ground between the monarchs. He would also handle boatmaking for the battles ahead and writing contracts for ally merchants to ensure everyone was fed.

Bliss would take the military-occupied Gullies back and be in charge of disrupting Cross's supply chains if the merrow agreed to help, which they likely would.

Violetta had some of the best blacksmiths in the Isles under her charge, so she would handle weaponry. It would also be her responsibility to dispatch any unaligned bandits or recruit them.

Power in numbers.

But there was still one question left unanswered.

"Who would we answer to?" Bliss asked. "I don't want to answer to either of you blokes."

"Someone unaligned with us. Neutral. Someone with a good head on their shoulders. Someone capable of bringing three distrustful pirate monarchs together to get along," Lucky answered, glancing at me. "Someone I would put my colors behind."

A warmth unfolded in my chest.

"Someone born for this," Violetta concurred. "Captain Leviathan is the obvious choice. Not only does he have the Princess of Farlight at his side, but he's got the most loyal crew this side of the Algarian Sea. That speaks volumes."

Bliss narrowed their eyes but then shrugged. "I can live with that. I don't like you, but Udine has taken a liking to you." They took a drink and waved their arms dismissively. "*And* it helps that you've never had any documented mutinies in almost nine years of captaining. I'll work with you."

"Then it's settled," my mother claimed. "Onto the next course of business—"

A distant bell went off. *Once.*

Only once.

Barely audible over the heavy rainfall and the thunder booming outside. It was customary to ring the bell three times in an emergency. But something sank in my belly. The hair stood up on the back of my neck. The leviathan within me stirred, rearing its head in warning.

All the monarchs straightened up. "What in the Nine Hells was that?" Lucky asked.

The taste of dread filled the air. We could clearly all feel it, as each of us bristled one by one.

"It sounded like a warn—" Violetta began before she was

cut off by a cannonball pummeling into her chest with a sickening *crunch*.

It happened too fast for anyone to react.

"*Captain!*" Gunny's voice pummeled through us as he slammed the door open, eyes wide and *spooked*.

Nothing ever spooks my gunner. Nothing.

"Pike—" Another cannonball took the door off the hinges, sending Gunny flying into the street.

Mae was on her feet before I could comprehend what was happening as another round of ammunition split through the tavern, a rain of splinters around us. Screams ripped through the rain as a—

Boom.

Boom.

Boom.

—filled the air.

As the tavern collapsed on top of us, I caught sight of a barracuda family crest flying high on the flag of a man-o'-war. *Pike's ship.*

The raid was here.

Now.

We were out of time.

44

MAEVE CROSS

Chaos unfolded right before my eyes.

Wesley shoved Enya out of the way as a beam fell on top of them. Luella pulled Andra out the door on instinct, barely ducking under another cannonball. Bliss shouted as a blast sent them flying into a crumbling wall.

Lucky uttered a phrase of magic, but it wasn't fast enough as Ethan dove in front of him and was shredded by the shrapnel.

Pinky sat frozen in his seat by shock with Violetta's blood painted across his face. "Vee?"

There wasn't time to react. I could only move.

There was no saving *anyone*. I could only hope they made it out.

I grasped Ronin's arm, yanking him out of the path of destruction. As wood rained down on us and water spilled through the roof, we ran toward the door. The whistle of another attack tickled my ears, and I slammed my body against Ronin's, tackling him into the mud as everything exploded into debris around us.

"Come! Now!" Luella shouted. She and Andra pulled us to

our feet and behind cover as cannonballs tore through Shipwreck Bay.

My back was flat against the wall. Unimaginable horrors
filled my eyes as Nathaniel's ship was poised in the harbor,
reloading ammunition and firing.

And firing.

And firing.

One deafening boom after another.

A never-ending hail of cannonballs.

They shredded the ships in port. They demolished buildings. The rain became so thick that I couldn't see the ship in
harbor, but I could see the gunpowder ignite as another bolt
of ammunition destroyed the church. The elvish temples.
The townhouses. The market. Everyone was inside seeking
shelter from the storm, making it the perfect cover for a
pirate hunter.

I squeezed my eyes shut, trying so hard not to feel
helpless.

What can I do?

What can I do?

What can I do!

Nothing. I could do *nothing* but hope.

Thunder and cannons sounded the same.

"Howler? Mama? Where are they? Did you see them?"
Andra shouted, grasping Ronin's arms with mud-crusted
fingernails.

I could hear the pain in his voice when he replied, "I don't
know. I don't know."

Andra released a sob, but Luella dragged her into her
arms, physically protecting Andra with her body as the
explosions continued around us.

Was Gunny okay?

Did Wesley and Enya survive?

What about Lucky?

Udine, Butcher, and Conway?

Spider?

Isa, the babies, and all the crew at Anchorage Cove. How long did they have?

My eyes shot toward the port town.

I'll be okay.

They won't.

I need to help them.

Before I could move, Ronin grabbed me, keeping me seated and covered by the wall as everything was destroyed around us. "Don't even fucking *think* about it."

My breathing was fast and heavy. "I can help them."

"*No.*" His eyes bore fire, his grip on my arm even tighter. "Stop trying to be a godsdamn hero, Mae."

Panic bloomed in my chest, tears welling in my eyes. "They need help!"

Ronin's eyes softened, and I knew he felt just as helpless as I did. But I'd survive and he wouldn't. Not like this.

"You're right," Luella snapped, her voice a roar as she held Andra close. "They do need help! But even if you can't die, they will *take* you. And you can't help people if you're in a fucking brig."

She was right. And it *crushed* me. My tears became indistinguishable from the rain pouring down on us. We couldn't move from where we were, just *pray* that the ammunition wouldn't hit us.

"When it stops, we run for the tunnels," Ronin said. "Then we regroup. *Then* we plan a rescue."

I looked away, my chest shaking with silent sobs. He cupped my face in his hands, smearing mud and debris across my cheeks. Devastation was apparent in his eyes, in the way his leviathan glowed through the blue flecks.

Not even a dragon could survive the onslaught of cannon fire. Even if he could shift, it wouldn't help us. We were in the open. He'd be torn into pieces by shrapnel. Being a dragon only made him a bigger target.

"It *has* to be like this. I'm sorry."

I know. I swallowed thickly and nodded.

He pressed his forehead against mine, a million things he wanted to say in his eyes, but we didn't have time. Pain seized my chest, fear a cold breath down my spine.

I could lose everything today. My love and my family. Everything that matters to me.

The blasts slowed down. The entire time, Ronin held my face as he tried to commit everything to memory. I did the same. The curve of his mauve lips. The intense soulfulness of his dark eyes. His nose, crooked from being broken a few times. He was covered in muck in the pouring rain but was still as magnificent a man as he'd always been.

I love you.

I love you....

"Now!" Ronin shouted, pulling away from me once the cannonballs stopped firing.

I looked around the corner and saw sloops and rowboats dock at the pier. Full of pirate hunters. Navy officers. There were more ships than just Nathaniel's. Several of them loomed in the distance, all dropping anchor to let their soldiers raze Shipwreck Bay to the ground.

We weren't the only ones who moved. As pirate hunters stormed the pier, pirates and retired sailors came out of hiding to attack. To defend their home. Beside me, Luther sprinted out to the others, a cleaver in hand.

He was too young to die, but he bled red like the rest of them.

Luella, Andra, Ronin, and I ran toward the tunnels, an underground system of escape routes that doubled as the sewer. We pulled our cutlasses, and Ronin fired a bullet from his pistol, hitting a hunter in our way.

I watched him reload, tearing a packet of gunpowder with his teeth to plunge it into the barrel. He tamped it down and followed it with a bullet, all of it done in a matter of seconds before he had to do it again.

We ran down the pier, weapons drawn. Not to attack but to defend ourselves. We wouldn't survive a head-on attack.

Dread bubbled up in my chest as I watched a figure with yellow eyes stride past the pirate hunters, carrying a broadsword in both hands. A winter smoke billowed around him.

The Skadian heir.

The dread quickly turned to seething rage.

He followed us. He intercepted the messages. He was in the cabana that night.

He did this.

But there were too many hunters to face him directly. They scattered behind him, fanning out and following his lead but maintaining a healthy distance. We deflected the attacks and headed straight to the tree line, hoping to lose him in the thicket.

It was pointless.

This was the man who followed us to the gully and attempted to assassinate us. This was the man who taunted me when he could've killed Ronin back at Violetta's Haven. He could've killed us in our sleep at Ronin's cabana.

He was *unpredictable.*

But he was working for Varric. He was working for Nathaniel. He was playing his part and becoming yet another Scourge of the Sea.

I didn't give a fuck where he came from or what was in it for him.

I will not let him hurt my family.

I didn't understand why the hunters were so far behind him, giving even more distance than before.

Until he *berserked.*

A pure wave of rage radiated from him like a brutal breeze.

He caught up with us, swinging his broadsword through trees and collapsing them with incredible strength. The trees cracked and crashed, shaking the earth under us.

"Do not run from me!" he roared, his voice cutting through the sound of thunder. "Face me, coward!"

He will follow us.

He will kill us.

And everyone who stands in the way.

I knew this. Ronin knew this. And so did Luella.

Luella stopped in her tracks, and the rest of us followed suit. My heart was in my throat as I looked back at her, red hair saturated down her back, no hat to hide her ears. Her piercing eyes met mine before they drifted over to Andra.

No, Lulu....

"What are you doing?" Andra shouted.

"If he follows us, we'll lead him straight to the safehold." Luella swung her cutlass, taking a deep breath. "One of us needs to hold him back."

Andra squared her shoulders and took a step next to her wife. "Then we hold him back together, love."

"I'm not leaving you!" I snapped. I glared over at Ronin. "You're not pulling me away this time."

Rain washed over all four of us. Ronin stared up at the sky as lightning cracked through it, splitting the dark clouds. He looked down at his pistol, now saturated from rainfall. It wouldn't fire any more than any waterlogged firearm would.

He drew his cutlass, eyeing the perfectly sharpened blade. "Let's send this fucker to the Hells."

Hope emboldened us as the winter fog licked at our ankles, the scent of smoke in the air. The sound of flames crackling, gunfire, and screams drifted from the port. My hair was saturated, clothes plastered to my skin, toes squishing in drenched socks.

When the Skadian heir reached us, his blade clashed off Luella's in a blaze of rage and thunder. He moved like the fog that circled us, bouncing between all four of us. His berserk outlasted us, the sheer seething fury enough to empower him beyond normal magic.

He flung Luella back, using magic to smash Andra's sword out of her hands.

Luella scrambled to her feet, but then a crack of lightning struck the ground, the force of it shooting both her and Andra back into a tree.

The hunters kept their distance, watching and at the ready.

Why?

Then the dark elf bounced between Ronin and me. We swung with everything we had, but he was a formidable fighter. Faster. Stronger. Enhanced by his own blood and not stolen magic. I couldn't feel any draconite. He didn't use it.

Sparks ignited when my cutlass met his broadsword when I got between him and Ronin as he ducked under my hit to strike Ronin.

No.

The yellow of his eyes gleamed as if they were spitting sunlight. "Get out of my way," he seethed. "My fight is not with you, Princess."

I dodged a hit, not letting up even as my muscles screamed and burned. "No!"

The Skadian heir hissed, shoving me backward with brute force. "I *will* take my revenge, even if I have to go through you to get it."

I flopped onto my back, splattering mud across my clothes, losing Ronin's hat in the floodwaters. Ronin met the heir hit for hit, defending himself while Luella got up behind the dark elf. She had a dagger in her hand, prepared to dig it into the Skadian's ribs, *ending him.*

But he could hear her.

I caught the glimmer in his eyes as he glanced at her. He

kicked Ronin's foot out, swinging the broadsword toward Luella's belly.

Time slowed down.

Heavy droplets seemed to still as I shoved myself off the ground.

I will be okay.

They won't.

Without thinking, I shoved Luella out of the way.

Agony tore through me as blood fizzled out of my mouth. My body seized as the broadsword bit into my belly, spearing through me. Tears of unrelenting pain streamed down my cheeks as I stared up into yellow eyes.

The Skadian heir's eyes rounded as he froze, the blaze of rage evaporating.

"I—" I spat out, grinding my teeth through the suffering. *"You will not hurt my family."*

Distantly, I heard Ronin scream my name. By sheer force of will, I grasped the blade, slicing my hands and bringing it deeper into my body.

Flickers of memories danced behind my eyes as they came into focus, blurring me between this world and the next. Warmth spilled down my belly, pooling around my feet. I could taste metal in my mouth, everything growing cold and distant.

I grasped the blade tighter. Holding on.

I was the shield. Maybe that was what I was meant to be all along.

The moments might have been eternity as my head lolled back, and with my dying breaths, I begged the Gods that this would be enough.

Let it be enough to save them.

The abyss beneath me opened up like a gaping maw and swallowed me. I sank deeper and deeper into the inky black until I became nothing.

45

RONIN MURDOCH

"Mae!" I screamed, but it was too late.

Everything happened too fast.

Before the Skadian heir could slice into Luella, Mae was there. She shoved Luella out of the way, taking a broadsword through her gut. All I could do was watch as the color left her face and she spat bubbly blood out the sides of her mouth.

She grasped the sword and dragged it deeper, excruciating anguish flashing across her face.

"*You will not hurt my family,*" she cried with her dying breaths. The light ebbed out of her eyes as she fell slack on the blade.

The pain that followed was a well-placed strike. A fissure splitting the earth beneath my feet. A billowing darkness shrouding the clouds, snuffing out the sun. A tidal wave of devastation ripping me in two.

I couldn't feel my injuries. Not the slices I'd endured during the sword fight. Not the burns on my fingers from igniting gunpowder. I could feel nothing but my chest aching as if I'd fallen on the blade instead.

You couldn't save her.

You let her die.

Again and again, the tar threatened to swallow me. Take me down into the depths of despair. She slipped off his broadsword and into the mud. He stared at her, eyes rounded in disbelief. Her blood spattered across his face.

He's wearing Mae's blood.

My breathing deepened as pure, blistering *fury* blazed in my own blood, boiling under my skin. Curling violently against the rousing leviathan spirit. Steam as hot as a summer scorch ripped through me.

I will rain Hellsfire upon them.

Luella unleashed a broken sound of despair as she shoved herself off the ground, blade in her fist.

The dragon tattoo *burned*, coming forth as it enveloped me. Claws emerged from my hands as I roared, "Get behind me. *Now.*"

My leviathan came forward, contorting my bones and ripping through my flesh. It had been so long since I claimed my birthright. So long since I embraced it. But I couldn't feel the pain of the shift, only the anguish of seeing Mae on the ground.

Barely more than a bloodied heap.

She didn't move.

The color didn't come back to her cheeks.

The light didn't return.

Was that the final death? Has she been stolen from me like everything else? The one good thing that's come from any of this pain... ripped away from me?

Sinews expanded to my wings as they tore from my back. Horns like a golden crown encircled my head. Four massive paws rumbled the ground in a way that rivaled the thunder overhead. My clothes shredded into ribbons as they tore apart at the seams. I tilted my head up to the sky and opened my jaws, and a deafening noise cracked through the sky.

I am the thunder.

I am the lightning.

I am what the sea fears.

Trees fell around me as I was reborn in the skin of my ancestors. Pirate hunters balked behind the Skadian heir, turning to run away as they caught a glimpse of me.

I was the last *fucking* leviathan, ready to take my pound of flesh.

My eyes locked on the pirate hunters.

On the debris of my home.

On the Skadian heir who wore the blood of my love. Her body crumpled there. My magnificent woman who loved our family and would do *anything* for them. Even die.

She'd died for me.

Died for the crew.

Fell on the sword for us time and time again.

And now she was in the *mud*.

Those yellow eyes bored into mine, wide with a mixture of awe and terror.

You will feel this death long into your next life.

A plume of winter smoke enveloped the heir and Mae's body as my throat opened and I released a scourge of electricity. It crackled through the air, catching on the rain and sizzling the fleeing pirate hunters.

The smell of melting flesh surrounded me, as did the sound of screams as the hunters seized as soon as my electricity hit them. I released all my energy. All the brewing power stowed away in my soul.

My roar shook the Isles. Trembled the very stone walls across oceans that had claimed the lives of my people. I knew that even Varric could feel it while he sat atop *my* throne and wore *my* crown.

The lightning struck trees, hit hunters, burned rowboats in the harbor, a chain of destruction. But like any natural magic, it evaporated from my throat, depleting the spirit faster on land than it would have if I were in the water.

My leviathan spirit embraced me in a fleeting warmth as

it left my body, sinking back to where it belonged in the tattoo under my skin. The massive form retreated in a blue shimmering light, as exhausted as I was.

After so long trying to find it, my leviathan and I were one.

I collapsed onto my knees in the mud, naked as the day I was born. By sheer will, I kept my eyes open. Scorched bodies decorated the tree line. Cracked, burning thickets released plumes of smoke into the clouds.

Mae's body was gone. All that remained was my hat smashed into the mud.

That fucker took her.

I stumbled to my feet, crumpling on the first step.

"She's gone," I uttered, grasping my hat as if that would bring her back.

"I'm sorry, Levi. I'm so fucking sorry," Luella said, voice cracking as tears spilled down her cheeks. She threw her jacket around my shoulders, and both she and Andra tried to lift me up.

My words were barely more than slurs as exhaustion wreaked havoc on my body. "What if that was the final death?"

"Then we make it count," Andra said, swallowing thickly as she fought her own tears.

"She saved me," Luella muttered. "We have to save her. We have to go." She was distraught, pulling her fingers through the bloodred strands of her hair hard enough to rip them out.

"We can't go after Mae."

It took me several moments to realize that *I* was the one who said it. My chest fucking hurt as an ache reverberated through it again. I knew that going after Mae meant turning our back on everyone else.

Our family.

Our friends.

The monarchs.

Innocent people caught in the crossfire.

I let Cross survive. My mercy damned us.

I could hear the destruction of Shipwreck Bay. I could hear the cries and the screams. Everything fell apart, but we had to be the ones to put it back together.

Luella shouted, "What are you talking about? Mae is *family*. We can't just let them take her!"

I mustered everything I had in me and shook Luella's shoulders. "That is an *order*, Wraith."

"Don't you fucking pull rank on me!" She shoved at me, but I didn't let go.

I pointed to the port town. "Look! Look at our home!" My voice was full of authority, and I knew it blazed in my eyes as well. "We *can't* leave them. I trust Mae. She can handle this. I know she can."

She has to.

Pain shone in Luella's eyes. A tic formed in her jaw, and I knew she was about to strike.

Andra curled her hand around Luella's clenched fist, and it loosened, softening to thread their fingers together. "Mae wouldn't want us to go after her."

She wouldn't.

Agony thickened in my throat because I knew what it meant. Either Mae had perished and we'd be retrieving her body, or she'd be going right back to Pike and Cross. Both options felt as if a piece of me had broken away and Mae had taken it with her.

Luella released a shaky breath. "Gods, I *know*. Fuck, I know."

"We need to move before more soldiers find us." I glanced up at the smoke, a fucking beacon to where I was. "To the tunnels first, then to Isa's. We can defend Anchorage Cove from the hunters. Let's go."

With Luella on one side of me and Andra on the other,

they supported my weight as I fought against the exhaustion. I didn't know who survived the attack, but I did know that I was going to save who I could.

Cross wanted a war.

I'll give him a fucking war.

46

MAEVE CROSS

I FLOATED THROUGH OBLIVION.

Memories hovered beside me like panes of broken glass. Some I recognized…

The echo filling my lungs with water.

Being thrashed under the water as a baby.

Having my neck slit open as a child.

Varric silencing me in Farlight Prison.

Pools of crimson at my feet.

Some I didn't recognize…

A rapier embedded in my belly.

Painful warmth as fire eats through my clothing before reaching me.

The crack of my skull as something hard strikes me down.

The inkiness of oblivion split open underneath me, giving way to a blinding, dappling sunlight. I sank down into the endless trenches I'd experienced through every death. A shadowed figure waited for me in the black. Never close enough to make contact.

But this time…

I hit the bottom.

My bare feet grazed a marsh of tender grass as a forest

appeared around me. Massive trees canopied the sun, leaving thin streams of golden light to caress the ground. The sound of rushing water filled my ears as I looked from side to side, seeing an impassable river of white rapids.

I've been here before.

It went beyond the sights I'd seen in Farlight. Beyond mortal existence. Red vines draped through the trees. An abnormally beautiful color palette painted the plains and the trees that went on for eternity.

I'd explored it once before.

While it was vivid in color, it was void of life. This was merely an illusion to make travelers comfortable. But the sun had no warmth. The grass had no smell. The trees were silent without the songs of birds or chittering of woodland creatures.

"You're a difficult woman to get a hold of."

I whipped around toward the shadowed figure standing on the edge of the rushing river, a shallow boat behind them. The shroud surrounded them like a cloak of nighttime until moonlit hands reached out from within it and pulled their hood down.

Black hair spilled past the ethereal fabric as the shadows flittered and vanished. It was hard to comprehend how they looked. Neither male nor female. But perhaps they were both. Appearing as whatever the soul needed to let go.

They were tall and narrow with a well-worn scythe hooked around the leather strap on their chest. Tawny golden flesh gave way to moonlight around their mouth where it had lost the pigment. They looked rather gaunt, the silhouette of a skull appearing and disappearing as they approached me.

I didn't need to ask who they were. I already knew the answer.

Death—Reaper of Souls.

"What am I doing here?" I asked.

This plane of existence—Death's realm—gave me an odd sense of peace. Life could be chaos, so perhaps peace was the lack of life.

A knowing smile pulled at Death's mouth as they stood a mere few feet away from me. "Don't worry, you won't be here for long. This skiff behind me is not for you."

"That doesn't answer my question."

"Always so full of questions. I've always liked that about you," Death mused. "It's nice to see that your spirit remains unbroken. What comes next will test you, but know that you *will* survive."

I narrowed my eyes, uncertain what they were getting at. "I don't like to repeat myself. What am I doing here?"

"You've been here every time you perished. You just don't remember. You weren't ready." Death brushed a moonlit finger along their scythe. "So I'd give you bits and pieces. Enough to open your mind, but not enough to break it."

All my suspicions had now been confirmed. Each death gave me something new, something to help piece it all together. I pressed my hand against my chest, expecting the anxieties to send my heart pounding, but it was silent. All my mortal tethers had been stripped away. No pain. Just peace.

"I need to leave. I need to get back to—"

"Worry not about your lover or your kin. They escaped. Your mortal body isn't anywhere near them. You've served your purpose for now."

I felt relief like a warm beam of sunlight. "Where am I? My mortal body?"

"Patience, patience. Now I remember why I kicked you out of my realm all those years ago."

Did Death just roll their eyes at me?

They waved their hand. "There is much to discuss and little time."

"What am I?" I asked.

"You already know what you are, Maeve. You're a sentry. You always have been. Let me show you."

The forest around me shuddered before that dark shroud that once covered Death was cast over all the greenery. Shiny shards of my memories surrounded me. This was the one I didn't recognize.

I wasn't seeing it from my eyes. Death was showing me this memory from theirs.

Farlight Castle. But it wasn't as I would later remember it. Different tapestries hung from the windows. The queen was away for dinner, giving lessons at the orphanage while the king and princes enjoyed a spread.

Vitrophine poisoned their food.

A swarm of guards—no—sentries formed a line in front of the dining hall. Nobles and their assassins struck, taking the opportunity to slaughter the oath-bound sentries.

Blood ran down the hallways as they gave their lives to protect the royal family. The Murdochs. I recognized Varric Cross. Younger, but wearing his amulet of draconite. He blasted through the sentries with unnatural, powerful magic.

Queen Enya had a smaller sentry detail around her to escort her back to the castle. Standing beside her was a young sentry, barely nineteen, who had just taken her oath.

Me.

The guards at the front of the gate were acting odd, and something felt off.

When we entered the castle, my superiors were the first to wield their blades. Samuel Pike led this second charge. Nathaniel's father. His goal was to murder the queen. My commanding officers ordered me to take her and run while my superiors held off the brunt of the attack.

I obeyed.

Blurred chaos. I grasped Queen Enya, taking her to one of the side rooms. I shoved a desk against the door, but the guards were banging on it, threatening to knock it down. I'd never wet my sword with blood before. I didn't know what to do.

Queen Enya was in a state of panic, and I was trying to keep my head on straight.

The windows.

I threw the window open, telling her that I needed to get her out of there.

I was terrified, my heart in my ears.

I prayed to the Gods above. To anyone who would listen. All I knew was that I needed to protect the queen, as my oath demanded. But I didn't know if I was strong enough to do it.

I wanted to flee. I wanted to cower and hide.

But I didn't.

I tied a rope to a secure place, readying myself to grapple Queen Enya away from harm. The rest could come later.

"Come with me, Your Majesty. I must get you to safety."

A hand fastened over my gauntlets, all five fingers, gripping hard. "Not without my boys. Please. I must get to my sons."

The desperation in her voice. The pleading in her eyes. Fear licked the back of my neck like the looming presence of Death. The banging on the door got louder. The desk shifted as it scraped along the floor.

Queen Enya kept my gaze. "I know what I'm asking you to do, Sentry. But I will not leave without them. You took an oath to the crown, but my oath is to my family."

Terror seized me completely, but I gulped it down.

I will not be afraid.

"Then hide," I uttered. "Hide. You're no good to anyone dead."

My armor was too bulky to allow me to hide as well or sneak around the castle. There was only one way she'd succeed.

I needed to be the distraction. For the queen. For my kingdom. The most noble death a sentry could wish for.

Queen Enya knew what I was telling her to do, and there wasn't any time to argue. She discarded her silks out the window and crawled inside a wardrobe, a drapery of hung clothing in front of her. I closed the wardrobe tightly, clicking it quietly into place as the desk shook harder and harder.

I ran over to the window, where the breeze tickled my face. The moon was full, beaming down on me. I clutched my hands into fists and placed one on my sword. "Run!" I called out the window, trying to give the impression that Queen Enya had escaped.

The wind blew her silks down the road, adding to the ruse.

With one final bang, the desk was shoved out of the way. I heard half a dozen footfalls and turned, holding the hilt of my sword. "I will not let you get to the queen," I declared, drawing my weapon and taking a stance in front of Samuel Pike.

A cruel smile pulled across his lips. "You cannot save them. But you can die for them."

I fought as hard as I could, absolutely terrified as his rapier struck my longsword. I'd taken my oath a few weeks prior. I wasn't ready to fight. I wasn't ready to die. One of the treacherous guards struck the sword from my hand as Samuel Pike's rapier dug into my belly.

I grasped the blade, holding on as the wardrobe opened behind them. I wouldn't die. I wouldn't let go. Not until Queen Enya slipped away completely. I pulled it deeper into my body, spitting foamy blood from my lips and clawing onto the light of life.

Agony ripped through me, but I held on.

"You're a determined one, aren't you?" Samuel Pike chuckled. He took several steps forward, knocking me back against the window frame. I grunted as anguish stole my breath. "Don't worry, you'll be seeing your queen soon enough."

The rapier ripped through me, and he shoved me out the window. The sensation of falling enveloped me. I didn't feel the impact of the fall, but I was still alive when Samuel Pike and his band of assassins came down the rope to pursue Queen Enya.

A smile pulled at my lips because I'd succeeded. She was safe.

It felt like eternity.

I was cold.

I was alone.

I was terrified.

And then I was nothing.

Death's realm came into focus around me, the shroud disappearing.

"What happened after that?" I asked, tears welling and spilling from the corners of my eyes at the intense emotions that had come with the vision.

"You know what came after that," Death said. "Because of *you*, Enya could save one of her sons. You were never meant to be the sword, Maeve. You were meant to be the shield."

"But… why am I here, then? Why did I live?"

Death gave me a fond smile. "You stayed in my realm for years, refusing to cross over. As the war waged on, the balance of life and death fell into chaos." They tapped their chin. "As a god, I couldn't interfere with mortal matters. But our champions could."

My eyes rounded. "Me?"

"Who else but the stubborn spirit who refused to cross over until the queen and prince joined them? Who else but the spirit who did the right thing even if they were terrified? Who else but one who upheld their oath, even in death?" They continued on, and the surroundings changed again, flittering between darkness and light. "You see, your body perished. So you gave me the extraordinary opportunity to create *life*. It wasn't easy. I had to ask Cliohde to assist me."

The Goddess of the Ocean and Death themselves came together for me?

"After all, a sentry meant to protect her leviathans ought to have her touch."

That's why I don't have parents.

"I gave you the ability to transcend my realm. Cliohde gave you the ability to withstand stolen leviathan magic. You, my child, can set them free. This is not infinite, mind you. Once you fulfill your oath and unseat the usurper, this will be gone. You would've earned mortality."

"Earned?" I wondered. "Why is mortality the reward?"

Death smiled, outstretching a moonlit hand to stroke my chin, leaving a trail of cold in its wake. "I can be violent. I can be a thief. I can be the embodiment of murder and sickness. But when everything is over, I am mercy. I am peace."

The darkness devoured the moonlight, and the force holding me to the ground reverted, dragging me upward into the abyss above. Death watched me as I floated, returning to the land of the living to fulfill my mission.

I'm not a princess.

I'm not a warrior.

I'm Death's champion.

The Skadian heir sat on his sloop, tapping his foot incessantly as Varric Cross spoke to him through the shimmering bowl of liquid on his lap. The elf didn't have his bloodied sword. Only the body of a dead woman on the floor of his sloop, covered in a blanket. He couldn't bear to look at her face, knowing he was the one who murdered her.

"I didn't agree to this, Cross," he hissed into the bowl. "You told me that I'd have my revenge against the leviathan, not that you'd destroy a whole fucking town behind me. When I sent you that correspondence, I didn't agree to a siege. You *told* me that Pike would help me secure the leviathan. That's it."

Varric raised one brow. "I remember telling you that if you brought the leviathan back to me, you'd have your revenge. I see you've failed me, Freynir. Again. The leviathan is no good to me dead, but you ignored my order last time."

Freynir bared his teeth, elongated canines exposed in a visible threat. "You certainly didn't tell me that *your daughter* was in love with him. You told me he kidnapped her! Forgive me if this is a Farlight custom, but I don't think a kidnapped woman would willingly fall on my fucking sword to protect her kidnapper."

He didn't tell Varric that he'd taken a boot to the face when he tried to snoop around the leviathan's cabana. He didn't tell Varric that he'd seen his daughter solidify those alliances Varric was so desperate to dismantle. And he certainly didn't tell Varric that Maeve had gotten between him and the leviathan numerous times.

She made the ultimate sacrifice, and that was enough to plant a seed of doubt in Freynir's head.

A smile curled the side of Varric's mouth. "Do you have her?"

"Her body." Freynir frowned, noticing that Varric's reaction was *not* that of a grieving father. He grew more suspicious, but what other option did he have?

"Forget the leviathan. Pike will succeed where you have failed. Your new course of action is to bring Maeve's body to Nathaniel Pike's ship," Varric declared, fiddling with his odd blue amulet in the reflection of the communicative bowl.

"No. I will bring her body back to Farlight Harbor, and you are going to send me home," Freynir argued.

Varric laughed. "Obey and perhaps I'll send you home. You won't get back to your people without me." He tapped his chin. "Isn't there a war about? Your kingdom will fall to ruin without their heir."

"You don't own me, Cross."

"Wrong, yet again. I do. And you will obey."

The shimmering blue light flickered out. Varric had severed the connection.

Hot air blew out Freynir's nostrils. He got to his feet, and in a sudden bout of rage, he flung the bowl out to the ocean. "Fucking prick!"

He ran his hands through the white tufts of hair poking out from his braid and sank down into a crouch. With a huff, he rolled his shoulders, obviously pissed off, before he stood back up and strode over to the helm, rotating it to get on course to sail to Nathaniel Pike's primary ship on the edge of the horizon, just out of view from the pier on Shipwreck Bay. The other man-o'-war stayed positioned by the pier, still smoking from unloading all the cannon fire.

He reached under his collar and pulled out his marital pendant. He eyed the icy magic, bringing it to his lips for a tender kiss.

"To the Gods, I wish you were here. Give me a sign, *skelmis*. Tell me that I'm not fucking everything up."

Out of the corner of his eye, he saw the blanket covering the dead woman move. He froze, turning slightly toward the body. He'd had encounters with the undead before in Skadi, but this would be the first time an undead rose from a body he'd slain.

Another way to torment him for his crimes, perhaps?

"*Draugr*," he hissed, one hand on his blade as he backed away from the helm.

The body rolled over, pulling the blanket back, and Freynir came eye to eye with the not-so-dead Princess of Farlight Isles.

Fresh-faced. Pinkened skin, not grayed or void of color. Bright eyes. Not at all like an undead. In fact, if it weren't for the blood caked across her chest and clothing, she looked as if she'd never met with Death.

But he *knew* he'd killed her.

He knew her lifeblood had pooled at his feet. He'd even tasted it when it splattered across his face. She couldn't have survived that. No one could have.

She was *dead*.

"*What the fuck?*"

To be continued in Book Three, "*The Sentry*."

ACKNOWLEDGMENTS

The Monarchs was a labor of love at a very challenging time in my life. I saw a lot of myself in Ronin's strife and Mae's struggle to connect. As I wrote them progressing through this healing journey, I also healed little bits of myself.

But I couldn't have done it alone. I would like to thank my husband, Joseph, for always supporting my dreams. I love you, sweetheart.

To my mom, Libby, and my mother-in-law, Carolyn. Thank you for being my first readers and for not talking to me about the sex scenes.

Special shout-out to Deana and Kendra for being my biggest supporters and my most cherished readers. You have no idea how much I love you guys!

I would also like to thank my publishing team, Becky, Kristin, McKinley, and Lori, for making my dreams come true.

And finally, thank you to all my readers! You are my bread and butter. From the bottom of my heart, I adore you. You empower me to keep writing even through those challenging times and those hard days.

I'll see you in the next one! Until then, hoist your sails, set course, and get ready for an action-packed book three.

ABOUT THE AUTHOR

Anacostia Miller is a novelist and screenwriter with a background in filmmaking and prop creation. After ten years of writing and two years of ghostwriting, she found her niche in romantasy. She loves exploring different themes like found family and showcasing inclusivity.

World-building and developing intricate histories in her novels are some of her favorite things to do. She also grew up on classics like *The Lord of the Rings* and *Buffy the Vampire Slayer*, which have inspired her writing. Developing complicated lore and having moments of happiness are vital to the stories. Also, humor plays a big part. As dark as things will get, readers can always hold out for that moment of happiness to make it worth it.

During her days, you can find her trying out a new recipe to figure out how to describe it in her writing, daydreaming, or annoying her husband by telling him exactly how the lighting conveys emotion in every movie they watch together.

instagram.com/anacostiamillerauthor

tiktok.com/@anacostiamillerauthor

ABOUT THE PUBLISHER

Hot Tree Publishing loves love. Publishing adult romantic fiction, HTPubs are all about diverse reads featuring heroes and heroines to swoon over. Since opening in 2015, HTPubs have published more than 300 titles across the wide and diverse range of romantic genres. If you're chasing a happily ever after in your favourite subgenre, HTPubs have you covered.

Interested in discovering more amazing reads brought to you by Hot Tree Publishing? Head over to the website for information:

WWW.HOTTREEPUBLISHING.COM

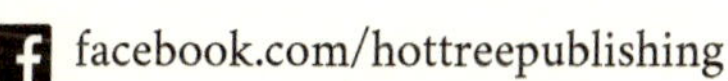

facebook.com/hottreepublishing
x.com/hottreepubs
instagram.com/hottreepublishing